TIME STAMPS

K. L. KREIG

TIME STAMPS

Copyright © 2021 by K. L. Kreig

Published by K. L. Kreig

ISBN-10: 1-943443-30-0

ISBN-13: 978-1-943443-30-7

This book is a work of fiction. The characters, events, and places portrayed in this book are products of the author's imagination and are either fictitious or are used fictitiously. Any similarity to real persons, living or dead, is purely coincidental and not intended by the author.

Cover Art by Veronica Larsen
Editing by Nikki Busch Editing

Published in the United States of America.

To my love ~ you are my reason, my imperfection, the very breath I breathe. I love you today. I will love you tomorrow. My love for you withstands the cruelty of Time.

PROLOGUE

LET ME
HOLD YOU

Roth
Present
June 15, 11:15 a.m.

"ARE YOU SURE?" she asks.

Her words wobble. Her body shivers uncontrollably. I squeeze her hand tighter, unable to look at her when her whimpers resemble that of an injured animal. It makes me feel like shit.

"I am sorry, Laurel."

That's it? *I'm sorry?* Never was a more worthless apology spoken.

Dr. Nuess gauges us both. He looks sorry. He sounds sorry. His body language even screams sympathy.

None of it matters, though. I am in another place entirely. It's dark and dank and stinks of mortality. I fly through a dozen emotions in a blink, watching the prize wheel spin.

Click.

Click.

Click.

The wheel slows.

Click.

Cliick.

Cliiiiick.

1

The metal needle bounces between two rubber stoppers until it finally comes to a complete halt, my spoil chosen.

White. Hot. Fury.

Seems appropriate, because I am hemorrhaging rage at the unfairness of it all.

Why her? Why me? Why us? Why now? Why ever?

Why? Why? *Why?*

I force myself to look at Laurel now. Her lips tremble. The color of them always reminds me of cotton candy. I fell in love with those lips the first time I laid eyes on them. I watch them when she talks and smiles and yells at me. Those lips. I still dream of them, ever grateful that they're awaiting me when I wake.

My breath catches. Frozen.

I can't wrap my head around this. I refuse to. This cannot be it.

Looks like my prize wheel has slipped straight to the next square: denial.

With my free hand, I cup my wife's cheek, round and rosy. Her long, inky lashes are dampened with droplets of grief. Her brown eyes, the shade of mud puddles I used to play in as a boy, are glassy and wild with unspoken apologies. She has nothing to be sorry for. Nothing at all.

Even blotchy-faced and snot-nosed, she is so beautiful, so pure. I love her with all that I am, all that I will ever be. I attempt to wipe the moisture away with my thumb, but it's futile, immediately replaced by an overflowing river of anguish. She tries to stifle a sob, but she fails and, "It's okay," I tell her softly, reverently. "It will be okay."

We both know I lie, but in this moment the lie serves to fend off the reality we're now forced to face, even if for the briefest of time.

Time. Something we are severely short on.

Click.

Cliick.

Cliiiiick.

My rage burns out of control, as if fueled directly from the center of the Earth.

I turn my attention back to the Harvard-trained oncologist, best in his field, who was unable to save our future. "How long?" I demand.

My throat feels as if it's been lit by a backdraft of fiery blue flames. An inch of ash now coats my vocal cords.

"I don't—"

"No *I don't* bullshit," I grit out through the muck. You don't get life-shattering news and say welp that's that, dust your hands off, and walk away. You cry foul. You demand answers. "You do. Ballpark it."

I know. I already know. I can Google as well as the next guy.

"Mr. Keswick, I don't have a crystal ball."

I snort. It's filled with vile derision and acrid bitterness.

"Roth, it's okay," Laurel whispers, sensing I'm about to break. I should be the one comforting her, not the other way around.

"No." I need to get out of here. The walls are closing in. "No. It's not fucking okay." I pin Dr. Nuess with a demanding glare. "We came in today thinking we'd discuss the next treatment plan and instead we're told all bets are off. That there is nothing more you can do for the person who is my entire..." *Universe. Life. Existence.* You name it. She's that. "So..." I begin to stand, my six-foot-four, 202-pound muscled frame rather intimidating to most, and ask him again, "How. Long. Do. We. Have?"

But my petite, fragile Laurel is strong in so many ways. So much stronger than I am. One quick pull on my arm and I'm back in my seat and Dr. Nuess can breathe again. He swallows, his oversized Adam's apple bobbing up and down, up and down. I want to punch it in until it's sunken deep in his neck. I want to unleash this pent-up, all-consuming, violent tempest and destroy everything in this frosted-glass office until it's shredded and lies in pieces. Like me.

"You'd better start talking," I tell him evenly.

I fully realize I shouldn't act like a spoiled, whiny toddler demanding a candy bar at checkout, threatening a meltdown if I'm not rewarded. Dr. Newcomb Nuess is a smart, caring man who has done all he can for us. Logically, I know this, but when you're facing the end of life as you know it, when all of your hopes and dreams shatter on a single exhale, you become a different person. One you don't like much.

"The mean survival rate is..." He stops and shifts uncomfortably. Then his forked tongue spits out my worst nightmare. Its metal tines embed the writhing entity deep into the floor, holding it firmly in place as it bleeds in front of me. "Less than a year."

"Fuck," I mutter.

Three-hundred and sixty-five days? Less than? How many hours is that? Minutes? Seconds?

I feel sick.

Two weeks ago, we were sitting in this very room, having our first consultation with the top hematology oncologist in the country. The best of the best. Test after test, he assured us we'd get answers.

He never assured us we'd like them.

The best of the best has failed.

A sharp bite nips the backs of both eyes. Laurel is now perfectly still beside me. She's not shaking. She's not wailing. She's not breaking apart. She's probably thinking the same thing I am. In fact, I know she is. We've talked about it late at night when the lights are off, and we don't have to bear witness to each other's pain. We don't need to. We can feel it coursing through our entwined hands.

"What's next, then?" I hear Laurel ask in a voice so calm she may as well be ordering a burger and a Coke.

I don't know who she's talking to. If it's me, I have no answers. I don't know what's next. Dr. Nuess was our last chance. We've had second opinion upon third opinion upon fourth opinion. Dr. Nuess speaks, but I can't pay attention because I am lost. So very lost and in so much pain I don't know if I can survive it. Every muscle, every organ, every bone is constricted, like my entire body is folding in on itself. Turtles do that...hide in their shells for protection. Why are humans left so exposed and vulnerable?

"Thank you, Dr. Nuess." Laurel stands. I don't how, but I stand too. We exit his office. I'm on autopilot as we start our trek to the lobby. We're both silent as the elevator doors open, then close, and in those ten seconds we have alone while we descend, we wrap ourselves around each other, unable to get close enough.

When I look back on this day, I won't remember much, but I will remember the shaky cadence of her breath, which seeps through my shirt, and the faint flowery smell of her shampoo lingering in my nostrils. I will remember how tightly her fingers grip my sides in fear and grief. I will remember how perfectly she molds her body to mine and the sound of her whispering *"I love you"* and *"I'm sorry"* over and over.

Like a hoarder, I start stuffing memories and tidbits away in every shadowed corner of my mind, terrified I'll forget a single one of them. How many have I already forgotten? They are all important and meaningful, now more than ever. And there will never be enough of them. Never.

Some people want to know which day marks their last. At least that's what they say, anyway. They claim they will live differently if they know, but I've always wondered, why wouldn't they have lived that way in the first place? Why not tell the people important to you that you love them every single day? Why stay at a job that makes you miserable? Why put off traveling to the places you want to see until you can afford it?

Why go to bed angry? Why wake with regret? Why not forgive those who have wronged you? Why not appreciate that sunrise or thunderstorm for the slices of wonder they are?

Now I know.

One's mortality lifts the veil of uncertainty. And under that veil is a whole new world. Colors pop. Passions intensify. Indignation wanes. Priorities shift.

Finality is embraced.

The automatic doors of MD Anderson Cancer Center open with a soft whoosh, and as we walk from the sterility and stench of death coursing through its veins into the sticky-sweet hum of energy on the outside, I think to my myself...

This is it.

The countdown has begun.

And there is not a damn thing we can do to stop the omnipotent hands of Time from moving forward, click after motherfucking click, inching us closer to the end of forever.

ONE

NICE TO MEET YA

Laurel
Ten Years Earlier
February 9, 6:21 p.m.

"Yo, chica. Vamos a darle."

The door slams behind the lilt of Carmen's voice. I hear the refrigerator jingle open and close and the distinct hiss of a bottle top being opened.

Help yourself. I roll my eyes. I'd bet last week's meager paycheck she's drinking my lone wild berry wine cooler—the one I meant to grab and chug as I primp for a girl's night out I'd give anything to ditch. A nice serial killer novel sounds far more appealing.

"You ready yet?"

I pause midmascara application, noting Carmen's reflection in my dresser mirror.

Yep. There it is.

Standing in my bedroom doorway, shoulder wedged against the jam, my fortification is nestled loosely between my best friend's perfectly manicured fingernails that are so long and sharp they should be registered weapons.

"I was going to drink that," I tell her. I let my gaze fall to her hand, the bottle already half-empty.

"This?" she replies with more than a hint of disgust. "I don't

7

know how you can drink this crap." She takes another deep swallow.

I chortle and shake my head, not bothering to state the obvious. Stuffing the black goo-covered wand back into its container, I give myself a once-over. Even with a moderate dusting of makeup and a few well-placed curls in my hair, I still look plain. Boring. Someone whom you wouldn't give a second glance. I grab my can of Aqua Net and spray until a cloud of chemicals settles into my hair and pores.

Eh. Good enough.

"It's suffrage, is what it is," Carmen prattles on between gulps.

"You didn't use that word in the right context." I toss the tube of mascara down and turn toward her, gripping the worn wood behind me.

"What?"

"Suffrage is the right to vote."

I want nothing more than to crawl into bed with a cup of tea in one hand and a book in the other until I fall asleep. Boring. Both in looks and charisma. That's me.

"Weeell..." Her eyes widen in challenge. "I think I used it perfectly, then. My *vote* is that this tastes like ant piss."

"And yet you finished the entire contents in under two minutes."

"I am forced to drink what's available."

"You weren't *forced* to do anything of the sort," I counter, cocking my head.

Carmen mirrors my stance. Her brown skin shimmers as if dusted with gold flecks. She looks far sexier than I ever could in pale pink skintight pants and a white V-neck tee that showcases her expensive black boutique push-up. Eyelash extensions to fuchsia-painted toenails, every inch of her is toned and appealing.

"We need to go." Tick. Tick. Tick. She taps her watch with one nail, impatient.

"Ready."

She runs her eyes quickly over me. "Whaaat?" she cries so loud that Meringue, my Russian Blue-Persian mix, scrambles from the edge of my bed and dives underneath it in search of safety, "in God's green Earth do you have on?"

The disgust she displayed at my choice of alcoholic beverages pales in comparison to that of her favorite subject: scrutinizing my wardrobe. I hate to admit I may possibly give her cause to. My fashion sense is a little...well, some call it dated, but eclectic is the word I prefer. Everything comes back into style eventually, right?

"You're not wearing that." She's so matter-of-fact that almost anyone else wouldn't dare argue. I am not anyone else.

Throwing a hand on one hip, I kick it up in challenge, not bothering to glance down at the loose plaid baby-doll dress I paired with neon-green capri leggings. "I am." I was half hoping it would get me out of tonight.

"Girl, you look like you were spit out of a nineties time warp. All that's missing are the bangs and oversized gold hoop earrings."

"Hey..." I *like* bangs. "Now that is uncalled for." I scoop up earrings that brush the tops of my shoulders and slip them through the holes in each ear. They happen to be gold. I smile. I wasn't going to wear them, but...

"I'm gonna let you in on a little secret, chica." Carmen stops talking for the half second it takes her to walk to my standard-sized closet that's not much bigger than a bread box. "That"—she looks over her shoulder and gestures up and down my body, lingering on my ears—"wasn't a fashion statement in the nineties. And it ain't one now, either."

"Carmen, it's fine."

"It's hideous." She snorts. "Are you trying to scare men away?"

Like men give me a second glance.

"No."

Besides, I don't need to do that with Carmen around. I envy the sultry, 1-800 voice of my best friend. One *hello* and men fall at her feet, not because she's drop-dead gorgeous. Don't get me wrong, she is beautiful, but it's something else. She has the "it" factor. I don't know exactly what "it" is, but she's got it in spades. When I'm with her, it's a given I'll be invisible. And truth be told, I am perfectly okay with that. I excel at floating under the radar. It's freeing to go unnoticed. So much less pressure.

"Here." She thrusts a gawdy short-sleeve wrap dress the color of dried mustard my way. I snag the edge of it before it falls to the ground, holding it with my index finger and thumb as if it will stain me.

"This is awful," I lament, studying the little white misshapen flowers that are scattered on it. "Where did I even get this?"

My mother. It has to be from my mother. Christmas. Three years ago. Ah yes, it's all coming back to me now.

"It's cute and summery."

"It's revolting. And it's February."

"These will look adorable with it." She hands me a pair of plain ivory Sketchers with matching silk laces, as if I haven't said a word in protest. Dammit, I hate that she's right. They would look cute. On someone else.

"Carmen, no." I toss them to the floor. "I am perfectly capable of dressing myself."

"Laurel…" She turns me around, so my back is to her. She starts to lift my shift up and over my head. Like a child in defiance, I shove my hands across my body and beneath each opposite armpit, a death grip now on the silky fabric.

"Oh my God, stop," I demand.

"I refuse to let you out of this house looking like you've walked straight from the pages of a comic book. Dios mios."

Not giving up, Carmen abandons my dress and moves to my leggings, and because my hands are otherwise occupied, she successfully strips them down to my ankles in one fell swoop. I screech and fight her, but they're like soft, stretchy shackles holding me prisoner.

"I'm not even going to comment on the undies. Gross."

"Except you just did," I tell her.

While Carmen wrestles with my pants, mumbling something in Spanish, I catch our reflection in the mirror.

Carmen's midnight-black hair is tousled, now wild and out of place. The ruby-red lipstick she applied with perfection is smudged on the two pristine-white front teeth she's dug into her lower lip. Her eyes are bugged and crazy. My dress is bunched in a wad beneath my utilitarian white bra, which matches the white grannie panties settled neatly over my belly button. They *are* gross, but dammit, they are comfortable.

I look so ridiculous; *we* look so ridiculous that I start to laugh. I laugh so hard that Carmen, still fierce and determined, joins me and gives up her fight with my leggings. I laugh so hard Meringue runs from the room, hissing her displeasure. I laugh so hard, I eventually lose my balance and topple to the floor, luckily missing the corner edge of every piece of furniture in my pint-sized bedroom on the way down. I laugh so hard I pee myself a little.

"I think I dislocated my shoulder," Carmen whines between giggles and hiccups.

"You'll live."

"You're heartless."

"I love you," I tell her, turning my head to face her. Carmen has been my best friend since college. I am an introvert and keep my circle intensely small, but when I met Carmen in an elective drama class in a failed attempt to "open up," she stomped her way right into my life and locked the door behind her.

She clutches my hand in hers. "Te quiero tambien, hermana." *Sister.* She's the closest thing I have left to one.

I squeeze my eyes shut, remembering the smattering of freckles dotting the bridge of Esther's nose. *She* would have liked the dress. *And that's always the point, isn't it?*

"Hand it over." I am resigned as I hold out my hand for the butt-ugly dress that's fallen on the other side of her, just out of my reach. I turn it over in my hands, keenly aware the tag is missing. Another of my mother's tricks, so I can't return it. "Did you get this from the back of my closet?"

"Of course." With ease, she pops herself to her feet, not bobbling at all on her strappy cream wedges. She extends a hand to help me up. "That's where all the good stuff is."

"You mean Candice's collectibles?" That's what I've named my mother's attempts at changing my wardrobe to her liking instead of mine.

"Hey," she says gently, placing a hand on my shoulder. "You be you." She knows the struggles I've had with my mother over the years, this being one of many. "Lo siento. I'm sorry. If you want to wear that—" She pauses, visibly choking the words out. "You should."

"Nah. You're right. It's...what did you say?" I toss my gaze up to the ceiling, pretending to think. "Comic-bookish?"

She winces. "That may have been rather harsh."

"But true."

With a few ballet-like moves, I rid myself of leggings that could be seen from the space station. In short order I don the new dress and try not to pull at the stretchy fabric that I think shows too much cleavage and clings too tightly to my full hips. I tie my shoes quickly and primp my hair, more for effect than concern. Finally, I remove the large hoop earrings and stick a classic pearl stud in each ear.

"You look great," Carmen tells me, adding on a catcall for effect.

I stare at myself for a full ten seconds. I actually do. Sleek yet casual. Dirty mustard looks good on me. Not sure how I feel about that.

"Guess I'm ready."

While Carmen beelines out of my bedroom, I slip my hands between my legs to check the status of my underwear. Damp. I should probably change them, but...nah, they'll do. Not like anyone's going to be up in them anyway.

I quickly follow her to the door and swipe my cross-body purse as I pass the island. I lock my apartment door behind me with a snick. Carmen throws an arm around my shoulder as we head to my car. I like to drive. I like being in control of my own destiny, or the illusion of it anyway. We each slip into our respective sides. Carmen immediately puts down the sun visor and opens the mirror. She smooths her hair back into place and reapplies her lipstick, removing the stain from her teeth. She then grins from ear to ear.

"You ready to meet tu amado?"

Your beloved.

"Carmen."

"What?" She is as transparent as saran wrap.

"I thought this was a girl's night?"

"It is."

Carmen may be a brash, sassy, rough-around-the-edges Puerto Rican woman on the outside, but inside she's all goo. A romantic at heart. She's been with her boyfriend, Manny, since she was sixteen. They'll marry, but she she's making him earn it. *"Don't propose to me until your credit score is at least seven-hundred and fifty,"* she always tells him. He thinks it's in jest. I know otherwise.

She wants me to have what she does. I don't know that I ever will, because the love that Carmen and Manny share is uncommonly rare. It's both sickening and enviable. I have had one serious relationship in my twenty-eight years. Johnny "Ace" Wallace. I dated him for precisely six months and two weeks in my junior year of college. He had a big ego and even bigger gambling problem. You'd think the nickname would have been a dead giveaway. Things sort of fizzled out when I discovered he'd stolen and pawned my dead grandmother's three-carat emerald ring, which was handed down to me. I got the ring back. He got prison time. I've been pretty gun-shy since then.

"I have a good feeling about tonight, Laurel."

Carmen and her "feelings."

"I'm glad someone does," I drone, my skin suddenly a bit too tight for my body. Isn't there a liquor store on the way to the restaurant?

"You'll see."

Carmen fiddles with the radio and starts singing along with Michael Bublé's smooth jazzy beat on "Haven't Met You Yet." She croons at the top of her lungs and sways to the music.

She keeps singing, turning to me as if to say, "See? It's serendipity. Today is the day."

Arguing is pointless. Two can play this game.

I ease out of the parking lot and take a left, heading in the direction of downtown Nashville. I love this city that I've called home for the last nine years. It vibrates with life and vitality. It also vibrates with tourists trying to get in a one-night stand before they fly cross-country back to their fiancées or wives. No thanks. Hard pass.

"Don't try to hook me up, Carmen. I mean it."

"Would I do that?"

I press the brakes a bit too hard at the four-way stop, and our seatbelts kick in as the force of gravity drives us forward. "Yes. Yes, you would. You have. You do it All. The. Time. I am happy alone."

"No one is happy alone," she counters, believing what she says to be true.

"*I* am." I poke my finger into the middle of my breastbone a little too hard. Ouch. "I am happy alone." Mostly. Sometimes. Fine...someone to cuddle with could be nice once in a while. Definitely not on the regular.

She shrugs, but those large dark eyes belie her *If you're happy, I'm happy* speech.

We stay this way, our gazes locked in a duel, until the impatient honk of a horn behind us forces me to move.

I skip the liquor store, eyeing it longingly as we drive past. Our twenty-minute ride to the Gulch ends up being filled with meaningless chatter, and by the time I pull up to the valet outside of Sambuca, I'm feeling marginally better. We quickly spot our friends, Wendy and Yvette, whom I absolutely adore. They gush over my outfit and the touch of rosy posy matte lipstick I swiped on earlier, and I relax even more.

A round of hugs and kisses later, I enter one of my favorite restaurants in the city, all but forgetting the man I haven't met yet.

TWO

NICE TO
MEET YA

Laurel
Ten Years Earlier
February 9, 10:48 p.m.

I SIT COMFORTABLY in a worn and oversized armchair that doesn't match any of the others around me. It wobbles and protests every time I move, and I wonder how many people have sat in it before me, enjoying the wash of smooth jazz flowing through their blood the way I am.

We're so close to the stage, I could reach out and touch the pianist. He's good-looking and I'm feeling so sassy in my mustard yellow dress that I might even flirt with him if he were paying me any attention. But he's not. It's Carmen who has his eye, though she's doing nothing to overtly encourage him. She has her Manny and while men may fall at her feet, she does nothing to bring them to their knees. They do that all on their own.

Wendy and Yvette left us after a fabulous dinner. Wendy teaches Sunday school and has to be up at the crack of dawn and Yvette has a two-year-old at home, with another on the way. I was tired and looking forward to getting home early myself, but Carmen insisted that ten o'clock is when the party starts, not ends. Sometimes it's easier to give in than to argue, so here we are after leaving Sambuca, at one of the best jazz clubs in Nashville in my opinion.

"What can I get you?"

I take my attention from hot piano man to the petite waitress now standing over me. Her skirt is short, and her bulb cheeks are flushed. It's clear she is hurried and stressed. Her gaze bores into me urgently, making me feel as if I don't order right now, I will forfeit my right to order a drink altogether.

"Water."

"Water?" she repeats with no shortage of contempt.

Suddenly I feel pressured. This venue is small. She's likely living on her paltry tips to pay her rent or perhaps her father's medical bills, and even though I limit myself to one drink when I'm driving, a free water isn't going to help her in the least.

"Ah...a lemon drop martini?"

"You sure?" She blinks rapidly. I know she knows she's capitalizing on my distress.

"Do you have beer instead?"

She heaves a sigh and cocks a hip, clearly annoyed at my stupid question. "Yes, we have beer."

"What kinds do you have?"

She rolls her eyes toward the ceiling and with an overexaggerated sigh starts reciting your standard list of domestic beers: "Bud, Bud Light, Coors, Coors Light..." None of which I am interested in. I don't even really like beer.

"Is the martini not good?" I ask after she finishes her beer dissertation, indecision on the best cocktail weighing me down. To my right, Carmen is snickering with a shake of her head.

I do this all the time. I will agonize over a meal or a drink or a pair of sandals before I am forced to make a decision. Which may be the real reason my closet hasn't seen an influx of new items except for my mother's in nearly a decade.

"The martini is fine." The waitress, sans name tag, glares down at me. She's about over me. I don't blame her. "Best martini in town," she adds, unconvincingly, before throwing a glance to a table about six feet to my right. They are starting to get impatient waiting on me to make up my mind so they, too, can get their drink on, though it appears they've had a few too many of those already.

"You know what, just surprise me."

"Surprise you?"

Wow. You'd think I'd asked her to donate her only remaining kidney to a serial killer.

"Yes. House special is fine."

"Okaaaay." Without a second glance, our brusque waitress bounces off on her high heels, relieved to be rid of me. I'm slightly worried what she'll bring back.

"What'd you go with?" Carmen asks me, voice pitched low as to not interrupt those around us.

This isn't a traditional downtown Nashville bar. There aren't throngs of people packed wall to wall like sardines. There is no drunk groping or girls puking in bathroom stalls. There aren't hookups in dark corners on rooftops or dirty dancing around the stage to music so loud you'll end up hoarse by the end of the night trying to scream over it. Rudy's Jazz Club isn't what I'd call classy, per se, but it is eclectic and intimate and, in my opinion, the best place in town for Louisiana-style red beans and rice and incredibly talented musicians who simply love their craft.

I shrug in response to Carmen's question. She smiles that engaging smile of hers before fishing her phone out of her clutch. By the way her entire being lights up, it has to be Manny. Her fingers fly across the lit screen, clearly replying to a text, and as she easily slips the phone back into her purse, she swings her eyes to me.

"What's wrong?" I ask.

"Nothing, chica. Everything is fine."

She taps her fingers in a quick rhythm against her leg. I

know that particular fidget. And I generally don't like what follows it.

I squeeze my eyebrows together, my forehead bunching up as I scrutinize her. "What are you up to?"

"Why do you always think I'm up to something?"

"Because you always are," is on its way out of my mouth, but there is a lull in the music at the tail end of Carmen's reply as the band ends one song and starts up another, and Carmen's high-pitched "something" echoes off the walls in those few empty seconds. I sense eyes from the entire room fall upon us in judgment. Someone whispers a rather uncalled for, "Shut up, bitch," and Carmen slowly turns around in the general direction our little scolding came from.

Uh-oh.

This is the thing about Carmen. She grew up in the one of the roughest parts of Miami referred to by the locals as "down south." Her father was killed in a bar fight when she was eight years old. Her three older brothers are all currently doing prison time. One for drug running, his fifth count. One for domestic assault. And one for first-degree murder and attempted robbery. Carmen's mother was chronically ill, but she still worked odd jobs in an attempt to bridge the gap of what the government couldn't provide and the basics of what was needed for her family to survive. Though Mrs. Morales was not about to let her only daughter travel down the same path as her three older brothers, no one escapes that type of environment unscathed. Carmen was molded straight from that Miami neighborhood where she grew up and when she feels attacked in any way, shape, or form, she quickly morphs back into the girl who ultimately won every street fight she was in and has the scars to prove it.

But while Carmen could absolutely hold her own, I would just as soon avoid getting the snot beaten out of me in some alley after we leave. Reaching across the space that separates us, I grab Carmen's hand, attempting a not-so-sly diversion.

"Hey, where do you think our drinks are?"

The band has been playing on, but a quick sweep of the room shows that we have now become everyone's entertainment, instead of the best jazz and R&B in all of Nashville.

"It's been a good fifteen minutes, I'm sure of it," I blather on. *It hasn't. It's been a good fifteen seconds.* Still, I pretend I'm searching for our waitress, but instead I make eye contact with the table of girls who stared me down earlier for taking too long to order and mouth, "I'm sorry." Luckily, all but the one with pencil-thin lips and a bride-to-be sash seem to be aligned with me in avoiding an all-out catfight. Three sets of hands land on the woman who told Carmen to zip it—she's half Carmen's size. *What was she thinking?* As they yank her back down, I jerk on Carmen's arm until she rips her attention back toward me, a string of Spanish expletives rolling fluidly off her tongue.

Suddenly I'm grateful for my earlier indecisiveness. I could use that "house special" about now. I scan around and lament, "Where is she..." but my voice fades into nothingness when I spot an insanely magnetic man with the most intense smoldering stare, I've ever seen.

And he's watching...*me?*

No.

Why would he be watching *me?*

Everyone is watching you, Laurel. You're nothing special; you're a spectacle. *That's all.*

Self-conscious, I ignore him, turning my attention back to the band. But try as I might, I sense his eyes on me. Assessing. And I begin to fidget like I have fire ants nesting in my granny panties. I smooth down my skirt. I cross my legs. I uncross and cross them the opposite way.

Those eyes. Wow.

I twist a chunk of hair into a corkscrew. I shake my foot and lick my lips.

Don't look. Don't. Look.

I don't. But I do pick at my peeling nail polish. I do chew off a hangnail on my left ring finger. And I do resist the urge to validate that the gorgeous man has moved on to someone else.

Because why wouldn't he?

Mi amado.

My beloved.

Could it...?

Nooo. It can't be. He's not. *Don't be ridiculous, Laurel.*

I scratch a nonexistent itch on my knee.

I pluck out an eyelash and blow it to the ground.

I pull at a stray thread in my hem, not realizing it's a bad idea until it's too late.

Finally, I can't take it any longer. I have to know if he's still there. Still watching.

When I turn my head his way, I am surprised to find he is. He absorbs my confusion.

Of course, there is doubt, gorgeous stranger. I am wearing mustard and you look like a ketchup kinda guy.

A slight smile upturns the corners of his plump lips. They resemble delicious ballpark franks. Almost makes me rethink my aversion to hot dogs.

I want to smile back, but he can't be flirting with me. Can he? Though who else would it be? It's definitely not Carmen this time.

Because of the way this room is narrowly shaped, Carmen sits at a forty-five-degree angle to my right, facing the stage. If she kicked out her foot, she'd almost kick mine. And I face the bar with the stage to my left. I face the stranger. There is no one behind me. I know this because my seat is flat against a brick wall that my long hair keeps getting stuck to.

Still, I have to weed out all other possibilities, so I glance to my left knowing very well the only one there is the hot pianist, and while hot pianist is quite attractive, I'm pretty sure he's not this man's bailiwick. Carmen's to my right, and as we've already established, she is out of the question for once. Out of stupidity or insecurity, or both, I turn around and stare at the wall behind me. Still brick. I slowly return to the stranger. He's laughing as he tips his half-empty glass of beer in my direction.

A mock "cheers."

My face burns hotter than the engine of Dale Earnhardt Jr.'s race car after five hundred laps at the Daytona 500. Instinctively, I reach for a drink that I still don't have yet.

"Where's that waitress?" My taste buds water wildly. I am so thirsty my mouth hurts.

My beautiful stranger—*my*, as though I've claimed him already—stands up from his place at the bar and begins walking in my direction.

Crap. Crap. Crap. Seriously?

I start chewing on a nail.

What is he doing? What am I going to say? Why am I so nervous?

I wince when I take out a chunk of flesh with nerves still very much attached. I shake my hand before twining all ten fingers together, clenching so hard my knuckles cry out.

Why are you acting like a zit-faced schoolgirl, Laurel? Get a grip.

I'm so busy practicing *hellos* and *how do you do's* and *who, me?* in my mind, that it's not until he's nearly upon me that I notice Manny is right behind him.

I deflate faster than a sliced balloon.

"Senorita." Carmen's boyfriend greets me with a quick kiss to the back of my hand as he always does. He doesn't look contrite in the least, and neither does Carmen.

This is a setup. I should have known.

Gorgeous stranger isn't into me at all.

I am angry. Humiliated. My breaths are shallow. I feel like

I've run a marathon and fell just short of the finish line, unable to cross.

"What are you doing here?" I spit.

I direct my irate question to Manny, but the stranger's gaze hasn't let me go yet. It's warm and inviting and...unnerving how much I like it, even if he was forced to be here.

"May I?"

Stranger waves to my seat but doesn't wait for a reply before he proceeds to turn his body and bend his long legs until he's perched in the chair with me. *With* me. I am now squashed between his warm, firm thigh and the arm of a chair that's roomy enough for one but is definitely not made for two.

He pitches an arm around the back of our chair—around me—and wedges his muscular self in a bit further until he's nice and comfortable. As if we are lovers or it's date night. As if we've known each other our whole lives and haven't just met.

And what can I do? We've already garnered enough attention that I'm worried we may be asked to leave, so there I sit. Fuming. Flustered. My face on fire and my body quickly catching up.

"I'm Ross," stranger says, leaning over to whisper in my ear.

Ross. Stranger's name is Ross. I had a great uncle named Ross. He would tap me on the patootie whenever I walked by.

"This is the part where you tell me your name," he jibes.

"Uuuhhh..." *Hot as you are, I can't date someone with the same name as my creepy great-uncle Ross. Sorry.*

He waits, expectantly. Damn, you smell a-freaking-mazing, Ross.

"Uummm..." I swallow, hard and awkwardly loud. Maybe Ross wouldn't mind being called by his middle name? Unless his middle name is Johnny. Or Ace. Or Wallace. *Like you have so many men lined up you have a right to be picky, Laurel.*

Out of the corner of my eye, I spy Carmen watching me, once again shaking her head in pity, as I search for appropriate words to string together that won't me look a) like an idiot, or b) desperate. But when I remember the circumstances of why Ross is practically sitting on top of me those words are misplaced, along with my manners, because I don't offer my name. No. Instead, I turn my back to him in favor of piano man, who now has his gaze squarely fixed on me.

Of course.

The edges of my mouth turn up wryly.

His turn up in amusement.

Stranger—Ross—shifts beside me, reminding me he hasn't gone anywhere, like he isn't aware the waft of his subtle, spicy cologne hasn't already hypnotized me.

"Tonight is a night for lovers, old and new," piano man says to me, fingers caressing his keyboard as lightly as if he's running them down the spine of a woman's back.

Good Lord.

I choke on the lake of spit now pooling in my mouth.

Ross slaps me on the back a few times as the crowd whoops and whistles. He genuinely seems concerned.

"I'm fine, I'm fine," I assure him, my voice wheezy. I wave him off, but when I lean back, it's right into his open arms. I fit as if I belong there. His palm curls around my shoulder and gently squeezes before retreating. I stiffen and manage another look at piano man. He winks. I'm sure he's playing me now, or perhaps he's playing Ross.

"Hardin, why don't you turn the house lights down for this next one."

No. Please no.

The lights go low, the music kicks up, and piano man starts crooning about the heavens and a rare night for romancing, but when he sings the title of the song, "Mind if I Make Love to You," I feel like I've been inserted into an episode of *Friends*.

And Ross and I are in the spotlight in this one.

Literally.

There is a wall sconce smack over our heads, which seems not to have dimmed in the slightest. Heat from the lightbulb is singeing the crown of my head. Half of my hem is hanging loose, and my thumb is now bleeding from where it's chewed to the quick.

I am a hot, bloody, unkempt mess.

As if Ross is only now understanding the horrible predicament he's let himself be talked into, he starts chuckling. And as the song goes on, with the day of our meeting and how time is fleeting, circling back around to the main lyric about making love, his body shakes with suppressed laughter.

I use the span of my right hand to cover my face in shame, hiding myself from Ross. But he's not having it. He peels my hand back and says lowly, "Your virtue is safe with me."

See? This is where I should have taken two seconds to interpret what he meant, which really was, *I'm a nice guy, not a dick who will try to get into your pants on a first date,* but nooo...I went all exorcist on him instead.

I whip my head toward him, my wrath as pungent as spewed vomit. "Why? You don't find this attractive?" I swipe down the length of me, lingering on the frayed edges, which in truth felt like every inch of me. I detest mustard. "Ketchup more to your liking?"

"What?" he says on a barked laugh, his brows furrowing in wary confusion...or perhaps fear.

"Ketchup? Do you like ketchup?"

My chest puffs out, my eyes feel bugged, and my jaw is clenched tight. I'm quite sure I resemble eleven shades of crazy.

He opens his mouth, then closes it again. He scratches the stubble lining his jaw, clearly contemplating his options. *Save yourself,* I think. But he doesn't flee like a sensible man would. He starts to say something, only he's interrupted by the waitress finally handing me my cocktail. She holds out a small goblet with a mint leaf floating in tannish liquid. It looks as if it came from the bottom of a well. I take it and sniff. It smells like the bottom of a well too.

"What *is* this?" I ask, turning my nose up.

"The house special," she answers me with a slight snap, but when she notices Ross, she becomes sweeter than rock candy. "It's called the Maiden Voyage."

I am in the middle of taking a sip when she announces this. Unfortunately for me several things happen in quick succession, none of them good.

I inhale a mouthful of the Maiden Voyage, which is made almost entirely of gin and ginger beer, neither of which I care for. I choke for the second time, and between my sputters and attempts to expel this sludge from my lungs, I faintly register the groan of the chair Ross and I are squeezed into. The groan turns into a creak, which morphs into the echo of wood splintering under too much pressure.

The legs beneath us give way and we crash hard onto the floor before we tumble in a heap of flailing arms and legs.

The music stops cold.

A hush comes over the crowd.

Once again, we are the center of unwanted attention.

"Are you okay?" Ross asks, running his hands over my hair, my face.

"I—"

There is commotion all around us. Strangers rush over. Concerns rain down on us. Several drops of liquid roll from my hairline down into my ear. I smell of pine and humiliation.

"Christ, are you hurt anywhere?" Ross pushes himself up on his forearms and washes a frantic gaze over me.

"I—"

"Talk to me," Ross demands when I don't finish.

I can't. I'm still gasping for air, but it's no longer because I'm choking, it's because Ross is squarely on top of me. And the man is thick, solid muscle.

Over Ross's shoulder I spot Carmen and Manny. Carmen appears slightly alarmed. Manny, however, is laughing his butt off, though he's trying to cover it up with his drink.

"Chica, you hurt?" Carmen asks.

"I'm fine," I rasp. I set my hands to Ross's chest to push him off of me, but holeeey cow. He is built like a brick wall or a linebacker in training.

"You sure you're okay?"

I nod, my palms still stuck securely to his pecs. They are unreal. Warm. Firm. *Wow*.

"You can move now," I tell him, licking my lips.

"You're sure?" With a grin and a wag of his brows, he flexes first one pec, then the other. I gasp, pretending to be affronted. We both know I'm not. More than moderately turned on, I squeeze my eyes shut.

Lord, take me home now. I'm ready. Please, I'm begging you. Open your pearly gates and let me on in.

Ross laughs before standing up with ease. He holds out a hand to help me up but just as I'm noticing the cool air on certain lady parts, Ross's gaze zeros in on my utilitarian, white, pee-stained underwear.

Sweet baby Jesus in a cradle. *Why me?* Perfect way to round out a first fake date.

"Here."

He bends down and covers me back up, like I am his to care for. The move is so tender, so gentle that I can't breathe. My eyes sting. Why would he do that? He didn't laugh. He didn't make fun of me. He didn't seem appalled by my lack of lace or a string splitting my butt cheeks. As I let him help me up from the floor, he tries to catch my eye, but I refuse to acknowledge him.

By this time the manager has rushed to our side and is babbling about drinks on the house for a year, apologizing profusely as they clean up the mess we made. Ross assures him we are fine. He says something to the band, which I don't catch, and they begin playing "September."

Ross brushes off some stray wood splinters from the front of his cabernet-colored button-down. I take the time he's using to right himself to really look at him. I would put him at well over six feet. He's handsome, but not as handsome as he is beautiful. And there is definitely a difference. His sandy brown hair is short but stylish, curling a drop below his ears. His jaw is square and rugged, and his hazel eyes are lined with bushy, manly brows that are neatly trimmed. His nose might be a tad big for his face, but the longer I stare, the more I decide it's perfect too. He is the perfect specimen of a perfect man and I am...well I'm bumbly and awkward and insecure. And to top it off, I've no doubt given him the impression that a thirty-day "vacation" in a hospital that specializes in the unstable would be well worth my while. I'm sure he will chalk this up to a bad attempt at a blind date and carry on his merry way.

Mi amado, my ass.

"Are you sure you're not hurt?" he asks one more time.

"Just my pride," I answer quietly, gazing around the room. Most people avert their eyes, some to where my undies are now hidden. "I need to go."

I swipe my purse from Carmen's hand and without so much as a goodbye to anyone, I head down the ramp that leads to the front door. The door attendant asks if I'm okay and I stall long enough to assure her that I am. Then I shove my way out.

Cool, crisp air hits me as I walk into the winter night. Wishing I'd brought my jacket, I make haste toward the direction I parked my car, two and a half blocks away. I walk through a wash of cigarette smoke from a couple leaning against the side of Rudy's. I heard cigarettes give you a quick buzz if you're not used to the nicotine. I almost stop to bum one, but I won't be able to stomach one more leer of pity.

I'm only half a block from ground zero when I feel, more

than hear, someone on my heels, and I may be incensed and embarrassed, but I am not stupid.

I spin around, shoving my hand in my purse like I'm palming a weapon. Tennessee is a conceal-and-carry state, and I have often thought of getting a small gun for protection, but I haven't taken the time to do it. So, most of the time that simple action of *acting* like you're carrying is enough.

"Youuu..." I can barely look him in the eye as I drag out the word longer than I need or intend to.

Ross squeezes his brows together before widening his stance. He crosses his arms. It stretches his shirt over his biceps very, very nicely.

Damn him.

"Boy, I was under the impression that Southern women were genteel and sweet."

It's obvious he doesn't have a lick of the South in him. I'd peg him as Midwestern. I want to ask, but I don't.

"If by that you mean pushover, someone has misinformed you."

That draws a bark. It's so loud, the smoking couple is now eyeing us, puffing away. I am tired of being tonight's main event.

"Goodnight, Mr...." I let it hang because not knowing his last name kinda ruins my haughty exit. I give Mr. Beautiful my back and double-time my pace.

In a flash he's beside me. I want to tell him that I am fully capable of getting myself home. Yet I keep my mouth shut. Shocker, I know.

It doesn't last long, though. "Didn't get enough in round one, Ross?"

"Ross? Who is Ross?"

He's so close to me that when I stop suddenly, he runs into me and I stumble a step or two forward before spinning around to face him.

"What do you mean who's Ross. *You're* Ross."

"I assure you"—he chuckles—"I am *not* Ross." All five finger-tips on his right hand come up to rest against the center of his chest. They're long and lean. I wonder what they'd feel like running down my back.

"But you told me your name is Ross. In there." I point dumbly to the club.

"No." He takes a full step toward me and I have to crane my neck to keep eye contact. "I told you my name is Ro*th*." He punctuates the "th." As if he didn't make his point clear enough, he goes on to spell it out for me. "R. O. *T. H.* Roth Keswick."

Roth. Roth Keswick. I almost laugh. So much better than pervy great-uncle Ross.

"What's your middle name?" I blurt, because that's the next most logical question a person could ask, right?

"Uh, Warren. It was my grandfather's name." He shrugs nonchalantly, as if he needs to rationalize the most regal name I've ever heard.

Roth Warren Keswick.

Well, that changes things, doesn't it? a little voice whispers in my ear.

No. No, Laurel. That doesn't change a thing. Even if he wasn't a setup, he's out of your league. Utilitarian, stained, tattered underwear is pulled up past your navel and you don't even mind. And Roth seems like a ketchup-loving, sexy-panty type of guy.

"Roth," I parrot.

He nods slowly, as if silently congratulating me. I don't even have steam left to be indignant about it.

We stand in silence for one breath, two, and with a flourish of his hand, Roth motions in the direction we were originally headed, so I begin to walk again, with him by my side. I won't realize how profound this small, seemingly inconsequential gesture is or how much I will come to rely on it over the years ahead of us. But I will learn in my weakest moments that this man's tenacity is the unshakable foundation that allows me to face each and every day, especially the ones you can't bear to face at all.

"You carrying?" he asks, noting my left hand still tucked inside my handbag.

"A woman can't be too…"

"…careful."

"Jinx, you owe me a Coke," we both say simultaneously again.

I give him a side-eye. His broad, genuine grin gets to me. I'm not even going to pretend it doesn't. His gaze drops to my lips, lingering on them, and my heart skips a half beat. *What is he thinking?* While I am distracted ogling my best friend's boyfriend's friend, the toe of my sneakers catches a crack in the sidewalk and the next thing I know I'm pitching forward toward the ground.

I'm bracing for impact when a thick arm snakes around my waist and breaks my second fall of the night. I am momentarily suspended in midair by strength and what has to be pure will, because light as a feather I am not.

"Once wasn't enough?" Lips brush against my ear, his question hushed but gravelly. He sets me back on my feet, making sure I am steady before he lets go.

"Th…thank you. I don't know what happened." I smooth down my skirt, which rode halfway up thighs that I think are too thick.

"At this rate, I'm worried about you driving home. Are you okay?"

"Oh, I'm fine," I assure him. "I've only had one drink and that was about two hours ago now. I don't drink and drive. Ever."

I don't know why I feel the need to justify this to a virtual stranger, but I can't have him thinking I'm both mentally unstable *and* irresponsible.

"I didn't think that."

I kick a pebble down the sidewalk. "Oh, okay. I just didn't want you to think worse of me than you already do."

"What I think of you is quite the opposite of poor."

Oh.

He scans our surroundings, noting a group of about ten young men walking toward us. Suddenly I am grateful he's there. As if we were headed that way anyway, he casually ushers us to the sidewalk on the other side of the street, away from the men. "But maybe I should—"

"No." No to whatever it is he is about to offer. "I'll be fine. In fact, I can get it from here. You can go back to..." I let it hang and simply nod back toward the bar.

"Not on your life. I'm at least getting you safely to your car."

The set of his jaw tells me he won't take no for an answer. "Okay, then," I say.

"Good."

We go the rest of the way in a silence that is quite peaceful and serene. By the time we make it to my car less than five minutes later, I sort of wish I'd parked farther away so I had a few more minutes to enjoy it.

"This is me," I say, pointing to my spicy red Kia Optima. I unlock the driver's door and open it. "Thank you, Mr. Keswick."

"Roth," he corrects. "I am not my father."

I let an amused smile slice into my cheeks. "Roth." I nod. "Thank you, Roth. I would say it was nice to meet you, but..." *I'm sure you don't feel the same.*

"It was very enjoyable. Thank you for an eventful evening."

I snort. It's unladylike and sounds like I'm trying to hock a booger. "You don't get out much, do you?"

"Enough."

There is no logical reason for it, but jealousy is difficult to keep at bay. Thinking of him on a date with another woman, her flirting with ease while he laughs at her jokes, is probably a chance I will never get with him. It's painfully clear I don't excel at flirting. Or ease. Or people, for that matter.

"Do I at least get your name before you get into your car and drive off into the night?" he asks, shoving his hands into his jeans pockets.

I tip my head to the side, studying him. "You didn't get a dossier on me from Manny?"

"A dossier?" He seems sincerely perplexed. Then his face lights up. "If a dossier exists, I would very much like to read it."

Now it's my turn to laugh loudly. I relax for the first time since I saw Roth Warren Keswick staring at me from across the bar. I almost wish I would have decided to stay. "I wouldn't be surprised if one does. Carmen is bound and determined to find *mi amado*."

"Mi amado?"

"Never mind. I, uh…I should go."

"So, your name shall remain a mystery, then?"

He's teasing, but he's also so brilliantly bashful that I offer, "Laurel. It's Laurel." He'll find out anyway the minute he returns to Rudy's, I rationalize.

"Laurel." He repeats my name slowly and deliberately. The deep vibrato of his voice makes it sound like he's reading a steamy passage from *Lady Chatterley's Lover*.

Time to go.

"Good night," I say quickly. Of course, my exit goes about as gracefully as the rest of the evening has gone. I throw my purse onto the passenger seat. It rolls to the floor and spills. I hit my head on the jam in my haste to get space between us and when I close the door, the edge of my dress gets caught and rips at the waist.

"Leave them wanting more," my mother always tells me about dating.

I can't imagine there's much more to leave Roth Keswick wanting. Except to run.

I start the car and am shifting into reverse when a rap on my window startles me. Through the glass, I stare up into kind eyes that would be easy to sink to the bottom of. Roth makes a "roll down your window" motion with his finger. I take in a fortifying breath before I do his bidding.

"To answer your earlier question, I do like ketchup."

Thought so.

I'm searching for a reply that doesn't make me sound pitiful, when he adds, "But mustard is my condiment of choice." He winks. "Drive safely, please...Laurel." Then leaving me with my mouth hanging open, Roth Keswick turns on his heel and is swallowed into the night.

For the longest time I sit there, waiting for him to return, wondering why I want him to. When he doesn't, I push away unwanted disappointment and pull out of the parking lot, heading toward I-40. Half a block down, there he is. Standing on a corner. Watching for me. Every part of me warms.

Roth brings two fingers up to his temple when I drive by. I give a small, tentative wave and watch him in my rearview mirror after I pass. I almost run a red light I'm so distracted. He sees, of course, and shakes his head. I watch him watching me until I have to turn to enter the interstate.

Later that night, after I've stripped and showered and settled into bed, my phone vibrates with a text message from an unfamiliar number. The only thing in the text is a link to YouTube. I almost ignore the message and delete it as phishing, as the message didn't load properly. Only there's something about it that compels me to click despite the risk.

When I do, tears instantly spring to my eyes. A shaky smile plays on my lips. And I swear my heart grows three sizes.

No man has ever sent me a song before.

My fingers linger over the keyboard, hesitant to respond. What do I say? Should I send a song back too?

Ultimately, I can't think of one that doesn't make me seem

clingy or like we should set a wedding date, so I settle for one that I hope will make him laugh instead. I text back a YouTube link to Gnarls Barkley's "Crazy."

My phone vibrates in under ten seconds.

Unknown: *Warning me off?*

Me: *I thought I did a good job of that already*

Unknown: *Oh, I'm afraid you'll need up your game considerably*

I sit on that for a long time. What if I don't want to up my game? What if I am tired of being invisible? What is it about Roth Keswick that has me feeling completely defenseless?

I have a thousand snarky comments running through my head, any of which would solidify my song choice, but instead I finally settle on a one-word reply.

Me: *Good night*

Unknown: *Until we meet again, Laurel*

I stroke the words a time or two with my thumb, thinking back to our debacle of an evening. Why on Earth would he want to see me again after tonight? I think *he's* the one who's crazy. Then I do something I haven't done with a man since my junior year of college. I add Roth Keswick to my contact list, because crazy as both of us may be, I'm not sure I can let this man go quite yet.

I go to sleep that night with Niall Horan's "Nice to Meet Ya" playing and a grin pasted on my face that is still there when I wake up.

THREE

**TODAY WAS
A FAIRYTALE**

Laurel

Ten Years Earlier
March 1, 12:32 p.m.

DESPITE WHAT ROTH KESWICK had assumed, I grew up in a small town outside of Omaha, Nebraska, not the South. I went to college at Vanderbilt, a "far too expensive education to be *just* an elementary school teacher," per my mother, but it was my grandfather's alma mater and it thrilled him that I wanted to attend as well. My PooPa, which is what I affectionately called him, wanted me to experience culture, diversity, and "the grandness of life." He knew that couldn't be accomplished in small-town Nebraska, population 1,092.

"Sow your oats," he'd tell me. "Just be careful what you reap." Then he'd smash me into him in a bear hug and tickle me behind the knees until I begged for mercy. He didn't want to hold me back, like my mother did, but it was hard for him to see me go, and it was just as hard for me to be away from him.

My grandfather died of a massive heart attack two months before I graduated from Vanderbilt. He was my rock, my guardian, my mentor, and most of all, my best friend. I think about him every day. Six years later, sometimes I still dial his number to tell him about a funny license plate I saw, or I start to text him when I run across our favorite movie, *Gremlins*, before I remember he's gone.

After college, much to my mother's chagrin and shaming, I made Nashville my home. I'd grown to love it here. Though our relationship was—still is—strained, I am all she has left. There was a teaching position open back in my hometown, mine if I wanted, but there was nothing left for me in Leone, Nebraska but heartache. My PooPa knew a small place wasn't what was best for me. On my last visit home, only three weeks before he died, he encouraged me to spread my wings, which was his way of saying don't come back. And my worst fear was ending up like my mother. A divorced, sad, bitter, lonely, tragic gossip-monger who most people in town avoided. She had her reasons. I'll admit some of them are valid, but some of them are chips she proudly keeps glued to her shoulders. For martyrdom? Pity? I truly don't know, but it doesn't matter. What matters is that I have strived my entire life to be the antithesis of my mother.

And a few weeks ago, I failed miserably.

So, while I don't suppose I grew up with traditional Southern manners, I am generally a far kinder person than I presented myself to be to Roth Keswick. My PooPa will be turning over in his grave at how I treated a man whose only crime was trying to be kind to me. Despite the trickery involved, he could have been a jerk. He wasn't. He was a gentleman in every way.

That's why I'm currently sitting at the Frothy Monkey, a fabulous café in a historic old house in downtown Franklin, intending to make it up to him. And to make PooPa proud.

"Your cappuccino, ma'am," the waiter says, setting down a large creamy cup balancing in a matching saucer.

"Thank you." I lift the cup to my mouth and blow on the steaming milk before taking a sip. "It's delicious, as always."

"Is there anything else I can get you?"

I rub my sweaty palms down the sides of my dress. Another

from the back of my closet, tag missing. This one is a fairly simple tealish-blue sleeveless smock, with intentionally frayed edges around the neck and hemline. Upon inspection this morning, it's not as horrible as I originally thought when I shoved it back there. Especially with the cute, shimmery gold long cardigan Carmen helped me pair with it.

"Some courage maybe?"

My waiter, who would be a bit dreamy if I were a few years younger, blinks a couple of times and cases the room quickly to see if anyone is in earshot. A shy grin appears, and his cheeks go red, like he's...

Oh no. *He thinks you're hitting on him, Laurel.*

I've been to this coffeehouse a hundred times. I think I've even seen this waiter before, and he's never paid me a lick of attention. Is it the dress? Maybe the two curls I put in my hair versus the messy ponytail I usually throw up?

He licks his lips and now they are glistening, which makes him appear as if he's aged backward five years right before my eyes.

"My shift doesn't end until four, but I'd be ah..." His blush deepens. *Don't say it. Don't say it.* "Free after that."

"Uh—" Crap. He said it. "I—" I don't want to hurt this kid's feelings. How do I let him down gently? I'm not used to being seen, let alone hit on.

"I know a great little dance club downtown," he throws out.

I'm wondering if he's even old enough to get into a dance club when a rough male voice from behind the kid belts, "I think the lady's dance card may be full tonight."

I have to stifle a laugh at how high he jumps.

"Oh, I...I'm sorry, bro. I didn't mean..." He motions back and forth, his gaze volleying wildly between us. "I didn't mean anything. I thought..." He ducks his head, embarrassed, mumbling, "My bad," before scurrying off.

"Well, that was awkward," I say, watching the mortified

waiter almost run into a customer on his way down the stairs. "I'll never be able to come here again."

The legs of the chair across from me scrape against the hardwood floor. I feel more than see Roth take a seat. "I'm a couple of minutes late and they're already buzzing like flies."

"No. It wasn't..." I glance up at him and stop cold. It's clear he heard this kid asking me out. I take in a breath and change the subject. "You're not late. I'm early."

I've actually been here for an hour. This is my third cup of coffee. I am thoroughly, tightly wound. My hands are shaking. I stuff them under my thighs.

"I was sort of surprised to hear from you," he announces, unzipping his jacket.

"Were you?"

This coffee "date" was my idea, but only after I'd ignored several weeks of texts from Roth. What was possible the night I went to sleep, after the song text, was improbable in the light of the next morning. When this graceful, gracious, confident man got to know me, he'd no doubt wish he'd made a different choice that night, leaving my grannie-panty, gin-soaked fanny sprawled on the floor of Rudy's.

It wasn't until Carmen chewed me up one side and down the other that I decided to reply to Roth. She rightly pointed out that I was being unfair and rude and just plain chickenshit. I told Roth I'd lost my phone. I'm sure he knew I was lying.

"I'm sorry about that."

"Don't be. I'm just glad you found your phone." He closes one eye in a quick wink. Buuusted.

A pretty young waitress interrupts, setting down what I recognize is a Monkey Cristo in front of Roth, a delicious mix of ham, swiss, and strawberry jam on bread, dipped in egg and grilled to perfection. He opted for the breakfast potatoes instead of the fruit. My stomach protests. Loudly.

"Did you eat?" he asks me.

"No, I—" I was too nervous and jacked on caffeine. "I'm good."

His brows scrunch together momentarily before asking our waitress, "Could you please bring an extra plate?"

"Of course, sir." She nods and hurries off around the corner, returning in a flash with an extra plate and set of wrapped silverware. "Anything else?"

"Yes, another side of the potatoes, please." He eyes me. "And some yellow mustard?"

I cover my smile with my coffee cup.

"You got it." She bops away, leaving us to be.

And it's at this time that I allow myself a full take of Roth Keswick. He's clean-shaven today. His hair is mussed a bit from the wind outside. He has on a pair of black wire-rimmed glasses he didn't have on when we met. They make him look smart and sophisticated. Apparently glasses on men *can* be hot. Who knew? I could sit and stare at him all day.

Then I notice the T-shirt he's wearing. At first, it was unremarkable because it's charcoal gray, but the yellow mustard bottle only now jumps out at me as if it's slapping me across the face screaming, "See? I told you I'm a mustard lover." There's something written underneath the bottle, but the table and his food are in the way so I can't read it.

"What on Earth..." I stop and giggle. I can hardly get out the rest of the question. "What do you have on?"

"What do you mean?" He adjusts his glasses up the bridge of his nose, then sets half his sandwich on the plate in front of me. He spoons some of his potatoes onto my plate as well.

I nod to his mustard bottle. "Your shirt."

Our waitress stops by with Roth's condiment, telling us the extra potatoes will be out in a couple of minutes.

"What about it?" He licks a splotch of yellow off of his pinky finger.

"It has a caricature of a mustard bottle on it," I articulate slowly, as if I'm speaking to a child who doesn't realize he's put his pants on backward.

Roth sets down the half sandwich he'd picked up and places both palms flat on the table. With a completely straight face he tells me, "I like mustard, what can I say?" Then he holds it out from his chest so I can read what's written below.

Oh. My. God.

The Mustard Whisperer.

In big, chunky, yellow letters.

This manly man is out in public in a mustard whisperer T-shirt. On purpose. It's a statement. A declaration. For me. It's ridiculous. And goofy. And insanely endearing. And what I will discover is the perfect representation of his personality. Bold. Daring. Uncaring of judgment.

I snicker.

"I thought you liked mustard."

"I..." I can't stop laughing. What a ludicrous conversation. "I don't."

"You don't like mustard?" He seems taken aback, likely thinking we are united in our love for this versatile condiment. Go team mustard! He's really going to think I'm a basket case.

"Nope." I shrug. "I hate it, actually. My sister and I..."

Mentioning Esther sobers me right up and I have to take a couple of moments to collect my thoughts. I don't talk about my sister with just anyone, because if I mention her, I ultimately have to talk about losing her, which is still devastating all these years later. But Roth...he seems like a safe space, so I swallow hard and make the decision to forge ahead, ignoring the sweat that's gathered in my armpits.

"My sister and I...we had a hot dog eating contest one year. We took two packages of hot dogs my mother had bought for a barbecue the next day, along with a giant bottle of French's mustard and we snuck down to our treehouse in the backyard. Esther got seven of her hot dogs down before they came back up, but she was smarter than me." She always was. "She didn't use mustard. But see, I didn't like hot dogs to begin with, and the only way I could eat them was with loads of mustard. I got all eight of mine down."

"Why did you have a hot dog eating contest if you didn't like hot dogs?"

The warm smile on his face is enough for me to continue. "Because Esther wanted to." And what my twin wanted to do; I did. She'd do the same for me.

"How old were you?"

"Eight."

He stuffs three potatoes in his mouth and chews. "I always wished I had a sibling to do those kinds of things with."

So do I. I swallow past a lump forming in my throat. "You mean get sick on hot dogs?"

"Absolutely."

"So, you're an only child?"

"I am, but we'll talk about me later. Tell me where your hate for mustard comes in. It gave you a win, so I'd think you'd be in the pro-mustard camp." He opens his mouth to take a gigantic bite of his sandwich, humming with pleasure.

I have to admit while I haven't given many men a chance to get to know me over the years, much of it is because I haven't found one who is genuinely interested in me. Who asks me questions about myself instead of trying to the turn the conversation back toward themselves at the first opportunity. It's refreshing and a little unnerving. I don't like talking about me.

"I did. But you know what goes up must come down...or in my case, what went down must come up."

"Ooohhh. Yikes."

The clench of his teeth sums it up nicely.

"Yeah. It wasn't pretty. I threw up all night long. We told our mother we wanted to watch Disney princess movies in the basement. She hated Disney princess movies. So, she let us have a sleepover down there instead of sleeping in our room." I think back to that night and how Esther never left my side. She held my hair and rubbed my back and told me she threw up on purpose so I would win. "The next day when our mother discovered the hot dogs missing, of course Esther and I were the most logical cause, but Esther...she was a pro at snowing her. She convinced our mother that she'd forgotten to buy them altogether."

I push a potato cube around the edges of my plate before stabbing it with my fork.

"Did she buy it?" he asks and takes another bite. It wouldn't be a hardship to wake up to this man's face every morning.

"She did. To this day she doesn't know the truth about those hot dogs or why we spent the night in the basement." I shove the potato into my mouth, so I can stop talking. Only he waits for me to finish, spooning a new stack of hot and steamy potatoes on my plate when they arrive.

"So, I take it you also never ate a hot dog again, either?"

"Ah...you would be correct on that assumption."

"Got it. Stay away from hot dogs. And mustard. Good to know. I'll burn the shirt." He plucks at the fabric, leaving a pinch mark where his finger was. It settles over his left pec and I have to cross my legs and look away.

"You don't need to do that on my account. I mean, if you're a mustard lover, you're a mustard lover."

His shirt hasn't lost its luster, unlike one that's a go-to and has been washed and dried a hundred times. In fact, I'm pretty sure it's new, if the crease marks are to be believed. That warms me in places that have long gone cold.

"I *am* pretty attuned to mustard, I must say."

I wrap my hands around my cup. I can tell by the temperature that the insides have already cooled. I want to order another, but I don't dare. My heart is already racing, and I'm going to blame it on the caffeine...not the man across from me.

"I didn't realize there was such a thing as a mustard whisperer." I egg him on, enjoying this inane conversation immensely.

"It's a little-known skill. Quite rare, in fact."

"Is that so?"

He is funny and kind and quick on his game. I like him. Sort of a lot. I think I could see forever in his eyes.

"There are all kinds of whisperers, Laurel." He leans back in his chair and bunches up his napkin, tossing it to his now-empty plate. "The horse whisperer is the most common, of course, but then there's the dog whisperer, a baby whisperer, a quarterback whisperer...even a love whisperer." The last part is said in a dropped voice that zings across my skin like static electricity.

"Wow. And you got the great fortune to be a *mustard* whisperer. How lucky." I tip my cappuccino in his direction and take a drink of the chilled liquid, much like he did to me at Rudy's.

He lets loose a howl that brings every patron's eyes to our table. But this time, I don't shrink or wish the floor would swallow me up. I laugh along with him.

"Beautiful, crazy, *and* clever," he says, wiping one eye. "Yes, I would say I *am* the lucky one, indeed."

I don't know what to say to that. He's rendered me speechless and that's hard to do.

"So, what do you do, Laurel?"

I'm relieved he didn't ask me more about Esther, but I hesitate in answering him. I'm proud of what I do. Being a teacher is a sixty-hour-a-week, sometimes thankless job, with mediocre benefits and a wage that definitely will not put me on the annual *Forbes* "Richest" list. But it was in my blood from the time I was born. My meema was a teacher. Her mother was a teacher. Her mother's mother was a teacher. And surprisingly, even my mother was a teacher, but instead of seeing the honor and reward in this incredibly challenging profession, she wanted "better" for me.

So, will this man think a teacher is enough? I decide I don't care. If he doesn't, he's not for me. *"Your partner should support your passions, sunflower. They don't need to necessarily share them, but they need to support them, at minimum,"* my PooPa once said. He was a wise man.

"I'm a second-grade teacher at Harpeth Mills Elementary School."

His face lights up. "That's fantastic. My mother is a retired high school principal. Forty-two years on the job."

"Really?" Every tense muscle I have relaxes, and I settle into my seat for the first time since I arrived. "Where?"

"Brooks High, Sarasota, Florida."

"That's where you grew up?"

He answers wistfully, "It is."

"How long has she been retired?"

His forehead wrinkles as he thinks. "Three years maybe. She's sixty-one."

"She's young."

"She acts like she's thirty-one." He snickers. "That woman doesn't stop for one minute of the day. She volunteers at the homeless shelter and is in three book clubs. She delivers Meals on Wheels for the elderly. She bakes for church funerals. She knits caps for babies. She even mentors new teachers. I mean, she is a one-woman wonder."

She sounds like a saint. One hundred eighty degrees different from mine. "She sounds wonderful."

"She is an incredible woman, Laurel," he replies. The love he has for his mother is evident, both in his voice and on his face. Another check in the box for him.

He picks up a glass of water the waitress brought and drinks half the contents in two gulps. I wonder if he doesn't care for coffee. "How long have you been teaching, Laurel?"

"When do I get to ask the questions?"

He tilts his head and studies me. "You just did. Several in a row, I might point out."

"Touché."

We fall quiet and the short distance between us seems to shrink even further as we stare into each other's eyes. Something I'm not all too familiar with starts low in my belly. It twists and dances and flutters against my insides.

Butterflies, I realize. I have actual butterflies.

I have to fight these weird urges to jump in his lap and kiss him senseless or ask him what he's doing for the rest of his life.

"You're not in the witness protection program, dodging the mob because you're a star witness in a federal money laundering trial, are you?"

His dimples are brilliant. Absolutely, mind-blowingly brilliant.

"I think you're reading too many crime novels."

Oddly, he is *not* wrong.

"Only someone who is in the witness protection program would dodge the question."

"No, Laurel," he answers, drawing out my name. Reaching across the table, he snags the tips of my fingers in his. I audibly suck in a breath.

This touch is different from the other day when my hands were cemented to his pecs. It's charged. Intentional. A little bit dreamlike.

"I am not in the witness protection program. I am not a criminal or unemployed or a closet serial killer. I am gainfully employed as a marketing director at one of the largest entertainment distributors in the US, and trust me, that sounds far more exciting than it actually is. I'd rather save for a rainy day than live beyond my means. I run five miles almost every day. I am an only child who loves his parents dearly and isn't ashamed to say so. Florida State Seminoles are my favorite college football team, but I'd forgo watching them on a Saturday in favor of a hike or a day at the lake. I love salmon and brussels sprouts but am allergic to shellfish. I enjoy grilling and the mastery of smoking brisket. I am team Apple all the way. I have an aversion to snakes and pumpkin pie. I drive an old, beat-up Jeep Wrangler that has over one hundred fifty-five thousand miles on her. I sing in my car. And in the shower. My brain is basically like a browser with twenty-nine open tabs all the time. I'd say I can move better than the average white man on the dance floor. I crave simplicity, yet always strive to be better. I'm a planner. I like a routine. My memory is a steel trap. I play a mean round of golf. And I do quite like mustard."

He finally stops and I am statue still, gaping at all he just told me about himself in ninety seconds. Inhaling, he adds, "All in all, I'd say I'm your average Joe living an average life."

Average?

He thinks he's *average*?

He is anything but ordinary or mediocre. He is extraordinary. Unique. Modest. Genuine. A rare find in a sea of crap.

So, I have no idea why, when I open my mouth, "If you're so amazing, why are you still single?" comes out.

His pause is only a blink and a breath. And in that briefest span of time, he somehow manages to turn the tables on me. "You think I'm amazing?"

"I—" I chorth, as my PooPa used to call it, which is a combination of a laugh and a snort that ends on me sounding as if I'm choking. It's unrefined and unbecoming, and sometimes something comes out of my nose. Yet it doesn't seem to faze Roth Keswick at all. In fact, he interprets this reaction exactly as it was meant.

"I will have to take that as a yes."

Again, all the words have fallen out of my head. When I don't deny it, his eyes sparkle. He wags his brows once, and once again, and he says, "So, now let's talk about you."

And that is how we spend the next eight hours. It turns out Roth does like coffee. Black with one packet of Splenda. We drink it until the middle of the afternoon, when we switch to beer. I try three before I find one I like. We share a charcuterie board and order two desserts. Roth has the banana pudding and I get the peanut butter bar. We end up swapping.

We talk until my voice hurts and my butt is sore from the wood bench beneath it. And we keep talking some more. Roth has been in Nashville for less than a year. He was at a small marketing firm, but when his current job opened, he couldn't pass it by, even though it meant leaving his friends and parents back in Sarasota. He met Manny a few months ago in a basketball league at the YMCA and happened to be having drinks with him the night we met. Carmen had forgotten her house key and Manny came by Rudy's to drop it off. It wasn't a setup after all, though I still think Carmen knew Manny's friend would be "tagging along."

I learn Roth is a surfer and a snorkeler and an accomplished sailor. I sink better than I swim, but I impress him that I can recite every word of *The Lion King*. He eventually begs me to stop after I prove my point. I never tell him about Esther. I didn't want to bring us down, but I decide on the next opportunity I want him to know. *If* there is another opportunity. I hope there is.

By the time he walks me to my car in the parking garage a few blocks away, the sun has long already set in the western sky. It's chilly.

"I didn't mean to take up so much of your day," he says, once again shoving his hands deep in his pockets. He rocks back and forth on his heels.

"You didn't. I mean...I didn't have any other plans." *Not cool, Laurel. You should play harder to get.*

"Laurel..." He lets my name hang, his gaze dropping to the few inches between us, then back up. When our eyes reconnect, it's as if he's found what he was looking for, in more ways than one. "I had a marvelous day. I enjoyed every single second of it, more than I could have imagined."

I feel all those things too. And more. So much more. "So did I."

He takes a step toward me. "I want to see you again."

I want to ask him to come home with me, but I settle for "Me too."

"Where did you come from?" he asks me as if I'm sort of a mirage come to life.

"From the cornfields of Nebraska," is all I can think to say. Lame. So lame.

He chuckles for a moment, then sobers as he caresses the side of my cheek. "They grow beautiful woman in Nebraska, I'll give them that." He brushes a few strands of hair behind my ear and his fingertips linger. How can a single soft touch hold so much power? "Will you please let me know you've made it home safely?"

I nod. *Where do I live again?*

He slips a finger under my chin and edges it upward. My mind blanks at the heat banked in his eyes.

"Can I kiss you, Laurel?" His attention drops to my lips. Like a bad chick flick, my tongue slips out to wet them, but by the set of his jaw, Roth must like it. Maybe they've got it right in the movies after all. "I want to kiss you."

I could have said anything. A simple yes or a silent nod would have sufficed. But I whisper, "Please," almost as if it were my first kiss and would be my last. And when Roth Warren Keswick's lips land on mine a moment later, I can honestly say it feels like both.

Kissing him is akin to landing in an indulgent, pillowy mountain of clouds. He is reverent, unhurried, and chaste. There is no tongue, no moaning, no thrashing of limbs as we try to stroke each other's bodies through our clothes. It's the best kiss I've had in my life. And as we both slowly open our eyes, I know that I am already falling for this man and I don't know how to keep him from seeing it.

"Good night, Laurel."

"Good night, Roth," I whisper just as hushed.

I don't move. Neither does he.

Eventually, he reaches around me to open my car door. He helps me in, and with a brief touch of his lips to my forehead, shuts the door. He steps to the side and watches me work my way out of the tight parking spot and out of the garage. I watch him until he's a blip in my rearview mirror.

Twenty-five minutes later. I enter my apartment and follow through on my promise to let him know I arrived home safely. This time, though, I flay myself open and do so with a *safe and sound*, and a song link of my own: "Today Was A Fairytale."

Within seconds, I get a screenshot of a song back, as if he was listening to it at that very moment. And if I didn't think I was falling in love with this man when he kissed me, I certainly do now.

Like a silly starstruck teenager, I make a playlist that includes both songs Roth has now sent me and the one I sent him. Turning out the light, I listen to "Today Was A Fairytale," "Nice To Meet Ya" and the newest, "Nothing Like You," on repeat until I fall fast asleep.

FOUR

SHE'S GOT
A WAY

Roth
Present
June 16, 3:12 p.m.

"Fuck me," my best friend Manny says. *My sentiments exactly.* "This just doesn't make any sense."

No. It doesn't. It doesn't make a damn bit of sense.

Laurel has no known risk factors that we're aware of. She doesn't smoke, has no previous cancer or genetic predisposition. She's not been exposed to dangerous chemicals or radiation, she's not of the right age group, and she's definitely not male. She was seemingly perfectly healthy, until she wasn't anymore. But that's the thing about monsters. They *do* lurk in the dark, unknown until they want to be seen.

A little over a year ago, Laurel's monster stepped out of the shadows and made its presence known with a venomous roar.

At first, we thought the sporadic fevers she had were attributed to the repeated respiratory infections she couldn't shake. She was exhausted to the point she struggled with her demanding job teaching seven-year-olds, but again, we thought that was tied to her constant illnesses. She lost weight, but because she was sick often, she also didn't eat much, so we didn't think as much of it as we should have.

In retrospect, the signs were clear. She had unexplained

bruising, but she always bruised easily, so we didn't give that the necessary attention. We certainly didn't tie it to her other symptoms. Her back and her legs ached, but that was because she spent more time than usual resting, trying to recover from constant illnesses, right?

Wrong.

Add them all together—fevers, weight loss, bruising, exhaustion, infections, bone pain—and you have a completely different picture.

A dire one.

One every doctor we saw missed, until October of last year when my wife was diagnosed with acute myelogenous leukemia, aka acute myeloid leukemia, aka acute myeloblastic leukemia, aka acute granulocytic leukemia, aka acute nonlymphocytic leukemia.

Doesn't matter what you call it; it's bad news. And in even worse news, she has the rare, tumor-forming subtype known as acute panmyelosis with myelofibrosis.

She was immediately hospitalized, where she started an intense regimen of chemotherapy. She responded well to the first three rounds, though she experienced most of the common side effects: nausea, vomiting, hair loss, fatigue. But she had her good days too.

Laurel never lost her positivity, even on the worst days when she could hardly get out of bed, or when the sores in her mouth became so painful she couldn't eat for two weeks. She endured countless blood and platelet transfusions, four days in the ICU from sepsis, and blood clot after blood clot. She has every right to be angry and hopeless, yet she has been *my* strength on the days when I didn't know how I could watch her suffer a second longer.

Three months ago, after the last round of chemo, Laurel's blood tests showed she'd gone into remission, which was completely unexpected given the gravity of her cancer. I bawled on the spot. I had my wife back. I had my *life* back. A bone marrow transplant was the next step and Laurel was added to a match registry. Though we weren't out of the woods, not by a long shot, we could see the path out.

Except we foolishly let our guard down, and we have been burned. Badly.

The elation we were basking in has spanned the length of one long exhale and now we are squarely back in the white-hot grips of perdition.

"I don't know what to say, man. I'm sorry just doesn't cut it."

Of course, it's doesn't. *Sorry* is appropriate when the Tennessee Titans lose, or your aunt fucks up your bowl cut the night before junior prom. In this scenario, *sorry* is an offering rooted in one's attempt to provide you comfort. It's futile. They know it. You know it. You appreciate the gesture anyway, though sometimes you simply can't tell them so.

"I mean, she's too damn young. It's not fair."

Taking another swig of my Red Bull, I let Manny continue his one-sided conversation. What I'd give for a fifth of vodka about now. Wouldn't even have to be the good stuff. A ten-dollar shit-store brand would do. But if I start, I won't stop until I'm passed out, and that won't do Laurel any good. Or me. I can't waste a single blink of our time together in a haze of denial, as much as I would like to.

Rubbing the middle of my chest where it burns, I gaze through the window into the kitchen, wanting to be inside with Laurel right now. She is sitting at the table with Carmen, her best friend and Manny's wife. Their mouths are turned up with smiles at the moment, Carmen undoubtedly trying to make light of this grave situation, which is her way to muddle through, but they've been crying. The giant wad of used tissues on the table between them isn't the only dead giveaway.

Even with a tear-streaked face and dark circles under her

eyes from little sleep, she has this indescribable light that surrounds her. She has a way about her that I've never quite been able to articulate. She is the most ethereal woman I've ever laid eyes on.

What am I going to be without her?

"Isn't there all kinds of experimental shit you can do? Like in Germany or Sweden or hey, Mexico?"

How many times will I have to answer this same fucking question over the next several months? Too many, to be sure.

"There is nothing, Manny."

Or maybe there is. But we're not going to pursue it. We agreed no extraordinary measures if it returned or the bone marrow transplant failed. Cancer ravages the body, but from my perspective the treatment itself is just as bad. The fact we gained an additional few months is a miracle in and of itself. I know this. It's one I should be grateful for, I suppose, though it's hard to feel anything but anger and bitterness right now.

Laurel laughs at something Carmen says. How she still has the ability to do that is a testament to her character. And her smile...it's always been contagious, so I find myself smiling too. It feels foreign. Wrong. Like a middle finger to the nightmare we are now special guest stars in. Holding my proverbial middle finger higher, I force the smile wider, but Manny's next attempt to make me feel better flattens it out in an instant.

"Maybe something will come up. They have new treatments all the time."

"They do," I agree half-heartedly, never taking my eyes from my wife. And in truth, though I am a realist, this is the only thing that keeps me from breaking down into a blubbering ball of despair on our bedroom floor. The *maybes*. Try as you might, they are impossible to let go of.

Then I wonder...is acceptance synonymous with giving up? Or is acceptance just your ability to move on to the next phase of managing through a crisis? Can you still hold on to hope, to the maybes, while planning for worst case scenarios? Or are these two separate worlds entirely?

I don't know. I truly don't. What I do know is that we can either spend our precious time chasing an impossibility or we can live what time we have left together to the fullest. Is it possible to do both? It's something I've given a lot of thought to since we first found out Laurel has cancer.

"Do you remember what I said the night I met Laurel?" I ask Manny. I dig my thumbnail into the flesh of my palm to quell this razor-sharp ache in my soul.

Manny's gaze follows mine into the house. To the one woman he's devoted his entire life to and to the one he loves like a sister. "Who the hell is that hottie?" he replies, laughing.

I did say that, but "No, I told you the fact she thought herself so unremarkable was incomprehensible to me."

She tried not to be seen or noticed. She thought she could shrink and that others outshone her. Instead, she was like a smudge of red lipstick on white satin, its indelible mark noticeable from a mile away. She's the only one I saw. How she didn't recognize that in herself was beyond me. It still is now.

"Yeah, I remember. That was an interesting night."

It was that and more.

"She is everything good about me. Earning her love is my greatest accomplishment in life." Without taking my eyes from Laurel, I add, "Thank you, Manny. Without you..." I'd never have met this incredible, fascinating, quirky woman who has given me the greatest life a man has the right to ask for.

"Don't give up, man." He clasps a hand to my shoulder and gives a quick squeeze.

I have to clear my throat a time or two before I answer, "Yah." I still sound like I'm choking on a frog.

Laurel catches me staring. I don't even bother pretending I'm not. Her eyes soften and even from this distance, I watch tears gather at the edges, surface tension working hard to keep them trapped. She reaches up to tuck hair behind her ear, something she used to do frequently. Flushing pink, she realizes her mistake. There is no hair, only the decorative scarf covering her nearly bald head. Her finger snags on the inside of the large hoop earrings she sometimes wears, and her cheeks burn brighter.

"Stop," she mouths. Her gaze keeps darting away, then back to me again, the shading on her face deepening each time.

"Why?" I mouth back. Grinning, I spread my legs farther and set my elbows to knees, letting my hands clasp loose between them. Then I say quietly, "I love you."

"I love you more."

No, you don't, I want to tell her back. *No one could love another the way I love you, Laurel.*

I'm not sure what she says next, exactly. I understood *pick* and *later*. I wonder if she's speaking out loud or silently like I am. I hope it's the latter. It's juvenile, but I want our private conversations of devotion to remain private. They are for me and me alone.

If Manny notices what we're doing, he doesn't let on, but Carmen sees our flirty, teenage exchange and I expect her to do something obscene, as is her usual MO, but she leans back and hangs her head. She snatches a clean tissue from the box and surreptitiously dabs the corner of one eye. She is suffering too. Just as I am.

I blow out a long, long breath of despair.

"What's next?" Manny asks. He crumples his empty beer can and lets it fall to his feet, reaching for the extra in his cup holder.

What's next? It's the question I've been tossing around since we left Dr. Nuess's office. Life cannot go on as normal, because it is *not* normal. I can't wake up and go into work on Monday and walk through the door at five thirty, wondering what's for dinner, anxious to watch the next episode of *Dexter* with Laurel while eating popcorn. Absolutely nothing that was important to me before is important to me now...except Laurel and making each moment we have left count.

"I've been thinking about something," I start. "It may be a little crazy, but—"

I don't get a chance to finish, because a car pulls into the driveway and the engine shuts off. I'm irritated at the unwelcome visitor. I simply cannot deal with a barrage of questions or blatant airs of sympathy.

I just can't. Not today.

"Hey, isn't that your—" I follow Manny's gaze to the person rounding the house and bolt out of my chair when I realize who it is.

"Mom?"

My parents live in Sarasota, Florida, which is a good fifteen-hour drive for a man who won't go a tick above the posted speed limit or refuses to let his wife drive because he's old-school and believes "driving is a man's job." I talked to my mom yesterday afternoon on the way home and broke the bad news. My parents, who are like parents to Laurel, were distraught. They wanted to come, and I told them no. We needed time to process and figure out our next step. I told them I'd let them know when they could make the trip.

Yet here they are, not listening to a word I said. They must have driven all night. They watch my reaction, and while I am feeling a plethora of emotions race through me at top speed, anger is not one of them. In fact, I am so overcome with the events of the last twenty-four hours, I am so overwrought trying be strength enough for two that I completely lose my shit and break down in sobs.

My mom can't get to me fast enough.

My dad is right behind her.

And as both sets of their loving arms surround me and their whispers of empathy envelop me, I am helpless to keep this shitstorm bottled inside any longer. All of it gushes out in unmanly hysteria. The anguish, the fear, the uncertainty. The love of my life is being unfairly ripped from me and I can do nothing to stop it or change it. I mourn like an inconsolable child out in the open for all the world to see and judge.

I weep while they hold me up, literally and figuratively. They are my armor, my bones, my momentary refuge in the eye of an EF5 tornado that will swallow me whole again and leave me with nothing after it passes. They refuel me with the courage and fortitude I will so desperately need to carry Laurel and me through this.

I have never been more grateful to see anyone in my life.

"How did you know?" I don't add *I needed you*, in an attempt to regain a shred of the dignity that I've publicly lost. I don't know that my parents have ever seen me cry as an adult.

My mom takes my face in her hands. They're weathered and spotted from the sun, but they're soft and tender and smell of the lavender lotion she's so fond of. She looks up at me, eyes wide and glistening, wearing her own pain without shame. And when she answers, "Mother's intuition," it breaks my heart fresh in two again, because it's a moniker my Laurel has desperately wanted yet will never get the chance to have.

FIVE

JUST A KISS

Laurel
Ten Years Earlier
March 22, 6:22 p.m.

"ARE YOU SURE THIS GOES TOGETHER?" I ask Carmen.

Balancing my phone on the dresser so she can see me, I grab the pair of new canvas Mary Janes from their box and hold them up next to my brand-new dress. Tonight, is my first official "date, date" with Roth. Well, what feels like a real date, that is. The coffeehouse was just...coffee.

I am nervous as all get out.

"Si," she tells me while fetching a sparkling water from her fridge.

"Carmen, you didn't even look."

"Laurel, we picked them out together." She twists the cap off of her water and takes a swallow.

"But the dress is red, and the shoes...are also kinda red. Are you sure it's not too much...red?" It's too much red. Why did I pick red? Red is a "power" color. Red draws so much attention. "I should have gone with blue. Or camouflage."

Carmen's eyes roll straight into the back of her head. "Laurel, the dress is burgundy. The shoes are mauveish, not red. The palette goes perfectly together, and it's a fabulous shade against your fair skin."

I study the shoes again, unsure. "Maybe plain white shoes would be best."

"No. That would definitely clash."

"I don't know."

"Laurel, don't you trust me?"

"I...yes?" I don't. I am so out of my comfort zone, I'm getting hives. I don't even like dresses. I hate them, actually. Yoga pants and baggy sweatshirts are more my style. Staying in is more my style. "I am so bad at this."

"Bad at what, chica?"

"Fashion. Dating. Dressing myself. All of it."

How I managed to get myself together for our last date must have been divine intervention. I toss the shoes to the floor and drape the dress over the end of my bed before flopping down on it in frustration.

"Where'd you disappear to?"

"Heeere," I lament, sounding incredibly pitiful.

"Hey, don't leave a girl hanging."

I sigh and pop up to snag the phone. I lay back down, propping myself on an elbow. "I should just cancel."

Carmen walks from the kitchen to my favorite piece of furniture in her apartment. A large, multicolored wingback chair that she has stuffed into the corner between two full-length windows. It's loud and boisterous, just like her. Dead opposite of me.

"What's wrong?" she asks. Sitting in the chair, she draws her knees up to her chin.

"I..." I pause, biting my lip. "I don't know."

"Don't you like him?"

Very, very much. That's the problem.

"I do."

"Then what is it, Laurel?"

"That's the same question I keep asking myself, Carmen. What is it? What does he see in me?" I haven't seen Roth since we spent the day together at the café, but we've talked and texted every day for the past three weeks. The conversations are light, and the texts are flirty. My playlist is mounting by the day. And my feelings for him grow exponentially with every passing minute.

But I don't get it. I am not the prom queen or the high school cheerleader. I was on the yearbook committee and in book club. I played in the shadows, comfortable on the periphery. I was a nerd. I still am. And he is…well, he is everything I am not.

"I am geeky and insecure and—"

"Unique and warmhearted and selfless and—"

"Clumsy and comic bookish and—"

"Excessively hard on yourself," she interrupts again before I can spit out more character flaws. "Laurel, you have this draw that is irresistible. Your wholesomeness and authenticity are arresting, really. I remember thinking that when I first met you in Mr. Hannifer's drama class. You were this beacon in the dark of night or a soothing serenade floating on a soft breeze. You, my friend, are everything I strive to be when I grow up someday."

My eyes prickle as tears spring to life. "Carmen," I whisper, all choked up.

"That is what he sees in you because that is what is there to see. You are beautifully perfect inside and out. Now, wipe your face, blow your snot, and get out of your head. And put the dress on. Let me see it."

"What? Now?" I rub my cheeks until they're dry, still feeling a bit sticky on the inside from all the unexpectedly wonderful things she said.

"No, tomorrow." Carmen scrunches up her face. "Yes, now. Isn't he picking you up in, like, forty-five minutes?"

I glance at the clock. Shoot. How did it get so late?

"Yes."

"Jesucristo. Darse prisa. No time to waste."

"Okay, okay." Feeling like I'm coming out the other end of a time hop, losing hours I can't account for, I shuck my sweats and tank and throw the dress on over my head.

It's a swing dress, per Carmen. The fabric is a soft, silky chiffon. I wouldn't know. A dress is a dress is a dress to me. It lies neatly over my breasts and hangs loosely over my torso, ending a couple of inches above my knees. The neckline is demure, which makes me feel less on display.

I spin one way and then the other. While it is girlie, it's also prettier than I remember in Nordstrom when Carmen bullied me into buying it. And she may be on point about the color.

"What do you think?" I ask her, continuing to twist in opposite directions, mesmerized by the flow of the forgiving material.

"Shoes, shoes," she commands. I snatch them from beneath my feet and quickly slip them on. I set Carmen back on the dresser and walk far enough back from the phone so she can see the full length of me. "Sleek and stylish yet relaxed at the same time. Perfecto."

She's right, once again.

"Do you know where he's taking you yet?"

I received very specific instructions from Roth for this date: Wear comfortable shoes, similar to what you had on the night we met. When I asked him why, he asked me if I was always this difficult. When I replied yes, his response was, "My mother always says I am a glutton for punishment." It made me laugh.

"No. He just said we'd be outdoors and to wear comfortable shoes."

"And what about the panty situation?"

Flames lick at my cheeks. I found a lacy pair of black panties in the far back of my "lingerie" drawer, a term I use loosely. I don't even remember buying these. Probably another gift from my mother. Weird, I admit, but for once I am grateful for her boorish attempts to turn me into something resembling a girl.

"They're clean," I reply.

Carmen laughs. "That's not what I meant, but okay. We'll make that our next shopping trip."

"Hmmm. Sounds fun." Truthfully, it sounds painfully...painful.

"I know this amazing lingerie boutique in an 1800s train station on Houston Street."

Of course, you do. Carmen has the most exquisite sets of undergarments I have ever seen. Makes sense she'd get them at some posh boutique that's unaffordable for regular people.

"Now it just sounds expensive," I mumble. "I can pick up a six-pack of Hanes at Walmart for under twenty dollars."

"Pfft." She waves her hand at me in a dismissive manner. "A girl needs to splurge once in a while."

"Easy for a girl to say who makes a healthy six figures a year as a top executive recruiter. Don't forget I live on a teacher's salary."

"I haven't. They even have sexy grannie panties," she says in a singsong voice, trying to entice me. "We'll shop the sale rack."

"I'll think about—" My phone vibrates and a banner across the top indicates it's my mom trying to FaceTime me. "Great."

"What?"

"It's my mother."

"Don't take it."

"I have to. This is the third time she's called."

"I don't think it's a good idea, Laurel. Not before your big date. You know how your conversations with your mother go."

She doesn't need to remind me.

"I gotta go." My phone chimes and chimes, as my mom tries to reach me. "She'll just keep calling."

"Fine. Don't let her guilt you into anything." Fat chance. "And text me when you get home, no matter how late. I want to hear how the big 'd' is."

"The big d?"

"Yeah." Carmen wags her microbladed brows up and down.

"Carmen," I chastise, but it's not entirely heartfelt, because I go warm in the center of my body at the mere thought. "I'm not going to have sex on the second date for crying out loud." Although I may have thought about it a time or two...or twelve. But...no. For sure, no.

"I meant *date*, Ms. Prude. Get your head out of the gutter."

"Sure, you did."

Her grin widens. "Go talk to Candice. Text me later. Love you, chica." Carmen puckers her lips, then presses them to the camera lens.

"Love you too." I click over to catch my mom in time. "Hi," I say, a little breathless, though I have no reason to be, except that it's my mother and well, it's my mother.

"Hi, sweetheart. Nice to see you."

"You too." I sit down on the edge of the bed, careful not to wrinkle my dress. As if she knows she'll be needed, Meringue strolls into the room and gracefully jumps into my lap. I rub her from head to tail, then start over again, not even caring about the white dusting of hair she'll leave behind.

"You sure must be busy these days." Candice presses her dark coral coated lips together ever so slightly, waiting for a reply.

Aaand here we go. My mother has passive-aggressive down to an art form. From the sugary tone to the schooled facial expressions, she is a master at making you feel like a criminal for anything and everything, even when you're innocent. I used to confess to most of what Esther did when we were kids...she is that good.

"Yeah, I'm sorry I missed your other calls. I've been a little busy."

"What's got you so...focused?"

"Oh, you know." I shrug and attempt nonchalant. *Not a date. Not a date.* "Same old, same old. School. Books. Stuff."

I don't say a word about Roth. For one thing, it's far too soon. For another, she would spend the next hour grilling me or start poking holes in a man she's not even met yet.

"You look like you have makeup on, dear." She brings her face closer to the screen, squinting. Oh nooo. "You do. What's the special occasion?" She knows me. It's rare that I wear makeup.

"Nothing, Mom. Just...ah, trying out some new stuff Carmen picked up."

"Oh." She pauses, and her pause gives *me* pause. "It looks nice, dear."

Does it? I had thought so, but now...

I glance up to catch my reflection in the mirror. I blink a few times, not knowing what to think. My mother doesn't dole out compliments unless they are on the back of her hand.

Is my foundation blotchy?

Is my eyeliner too thick?

I rub two fingers against my cheek, smudging the coat of blush I'd brushed along it. I thought it was just a touch but now I'm not so sure.

"What is that you're wearing?"

"What?" I ask, still staring at myself.

"Do you have a dress on?"

"Ahhh..." How could she see the dress? I must have tilted the phone down just right. "Ah, yeah."

"Makeup. A dress. And your hair...it looks like you've fixed it up. Do you have a date?"

Could she sound more surprised?

"No. No, of course not," I tell her with a fake adamance I am quite proud of. "I...it's a...a costume. For a school play."

"Oh." Now *that* tone I am used to. Resigned disappointment. "Well, I'm sure it will happen for you someday, dear."

"I'm sure," I mumble in stoic agreement. And for not the first time, that careless comment she flings about without thinking twice...it sticks, and it simmers and bubbles until my mind whirls and questions and worst of all...doubts.

"Did you know that Pastor Schefft's wife was caught cheating on him with that sketchy tattoo shop owner? Can you believe it?"

"How would I know that?" or "Who didn't see that one coming?" or "Maybe you don't know the whole story," are all replies I want to lob back. Instead, I answer, "Really?" as if I care who is cheating on who in Leone, Nebraska. And for the next twenty minutes while my mom babbles on about this illicit affair and the scuttlebutt it has caused throughout town, I listen with cool disinterest, because the entire time I am replaying her benign comment. I know, which one do I pick? But I go with, "It looks nice, dear," and by the time I can get a word in edgewise to tell her I need to go to "play practice," I am convinced I look anything but nice.

What was I thinking?

Plain Janes aren't glamorized; they're white noise.

The second I hang up, I head to the bathroom and scrub my face clean. I scrub until it's irritated and red and I am almost in tears.

"I can't do this," I whisper to my empty apartment, defeated.

With a heavy heart and trembling hands, I snatch my phone from where I'd tossed it on the bed and start pounding out a Dear John text to Roth. I type and delete, type and delete and ultimately end up with *You deserve glamorous.* Only, the moment I go to hit send, my thumb hovers over the arrow and I hesitate. When I decide to delete that one too, the doorbell rings and scares the crap out of me and my thumb lands on the send button by accident.

"Shit," I curse, and I hate cursing. It's unladylike and I honestly don't need any more help in that category.

And now I am in quite the dilemma, aren't I?

How do I explain that text? Maybe I don't answer the door?

"But then he'll worry, Laurel," I say to myself. I pace the bedroom floor back and forth a few times, tapping the edge of the phone against my now-dry lips. I stop to apply some mint Chapstick that I keep on my nightstand. I coat my lips several times until the layers of wax are thick and my lips tingle.

Three quick raps on the front door startle Meringue and she scampers underneath the bed. She's as much of a scaredy-cat as I am. We're a perfect match.

"Laurel?" Roth's deep voice penetrates my thoughts, but instead of answering him, I snap off my bedroom light and pretend I'm not home. Only, it's a cowardly move, and he can't see in the bedroom anyway, so it's also stupid.

I pace and think. Think and pace.

He knocks again.

The easy decision would be to stay in the dark until he gives up and leaves. It's appealing, but gosh, this man has earned far better treatment than that from me.

So, with rocks in my stomach and moths tickling the back of my tongue, I walk slowly to the front door and jerk it open, like I'm ripping off a Band-Aid. The moment Roth Keswick gets a look at me, this will all be over anyway, I convince myself.

But...that is not what happens. Not at all.

Roth lights up like a thousand-watt bulb in a dark room, blinding me. Wait...*what?*

"Hi," he says, his voice a little rough.

"Hi." I shift uncomfortably from heel to toe, crossing my arms, one over the other.

As if he's highly attuned to my crazy already, he reaches for my hand and lets it rest in his. It's grounding and somehow manages to slow my heart to a dull roar. "Saving the planet?"

"Huh?"

He motions behind me.

I look over my shoulder into my gloomy apartment. "Oh, ah...power outage."

"Really?" His gaze goes up above his head where the outside light glows and he joins it back with mine.

"Yeah," I stutter, not able to hold our connection as I tell a completely unnecessary white lie. But once a web is spun... "It's...a...sporadic. Happens all the time."

"Maybe you should contact your landlord."

"I'll do that tomorrow."

"Laurel." I don't want to look at him again, but the way he says my name with such tender concern compels me somehow. "Is everything okay?"

No. No, everything is not okay. I try to fight it, but my emotions have always been worn on both sleeves. Water blurs my vision and I say, "Yes," at the same time I find interest in my mauveish Mary Janes.

But Roth isn't having it. He gently lifts my chin until our eyes meet again. I blink and tears run down each makeup-free cheek, the turncoats.

Now, at this point any other man would suddenly remember that he left his refrigerator running and make haste, but Roth is not just any man, as he keeps reminding me. He wipes them away and says quietly, "How about we stay in instead?"

"I—no. I don't want to ruin the night any more than I already have."

"Laurel, you haven't ruined anything."

I have, but I have nothing else to offer except a weak, "I'm sorry."

Roth cocks his head slightly. "Sorry? There is absolutely no reason to be sorry."

"I'm..." Clearly a hot mess. "A little out of sorts at the moment, I guess."

He drops his hand away, leaving me a bit bereft. And with the absence of his touch, I try hard not to start spinning again.

"Happens to me all the time," he tells me.

I highly doubt there's anything that could get this man out of sorts, yet I give him a swift smile that falls way short of my eyes.

"I'm afraid I may not be the best of company if you want to take a raincheck."

I don't want him to leave, but offering an out seems like the right thing to do.

"I appreciate the warning. If it's all the same, though, I'll stay. I have very much been looking forward to spending the evening with you."

"You have? Even like this?" I take a giant step back, surprised. Here I am, a makeupless, wild-eyed, snivelly disaster decked out in a shade of confidence that I don't feel at all, and yet he's still here, as though none of that matters a lick.

"Like what?"

That knot my mother expertly winds up inside my gut loosens marginally. "Like this." I wave a hand up down myself, wondering if those sexy glasses are for looks only.

"If by glamorous, then the answer is unequivocally yes." The corners of my mouth tip up. The ball unravels more. "Did I already say how very much I was looking forward to this evening?"

I don't answer for a few seconds, dumbstruck. Or maybe awestruck. "You may have said that, yes."

"You heard me say *very*, right?"

I giggle. No man has ever made me giggle before Roth Warren Keswick. "Yes. I heard."

"Good."

He ushers me back inside and reaches around to the switch on the inside wall. Giving it a flip, he hides a grin when the light obeys his command. I bite my lip and avert my gaze.

"Looks like it's working now," he announces.

"What do you know," I mumble, flushing all over in embarrassment.

Though I know he knows I'm totally busted, his teasing does

the trick. Everything I was feeling before I opened the door completely vanishes into thin air. Because of him and a resolve that's like nothing I've known before.

We stand in comfortable silence, both probably with silly smiles on our faces. Mine feels silly, anyway. His is incredibly sexy. Maybe staying in is a bad idea.

"Do you want to order some dinner?" he asks me. I see the second he spots a half-used tissue I left lying on the counter. I don't know why, but I feel the need to use them multiple times before I throw them in the garbage. Half-used tissues are lying all over the house. I snatch it up and wad it in my fist, because even I can admit it's a weird, unexplainable habit.

"Dinner. Yes. Food is good." In my head, I roll my eyes. *Back to your usual bumbling, I see, Laurel.*

"I agree. Food *is* good," he parrots. Chuckling, he pulls his phone from his back pocket and asks me what I want. We settle on Mexican, a decision I'll likely regret in a few hours, but I've been craving it all week.

While we wait for our delivery, I show him around my eight-hundred-square-foot apartment, begging him to ignore my unmade bed since I wasn't expecting company. We end up on the sofa, him in one corner, me in the middle.

He pats the arm in quick rhythm. "Little more room on this one."

"I was thinking the same thing," I reply. Actually, I was wishing this sofa was a cushion smaller.

"I hope it's sturdier or I might have to ask to see the manager."

I wedge an elbow on the back of the couch and rest my head in my palm. I'm hoping it comes across as flirty and not wooden. Imagining what an idiot I look like, I drop my arm back into my lap. "Maybe she'd offer you drinks on the house for a year."

"Hmm." His voice falls an octave and if I'm not mistaken, he suddenly looks rather smoldering. Maybe I *was* flirty before. "I may ask for an open-ended arrangement."

Does that mean what I think it means?

Actually, what *does* that mean?

"You may?" My heart pounds so hard against my chest I am sure the neighbors can hear it. I have to swallow before I ask, "Can I ask what you are thinking?"

"Oh, Laurel." He chuckles, shaking his head. "I'm afraid if I told you what I was thinking, you'd ask me to leave."

"Would I?"

Do I sound breathless? I do. I am. I am totally out of breaths.

Roth leans toward me until I feel his exhales inch down my cheeks. His pupils have exploded. His mouth is pursed just so. Good gravy, this man has sensual down to an art form. I think he's going to kiss me, but he runs two fingers through a few strands of hair and holds up a fuzz ball.

"Oh," I manage to push out. My chest expands and contracts in crisp, shallow movements.

"I want to, believe me."

"You want to what?" My lids are at half-mast and my face is tilted upward, waiting. I must appear either desperate or inexperienced. I may be a little of both.

"Kiss you, Laurel." *Then dooo. Please, do.* "But if I start kissing you now, ten feet from your unmade bed...well..."

Well, what's the problem? I wouldn't say no.

"You may think this a little unconventional..." Cool air crashes into the space he's now left between us by shifting away. "But I'm okay taking things slowly. I like you, Laurel. Too much to screw this up by moving too fast."

The disappointment and rejection that gripped me in the first part of his sentence is replaced by heat firing through my blood at the last part.

"You do?"

"Yes." His hand covers mine. He wraps his fingers tightly around the edges.

"But...why?" I ask, confused.

He drops his head and shakes it, a smile on his face. "I think we need to work on this compliment thing."

"Do we?"

He nods, his eyes now flitting back and forth between mine. "You are like a unicorn, Laurel, you know that?"

My eyebrows scrunch together. That does *not* feel like a compliment.

"And what I mean by that," he goes on, as if sensing exactly where my mind went, "is that unicorns are thought not to exist. They are fantasy, legend. Mythological symbols of purity and grace." When I don't say anything, he twists his fingers in mine. "I never thought someone like you existed, Laurel. You're like a fairy tale come to life."

I almost break down right on the spot. No one has ever said anything so nice to me. Not ever. I mean what Carmen said was amazing, but this...

Wow.

Before I have a chance to even form an adequate reply, Meringue makes her presence known by leaping right into Roth's arms. I immediately go to grab her but stop the second she starts purring under his touch...much like I do.

"Huh," I say in complete shock. "She doesn't like anyone."

"Well, I'm not just anyone."

I chew on that for several beats before whispering, "No, I suppose you're not."

And that is that. If Roth has Meringue's approval, he most certainly has mine. I mentally kick doubt to the curb and hope she stays there this time.

"Where were you taking me tonight?"

"That is a surprise."

I want to kiss the smirk off of his face. "But we're not going now, so you can tell me."

"We're going. We're just delayed."

Oh. "But I don't like surprises."

He tilts his head to the side and runs his eyes over my face. It might as well be his fingertips, it's so erotic. I bite the inside of my cheek, unbelievably turned on. "You do, Laurel." I open my mouth to disagree, but he sets a hand over it to stop me. "Don't bother denying it. The excitement in your eyes is a dead giveaway."

Hate to break it to you, Roth, but that excitement you're seeing is not *because of a surprise.* But when he runs the pad of his finger lightly along my cheek before going back to petting Meringue, I don't have the heart to argue.

The rest of the evening is like a dream. We eat chips, guac, and enchiladas and drink a margarita or two. We snuggle under a blanket, hold hands like teenagers, and laugh through *Guardians of the Galaxy* and *Guardians of the Galaxy Vol 2.* We lavish affection on Meringue and make popcorn. I am giddy the entire time. It was absolutely perfect. And when he finally tells me good night after 2:00 a.m., he holds my face in his hands and kisses me like I've not been kissed before. It's not chaste, like the first time. It's fervent and intense and pent up. I want him to stay, that messy bed calling his name, but I don't at the same time. I, too, want to take it slow.

By the time he finally walks away, my head is swimming. As soon as he's stepped out of sight, I'm already anticipating seeing him again.

I've barely shut the front door when my phone dings and I just know it's him. I race into the bedroom to grab it, anxious to see what song he sent me tonight.

Only it's not a song. It's a question.

Roth: *if you could go anywhere in the world, where would it be?*

Random, but okay.

Me: *i don't know...why?*

I watch the dots, waiting for his reply.

Roth: *answering a question with a question isn't an answer...*

Me: *okay smarty pants...* I type back. *give me a second*

Roth: *patiently waiting...*

I am not what you would call "well-traveled." I've only been to a handful of states and I've never been outside of the country, but I've also had no desire to because as illogical as it is, flying terrifies me. So, while I try to think on a grander scale, like the Alps or Milan or some fancy island in the Caribbean, I am a pretty simple person with pretty simple needs. And what I keep coming back to is the place that holds most of my fondest childhood memories.

Me: *branched oak lake*

Roth: *sounds special*

Me: *it is*

Roth: *btw..."just a kiss" was the perfect way to end a perfect night. i had a great time, laurel. sweet dreams.*

I grin like an utter fool. Perfect song choice.

I lie on the bed and click the YouTube link he sent before replying *so did i. good night, roth.* And then I end up falling asleep in my burgundy dress and my mauveish Mary Janes, knowing without a doubt that Roth Warren Keswick is my beloved.

SIX

HAPPY

Laurel
Ten Years Earlier
June 7, 7:02 p.m.

"So…" I watch the city whiz by, anticipation building. We're closing in on downtown, which I'm guessing is our final destination. "Are you going to tell me where we're going yet?"

I haven't been this excited about a date in…well, since the last one I had with Roth. We've been officially seeing each other for three months now, and I don't mind admitting—to myself anyway—that I have fallen madly in love with this man.

I've never felt this way before. I finally have someone worth losing and it is terrifying.

"Patience is not your strong suit, is it?" Roth reaches across the console and melds his fingers in between mine. We are two puzzle pieces snapping into place.

"How long did that take you to figure out?"

"Oh, I had you pegged the very first night, Laurel."

"Did you now?" I draw one leg underneath the other, tucking my dress between them to make sure my panties aren't showing. Yes, the dress hater is wearing another dress, because tonight is the makeup date from what I've dubbed as the *Just a Kiss* night.

Roth's finger grazes the inside of my thigh as he tugs play-

75

fully on the fabric, dislodging it. "You don't have to do that on my account, you know."

Oh. My. Word.

My face cycles through five levels of heat. And I am now uncomfortably damp. While we have come close, Roth and I haven't slept together yet, and it is not from lack of trying on my part, believe me. I even asked Carmen to take me to that posh lingerie store she mentioned. We drank champagne and spent hours trying on the scrappiest, sexiest outfits I've ever worn. It was the most indulgent day I've ever had, as my credit card can attest. Tonight, I am wearing one of many new risqué purchases, and I am bound and determined that he is going to remove it.

But right now, I need to change the subject before I demand he pull into the closest hotel and get us a room for the night. Roth exits from 440 to West End Avenue. Guess we aren't headed downtown after all.

"Just tell me where we're going, pleeease," I beg.

"You're so cute when you beg."

"Cute?"

"Sexy?" he counters, eying me for a reaction.

"Sexy?" My voice inches up and his response is a deep and booming laugh.

"Yes, definitely sexy."

Begging is definitely sexy? Well, then maybe I should change tactics in the bedroom. I tuck that little piece of information away for later.

He turns right on Thirty-First Street, which leads us toward the Vanderbilt campus. I have no idea what to expect. We could be going anywhere, but in minutes, he's slowing to pull into Centennial Park. Maneuvering his Wrangler between two other vehicles, he declares, "This is it," as he shuts it off.

"This is it?"

The park is packed with people of all ages, young and old

alike. There are a surprising number of college-age kids here, as well as several food trucks and what looks to be a beer tent.

With a wink and a grin, he says, "Yup."

His body is vibrating with excitement. Mine is vibrating with bad feelings.

We both exit the vehicle and the first thing that hits me is the music, which in and of itself is not unusual in Nashville. Music is everywhere. Street corners. Stores. Restaurants. Broadway. But what's unusual is the type of music that's playing.

Nashville is known for country, but this sounds like something from my PooPa's era.

Roth swings open the back hatch and slides two bag chairs over his shoulder. He slips a large, folded blanket over his forearm, closes the hatch, and holds out his free hand for mine. He leads me around the throng of cars toward the covered pavilion where everyone is gathered, dancing away.

Dancing.

Uh. Oh.

Finding an open spot on the grass, he hands me one of the chairs. I remove it from its holder as he spreads out the blanket.

"Have you been here before?" he asks as he works on setting up the other chair.

"No. I've done a lot of things in this city, but I never knew this existed."

Because it's *dancing.*

"It's a free concert series Metro Parks puts on every summer. Each weekend they focus on a different style of dance, like the waltz or the rumba or the foxtrot. But it's always big band themed."

Ah. That explains the Lawrence Welk vibe.

"I didn't peg you as a big band lover." I gnaw an imaginary hangnail I feel coming on.

He doesn't look ashamed in the least, answering quite proudly, "My parents took me to hear big bands when I was younger. Most kids would have hated it, I suppose, but I thought it was cool. Kinda stuck."

"Did your mom teach you to dance then?"

"She did, in fact. Do you dance, Laurel?"

Roth told me on our first date that he could dance better than the average white man. I should have paid more attention to that, dug deeper, asked more questions because now, it appears, I am in quite the pickle.

I stare at him. I knew this was coming, and sometimes the only way to answer a question is to paint a vivid, colorful, 3D portrait that pops right out at you.

"I don't suppose you ever watched *Dirty Dancing*, did you?" The way his eyes bulge, I'm quite sure he doesn't know where this is going. "Then you remember Baby?"

He smirks. "Nobody puts Baby in the corner."

I really want to ask him if he prefers Jennifer Grey before or after her nose job but debating that would get us off track. I'm in the before camp, by the way.

"Well, I am *not* Baby." I stab my finger into my chest. "There are no watermelons. No seductive pelvis rolls or elegant leaps into the strong arms of Patrick Swayze. *I* am the stiff older sister, Lisa. The one with zero rhythm and a singing voice that would scare a screech owl."

The edges of his mouth curl in amusement, only I am dead dog serious.

"If Baby can be taught to dance, you can too."

"Wrong." I chuckle nervously, trying reverse psychology instead. "Why? We didn't come here to dance, did we?" Silently I beg him to say, *"No, I just enjoy music of old and thought I'd expand your horizons,"* and I'd say, *"Oh, ha ha, you scared me,"* and he'd say, *"I'm sorry, it wasn't my intention to scare you, Laurel,"* and we'd *not* dance, eat Mojo Cookie Dough ice cream, and have another great date.

While I pray this pretend conversation comes to fruition, my gaze sticks to a couple closest to us on the dance floor. I wouldn't put them at twenty, yet it's obvious they are well practiced. Each spin is fluid, crisp, and precise. Each flick of their limbs as sharp as twin bullwhips.

This isn't like the box step we learned in gym class when I was in seventh grade. I shudder as I hear Mr. Romo's sharp rumble: *"One—Two—Three—One—Two—Three."* Tap. Tap. Tap. Tap. *"Laurel, no. You always start with the right foot. Walk, side, together. Walk, side, together in the shape of a box. It's not that hard. Now let's try again."*

But it *was* that hard. I didn't get it then. I don't get it now. And according to Mr. Romo, the box step is the foundation for all other dances, so if I can't master that, I certainly have no shot at whatever *this* is.

"Well, tonight *is* swing dance night," Roth declares. He's all keyed up.

Not the response I was hoping for.

Think, Laurel. Think. Quick.

"Swing dance night?" That doesn't bode well for me. "I'm afraid I don't know that one." Or any of them. I don't even know the box step for crying out loud!

Roth grins, but this time it does not make me feel warm and tingly inside. I start to sweat.

"They have lessons," he offers. "In fact, they start here in a couple of minutes."

He's been here so often he knows what time they give lessons? Who is this guy? Why has he never mentioned this before? Next, he'll nonchalantly announce he's a two-time swing dance champion.

"Ready?"

"Uh…" I take a step back and hold out my hands for him to stop. This is seventh-grade gym class all over again. No. No, no, no, no. No. I can't. "I promise you—you don't want me to dance."

"But I do."

"I am pathetically awful at dancing. Really. I don't move better than your average white man. Or woman, for that matter. Lisa...remember?"

He snickers. "Laurel. I don't care how well you can dance. I just want you in my arms."

Well...crap.

Really?

What's a girl to say to that? Thanks, but no thanks? I am truly flat up against a wall now.

I hear PooPa whispering in my ear to suck it up; this is what relationships are all about. Give and take. And Roth has given plenty. It's my turn. I try to ignore him, but his raspy voice grows louder and louder until I can't anymore.

Ugh.

I can't believe I'm about to say this.

"All right."

He takes my hand, squeezing it until I look up at him. I pull the inside of my cheek between my teeth and bite down.

"Laurel, I promise you it's not that bad."

"It *is* that bad. You have no idea what you're getting yourself into, Roth."

"Just want to dance with my girl is all," he says, wagging his thick brows, trying to lighten me up.

"You may need another girl then," I reply with what sounds like oodles of sarcasm but is one-hundred percent truth.

He pulls me close until our bodies join chest to knee. Usually touching him makes me melt into goo, but I am so taut, it feels like rigor mortis has set in. "If you don't want to try, then we can just watch."

"Really?"

"Really."

My body sags in sweet relief, but it only lasts a moment, because while that may be what *I* want, Roth's disappointment is palpable. And as much as he wants to make me happy, I want the same thing for him.

Fortifying myself with a big breath, I blow the words out before I chew and swallow them up. "I'll do it."

"Are you sure?"

"On one condition."

"Name it."

"Promise me you won't make fun of me."

"I would never make fun of you, Laurel." He throws his free hand over his heart. "You have my solemn vow."

"Let's go then, before I chicken out."

"That's my girl."

He leads me to the side of the floor where men and women are gathering for the instructors. They tell the leaders to go to the left side of the floor and the followers to go to the right. I don't really know what that means but when Roth lets go of my hand and motions for me to go to the right, I panic.

"What are you doing?" I grip his arm with one hand and ball his shirt up in the other.

"You need to go to the followers' side." He tries prying his shirt from my kung fu grip. Only in death will that happen.

"Why?"

"Because you're the follower and I'm the leader."

"For purposes of dance only, I can accept that statement, but today you're a follower too."

His lips twitch, but he comes when I drag him to my side. It may be because my nails are now embedded in his shirt and it ripped a little when he tried to pull away, but whatever. Extreme circumstances, extreme measures.

"Okay, okay, ladies and gentlemen!" A pretty, thin blonde taps on the tip of the microphone attached to a headset. I recognize her as the girl I was watching earlier. "If you're new to swing dance, do *not* worry. We'll break down some simple moves step by step, so even the most novice of you will be able to enjoy a twirl on the dance floor." The crowd whoops and claps and sways with restlessness. I think I might vomit. "As a reminder, those who will lead the dance should be on the left side of the house with Greg here." She points to the man she was dancing with. Greg, who wears a matching headset, waves gregariously to the group. "Followers are on the right with me. I'm McKayla. The steps will be a bit different, so be sure you're on the correct side of the room."

The girl is staring straight at Roth when she says this. I glance around to note he is the only male on our side, and with his height it's not as if he doesn't stand out. I roll my eyes up to him and he's watching me, amused.

"You're not going anywhere," I demand, sliding two fingers through the closest belt loop.

"Wouldn't want to lose my shorts too."

"Ha. Ha."

He is getting a kick out of this. I'm glad one of us is. When I mutter, "Thank you," he wraps an arm around my waist and kisses the top of my head, whispering encouragingly, "You're gonna do great."

Not likely.

Seeing that Roth is staying put, blondie asks, "Y'all ready?" with a great deal of enthusiasm that garners a wild round of "yeses" and my faint "no."

And before I know it, we're off.

The band stays quiet and both she and Greg turn around, so their backs are to us.

"Okay," McKayla starts. "There are many variations of swing, but tonight we're going to focus on the East Coast variety. We'll start by teaching the most basic swing step first. Put a bit of space between you and your neighbor so you don't step on any toes."

I reluctantly let go of Roth and take a half step to the right.

He says something about his toes, but I can't process it because McKayla is already shouting more instructions.

It's all happening so fast.

"Leaders you'll start with your left foot, followers start with your right." She slides her right foot out and points her toes to the floor. We all follow suit, holding steady until the next instruction.

"Don't look at me," Roth whispers, when he sees me checking out his form. "Keep your eye on McKayla." He says her name as if he's familiar with her.

I frown, muttering, "Okay."

"We're going to start with a rock step back." Moving her right foot back behind her left, McKayla shifts her weight back to that foot, then up to the left. "Then we're going to move to a closed step, also called a triple step." Her right foot slides back out to the right where she started and she moves her left foot over to meet her right, then moves her right foot one step to the right again. "Right, close, right," she explains at the same time she's demonstrating.

I'm already in way over my head.

They do a triple step back to the left and I bump into the lady next to me because I went the wrong way, of course. I make light of it. "We're starting off on the wrong foot," I joke, and she laughs hysterically as if it were original.

I get back on track and follow McKayla, chanting under my breath, "Rock, step, trip—le step, trip—le step." It's remedial but it seems to help. They repeat the steps over and over, first to the right, then to the left, and by the last time, I actually get through it cleanly before she moves on. I even manage a tiny sway in my hips the way she does.

"See? You're catching on."

I don't let Roth's praise, or his animation, go straight to my head. A lifetime of swing dancing couldn't get me to the caliber of McKayla.

"Leaders, it's time to grab your partners and practice with them. This time to music!"

Music. Great. How exciting.

As everyone scrambles excitedly to find their person, Roth turns to me and I tentatively step into his arms. He shows me exactly where to place my hands. My left on his shoulder and my right held in his left. I'm a little awed at how smooth he is.

"You're a natural," he tells me.

"And you are conveniently blind," I reply on a chorth.

"And you are so very beautiful, in case I didn't tell you yet tonight."

He did, but a girl doesn't get tired of hearing it even if she has a hard time always believing it. I don't get a chance to respond, though, because Greg calls out, reminding us which foot we're supposed to lead with first.

My heart leaps into my throat when the band kicks up and we take our first steps. I watch our feet and begin chanting under my breath, "Rock, step, trip—le step, trip—le step."

Ross brings us to a halt. "Let me lead, Laurel."

"I am," I insist.

"You're not. You're trying to take over." He runs his hands down my arms until he has my hands in his. He takes a step back and shakes them back and forth until they're semi loose. "Relax."

"Easy for you to say."

"Maybe. I admit I don't know what it's like to follow, but you have to trust your partner. Do you trust me?"

"Yes," I reply automatically, without a second thought.

"Okay." He takes a big inhale and exhales slowly, watching me as he does it. "Now you."

I grumble but follow suit. He takes me back into his arms and leans down to place his lips on mine. I close my eyes, forgetting everything around me as he kisses me tenderly.

"Much better," he mumbles against my wet mouth.

And I realize he's right. My muscles have loosened their pinch. "You may have to do that a lot."

Roth leads me right into the next step and floats us along effortlessly, even as we pick up the pace. "Kissing you is not a hardship, Laurel."

"It might be after we're done here tonight."

He flings me out and twirls me around. It's unexpected and I shriek in surprised delight, but as quickly as he does it, I am back in his hold and we're practicing the same old steps that I am getting more comfortable with.

When he slows his movements, I step all over his toes. He doesn't even seem to notice as he draws me close and whispers, "A lifetime of kissing you wouldn't be a hardship."

"Oh." My mouth floods with saliva as we stare into each other's eyes. Is that a declaration? An invitation? A promise? It feels like all three wrapped neatly into one. All that's missing is a bow. And a ring. I swallow. "A lifetime huh?"

"Does that scare you?" he asks as we sway, our rock, step, triple steps all but forgotten.

Does it?

No, I decide. It doesn't scare me at all.

"I should probably take you for a test run first," I say, tongue in cheek.

"A test run, eh?" He spins me again. Out and in. Then we're nose to nose. I'm breathing hard and fast. "What kind of test run exactly?" His eyes smolder like molten lava. The heat burns me so good.

"The, ah…" *The sex kind, you fool.* The hot, sweaty, dirty sex kind.

He runs the hand that's on my lower back to the underside of my tush. His fingers graze my crack and I swear to you, I'd call him a god to his face. If he stripped me naked right here right now, I would not object.

"A test run seems to be a reasonable request," he rumbles in my ear.

"It only seems prudent," I counter breathily, though he's already agreed.

He grazes the tip of his nose up the length of my jaw. Lord in heaven. This champagne music is distracting. "Prudence is practical, but one can miss out on the best adventures being too cautious."

Caution meet wind. So long! I wave her goodbye, the hanger-on.

"Laurel…"

"What?" I pant, exposing my neck in blatant invitation. I wait for the warmth of his lips or the flick of his tongue. Neither come. I pop one eye open and Roth's staring at me, his grin wide and toothy.

"You're standing on my feet."

"Oh. Whoops." I slide off, one foot at a time, bumping into a couple dancing behind us.

The hazels I've grown accustomed to are dark and ablaze as he assumes his dance position once again and waits for me to move in. I would be affronted if it wasn't unmistakable that he is as turned on as I am. The evidence is both in the sharp angles of his face and in the outline below his belt. "Shall we?" he croaks.

Good.

At least he'll struggle as much as I will.

"We shall."

I put thoughts of a test run in the back of my mind and for the next solid hour we learn variations of the same step, adding on turns and spins at various angles. I learn that the rock, step, triple step is the foundation for at least this version of swing. We put the moves we've learned together and all of a sudden, I feel as though I might actually be dancing. It's still a bit confusing and I stumble more than once, but Roth is always there to guide me back, his hold firm and confident. He's extremely patient and it's clear he's enjoying himself, even though I may very well be the worst partner on the floor.

Then the lessons are over and now it's open dance, and while I'm hungry and thirsty when Roth suggests we take a break, I decide I want to stay on the dance floor. I'm truly having fun. Who would have thought?

"Mr. Romo would be so proud."

"Who?" he asks, twirling me out, then back in.

"I'll tell you later," I yell over the throng of voices and live instruments.

Another thirty minutes goes by, and I beg for a bio break. After that, we skip the beer and drink water to rehydrate ourselves, and by the time we're ready to get back out there, an incredibly upbeat, happy song starts playing. A crowd forms a circle around the center. Roth grabs my hand and drags us up to the front.

Two girls and two guys stand in the middle, their poses frozen. One of them is McKayla and the other is Greg. Every few seconds they change their poses to the feverish beat of the music, freezing again. But they're all doing something different. McKayla shakes her hips. One of the guys wiggles his shoulders. The other girl knocks her knees together, while Greg decides to spin around. They're bold and fearless and when the music reaches a fever pitch, they all fall into a choreographed routine. And nowhere in that routine do they perform a rock, step, triple step. I am envious as their arms whiz fluidly over their heads and their legs flick crisply to either side. Their bodies move as swiftly and sharply as an ocean wave crashing into the horizon, yet it's honeyed and smooth at the same time.

As they transition from moving as one to their own individual displays of personality, I notice that McKayla has locked eyes with Roth. Now, I don't tend to be a jealous person and maybe that's because I've had nothing to be jealous of, but at the same time my vision turns various shades of green, Roth lets go of my hand and announces, "Be right back." Then he jogs onto the dance floor with three other people from the crowd.

I've seen flash mobs on YouTube and in movies, of course, but I have never been witness to one until this moment.

It's thrilling and fascinating. And my boyfriend is apparently part of it.

Wow.

I have a boyfriend.

With a quick, flirty wink to me, Roth seamlessly joins in their little act as if he was part of it from the very beginning, as do the others. About every fifteen seconds, another new person joins their group, and I stand there in absolute, utter awe.

Roth's moves are skillful. Flawless, as if he's been professionally trained.

His poise and self-assurance are not only commanding, they're beyond arousing.

And suddenly I envy everyone who is out there with him.

I want to be them.

I've never wanted to be able to dance more in my life, but I want to be a partner Roth is proud to have on his arm. I want to exude confidence and glide around the floor with finesse. I don't want to have to count steps. I don't want to be a Lisa.

The song ends. The crowd goes wild. The band begins playing again and people flood the floor, coupling up. Roth high-fives with his dance partners and jogs back over to me. He's barely broken a sweat.

"That was...wow," I say, flabbergasted. "I guess you weren't kidding when you said you could dance."

"I do okay."

"Okay?" I snort. "I'd say you're far better than *okay*. You were amazing, Roth."

And I am so, so inadequate. That doubt I'd given the old

heave-ho a while back pokes her grubby little head out of the gutter and waves.

"How did you do that?" I ask, still stunned.

"Practice," he answers with so much humility it warms me. "Hey." He sweeps me up in his arms. I wrap mine around his neck as he swings me around. "Want to get a snow cone?"

"A snow cone?"

"They're not just for kids, you know."

I check his face to make sure he's serious and he is. He surprises me at every turn. "You're right. I would love one."

The line is short. I choose cherry and Roth decides on blue raspberry. We split an order of nachos too, since we haven't eaten dinner and I'm starving. We sit in our lawn chairs and watch people laughing and dancing and having fun.

I pop a cheese-dipped tortilla chip in my mouth and look over, asking him in jest, "Tell me you're not a two-time swing dance champion or something."

Scooping up a spoonful of blue-shaved ice, he replies, "I can say that I'm not a two-time swing dance champion." He opens his mouth, and the shaved ice disappears.

Thank goodness. With that devil in his eye for a moment I thought he was going to—

"I only won the US Open Swing Dance Championship *once*."

I stop cold, watching for some sort of tell that he's teasing me. As his shoulders rise to his ears, I notice a blush creeping along with it. He's not.

"You're joking," I say, astonished.

"It was only the novice category," he adds. "Not a big deal."

I sit there with my mouth agape. If I'd won the US Open of Swing, I'd wear the medal around as a gawdy necklace. But not Roth. He is modest and unpretentious. He probably has his trophy buried in a box, as I've not seen it proudly displayed under a spotlight anywhere at his house.

"How old were you?"

"Nineteen."

"Do you still dance then? Like that I mean?" I gesture to the dance floor. It's obvious he does. The flash-mobbers clearly practiced together. That much was undeniable.

"Not much anymore. I'm a little rusty."

"But you knew what you were doing out there. You didn't look rusty to me at all."

He focuses his attention on me again. "Every major city has a swing club. It's a great way to meet people and stay up on your skills. I've been a few times. It didn't take long to learn that."

There are a dozen other replies that are far more appropriate than, "Oh. So that's how you know her," but nooo...that's the one I latched onto instead.

Roth crumples up his snow cone wrapper. He plucks mine from my hand and does the same thing, stuffing them in his cup holder. Then he tugs on my hand until I stand, and he drags me over until I'm sitting in his lap.

"I'm going to break your chair," I tell him, ashamed I let doubt's doppelganger, insecurity, get her claws in me too. I try removing them, one by one, but those suckers are impacted, like rotten wisdom teeth.

"You're not jealous of McKayla, are you?"

Yes. Yes, I am.

"Of course not." I roll my eyes for effect, but my tone is unconvincing, even to my own ears.

"Laurel." Roth palms my cheek and forces eye contact. "I have no interest in McKayla."

I should have kept my mouth shut or said, *"Hey look"* to distract him or kissed him until he grew hard again beneath me. Again, many, many options to choose from. But what I should do and what I *do* are usually on opposite ends of the spectrum.

"She's pretty. And peppy. And she's a far better dance partner than I am."

His fingers flex and he brings his face within inches of mine.

His breaths are still cool from his snow cone. "She's petulant and immature and condescending."

"Oh." I guess looks *can* be deceiving.

Roth moves me closer yet, his lips brushing mine when he says in a hush so low, I strain to hear him, "I have been blinded by you, Laurel."

A cohesive sentence doesn't come together for a minute. Maybe two. And during this tender silence, I let down every guard I have. I let him see the real me. Every scar, every imperfection, every weakness, every wound, every loss, every uncertainty. Everything that shaped who I am today I uncover and leave out in the open. And though he doesn't know the stories behind them all now, he will in time.

I let Roth Warren Keswick in completely and thoroughly. I let him in where I've let no one else before. And let me tell you, being *that* vulnerable to someone who you want to love you for you and not just who you portray yourself to be is paralyzing.

Because what if they don't?

But rejection or revulsion is not what I see when Roth gazes back at me.

What I see is...my heart runs wild. *Could it be?*

"That sounds like a nasty side effect," I end up saying, because sarcasm is my go-to when I get anxious.

"It definitely was unexpected."

Some guys would say this, and it's just a line...a way to reel a woman in and make her think you mean more to him than you do.

This is not a line.

It's not an act or a game or manipulation.

He's in as much amazement over us as I am.

"Roth," I breathe. My mind is swimming in need.

He is fixated on my mouth. Reverently, leisurely he kisses one corner, then the other. Then he kisses me like he means it.

I squirm. My new panties could be wrung out. I don't think I've ever wanted a man this much.

"Are you ready to go?"

His breaths have quickened, and he's hard as a rock beneath my thigh.

Yes. Yes. Yes.

"If you are."

"I am," he husks, leaning his forehead to mine briefly.

"Let's go then," I tell him, wanting nothing more than to get back to my apartment as fast as possible.

We pack up quickly. Roth drapes the blanket over his erection, and we giggle like children all the way to the Jeep. We hold hands, both quiet on the twenty-minute drive, but the anticipation is thick and electric. If I reached out and ran my finger through it, I'd get a slight jolt.

"Feel up to that test run?" Roth asks me, pulling into a guest spot outside of my apartment. He's peering at me, waiting patiently on my reply.

And this time I don't mince words. I don't think one thing and say another.

"Only if you stay."

Roth leans over the console and kisses me sweetly. His lips linger and he comes back in several times like he can't get enough. Each time, he becomes greedier. Each time, I become needier.

"Just try and get me to leave, Laurel."

He thumbs my lower lip, watching as he does it. His mouth finds mine again and he groans as he forces himself away. He exits the car and opens my door. As we walk hand in hand to my apartment building, I am not nervous. Not much anyway. I am ready, because I am certain of one thing.

Tonight, is the night that changes my forever.

SEVEN

THE ONE

Laurel
Ten Years Earlier
June 7, 10:28 p.m.

"Do you want a drink?" I ask.

Dropping my purse on the kitchen island, I open one cupboard after another looking for any stitch of liquor. *Didn't Carmen leave a sliver of rum in the bottom of a bottle a few months back? I just need to find—*

"Laurel." Roth says my name quietly, ending my frantic search.

The heat of him at my back has my stomach tumbling into a free fall. I close my eyes in anticipation of pleasure and wait. Wait for him to do something. Anything. Each quiet, patient exhale trickles over the back of my neck, making my muscles quiver and goose bumps explode.

"Yes?"

"I don't want a drink." As gentle as a breeze, his hands set low on my hips. His thumbs circle the sensitive spot right inside my hip bones in slow, drugging motions. God. I can hardly breathe as desire I've tried to keep in check unfurls and blooms. I tremble everywhere. I want everything. Pressing his lips against the shell of my ear, he whispers, "I want every one of my senses to be razor sharp."

93

Ohmygod.

Applying gentle pressure to my hips, he turns me to face him.

I lied earlier. I am so nervous I am shaking in my high-waisted thong that now feels like it's digging into my oversensitive flesh.

"Are you nervous?"

He deftly traces a line from the crook of my neck over the length of my shoulder, drawing an honest answer from me in the process.

"Yes."

I grip the countertop behind me for support and my knees knock in toward each other.

I have to look the exact opposite of provocative. Yet for some reason, Roth never sees what I see. And when he tells me, "You are so sexy, Laurel," with such sweet, unadulterated reverence I liquify on the spot.

"Make love to me, Roth," I beg him, reaching for the hem of his untucked shirt.

"Oh…" He wraps his fingers around my wrist, gently stopping my advances. "I plan on it." And in one smooth motion he sweeps me into his arms as if he's preparing to carry me over the threshold. "But I am definitely not making love to you in your kitchen."

He carries me into my bedroom with ease, as if I weigh nothing. I wrap my arms around his shoulders and nibble on a spot behind his ear.

"Fuck, Laurel," he grits, depositing me on my feet at the edge of the bed.

He reaches over to flick the switch on the lamp, casting a dim glow around my room. He's half-bathed in light, half-shadowed in the darkness. He looks disheveled and hungry. Starved, in fact.

"You, ah…you gonna leave that on?" I ask breathlessly,

folding my arms around my middle.

Removing a strip of condoms from his pocket, he sets them on the nightstand. *Oh, okay then. He came prepared.* I half wonder if he has more. Taking a step toward me, he tugs my arms apart. "I want to see you, Laurel."

"You already know what I look like," I counter, rocking back on my heels apprehensively.

Surely, he doesn't mean to make love to me with the light on, does he? He'll see that unsightly bulge on my belly and the cellulite on the backs of my thighs. Every imperfection will be magnified by a thousand.

"I would never ask you to do anything you're uncomfortable with." *Thank you, baby Jesus.* "But...I will point out that you didn't want to dance earlier and..."

He leaves that sentence hanging, waiting for me to fill in the blanks.

And it wasn't so bad after all.

Crap.

How does he do this? How does he manage to effortlessly push me out of my comfort zone?

If I want a life with this man, which I do, he'll ultimately have to see me naked, right? I mean, I could keep him at bay for a bit longer while I hit the gym and drink collagen, I suppose. *But your underwear does pretty much cover up your stomach fat.* That will only last so long, though. Eventually they have to come off. Maybe if I arch my back with my arms over my head, I'll stretch my torso, so it flattens out. Maybe we can start with the lights on and then I can convince him...

Laurel, good grief. Stop already.

Okay. Okay.

Deep breath in.

Deep breath out.

It's now or never, and never isn't an option, so...

Here goes nothing.

Silently, I shuffle until the backs of my knees butt up against the bed. I drop his hands and toe off my shoes. My stomach does backflips when I reach for the bottom of my dress.

He watches my every move, his breathing labored as I drag the fabric up over my head. His eyes grow darker, the slant of his jaw more severe as I drop it on his shoes.

Resisting the urge to fidget, I stand still in front of him, arms at my sides, positively defenseless in my red demi bra and matching thong.

Red. I know, I don't understand how that happened either.

But seemingly it was the right call, because the homage Roth pays me causes all focus on my imperfections to drop away. In a split second, I feel seductive and wanton.

And powerful. It's absolutely true what they say about red.

"Jesus," he whispers under his breath.

He runs his eyes over me in a rush, as if he doesn't know what to concentrate on first. Then he visually devours me, slow and savory, as though I'm a gourmet seven-course meal at a five-star restaurant.

His gaze trickles over my face and shoulders first, leaving my skin tingling without a single touch. He lingers on my breasts. They feel swollen. They ache. He swims over my ribs and belly with languid strokes, and the low growl that emanates from him when he gets to my panties makes me want to drop onto the bed in sweet surrender.

When he swallows hard and loud, it empowers me, this reaction of his.

"Touch me," I hear myself say. Raw need has me strung tight, my inhibitions all but gone.

"I'm going to do more than touch you, Laurel," he murmurs, now tracing the lacy fringes of my bra cups before feathering circles around my erect nipples. I moan lightly and close my eyes. My head feels heavy, my legs like damp tissue paper.

He winds an arm around me just in time and lowers me to the bed, laying me on my back before standing over me.

"My God, I wish you could see yourself."

He pretends as if he's capturing me in a picture frame, his index fingers and thumbs forming a loose square.

"Your hair is splayed in a hundred different directions. Your skin is luminescent, as though you've bathed in liquid silver. Your breasts, Jesus. Your body is sheer perfection." As he talks, I visualize. I see a sexpot that every man desires. I see myself through his eyes and though I know that's not me, at this moment it feels like it could be. Like maybe it *is*. Reaching for the button on his pants, he pops it open. He drops his jeans, then shucks his shirt. The air thickens. "You are undeniably sexy, but..." His breath hitches as if he's having a hard time breathing too. His erection presses against the confines of his boxer briefs, demanding release. I could help with that. "You are absolutely radiant, Laurel. So stunning I can hardly think."

Hook. Line. Drop shot sinker.

I am his.

For all my days.

"It's all you." I reach out my hand, begging him to come to me.

He hooks his fingers into the band of his underwear and removes them, and *holy shit*. Yes. I said it, because there is no other adequate description for what I am witnessing.

Roth Warren Keswick is not only buff, he is *built*.

His eyes gleam as I get my fill of him the way he did of me. I've had sex, of course, but I am not what you'd call sexually experienced. I haven't orgasmed at a man's hand, ever. And I've never had a man in my mouth, the thought of it demeaning and repulsive, actually.

But I had it all wrong. That is an act of pure devotion where *I* would hold all the power. And I'm wearing red to boot, which I fear is making me irrationally emboldened because now all I can think of is wielding all that command to make Roth cry my name as I swipe my tongue over that bead dotting his tip.

I reach for him, but he grabs my wrist right before contact.

"What are you doing?" I ask, highly disappointed he's thwarted my first attempt at giving a man oral pleasure.

"Going first."

"Oh."

His gaze drops between my legs and I feel myself gush. He licks his lips before telling me, "I'll get there, don't you worry."

I start to laugh, but it morphs into a drawn-out moan when he slips a finger underneath the crotch of my panties. I arch my back as he leisurely runs the back of his nail over my sensitized, wet flesh. I whine when he stops.

"Relax," he tells me softly, lying at my side.

"Easy for you to say." Every part of me is taut, ready to snap.

"You have to trust your partner." He said the same thing earlier tonight on the dance floor. "Do you trust me, Laurel?" His strokes down my belly are unhurried and featherlight. No woman could be more worshipped or adored or undoubtedly, unconditionally loved than I am right now.

"Yes," I reply without a second thought, the same way I did earlier. "I trust you."

"Good." His arousal jerks uncontrollably against my thigh. I marvel at the restraint he has, my needs coming before his. Another first. "Then close your eyes, please."

"Since you asked so nicely..."

I do. I close my eyes and allow myself to just feel.

Roth speaks to me in soft tones, telling me how much he loves the softness of my skin, which pebbles under his touch. He tells me how every curve and bend in my body, which won't stop undulating, is majestic. He tells me how beautiful I am and how lucky he is to have found me, and my heart swells with each devout word.

Each caress stokes the embers hotter. Every kiss steals my breath away.

He rids me of my panties and bra and gently palms both breasts. He thumbs my nipples, lightly pinches them, then sucks one into his hot mouth. I cry out and snake my fingers through his hair, holding him to me as I writhe in pleasure. He moves from one breast to the other but takes his time, alternating between gentle laps and harried pulls. It's as if he's fighting between his mind and his need.

I know because it's the same for me.

"Roth," I moan. Carving my nails into his back, I drag them down over his hips and dig them into the tautness of his butt. His erection flutters in a steady, insistent beat, growing more indignant by the second at being denied.

We can't have that, now can we?

With a surge of energy, I flip our positions. Now I'm on top, straddling him, and Roth is on the bottom at *my* mercy.

I am in control.

It's the red, I swear it.

"What are you doing?" he asks me, the cutest smirk cutting into his cheekbones. I'm suddenly glad the lamp is on, so *I* can see *him*. He pushes his thumbs into my hip creases, making me squirm. It tickles.

"I'm taking matters into my own hands," I say, flattening my palms to his pecs. His smirk widens until I flick my fingernails over his nipples. He sucks in a harsh breath as his eyes momentarily roll back.

"Is that so?" he moans.

"Uh-huh," I reply, proud of myself.

Wedging him between my wet folds, I rock my hips back and forth, sliding along the length of him easily. I move. I feel. I palm my own breasts as I let every pretense of what I should do go. Instinct takes over. With each pass, his face sharpens, and I revel in this authority I never knew I had. It's addicting. Red is my new go-to.

But Roth turns the tables once again. He slips one of those thumbs that were tickling me between—*Oh God*—right between my legs, circling my bundle of nerves with the right amount of pressure to throw me off my game. His other hand grips my hip, steadying me as he watches me get closer and closer with every rotation.

"I told you, ladies first," he murmurs, and I am on such a high right now I can't possibly form a sassy comeback even if I wanted to. My heart pounds, my skin is warm, my breathing erratic.

I drop my gaze to his hand, the one working me to new heights, and I'm surprised that I am on the knife's edge already. When I glance up, he's trained on me. I watch him watch me, and watching him watch me may very well be the most erotic experience of my life.

I come on the spot.

Head thrown back, eyes twisted shut, my body shudders and shakes as I ride wave after sharp wave of pure, utter bliss. And Roth's hum of male satisfaction only serves to prolong my gratification.

"That's it," he urges me on. "Christ, Laurel. You are magnificent when you come."

I feel magnificent.

Though he could stop with one and take his turn, he doesn't. He tosses me on my back and brings me up again and, "Again," he demands, my body responding to him as if he has been the lone keyholder all along. I orgasm under his tongue and his fingers and his tongue again until I feel boneless and atrophied and so tender I can't stand one more. Only once I am sated like never before does he slip inside me on a choppy groan.

"You feel so fucking good," he whispers in my ear. In one swift move, he hitches my hips upward until I moan. I wrap my legs around his waist and hold on as he hits the right spot with each lazy thrust.

"So...do...you."

Unbelievably, I am balancing on the precipice again. Is that possible?

Rising on his forearms, Roth hovers over me, spanning the whole of my face with his hands. When he tells me in a low voice, "You feel like mine," my thoughts momentarily freeze before I tell him back, "I am," though I've never felt like anyone's before now.

His stormy gaze bores inside me and I am unable to look away, nor do I want to. This is straight-up intimacy. We are as locked together as two human beings can be. It should be uncomfortable and terrifying. It would be with anyone else. But with Roth, it's the exact opposite. It feels so right I am a wound-up ball of raw emotion. *Don't cry. Don't cry.*

He moves inside of me, in no hurry whatsoever. Never breaking our connection, something between us clicks together. It's audible and permanent and by the gentleness on Roth's face, he hears it too.

He makes love to me so sweetly, so purposefully, tears gather in the edges of my lids.

"Pure beauty," he murmurs when I come undone for the countless time, and when he finally reaches his own pinnacle long, long minutes later, I stare into the soul of a man I love with every part of my being.

Even if I'm afraid to say it, a person's eyes can't hide the truth.

I hope he sees it while I build up the courage to say it. I hope he knows this isn't casual for me. That, while I am terrified of the dark, he'll always be the one lighting the way for me.

We lie together, arms wrapped around each other, legs intertwined. We let our breathing even and our slick skin cool.

Neither of us is in a rush to clean up and frankly, I don't want to leave him, even for the few moments it will take.

I wonder what he's thinking, though I don't ask. I hope he's still going to stay.

Eventually, he says, "I'm going to get you a warm washcloth, okay?"

Uh… "Okay."

I try to keep the question *Do guys do that?* out of my voice, but I know I've failed when he says, "Any man worth his salt takes care of his woman after he makes love to her," as he exits the bed.

And Roth Warren Keswick is definitely worth his salt.

Not only does he retrieve a warm washcloth, he makes it his mission to clean me as well, even through my protests of embarrassment.

Then he climbs back into bed and pulls me toward his chest.

While I miss the fact, he won't be sending me a song tonight, a smile turns my lips and satiation warms my body as Roth's heart beats beneath my ear, and I have one final thought before sleep thieves me away.

He's passed with flying colors.

EIGHT

FEELS LIKE LETTING GO

Laurel
Ten Years Earlier
June 8, 8:46 a.m.

WARM, bright rays wake me from a deep, peaceful sleep. An intoxicating scent invades my nostrils—it's woodsy and spicy and quickly followed by an inexplicable sense of belonging, as I lie wrapped between strong, sinewy muscles I want to wake up to every morning.

How long was I out?

I cup my palm and breathe into it, cringing.

Yikes. Long enough to have morning breath.

"She wakes."

The thickness in Roth's morning voice reminds me of gravel being raked through concrete. It is an unexpected turn-on.

"Morning. Sorry about that." I keep my face strategically pointed away from his. He draws circles on my shoulder blade. His touch is featherlight and so highly sensual I want him again; morning breath be damned.

But no. That's just gross.

"About what?"

"Passing out."

"Well..." he rumbles. "Multiple orgasms will do that."

I adjust how I'm lying so I can see his face. His eyes are a bit droopy, and he has a goofy smile softly curling his lips. He's sated and content and something bubbles up inside of me because *I* did that. I've never felt so much satisfaction making another person happy.

"Are you fishing for a compliment, Mr. Keswick?" I tease, twirling a few short strands of his chest hair between my fingers.

"I believe you gave me plenty of compliments last night if I'm not mistaken."

Heat washes over me as I remember how many times I came undone moaning his name. And I may have actually shown my appreciation by thanking him once or twice. Awkward.

"I can't believe you just said that." I swat at him, but it's mostly air.

"It's true, is it not?"

Oh, it's true all right. But should you feed into your man's ego or make him work that much harder next time?

"I have no idea what you're talking about."

Roth visibly frisks me, searching for the white lie I'm trying to keep hidden. Though he finds it with ease, he plays along nicely.

"Challenge accepted."

Smiling in my small victory, I reluctantly scoot out of his hold. Grabbing a throw blanket on the end of my bed, I wrap it around me as I slide off the edge. "Be right back," I toss over my shoulder right before I shut the bathroom door.

A couple of minutes later I emerge, bladder relieved and breath minty. I climb back into bed and Roth greedily yanks me into him.

"So, besides multiple orgasms, what else makes you happy?"

"More multiple orgasms?" I suggest cheekily.

"So, you admit to multiple orgasms now, do you?"

I feign indignance. "I did nothing of the sort."

"If you say so," he replies on a chuckle.

Who are you and what you have done with the real Laurel?

The Laurel I know would never banter sexual innuendos back and forth like she was some sort of field expert. It seems Roth has managed to unearth a part of me I didn't know existed.

A rather fun one.

Those three loaded, perilous words start to fall off the tip of my tongue, but I snatch them with my front teeth and bite down, managing to shove them back in. Then I shift the subject.

"What makes me happy, huh?"

"Yeah, you know...this." He points to his now exaggerated grin. It makes me laugh. "And this..." He places his palm between my bare breasts. My body reacts. The way his nostrils flare, he notices, yet he stays focused. "What warms your heart and feeds your soul?"

This, I think. *This does. You do.* A future with him plays out right in front of my eyes as if it's already been caught on film. A lifetime of love and fulfillment and dreams realized. Gray hair. Great-great-grandchildren. Arthritis. Alaskan cruises. Holding hands while we watch the five-o'clock news. Four thirty all-you-can-eat buffets. Celebrating a golden wedding anniversary.

That could definitely make me happy.

But I can't vomit all that because, well, that's obvious.

"I didn't know this was such a hard question," Roth jibes.

"I don't know, I guess."

"You don't know what makes you content?"

I shrug. "I've never thought about it before."

"Well, now's your chance."

Now's my chance. Great. I grasp at straws, coming up blank, so I go with the first thing that comes into my head.

"I like pina coladas and getting caught in the rain..." When he doesn't respond right away, I keep going, steeling my mouth into a straight line. Speaking the words versus singing them is harder than it sounds. "And the feel of the ocean and the taste of champagne."

Roth pushes himself up. "Go on," he encourages, eyes wide and bright.

Really?

I rack my brain trying to think of another line and can only come up with one. Dammit. I don't want to say it, but I don't know what else to do. In for a penny, in for a pound.

"I like making love at midnight in the dunes of the Cape."

No smirk. No flash of lust in his eyes. Just genuine interest. I almost feel bad I didn't take this more seriously.

"Well, then I guess I'm the love that you've been looking for."

He says this with such deadpan that my heart thuds in my chest.

It takes me a few seconds to catch on and when I do, strangely my racing heart takes a dive into my belly. My little ditty has backfired. He was onto me the whole time.

Then he grins and his grin quickly turns into a belly laugh. I ball up a fist and punch him in the meaty part of his arm to get him to stop, but it only serves to make him laugh harder. I find myself joining in, and we laugh until our faces are streaked with tears, our sides ache, and our cheeks hurt. We laugh like all of our laughs have built up over our lifetimes, as if reserved only for the other. We laugh until we can't laugh any more.

"You should have seen your face." His voice is pitched several octaves higher than usual, and it starts us all over again. "Classic."

"Stop. My jaw hurts." I squish my cheeks in, trying to relieve the tension in them.

"So, does mine." He does the same. He looks like a fish. I double over in hysterics again. As soon as one of us achieves some semblance of control, we simply need to look at the other and we're at it once more.

Fifty years. You could have this for fifty years.

I don't know how much time goes by, but finally I say, "I can't take much more," in between gasps. "Stop. I mean it."

"Okay, okay." He takes in a deep gulp of air and blows it out slowly, but it's choppy and nowhere near under control. When I start to giggle again, he stretches out his arm, palm facing me. "Don't look at me. If you don't look at me, maybe I can stop."

"Okay. I won't."

We both stare straight ahead, our bodies warm, our chests heaving. It's a good five minutes before I think I can talk normally again.

And then I decide to be real. To give him what he wants to hear.

"Things that feed my soul, huh?"

He nods, staying silent.

"Meringue, of course."

"Of course."

Deeper, Laurel. Get dirty.

"I love the summer solstice, the longest day of the year."

I chew on my lip. Why is this so hard? This fear of letting go? It's terrifying, like water seeping into your lifeboat when you're five nautical miles from shore, and the only thing you have to bail it with is a thimble.

He wedges himself so he's facing me. "I'm not familiar with this one."

I stroke the side of his jaw, scruff poking the pads of my fingers. "This is an original," I assure him.

"Ohhh...I love the creativity of a talented new author."

He's being playful, but his demeanor tells the true story. He's eager to hear more. He gives my hand a squeeze. I stare at that hand, wrapped around mine. It feeds me courage. And while I could offer up surface-level information about myself, like how reading is my Calgon or how yoga calms the madness inside, I dig deeper, dig into the chaos, his touch fortifying me. It makes me feel extraordinarily safe.

I bend my legs under the covers so the sheet tents over my knees, trying to figure out what to say next. Everything good about me also carries the burden of remembrance, the pain of loss. They are doors I keep tightly closed, the cracks purposely sealed.

Now there is reason to pry them open, though. So, I get out the proverbial crowbar and go to work.

"There is something very hypnotic about whirlers."

"What are whirlers?"

"You know...those winged seeds that fall from maple trees. They whirl through the air, floating madly to the ground as if they're in a hurry to get nowhere."

"You mean helicopters?"

"Is that what *you* call them? We called them whirlers. Esther and I used to lie underneath our hundred-year-old maple and watch them whirl to the ground around us. Our PooPa would sometimes lie down with us and tell us stories of when he was a kid and make us laugh until our stomachs hurt."

He doesn't say a word, but with the compassion he's emanating, he doesn't need to. It's enough for me to continue. The door hinge creaks loudly as I shove it another inch.

"I'm fascinated by old musicals. I sang *The Music Man* so many times it drove my mother up the wall. She finally forbade it in the house, so I'd watch it at my grandparents' house."

"You can watch *The Music Man* at my house anytime you want."

I tip my head up and catch his gaze. He means it. And he might regret it, but I don't warn him off. And I keep going, because that door is standing wide open now.

"I love roller skating. Or I used to. Is that silly?"

"Ehhh..." He twists his head and screws up his mouth, teasing me. I bump him with my elbow and he oofs, pretending to be hurt.

"And Christmas music. The classics, you know? "Have Yourself A Merry Little Christmas" always makes me nostalgic for some reason. And as odd as it sounds, I miss snow. We don't get much snow here but when I wake up on a cold January morning and the trees are frosted with a thin coating of ice, it's so peaceful it reminds me of home."

And Esther. So much reminds me of Esther.

"I hate the snow," he says.

"Most Floridians do. That's why they're Floridians."

"Got a point there."

"Do you want me to keep going or am I boring you?"

He kisses my temple and draws me closer. "There's not a boring aspect about you, Laurel."

I lay my head on his chest, and listen to his heart beat in a steady rhythm. I spend the next hour vomiting everything that sings to me, from a cup of chamomile tea by a crackling fire to movies that scare the bejeezus out of me to watching endless hours of cat videos on YouTube. I tell him of my love to fish that came from spending time with PooPa at the lake, but how I hate threading the hook with live bait. Strangely, he's never been fishing, though he grew up by the ocean. I told him I'd teach him but that he had to bait the hook.

"I always had a thing for fireflies. I don't know why, but there's something extraordinary about sitting outdoors on a warm summer night watching fireflies call to each other. I refuse to end their already short life in a small, sterile jar filled with grass when all they want is to find a mate."

"Me neither," he says thoughtfully, and that connection we have deepens. Over fireflies.

We move on to hiking and rock skipping and anything outdoors. I weave stories of Esther throughout our conversation. It's the most I've talked about her since we started dating. And when he asks, "Will you tell me more about your sister," I do.

I bite back my emotions and tell him about her epilepsy and

how she had a bad seizure in math class when she was twelve. She had a severe brain bleed and never regained consciousness. I tell him how she bravely fought in the ICU for six days, and how she died while I held her hand and told her it was okay to let go even though I didn't really mean it. I tell him about how Esther's death tore our family apart in more ways than one. How it hurtled my mother into a steep depression, and how she's stayed there ever since.

"What about your father?"

My father. He's a sore subject.

I have two distinct memories of my father. The day he left and the day he came back. Or tried to come back. He showed up to take Esther and me out for the day. It was Easter and we hadn't seen him since before Halloween. We'd dressed in our prettiest Sunday clothes and brushed our teeth extra-long, so we'd impress him with how sparkly they were. Esther wore a pink ribbon in her hair. Mine was white.

We were beyond excited to see him, but when my mother opened the front door, she did not share that same enthusiasm. She demanded he leave, locked us in the house, and we watched the rest unfold from the living room window. Father held two baskets stuffed with gifts, one in each hand. He was angry. Mother was crying. Father kept pointing at us. Mother screamed at him until her face turned red. We pounded on the glass. We couldn't get out of the house. Then my grandfather showed up with his shotgun and my father got into his car, along with our baskets, slammed the door, and drove away.

We never saw or heard from him again.

And I blame my mother for that.

"Absent. My parents divorced when Esther and I were four. I guess he remarried and had himself a new family and we were but a blip in the past. Not even a memory."

Roth twines our hands together and I experience a moment of such pure, sweet serenity I have to close my eyes to keep from losing it. Is this what Carmen feels with Manny? As though she's finally settled into her own skin?

"What a selfish asshole."

He sounds genuinely angry on my behalf, and something breaks loose inside me in a good way. It prompts me to speak my biggest fear aloud. And it's the real reason I keep my circle small and am still alone at the age of twenty-eight.

"Not only did Esther leave me, so did everyone else."

For the longest time Roth doesn't say anything, and me being me, I start to agonize. Maybe I should have kept quiet. Maybe this was too much for him. Maybe *I* am too much for him. I try to keep it all together, but sometimes it's a ruse. A heavy mask that I get tired of wearing in public and am scared to remove in private. Scars are ugly.

Roth resituates us, so he's hovering over the top of me. I hold my breath as he looks deeply into my soul. The moment is ripe with a tenderness I can't possibly put into words.

"You can stop running, Laurel. You'll never be alone again."

I find it mind-boggling sometimes how attuned to me Roth can be. He could have said anything, yet he said what I desperately needed to hear. He let me show him my heart, and now he's holding it tenderly in his open hands.

Fifty years, Laurel.

"It felt good to talk about my sister. Thank you."

"You can tell me anything, Laurel. You can trust me."

"It's hard for me to trust people," I tell him truthfully.

"I know."

"But I do trust you, Roth."

He pushes a wisp of hair behind my ear. "I'm glad. Tell me something else," he prods. He tries to move off of me, but I don't want him to go, so I wrap my legs around his waist, ignoring his low, male groan.

"What do you want me to tell you?"

"Anything."

This time I don't hesitate.

"Okay. Fireworks."

"Fireworks?"

That smile. It does me in every time.

"Yes, fireworks. I love everything about them. The thunk they make when they're shot from the cannon. The reverberation in your bones when they explode. The sizzle as they fall to the ground. The bright colors that stay behind your lids when you close your eyes. Fireworks are magical."

"Exploding things are magical, huh?" He twitches against my belly as he teases me. My body leaps to life.

"Some are more magical than others."

His hum is equivalent to a hand-calligraphed invitation to the Oscars being delivered by Ryan Gosling himself.

"You'd better knock that off," I say. I don't mean it at all.

"What?" he replies, all innocent like.

"That." I twirl my finger around in a tight circle. "That... glaze of longing you have in your eyes."

"You put it there."

I bite my lip to keep from smiling. "By talking about fireworks?"

"It's the *way* you talked about fireworks, Laurel. It was very...sexual."

"Sexual fireworks, that's a first," I giggle.

He pokes my side and I jump with a shriek. He does it again and I poke him back in his armpit. Then we're rolling around on the bed in a heap of thrashing arms and legs and squeals. And next, he has me pinned beneath him. He snags a hardened nipple between his teeth and sucks deep. My entire body arches in pleasure and soon I'm calling out his name again as he slips inside of me with ease and control.

He makes love to me again, holding me in his enthrall, and when he whispers, "I love you, Laurel," only moments before we both explode, I find myself with the courage to reciprocate, uttering words I've never spoken to another man, outside of my PooPa.

I'm glad Roth is the first.

"I think I will love you until the end of forever, Roth."

Then I proceed to fall into the most deep, peaceful sleep of my life.

NINE

TUESDAYS

Roth
Present
June 21, 5:41 p.m.

I walk into the kitchen and stop in my tracks, my blood turning to ice. "Laurel, for God's sake, what are you doing?"

My wife is perched precariously on a kitchen stool that I have asked her repeatedly not to use as a step stool. That leather-covered stool swivels, and more than once she's fallen from it. One time she needed six stitches on the inside of her upper lip.

In my mind's eye I envision my wife's demise. I see her hitting the floor. I smell blood as it spreads from beneath her cold, limp, battle-weary body. At this moment, I'm terrified I won't lose my Laurel to the cancer ravaging her body, but to her pride, because she refuses to ask me for help.

"I'm getting the punch bowl." She stretches until she's balancing on the extreme tip of a single toe.

My heart pounds violently against my breastbone. "Nonononono." As if we'd choreographed and practiced it a hundred times, I fly across the room and make it to her just in time, catching her in my arms as that stool sends her mercilessly spinning toward the floor.

"Jesus Christ, Laurel," I spit on a cross between relief and anger. "You could have killed yourself." My legs turn liquid, and I fall to my knees, still cradling her.

"But I didn't." She beams, holding up her prize: a ten-dollar plastic punch bowl that I'd like to smash to bits. "You're my savior, as always."

I'm not. If I were, I could rip this enemy from your body and destroy Him for good.

"Laurel." I bury my face in her neck and drink in her sweet smell until I'm drunk on it. How long will it take before it fades away from my memory completely? I can't bear that thought.

"I'm sorry, Roth." She runs her fingers through my hair, scraping my scalp lightly with her nails.

"Fresh-cut fingernails?" I ask. They feel so good.

"It amazes me how you can always tell."

"I notice every little thing about you, Laurel."

"Mi amado," she says on a hush.

God, that gets me every single time. When I found out what mi amado meant the first night she mentioned it, I swear I fell instantly in love with this sassy, quick-witted, clumsy woman. I can't believe my luck. My lips find the warmth of her flesh. I press them to her, enjoying the slight hitch in her breath. I nibble my way up to her earlobe and clamp hard enough to elicit a shriek, yet not hard enough to hurt.

"Am I interrupting?" my mom asks from behind us.

"Yes," I reply at the same time Laurel says, "No" with a giggle.

"Laurel," I moan. I would love nothing more than to take her into our bedroom, strip her naked, and spend the rest of the day making her shriek over and over. That can't happen for so many reasons, but damn, what I wouldn't give to have those carefree days back. I fear they are gone for good.

"Roth."

One word. One syllable. One demand. That's all it takes.

"Okay, okay." I stand and set Laurel gently on her feet,

kissing her temple before I let her go. I check her over against her protests that she is fine. She is not fine. She has dark circles under her eyes, though she's given it a good effort trying to hide them with makeup.

"How is the pain in your legs today?"

Her eyes go blank, flitting quickly to my mom, then back to me. "Gone."

"Gone?"

"Yes."

"Liar," I mouth. That tenacious independence rears her ugly head and I want to pound her into the ground. "It's okay to need help."

"I don't need help."

Stubborn, stubborn woman.

"Are you all right, dear?"

Laurel bristles at my mother's question. She's angry at me but directs it at my mother. "Fine, Elana," she snaps. Realizing her mistake, she softens her voice and nonverbally begs my mother's forgiveness, adding, "I'm good. Really. I'm sorry."

My mom tells her not to worry, but *I'm* worried.

Good. Fine. Perfect.

Lies. These past two weeks have already shown a marked change in Laurel. She doesn't sleep. She is in pain, intensely so sometimes. Her appetite is all but shot. I hate it here, where we are. I can't stand watching her suffer.

How am I going to do this?

Snagging the punch bowl from her, I wave it around, huffing, "Why are we doing this?"

"Making punch?"

"Funny girl." She's amused, but I am still quite irate. "No, this." I point to the stacks of napkins and plates and platters of food strewing every inch of our countertops.

"You'll have to be more specific." She plucks the bowl from

my fingers and walks around the island to the sink. She flips open the water spigot and squirts in a dollop of dish soap.

"Having this party, Laurel? Why are we having this stupid party?" Could I sound more insolent?

"Because we always have this party, Roth. Why wouldn't we have it this year?"

Because you're dying, I want to scream at the top of my lungs. Because having a house full of people drinking my alcohol and eating my food is the last thing I want to do. Because I can't stomach the thought of dodging sympathies and platitudes for hours on end. *How can I share you with others when this might be the last June 21st we have together, Laurel? How can you ask me to do that?*

She looks over her shoulder at me, pausing midwash. Can she see everything I'm thinking? By the frown pulling down her cheeks, it's most certainly a yes.

Once again, our nonverbal communication astounds me.

I need this, Roth. I need to feel normal. Please, please don't take this away from me.

"I love your Summer Solstice parties, honey," my mom interjects, trying to stave off an argument. I forgot she was even there.

"I know, Mom."

She pops a baby carrot in her mouth and chews it before draping an arm around me, squeezing me in understanding. This is foreign territory we're all trying to navigate and I'm doing a piss-poor job of it. I throw one around her shoulder and lean on her in more ways than one.

Laurel smiles a knowing smile and just like that, I've lost. Two against one is never good odds, especially when it's your wife and mother ganging up. But if she thinks it's my mother who turned the tide, she is dead wrong. I live to make her happy.

"What time are the freeloaders coming?" I scoop up a handful of what Laurel calls puppy chow and throw the powdered sugar-coated pieces in my mouth. The name belies the taste, believe me.

"Roth," Laurel scolds.

"What?" I mumble around chocolaty goodness.

"Roth, did I teach you no manners?" my mom piles on. I want to stick out my tongue, but it would only prove her point.

"Can you get the cooler of beer ready, please?"

"Can you ask me for help next time?" I counter Laurel's request, brows raised as high as I can get them.

"Yes."

She's placating me. A man knows when he's being patted on the head and told to scoot along.

"No more crawling on that thing, Laurel. I mean it. If I hadn't been here…"

"I know." At least she has enough sense to look contrite.

"I'll get the cooler ready," my mom offers, discreetly disappearing to leave us alone.

I close the distance between us and wind my arms around her from behind. Setting my chin on her shoulder, I remind her, "Your sense of balance is off, Laurel. You could have been seriously injured."

She swallows hard. "I know I should have asked for help, but you were in the shower and I—"

"Was impatient, as usual."

"I hate this. All of it. I feel like such a burden."

"A burden?" I spin her around to face me. "Laurel, you are *not* a burden. Never that. Ever."

"I am. And it will only get worse, Roth. You know it and I know it."

Everyone goes through their own personal hell when they battle cancer. For some, losing their hair is the worst part of it. For others, being unable to maintain the career they've spent all their lives building destroys their spirit. For Laurel, it's been the loss of her independence that's killed her the most. She is fierce about being able to care for herself, almost to the point of exasperation. It's as if she's failed somehow if she has to ask for help. Since her diagnosis, though, she's had to rely on others for all kinds of things, from bathroom assistance to meal delivery. And it's a small blow to her pride every time. So, while I get this stubborn streak she has, if it puts her in danger, I won't have it.

"I understand, Laurel, but my job is to keep you safe. Please let me do it while I can."

She throws her arms around my neck, hugging me tight. "I just want to be normal, Roth."

"Normal people ask for help too." That gets me a sweet half snicker, which is what I was going for. "I love you today, Laurel," I whisper.

"I'll love you tomorrow, Roth."

For as many tomorrows as we have left.

"Hey." I pull back so I can see her beautiful face. "What do you say to a little adventure?"

She clucks her tongue in reprimand. "We have guests coming any minute."

The man downstairs jumps at the insinuation. I'm not complaining, but it's been a while. "I like the way you're thinking. Unfortunately, that wasn't what I had in mind."

She weaves her fingers through my hair, massaging back and forth. "Oh?" Her voice is pitched low. Inviting. She's doing that on purpose, the tease. "What did you have in mind then?"

Focus, Keswick.

"Let's go on a road trip."

Confusion scrunches her big brown eyes together, made more pronounced by the absence of thick eyelashes lost to chemotherapy. "Road trip?"

"Yeah."

"We can't just go on a road trip."

I slide my hands to her waist. "Why not?"

This may be a bit unconventional, but we've talked about a

cross-country road trip for years. Something always got in the way. School. Work. Money. Priorities. One excuse after another. I'm done with excuses. If Laurel is game, then we're doing this. I even called her oncologist, who wasn't crazy about the idea in case Laurel needed immediate medical attention, but I reminded him there are hospitals all over the country and I promised him I'd never have her far away from the best one. I'd plan our trip around them.

"Because...I don't know." She tips her head, giving it some thought. "You have to work."

"Let's say I didn't have to work."

"But you do."

I haven't told her yet, but I'm handing in my resignation on Monday. I will not go on like time with her isn't ticking away at lightning speed.

"Laurel, just play along, please."

"Fine." She exaggerates her sigh, but it's all pretend. "Where would we go?"

"Anywhere you want. You've always wanted to camp, right?"

Why have we never done this? Regrets, I'm full of them.

She wiggles in my hold. "Camp?"

"Okay, glamp," I say, knowing women generally prefer that to roughing it.

"But we don't have a glamper."

"RV," I correct.

Her cute nose crinkles. "RV, camper, glamper, same thing."

They're not even in the same vicinity, but I don't argue with her. "For shits and giggles, let's say we had an RV."

"But we don't."

"Laurel."

"I, okay."

"Okay, what? Okay, meaning yes?" Could it be that easy?

A quick succession of knocks at the front door is followed by a high-pitched wail. "The party is here!"

"The troops have arrived," I say with a heaping dose of satire.

"Stop." She swats me playfully on the chest. I wasn't kidding.

Carmen, Manny, and their wild four-year-old beauties come bounding into the kitchen. The girls yell for Laurel. They absolutely adore their godmother. I am second fiddle when she's around.

"Okay, meaning we'll talk about this later." She gives me a dismissive peck on the lips and twists out of my arms and into the waiting ones of Sofia and Lucia, both of whom begin jabbering a mile a minute about their new dresses.

That was all I needed. Her "talk later" was as good as a *yes* to me. My mood instantly lifts, and I no longer dread the afternoon and evening to come as much as I did a few minutes ago.

"Manny." I nod in greeting.

"How is Laurel today?" he asks me, eyeing the puppy chow. The guy is a sucker for sugar.

I watch her talking with the twins and Carmen. Her eyes are drawn, her skin is pale, but her face is still lit by that wide smile of hers. She is ethereal.

"She's hanging in there."

"Manny, none of that," Carmen berates him as he reaches for the bowl. "Your diet, remember?"

"Diet, my ass." In defiance, he buries his hand in the dessert mix. Swiveling his attention from his scowling wife back to me, male satisfaction evident, he shoves the entire handful in his mouth after asking, "You ready for this?"

For some reason, I remember what my father said when I told him I was going to marry this woman a mere ten days after I met her.

"Marriage is hard. Being with the same person day in, day out, year in and year out is even harder, no matter what anyone else tells you other-

wise. *Your mother and I, we almost divorced when you were six years old."*

"What?" I never saw anything but pure devotion from my parents with one another. *"I don't believe you."*

"It's true, son. Go on and ask your mother if you want. She'll tell you."

"But...why?"

He scoffed. *"The why isn't any of your business, but the why not? Now, that's the lesson learned from this. Essentially, Roth, love isn't about who bought who the better birthday gift or how many carats her diamond ring is. It's that you can look at this woman on a regular ole Tuesday night and know you'd make the same decision to be with her as the day you asked her to marry you."*

"This feels like a Tuesday."

"Think you got your days mixed, bro. It's Thursday," Manny tells me.

I don't feel like explaining myself, so I simply answer, "Yeah, I'm ready."

And I'm surprised to find I mean it. We may have a house full of guests in under an hour, but very soon I will have Laurel all to myself. And we'll get the chance to spend quality time together, taking a trip we've always wanted to. Plans I loosely made over the past week start solidifying in my mind. This trip will not only be an escape, but most importantly, it's an opportunity to make memories that will have to last me for the rest of my life.

A life that will now not include my very best friend.

TEN

SONGBIRD

Roth
Present
June 25, 8:05 a.m.

"ROTH." My boss's boss, Pat, stands when I enter his office with a quick knock. "Nice to see you." He holds out his hand and I reach mine out in kind. "How is Laurel?" he asks with honest concern.

Pat Anderson is the sixty-three-year-old son of the owner. While his father still holds the title of CEO, for all intents and purposes, as the president, Pat is the one who runs this family-owned company. And Pat is a great guy. He gets to know each and every one of his employees personally. That's one of the benefits of working for a family-run company. They treat you like you matter. You're not only an "associate." He was the one who gave me a shot at this role even though it was a bit of a stretch, considering my skill set, and he knew it. I have nothing but respect for him and for a company that I consider extended family. I'm going to miss it here.

"It's not good, I'm afraid."

He sighs. Its weight is one I feel all the way to the soles of my feet, making them heavier than they already are.

I respect Pat and I respect his time, especially since I showed up unannounced. So, I don't beat around the bush. I get straight to the point. "I appreciate everything you have done for me over the years, especially this last one, but I'm here to give you this, then collect my things."

I lay the resignation letter I wrote last night on his desk. He picks it up and scans it, then his gaze lifts above readers he keeps perched on the end his nose at all times.

"Your resignation?"

"Yes, sir."

"Hmm." Pat sets the letter back down, then pushes away from his desk and walks around it to stand in front of me. He gestures to the long leather sofa that butts up against a wall of glass. "Sit. Please." I stand there for a moment. I have no desire to make small talk or hear that God doesn't give us more than we can handle. The fuck he doesn't. "Please," Pat says again.

"Okay." Peeling my feet from the floor, I put one in front of the other until I've reached the couch. "It's terminal," I blurt, once I've taken a seat. Not the gentlest way to deliver the news, but I can't stand the process of twenty questions before we get to the punch line.

"Shit, Roth. Are you sure?"

Pretty fucking sure. "I am afraid so, yes."

He removes his glasses and scrubs a hand over his eyes. *Is he crying?* He sets his glasses back on his nose. His whites are now red, and I definitely see moisture. *Jesus, Roth, you're an asshole.*

"I am so sorry, son."

"Thank you."

We sit in silence as a grandfather clock in the corner ticks off seconds in the background, and I have decided that outside of my wife actually dying, this may be the worst part of this ordeal. The awkward space between your grim announcement and their grappling platitudes.

"What is next then?"

Not the question I expected he would ask. I could almost

script this entire conversation, because every single one is a mirror image of the last.

"Have you gotten a second opinion?"

"Second. Third. Fourth."

"And there's nothing they can do?"

"No."

"(Enter expletive of choice)," followed by another, *"I'm sorry,"* followed by, *"How long does she have?"*

"A year, maybe less."

"(Enter expletive of choice)", followed by, *"I can't believe it."*

"Neither can I."

"What can I do?"

"I wish there were something, but thank you for offering."

"We're praying for you."

"Thank you."

"If you need anything, and I mean anything, we're here for you and Laurel."

"Thank you. I appreciate it."

I've thought about writing it all down and handing out fliers to family and friends, so I can stop repeating the same old shit, but Laurel wouldn't let me.

"We're going on a road trip," I finally reply.

"Road trip, eh?"

"Yes, sir." Laurel doesn't quite know it yet, but she'll thank me once we drive into the foothills of the Smoky Mountains. She'll see this is what we need.

"To?"

"To? I don't know, exactly."

That's not entirely true. I do have the first part of our trip worked out. First, we'll hit the Smokies for a few days, maybe a week. Then we'll head down the Carolina coast and continue on to see my parents. Eventually I want to get us out to Moab, Utah where we took our first vacation. I have a few surprises sprinkled in along the way too. And quite honestly, it's probably too much. I don't know how long Laurel will be able to hold out, so the whole thing is a crapshoot. The last thing I want to do is accelerate this horrible disease by wearing her down.

Maybe this is a bad idea.

"How do you plan to road trip?"

"I'm sorry?" I ask, confused. "Drive?"

"Drive?" Pat shifts, setting an ankle atop the opposite knee.

He's striking in a Johnny Cash kinda way. His hair is black. His suit is black. His shirt is black. His tie is black. His socks and shoes are black. His glasses are black. All he's missing is the black guitar slung over his shoulder and the rockabilly pompadour hair.

As I stare at this man in black, so benevolent, I now can't get the chorus of "Ring of Fire" out of my head. I even inappropriately hum a few bars under my breath. Then I begin to laugh. I laugh and I laugh, and I laugh until tears stream down my face, and I have no idea what I found so damn funny in the first place.

If Pat thinks I've lost my shit, he's right. Yet he hides it well. He doesn't even blink. It's as if he comprehends this mini meltdown is the fuel I need to keep me going and he's been tasked to stay by my side to see that I don't hurt myself.

He's so patient, so understanding, I wonder if maybe he's part of this exclusive club no one wants a membership to.

"Well," I stop to clear the phlegm from my throat, moderately humiliated. "After I leave here, I plan to rent an RV."

"An RV, huh?"

He kindly doesn't reference my breakdown.

"I want Laurel to be comfortable as we're traveling, and I need to make sure we're not around a lot of people with her compromised immune system. Plus, this is something we've always talked about..." I choke on the rest as I attempt to swallow past the anguish in the middle of my chest. But it's like a permanent appendage. My own personal malignancy.

"I have a better idea."

Pat pushes himself up and goes back to his desk. He rifles through a neat stack of business cards he keeps beside his stapler. He's very traditional, preferring paper to technology. His assistant complains about it constantly. But it's uncanny how he knows where everything is. About halfway through, he finds the card he's looking for. He heads back and hands it to me.

"What's this?" I run my fingers over the ridged fine print.

<hr>

Nashville RV Sales and Rentals
Hendersonville, TN

<hr>

"It's where I store my motor home."

"Your motor home?"

"Yes."

"Okay." I stare at the card, not getting what he means. Is he telling I should rent an RV at this place? "I don't understand."

"It's yours," he tells me.

"What's mine?"

"My motor home."

I look around for a white rabbit or red and blue pills lying on the coffee table. They are both noticeably absent, yet none of this makes sense. I gawk at him, blinking several times. Replaying what he said over and over.

"I'm sorry, sir. You're giving me your motor home?"

He chuckles and sits back down. "No. I'm not *giving* you my motor home, but I am letting you borrow her for as long as you need. She's big, though. Forty-two feet. Think you can handle her?"

"Uh, yeah," I answer slowly. "My parents always had motor

homes growing up. My dad taught me early so I could help drive on long trips."

"Perfect."

This man, this company, has been so good to me through all of this. They've given me all the time off I've needed, no questions asked. They've continued to pay bonuses I don't feel as though I've earned. They've kept up our health insurance. They've sent countless meals and people to clean our home. I can't wrap my mind around how well they've treated me, but this...

I take a deep breath and blow it out slowly. The very backs of my eyes sting.

"It's a very generous offer, sir, but I—"

He cuts me off, knowing what I'm going to say. "You can."

"I don't understand." My throat is dry, my voice raspy.

"But I do, Roth." Pat stares out the window. And as he does, I see that I am right. He's definitely a cardholder of the shittiest club in existence. "My first wife, Camilla, died when she was just twenty-six. We'd only been married for four years."

His *first* wife?

Shit. I've known Pat for over ten years. He has four beautiful children and recently celebrated his thirty-fifth wedding anniversary. He seems blissfully happy. "I had no idea."

His smile is thin and wistfully heavyhearted. "Not many people do. It's not something you lead off with after introductions."

I nod, not fully comprehending what that will be like for me in a few months' time.

"On our honeymoon, she found a lump in her left breast. We weren't too worried because she was so young, but as you know, cancer doesn't discriminate based on age or your bank account or the stage of your life. She gallantly fought it for four years before she finally succumbed."

"Shit, Pat. I am so sorry."

Christ, it's the script. *I am the one now reciting the script.*

"It was a long time ago." He stops to think, and I can see he's taking a walk down memory lane. "I love Natalie and the kids. I count myself lucky to have found her when I did. I have a wonderful life, mind you, and I know it, but...I still miss my Camilla every single day."

Now my eyes blister like someone lifted my lids and shoved white-hot coals behind them. I can't speak. My chest is heavy. I swipe my tongue over my top teeth, wiping off the salty gunk that's accumulated there.

This will be you, Roth. Missing Laurel every second you have left to live.

"The only thing Cam wanted to do before she passed was to go camping." Pat's voice has become softer and more gravelly.

"Camping?" My surprise can't be missed.

"Yes, camping." And it isn't. "Unfortunately, we didn't get around to it. Life always got in the way. And then it was too late, and she was too ill to travel. That was my single biggest regret, Roth. That I didn't fulfill my wife's final wish."

"I'm sure she understood." Clichés. We are full them when we have nothing else to offer.

He clasps his hands together. His knuckles turn a dim shade of white. "When I met Natalie, one of the first things I asked her was what was on her life bucket list."

I smile, then, because I know where this is going. "Let me guess...camping?"

Winking, he says, "I knew I hired you for a reason."

"I don't know if we should go," I confess. "I don't know how Laurel will do. She seems to be getting worse every day."

I talked to my parents about this last night after Laurel went to bed early. They were worried, rightfully so. They don't think we should risk it and when I asked them if we were supposed to just sit around and wait for Laurel to die, they didn't have a good reply.

"And if you don't?" he asks me. "What then?"

I shrug, but I know "what then" means. When I look back, I will hate myself.

"If Laurel is in good enough health to go now, go now. If you can make it even a day, it's a day you won't regret. Trust me."

I turn the card over in my hand, still in a bit of a daze. "Are you sure?"

"I wouldn't have it any other way."

"Thank you, sir. For everything."

"You are most welcome."

We rise and Pat tells me, "Call and ask for Justin. Tell him I'm sending you and ask him to get the *Songbird* ready."

"Songbird?"

He scratches his head in a nervous gesture. I can tell he's not sure he should elaborate. "It was Camilla's and my song."

"Oh."

Yowza. He named his motor home after his dead wife?

"And it actually was Natalie's idea," he chuckles. "In fact, she insisted. She thought I needed a way to honor Camilla."

What a woman. Pat truly *is* a lucky man.

"I like it." This meeting didn't go as planned at all. "Thank you, again. I can't tell you how much I appreciate everything you have done for Laurel and me."

"You're family, Roth. Family does for family. Now go soak in as many memories as you can."

That lump in my chest pulses. "I will, sir." I'm to the door when I turn back around. "You didn't ask me."

"Ask you what?" Pat peers up at me. He's sitting back at his desk, my resignation letter in his hand.

"How long she has. You didn't ask me how long she has."

He leans back in his chair and studies me. "The only thing that question serves to do is to satisfy one's curiosity. Whatever time you two have left, it won't be nearly long enough. That is all I need to know."

My teeth click together, hard. I acknowledge his graciousness with a sharp bob of my head.

"And Roth…" He rips the piece of paper he's holding and tosses the two pieces into the trash. "Your resignation is not accepted. There will be a position here for you whenever you decide to return."

"I don't know when that will be," I tell him honestly.

"Doesn't matter. Be it a month or year from now, we'll welcome you back. Don't worry about a thing in the meantime."

I don't know what to say.

"Thank you, sir," I croak, wholly overwhelmed with gratitude.

And then I leave his office before I do something stupid, like throw my arms around him and weep.

ELEVEN

SOME KIND
OF LOVE

Laurel
Ten Years Earlier
June 21, 9:06 a.m.

"DID YOU GRAB THE SUNSCREEN?" Roth asks me, leaning into the kitchen from the hallway.

He looks positively scrumptious today in his fitted olive shorts and a navy tee that says *Surely Not Everyone Was Kung Fu Fighting*. He has the most eclectic, comical collection of T-shirts I have ever seen, each making me laugh more than the last.

We are headed to Rock Island State Park for a weekend of sightseeing, hiking, kayaking, and fishing. Plus, they have the most spectacular twin waterfalls. We borrowed a tent and fishing poles from my friend Yvette, and we've loaded the back of Roth's Jeep with all the essentials we'll need.

At least I thought so.

"Shoot, no."

I wonder what else I'll forget.

"If you tell me where it is, I'll grab it."

"I think there's a bottle in the linen closet. Thank you."

He closes the distance between us and sweeps me into his arms, making me feel as if I'm one of those women on the front of a Tessa Dare historical romance that Mother used to read. All

I'm missing is an off-the-shoulder, cleavage-bearing ball gown sweeping the floor.

"I wouldn't want you to burn, you know. It would ruin my plans for tonight."

"Really," I pant. Now if I could master the alluring head turn, with pouty lips...

"What are you doing?" Roth asks me on a laugh.

"Nothing." I snap my face back toward his. "I, ah...I thought I dropped something on the floor."

My checks burn. Well, that was an epic fail.

"I love you, Laurel."

"Why?" I ask, genuinely confused. "I mean, I'm glad you do, but I don't get it at all."

"It's this." He makes sure I'm steady on my feet before he lets me go. "This whimsical behavior of yours. It's absolutely adorable."

Whimsical. Adorable. A nice way of saying I'm weird.

"I was going for alluring," I mutter, hanging my head in shame.

He slides a finger under my chin and lifts it until I am forced to look at him. He has to do that a lot. "Oh, you were definitely alluring."

"I was not. I was whimsical," I reply in mocking air quotes.

He brings me in for a kiss that's passionate and claiming, and I could almost feel as though I'm back there on that cover with Roth, the shirtless village blacksmith who is supposed to be wrong for me but is right in every way.

"You were whimsically alluring."

I slowly blink my eyes open, my lips still pursed and damp. "That isn't even a thing."

"Of course, it is, Laurel." He cocks his head as if he's truly bewildered. "It's you. You are original and playful and sexy and enthralling. You are whimsically alluring." His mouth quirks crookedly. "Trust me, it's a thing. And you're the only one with it."

"Well, when you say it like that..." Whimsically alluring. Huh.

"You should listen to me more. I am usually right."

He is. But it would be a disservice to the female race to agree with him outright.

"I don't know about that."

I tip my head again and slightly part my lips in hopes that I'm pulling off my newly coined phrase.

"I do." He bops me on the nose and shuffles backward out of the room.

I deflate. Looks like I need more practice.

But Roth's reassuring reply, "Trust me, Laurel," proves he knows me so well already. It pumps me back up.

"Hey, don't go," I beg, liking where we were headed a minute ago. I reach out for him, but he only winks.

"Sunscreen, remember?"

"Fine, be that way." I pretend to pout and he chuckles.

"You'll thank me later. I promise."

Promises. Promises. Roth is full of them. *And he's kept every one so far*, I remind myself.

"I'll hold you to that," I yell after him as he disappears around the corner.

I go back to packing a cooler with a few waters, sodas, and a couple of bottles of wine. I snag the wine opener before I forget, mentally running through the list I wrote down earlier.

Eggs for breakfast, check.

Sheets for the air mattress, check.

Bug spray, check.

Birth control—

"Laurel, your phone is ringing," Roth calls to me.

"Who is it?"

"It says..." He walks back into the kitchen, reading my screen. "Candice."

My mother. I roll my eyes.

"Yaaah."

"Do you want to take it?" He holds out the phone, but all I see is a king cobra wrapped around his forearm, coiled and ready to strike.

"Not really," I mumble.

The ringing stops and then starts up immediately again.

"She's very persistent, this Candice."

"Yes." I smirk. "*She* is."

I snatch the phone from his hand and ready for the attack.

"Hi, Mom."

Roth scrunches up his face. *Yes, Roth, I have my mother labeled by her first name on my caller ID. Don't judge, please.*

"Hi, dear."

I lean up against the countertop and start our surface conversation with a benign, "How are you?" Roth watches me warily, arms crossed.

I've talked to Roth about my mother, of course. A puzzle piece here and there. Not enough for him to even put the edges together. I haven't mentioned the abandonment I felt from her after Esther died. The loneliness that has followed me because of it. The longing still for a close relationship I want but know we'll never have, and the daily disappointment at that stark reality.

When someone you love isn't what you want them to be, that's a jagged pill that gets stuck repeatedly on each attempted swallow.

"Last time we talked, you were headed out on a date. How was it?"

I haven't told my mother about Roth yet, and I certainly never mentioned a date. I rack my brain as to where she would have gotten that idea.

"Date? What date?"

I avert my gaze from Roth's, ashamed. I have the urge to flee into my bedroom and slam the door shut so he can't hear the half-truths I tell her.

"Oh, that's right. You said you were dressed for school or something."

"The school play," I mumble, remembering the lie.

I don't think I'm a much better daughter than she is a mother. And that gives me great pause. Whose job is it to try to mend a broken mother-daughter relationship? The mother's? The daughter's? Both? Neither?

"How did it go?"

"Fine, Mom. Thanks for remembering."

"Of course, dear."

For the next few minutes my mother talks about our neighbor's ten-year-old German shepherd, Willis, who wandered off and has yet to be found.

"That's awful. The Hansen's must be devastated."

"They are. Blanche is simply beside herself. I think it's that raunchy tattooist, if you ask me. I'm sure he's responsible somehow."

I don't bother to ask why, but she bothers to tell me. She goes on and on without pausing for a breath. Roth quietly sneaks out, but I don't think he's gone far. Not really far to go in eight hundred square feet to be fair.

The longer she talks, the more wound up I get. It's not because of what she says this time, it's that when I get off the phone, I'm going to have some 'splaining to do. Roth wouldn't press me if I asked him not to, but this seems like another one of those natural segways into a part of my life I keep closed up tight. Like Esther.

When we come to an ordinary lull in the conversation, I tell her, "Hey, I have a spin class that I'll be late for if I don't get going, but I can call you early next week."

"That's fine." She's disappointed, which isn't like her. "One more quick thing before you go. It's the reason I called, really."

"Oh?" My Spidey senses kick in. "What's that?"

"Riverrun Rally kicks off next weekend."

A churn twists my lower belly into a cluster of knots.

"I know," I reply with hesitation.

I love the Fourth of July. I always have. I'd count down the days to Riverrun Rally the way one would to the start of a new year. I've yet to come across either a small town or the largest city that celebrates America's independence like Leone, Nebraska. Nashville, while it's impressive, is missing that warm, small-town, everyone-knows-your-name charm.

The massive celebration spans two full weekends beginning with Founders Day at the end of June. There are tractor pulls and watermelon eating contests and a carnival with a Tilt-A-Whirl. I took my meema on it once. She threw up the minute we got off and refused to go on it ever again.

Founders Day smoothly transitions into a week of Fourth festivities that starts with an antique car parade. Esther and I would ride in one of the cars, wave like we were famous, and throw loads of candy.

Downtown square is where the action is though. The center stage house's talent shows and the annual Ms. Leone contest during hot summer days. Then after the sun sets, they feature musical acts or comedians suitable for the entire family. People from surrounding towns bring their lawn chairs, blankets, and picnic baskets and make a night of it.

The entire celebration culminates into the grandest of fireworks shows over the river on the evening of the Fourth.

It truly is magical.

But after Ester died, it was never the same, and after PooPa passed away, I haven't been able to make myself go back.

"You're coming this year, right?"

"I, ah…" I scan the area for Roth, lowering my voice. "I don't think I'll be able to make it."

Same thing I've said for the last several years in a row.

My mother doesn't say anything. Awkward silence that I want to babble through makes me start sweating behind the knees and on my upper lip. I take a page from Esther's book and bite my tongue, tasting blood.

I don't know what I expected. An argument, maybe. A guilt trip, most definitely. But I didn't expect her to say, "Because he was a pillar of the community for so long, they are honoring your grandfather this year. I was thinking you'd like to be part of it."

My PooPa is being honored? As much as my grandfather wanted me to flee small-town life, he loved it. He thrived in it. As the mayor of Leone, Eugene Collins took pride in his town, its residents, the community. And he held that most honorable position for thirty-nine years, reelected term after term until the day he passed away, not because people liked him. They did, but it was his passion, his authenticity. He cared and it wasn't simply lip service.

It makes sense they are honoring him.

But why didn't she tell me this before? Surely, she's known about this for months. This wasn't something that was sprung on her during yesterdays' nail appointment. Mayor Burrell would have asked her if it was okay, and knowing my mother, she would have made a big deal of it before agreeing.

Or maybe it was *her* idea to get me back there.

Regardless, it doesn't matter, I suppose.

"I didn't know."

"Oh, well…" she starts in that nasal tone she sometimes gets, and when she does that, I know exactly what's coming. Every parent has a line, you see. A verbal gauntlet they throw down with the intent to manipulate you into doing their will. My mother has many of them, but she knows this one in particular works without fail. "Your grandfather would have wanted you to be here."

Roth chooses that moment to check in on me.

Roth.

Crap.

If I go back to Leone, what do I do about Roth? Take him with me?

God, no. I'm not ready to expose him to my mother yet.

But I can't *not* take him, either... *Can I?*

Double crap.

My PooPa wasn't simply the pillar of the community; he *was* the community.

I have no choice. I can't *not* go. Double negative, I know.

"Is there an official ceremony?" I ask, still hoping there's a way I can weasel out of this.

"There will be an award given to the family before the boat show starts at the Harlow Park Amphitheater."

The boat show happens in the late afternoon of the Fourth. Crowds gather at the banks of Harlow River for an exciting and daring show of skiing and water slalom demonstrations, then wait for the fireworks. Before food trucks became a thing, there were corn dog and cotton candy stands and people selling Cokes and Shastas out of huge travel coolers for twenty-five cents.

Then when it gets dark...thunk, boom...the first starbursts light up the sky.

"Of course, I wouldn't miss it, Mom. I'll be there."

Roth crooks his head. And now he's overheard that I won't miss "it" and "I'll be there" and when he asks what "it" is and I tell him the truth, which of course I have to, he'll be hurt if I don't invite him.

Crickets on a slice of toast.

We've been dating all of four or so months and he has to meet my mother already?

I'm suddenly light-headed.

"Oh, I'm so glad to hear it. I'll have your old room ready for you. And your favorite cover band, Hip Hop Hooray, is playing on the eve of the Fourth. Remember them?"

I hum, or something along those lines, unable to share in her excitement.

My ears ring.

I'll have to tell Roth about my mother.

And my mother about Roth.

Why does this feel like the moment of truth? Or sudden death?

Now Roth is beginning to look concerned. He walks over to me, takes my arm, and leads me to a kitchen chair. I sit, numb, tuning out my mother as she goes on and on about how nice it will be to have me home and all of the girl things we'll do together, all the while thinking...

Is the love we share some kind of love to survive a weekend with Candice, or has my fairy tale come to an abrupt, sad ending?

I guess we're about to find out.

TWELVE

TENERIFE SEA

Laurel
Ten Years Earlier
July 3, 12:48 p.m.

"You haven't said a word since we landed."

"That's not true," I reply, monotone, watching the cornfields fly by out my window. It's been years since I've been back here and man, things have changed. Most notably, the ten-year road construction project to widen I-80 right outside of Omaha is almost complete. It's slick.

"You gave me the address to plug into the GPS. That was twenty minutes ago. Before that you said, 'No,' when I asked you if you were hungry."

"I wasn't."

In fact, I'm pretty sure I could vomit the mocha soy latte and apple I forced down for breakfast before we boarded. I was just wondering if we had a plastic bag somewhere in this rental car. Otherwise, we may need to pull over.

"Laurel." Roth slots our hands together. "It will be okay."

My strangled laugh sounds near hysteria.

"You have no idea what you're getting into."

After I hung up with my mother, I broke out into an allover sweat and couldn't catch my breath. This horrific, intense pain radiated from my chest down my torso, and I was convinced, at twenty-eight, I was going to prematurely die of a heart attack. I told Roth to call 9-1-1.

Turns out it was a panic attack. I've never had one before, so I wasn't quite sure what it was. It was awful, is what it was.

Roth didn't call 9-1-1. He talked me through it, telling me to close my eyes and take slow, deep breaths. When that didn't work, he told me to hang my head between my legs and he made me a cup of chamomile tea. He handled me with care and concern, and eventually, with his help I worked my way out of it.

This man has the patience of Job or Mother Teresa or anyone who lives in Sweden, and there are many times I don't feel as if I deserve him.

"I think I can handle it," he tells me.

"I hope so," I mutter under my breath.

He squeezes my hand, and we drive the remaining few minutes in silence. As we pull into the outskirts of Leone, I feel strangely conflicted.

This place holds a sense of neglect, deep sorrow, and the remains of people I love dearly. But it also holds memories of hopscotch and knee scrapes and belly laughs and midnight eggings and tree climbing and countless July Fourths. So many good things happened here too. I haven't allowed myself to actually *feel* those memories in my bones for the longest time. And I think much of it is because of the man sitting next to me.

As much as I'm dreading the visit with my mother, I'm also sort of excited about showing Roth around the place I grew up.

Maybe this won't be so bad after all. Surely, we can make it through seventy-two hours without incident, right?

"Oooh." Roth turns up his nose at the same time the ripe stench hits me. "It smells like a—"

"Skunk in the middle of the road." I finish, suddenly remembering a long-forgotten game Esther and I used to play. "One-a-skunk."

"What?"

"One-a-skunk," I repeat. "Now you're supposed to say two-a-skunk."

"Two-a-skunk?"

"Three-a-skunk."

Silence. He's clueless about what's going on. Next time he'll learn to be quicker on the draw.

"Now you say four-a-skunk," I prompt.

"Wh—"

"Just say it."

His sigh is heavy. He's clearly not enjoying this as much as I am. "Four-a-skunk."

"Five-a-skunk," I say next.

He catches on. "Six-a-skunk?"

I grin and say, "Seven-a-skunk," and when we get to eight, when *he* gets to eight, he still doesn't realize what the game is all about. So, I spell it out for him.

"You ate a skunk," I tell him with kid-like glee.

"That's a stupid game," he laments, flipping the radio station. Bruno Mars blasts us with his "24K Magic" gold rhythm.

"You only think it's stupid because you lost."

He huffs and shakes his head, and I can tell he's replaying our little banter to see if there's another angle. There isn't. You just need to know how many people you're playing with and the order you need to be in *not* to be eighth.

A few miles later, we exit the interstate and Roth quips, "The *Hometown with Heart*, huh?" as we drive by the massive boulder on the right side of the road, which our motto is carved into.

"My grandfather's doing," I reply with a big swelling of pride.

"Really?"

"Yes. It was the first thing he did as mayor. He thought we needed a tagline of sorts. Something that would draw people from the big city."

"And did it?"

"No, not the way he wanted. But in 2006, Leone *was* on Charles Anderson's list of the best small towns in America."

"Well, that's pretty cool."

"Yeah. And while we are most famous for our Fourth of July celebration, it was his idea to start the annual fall festival we call AppleJacks."

"AppleJacks? You have a festival for cereal?"

"No, silly." I chuckle, forgetting that he's from sand-and-yacht country. "It's a three-day weekend to celebrate the fall apple harvest."

He eyes me with a cheeky grin. "Do they have an apple bobbing contest?"

"And water barrel fights and a craft fair and a classic car show. We don't do anything half-assed in Leone."

When we both laugh, I feel a touch lighter.

Until we pull into the driveway of my childhood home three minutes later, that is.

We sit in the driveway with the car running.

Roth doesn't speak as I stare at the house. The memories that rush over me are as powerful as the waves of a tsunami.

Ours is a sturdy, 1960s two-story white farmhouse with mint green stairs and porch floorboards. It reminded me of the outside of a Doublemint gum wrapper when growing up. I hated it when we had friends over. Oddly, now I think it gives the place character.

I spy the extravagant treehouse perched solidly in the back-yard maple, veranda fully intact. And the tire swing that still hangs from one of the thick branches where Esther and I would take turns pushing each other. In the tall grass, the outline of where we lay and let whirlers fall all over us is clearly visible, to me anyway.

Roth pushes the start-stop button, and the engine cuts off.

I coil my fingers together, anxious.

My mother swings the front door open as if she's been standing there for hours waiting for us to arrive. She probably has after my conversation with her the other day.

"You're bringing a man?" she asks with complete and total surprise.

"Yes, Mother, I am bringing a real man. Is that a problem?" I reply defensively. Daring almost.

"No...of course not. I didn't realize you were seeing someone." You didn't tell me, is what she meant.

"It's early." Please don't screw it up for me.

"Well, he must be important if you're bringing him home to meet your mother."

"He is." Which is the most honest thing I have said to my mother in a long, long time.

"You okay?" Roth asks me.

Ah, nope. How far from okay can one get, exactly? Recognizing signs from that panic attack I had a couple of weeks ago, I draw in a deep breath, purse my lips into the shape of an "O," and let it go in a steady rhythm. It's not working, but "Sure," I finally answer. "You ready?"

My gaze hasn't broken with my mother's since she opened the door. She's now stepped onto our minty-green wraparound porch. Minus the color, it's the kind little girls dream of having, complete with a Sunday porch swing. Esther and I used to spend hours in the summer on that swing, reading Judy Blume books and drinking lemonade until our bellies ached.

"Are *you* ready, is probably the better question."

I swallow past the angst and turn toward him. "You love me, right?"

"Yes," he replies immediately with this tone that is absolute, leaving no room for argument.

"No matter what?"

"Laurel..." My eyes immediately water. He can't possibly understand what I'm feeling right now. Every nerve is charged. Every muscle is wound taut. "I am so in love with you. All that you are is all I will ever need, and there is absolutely nothing that could change my love for you, including whatever is inside that house."

Heartache is what is inside of that house.

I twist the two rings circling my right thumb. Around and around and around they go. "You're sure?"

His gaze burns into mine. "Yes."

I look away. I repeat my deep breathing and my ring twisting. "Okay, then. I'm ready."

He has to know my mother is watching. Either he doesn't care, or he wants to show her how much I mean to him. It doesn't matter, because when he leans over to kiss me like no one is watching, I let everything go. I give it to him for safekeeping, trusting in him and in his love for me.

"I love you, Laurel. No matter what," he tells me, his forehead pressed to mine.

"Mi amado."

"Christ. You know what that does to me. Do they have hotels around here?" He adjusts himself and that makes me chuckle.

"Let's go."

"I need this hard-on to go down first." His eyes sparkle and I do what I *hate* when other girls do it...I throw my head back and barrel laugh, hand to chest.

My mother has to be wondering what in the heck we are doing, but I find I don't care. This right here is perfect. A stolen moment in heaven before a few days in hell.

"You'd better will it down."

"That doesn't help, love."

Love. Wow. The first time he's called me that. Now I *know* I can do this.

I open my door and while Roth moans, I step out of the air-conditioned car into the sticky humidity of Nebraska in July.

"Laurel," my mother calls, and then she surprises me by running down the stairs, meeting me halfway up the sidewalk.

She opens her arms and embraces me as if we are BFFs. I hug all five feet three inches of her petite frame. She's thinner than I remember.

"I am so glad you're here," she whispers in my ear.

Is this for show or did she truly miss me? She sounds genuine, only I don't say anything back, because I don't want to lie. I am so tired of the lying. I am tired of needing a *reason* to lie.

"Mom." I break from her and go immediately to Roth's side, twining my arm around him. He does the same, holding on tight. "This is Roth Keswick. Roth, this is my mother, Candice Collins."

"Candice, nice to meet you," he says politely, extending his free hand.

But for my mother, that isn't nearly good enough. "I'm a hugger," she announces, practically jumping into his arms. *She is no such thing.* He has no choice but to reciprocate, leaving me in the cold.

"Just look at you."

She holds Roth by both shoulders and scans him up and down as if he's an endangered species. It's the exact same thing she did to Johnny Mavin, my junior homecoming date. Then she repinned the boutonniere I'd stabbed myself six times getting just perfect and said, *"That's better."*

"Aren't you a handsome devil."

Roth's gaze snaps to mine. I raise my shoulders all the way to my ears, as if to convey, *"You're on your own, buddy."*

"Thank you, ma'am."

"Ma'am? No, no. That won't do at all. I insist you call me Candice."

"All right, Candice."

My mother hooks her arm in the crook of Roth's and leads him up the sidewalk toward the house. I am left in her rearview, forgotten, per usual. "Are you hungry?" I hear her ask him.

"I could always eat, yes."

Roth catches me over his shoulder to make sure I'm following, his eyes wide and round. I smirk and jog to catch up.

"Well, you're in luck. I've made my famous maidrites."

"Maidrites? What's a maidrite?" He holds the door open for her and waits for me to follow, kissing me lightly on the forehead as I pass.

"Why, Laurel hasn't made you a batch of maidrites yet?" She shoots me with a sear of disappointment.

"You haven't given me the secret recipe," I want to heave back. Instead, I press my lips together and force them into a thin smile.

"Laurel is a great cook, Candice. I believe she mentioned that's on her list for me try, but she wanted to surprise me."

No, I am not and no, I did not, but his little gray lie makes me feel all sorts of mushy.

"Oh, well that is sweet." Regarding me, she says, "I'm sorry I ruined your surprise, dear."

"It's fine, Mom."

"Well, a maidrite is simply a loose meat sandwich." When Roth scrunches his face up in disgust, she pats him on the arm and asks with horror, "You're not one of those vegetarians, are you?"

Oh God, Mother. Like vegetarians are a breed of their own or something.

But Roth takes it in stride, as he usually does. "I am a carnivore, Candice, but thank you for asking."

"Good, good. We live in meat-and-potato country here. Don't know what I would feed you otherwise."

'Cuz there's not a single vegetarian in the Midwest...*good grief.* Face palm.

"A bullet dodged then," Roth replies, biting a smile back.

"Well, why don't we get you one and see what you think. Laurel, could you get the plates, please? Roth, you can make yourself comfortable. I'm sure you're tired from all that traveling."

"Laurel is probably more tired than I am," Roth replies as I go and do my mother's bidding on autopilot. He comes to take the three plates now in my hands and walks to the table to set them out. "She didn't sleep well last night."

While that is true, it takes me aback when he says it. I've had no one to defend me since Esther died. My mother didn't make these subtle digs around my grandparents, or anyone, really. And the slight bite in Roth's tone makes me believe that Candice has managed to get under his skin in under three minutes. Maybe he sees what I've seen all along?

My mother is not outright mean. It's more of a subtle, molten undertone. I've often wondered if I'm overly sensitive or if I read between the lines too much. When she told Roth to make himself comfortable because he was probably tired, what I heard was, *Laurel, Roth is our guest, so it doesn't matter that you traveled the same distance as he did. If you're tired, suck it up.*

Is that what she meant, or is she oblivious?

"Where are the glasses?" Roth asks me.

I start to answer but my mother jumps in. "Laurel, grab the frosted mugs from the freezer. I bought a gallon jug of fresh A&W root beer just for you. I know it's your favorite."

And then she goes and does something like that...

"Thank you, Mom."

We stare at each other so long I get prickly. Then she hugs me, and I can almost imagine I am ten again. "It really is good to have you home, Laurel. It means a lot to me that you came."

Roth watches us. His face is passive, but his eyes brim with questions. A lump grows in my throat. "I'm sorry it's been so long," I choke out past it.

"I know it's hard for you."

It is, but does that excuse my behavior? It's hard on my mom too, and she lives it every day.

When she releases me from her hold, she hangs her head, but not before I notice a rare display of vulnerability. A lone tear streaks down her cheek.

"Why don't you sit down," I suggest, suddenly noting the shadowy circles under each eye. My gaze automatically gravitates to the faded inch-long scar above her left eyebrow, remembering the story she's told me many times about it. "I'll get everything."

"You're sure?"

"I'll help," Roth offers. "Sit, Candice. We've got this."

"Thank you. I am rather beat."

Should I be worried? Why am I so worried? I sneak a glance at her every few seconds as we grab condiments from the fridge and slap meat into our buns. But I don't notice anything else overt besides the draw of her lids as if she hasn't slept in days. Her facade is squarely back in place.

A few minutes later, we're all digging into our tasty maid-rites and frosty root beers.

"These are incredible, Candice," Roth praises her. He's already on number two.

"They are exactly as I remember. Amazing." I take another bite and moan.

My mother beams from ear to ear. "Just ground hamburger and a few other simple ingredients."

"I have never heard of this. Is it a Leone thing?"

"Not Leone, per se, but Midwestern." Then she goes on to tell the story of how the maidrite was born in Iowa one hundred years ago and how it goes by several different names, and that people try to fancy it up, but her mother kept it simple and so does she.

We finish our lunch amid rather pleasant conversation, I must say. My mom asks Roth questions, but in a polite "let me get to know you" kind of way, rather than "I'm judging every word out of your mouth" sort. She's open-minded and interested and most of the time I sit quietly confused, because this is not generally her operating rhythm.

"He loves you," she proclaims softly when Roth runs out to the car to retrieve our luggage.

"Why do you say that?" I ask, shocked.

"I have eyes, Laurel." She faces me. Roth spies us standing at the kitchen window, watching him. He quirks that one side of his lip up, and I always follow suit.

"You love him too."

Why lie? It's as plain as the smile on my face. I turn toward her. "I do, but—"

"There is no but. You love him or you don't."

I glance to Roth, then back to her. "I do, Mom."

Her mouth moves into a semi smile. It seems forced.

Is she not happy for me? Does she not like him? Does it matter?

I don't want it to, but it does.

We go back to watching Roth, who is taking his time pulling two small roller bags from the trunk.

"Were you worried about bringing him home to meet me?"

If I'd fallen and broken an ankle, I wouldn't have been too disappointed. You know, nothing too extreme. But I stay quiet, my silence speaking truer than I can.

"I don't blame you," she tells me. "I remember when I brought your father home to meet your grandparents. I felt as though I had swallowed a whole carnival and every ride was going full tilt at once. I was already pregnant with you and Esther, and I'd planned to tell your grandfather that night too, but…"

I shift my attention from Roth to her. She's still staring out the window, though by the fix of her stare, she's lost in the past somewhere. My mother never talks about my father. Ever. And while I knew my parents had a short courtship, I certainly didn't realize my grandparents hadn't even met my father before we were conceived. That is a shocker.

I wait for her to continue, but she leaves me hanging for so long I have to gently prod, "But, what?" *What happened? Was PooPa angry? Did he hug her and tell her it would be all right?*

It feels like I'm standing on a sea of nails as I wait for her to answer.

"Your grandfather drew me aside after dinner and told me he wasn't the one for me."

Whoa.

What?

My PooPa was the most loving, supportive, understanding man I knew and though he wasn't a fan of my father's, I assumed it was because he'd abandoned his family. I had no idea he didn't like him from day one.

"Why?"

"When I asked him that, he said..." My mother pauses, shaking her head as if she's trying to exit her old life and step back into the present one. But with as far away as her voice still is, she hasn't quite made it. "'He's missing the burn.' And when I asked him what that meant, he said, 'There's no sparkle in his eye when looks at you, peanut. No blaze, not even a glowing ember.'"

She sounds so sad that I'm at a loss for words. Out of my periphery, I see Roth pull his phone from his back pocket. It's almost as if he knows we're having a moment.

"I was devastated. Here I was, unmarried and pregnant, and my father hated the man I loved and wanted to make a life with. And the thing is..." She catches my gaze. The corners of her mouth now droop toward the floor. "He was right, and I knew he was right when he said it."

I had no idea, and I don't have to ask how it ends. Candice married Sean Collins, had Esther and me seven months later, and three years after that she was a single parent when he didn't come home after work, cleaning out their bank account on his way out of town.

"I'm sorry, Mom." It's meaningless and tastes stale, but I don't know what else to say.

And why is she telling me this? Why now after all these years? Does she think Roth isn't the one for me? Is that the reason? Because if that's what she tells me, I'm gonna lose it. Roth *is* the only one and no matter what she—

"Roth has that burn, Laureli." She interrupts my wild and erratic train of thought with a childhood nickname she hasn't used in years. "Your grandfather would have approved."

My chest puffs out, like someone's blown air into it with a straw. It's hard to breathe through the sensations now roiling around in there, bumping into each other.

What my mother thinks matters, even though I want to tell myself otherwise.

"I've no doubt your PooPa would have loved Roth."

She has no idea how much her words or this story mean to me, even though it clearly opened old wounds for her.

"Do *you* approve?" I ask, trying not to sob. I hate that I *need* it.

She nods, emotional as I am and working just as hard to squash it.

I want to ask her so many questions. She's opened a door that's been locked to me my entire life, which quite simply, is *her* life. But now I understand this story was about *me*...not her, and she only opened that door long enough to get a glimpse of what's inside.

Now it's closed again.

"You don't think it's too early?"

"Can you see this man staying by your side through the hard times? And I mean the low of the lows, when the hardest decision is *not* whether to stay *now* but wondering if he should have stayed to begin with?"

I find her question interesting and thought-provoking. Life takes unexpected turns that drive you to dark places your worst-case scenarios couldn't even conjure. When we're there, wherever there is, if Roth could go back and do it all over again, would he have chosen to walk me to my car that first night at Rudy's?

"Yes, I can."

"Then don't you let him go. Or I may just make a run for him myself."

The thought of my mother chasing after Roth makes me snicker. I think she may give it a go if given a chance.

"Thanks, Mom."

Something shifts between us in that moment. It's microscopic, and maybe temporary, but it's there. She feels it too, because she gives my hand a quick embrace as the front door opens.

"Where should I take these, Candice?" Roth asks, standing with a suitcase in each hand. He studies me first, then my mother. His brows furrow.

I'm not crying, you're crying.

"Your room is the first upstairs to the left. Laurel's is at the end of the hall."

"Yes, ma'—Candice," he corrects in time. His wink makes her giggle. Hmm...seems Roth Warren Keswick has the same effect on all women. At least the Collins women.

When I told him we'd likely have to sleep in separate rooms, I thought maybe he'd balk, but he said, "I wouldn't sleep with you even if you begged me to."

That man. He makes my head swim and my heart float. I'm getting used to being dizzy and weightless at the same time.

Roth disappears up the stairs, taking them two at a time, even with his heavy load. We watch after him.

"He's a keeper," Mother whispers.

And for once, I have to completely agree with her.

THIRTEEN

"I COULD NOT ASK FOR MORE"

Laurel

Ten Years Earlier
July 4, 5:54 a.m.

LIFTING THE SHEETS, I slide in beside Roth, then draw them back up over us. I nuzzle against his back, moving quietly so as not to disturb him. It's early, the sun barely breaking the skyline, but I've been awake for hours, staring at the plastic stars Esther and I painstakingly scattered all over the ceiling in a room that we shared until we were nine.

She was all around me yet nowhere at all.

I couldn't take it anymore.

I needed Roth.

Yesterday after we got settled in, I gave Roth the grand tour of Leone, and that included the elementary, middle, and high schools, the main drag, as well as the riverbend. It took all of twenty minutes. I saved Sumner's Square, our Main Street district for last. It was already buzzing with families, rides, street jugglers, and mimes. And the smells...freshly buttered popcorn and cinnamon-sugared funnel cakes. Yum.

We parked and walked around for hours.

We fed the baby goats and the llama in the petting zoo.

We watched the junior varsity drill team perform in the band shell. I gave them a B minus.

We moseyed through the art show. Even Roth was impressed.

We ate funnel cakes and slurped slurpies.

We got henna tattoos.

We played carnival games and Roth won me a cheap stuffed animal in the ring toss, setting him back thirty-six dollars.

My mother met us for the evening concert by Hip Hop Hooray, a local eighties cover band. Roth and I danced. I'd like to think the crowd was cheering on our swing dance skills, but there was no "our" about it. It was all Roth. He even convinced my mother to try, showing her a few basic moves.

We had a fabulously delightful time.

"I forgot how much I loved it here," I told him absently on our way back to Mom's, clutching my big-headed stuffed pig, which is about the most adorable thing I've ever seen. Last time I was here for my PooPa's funeral, I couldn't seem to catch my breath. I thought I would suffocate. I sensed my own mortality shadowing me everywhere I went.

The shadows are still here. I'm not naïve enough to think they'll disappear. Light doesn't penetrate the farthest-reaching corners after all. But they're not as bleak and foreboding as they were before. They don't hang over me quite as dense and heavy.

And that can only be because of a man who is as resilient as a willow tree in a straight-line wind.

"Then we will come back again," he said to me, as if he had our future together already penned in ink. I believe he might have. I secretly hope he does.

"How did you sleep?" Roth asks, his voice crackly from slumber.

He wriggles himself around to face me and blinks his mossy eyes open. They're murky when he first wakes up, I've noticed. More the shade of seaweed.

"I'm sorry I woke you."

"No, you're not."

I don't think I've known anyone who makes me laugh more than he does. Many nights my cheeks hurt when I go to bed. I laugh the entire time we're together.

"Okay, I'm not," I admit, grinning.

Slithering my arms around his torso, I press my pelvis into his.

"You'd better stop that, you little minx."

"What? This?"

I do it again, this time with a little twist. He stifles a groan, fully hard against me now. Then he flips the script. Rolling his hips, he hits me in just the right spot. I gasp. My eyes roll back in my head.

"All fun and games now, isn't it?"

When he grins, an unexplained naughtiness washes over me, and I morph into this exotic bedroom nymphet I've never seen before.

"I like games," I say in the sultriest voice I can muster.

Bait laid.

Wrapping my top leg over his lines me up against his erection quite nicely. I glide back and forth, and honestly, I didn't come in here for sex, but…well, good intentions and all have flown right out the window, and in their place is a coquette I think I like.

Roth sweeps my face to see if I'm serious. When he sees I am, a slow, sly smile curls his mouth. "What kind of games?"

Bait nibbled.

"Well…" I slip my hand underneath his boxers and grip his taut tush, making sure my fingers graze between his cheeks. He growls and the lines on his face sharpen. "I excel at the quiet game."

"Do you now?"

"Mm-hmm."

I bat my eyelashes and pray I resemble Marilyn Monroe and not Betty Boop.

"Isn't your mother right across the hall?"

Bait taken.

"Her bed is against the far wall. She's a heavy sleeper."

Knowing I almost have him, I boldly guide his hand beneath my panties and let him make his own decision.

"Fuck, Laurel. You're so wet."

Don't I know it.

Roth curves two fingers just so and slips them inside me. There's no resistance. I'm ready. It feels so good, I have to turn my head to the side and shove the pillow in my mouth to stifle my cry. He pumps them in and out, then circles my nub ever so lightly with the pad of his thumb. He whispers in my ear, "You're going to come already, aren't you?"

Yes, yes, a tiny wail of a "Yes" bursts through the Tempur-Pedic.

I wasn't entirely truthful. I *suck* at the quiet game. I always have.

"I thought you weren't supposed to make noise?" Roth teases, his chuckle tempered.

"You did that on purpose."

I blink up at him, my vision hazy shades of summer sun.

Wearing a lopsided grin, in a few practiced moves he has our underwear removed and me on my back. He spreads my legs with his knee, settles between them, and pushes my nightgown above my breasts so he can suckle a nipple.

"You have to be quiet too," I challenge. I'm weak. Wired. Flying through the clouds.

"I don't recall that was the game."

"But it—"

He cuts me off, driving inside me in one smooth thrust. Slamming his mouth over mine, he swallows my scream of heady bliss. Goose bumps race across my arms. My thighs tremble. I pulsate with need.

"You excel at quiet…" As he nips his way down my throat,

my walls tighten around him. He holds himself steady. "Said no one..." He nibbles the spot on my shoulder that renders me powerless. I beg him to move. He doesn't. "Ever," he croaks, giving his hips one sharp tuck and roll.

I want to dispute his sex-glazed accusation but a) he is right and b) I'm already dancing with an orgasm and can't exactly speak at the moment.

I lose all desire to argue anyway when Roth starts to piston like a man possessed. Sadly, our clandestine rendezvous comes to a tragic and abrupt ending when the bedsprings protest. And I mean, so loudly they could wake the dead.

Or my mother.

My eyes fly open. Roth reacts the same way, except his are stuffed with horror.

I slap my hands over my mouth and giggle uncontrollably.

My mother's door creaks open. Her footsteps pad slowly against the floorboards.

Roth's eyes round and pop. He doesn't move. He looks mortified.

I laugh louder. Her footsteps stop, then retreat.

"Busted," I whisper then snort. I'm out of control.

Her door creaks again and clicks softly.

Roth rolls off of me and flops onto his back. "I'll just pack my things and go now," he bemoans, throwing an arm over his forehead.

"I forgot this mattress was so loud."

His face whips toward mine. "What do you *mean* you *forgot?*" He squints, and I realize where his mind has gone.

"I..." My sides hurt. "Well, it's not what you think," I muster. I take a few deep breaths until I'm somewhat settled. "This is Esther's old bed. We may have broken a few springs jumping on it back in the day."

"That would have been a nice memory to surface *before* your mother caught me boinking her daughter."

"Boinking?"

I roll.

I don't even care that my mother will hear us. Peals of my laughter bounce off the walls.

"Boinking?" I parrot again, in hysterics. I start to hiccup.

"Would you rather I say fucking?" he asks, unable to stop chuckling himself.

"Yes." *Hiccup*.

"But you don't like swearing." Roth reaches over to pinch my nose and I swat his hand away, sitting up.

"*I* don't like to swear. I don't care if *you* do." *Hiccup*.

I hold my breath. One. Two. Thre—*Hiccup*.

"So noted. You need water," he proclaims, bouncing up from the bed. He's buck naked and beautiful as he searches the floor for his underwear, turning in frantic circles.

He reminds me of Meringue when she's chasing her own tail.

I lose it again.

"Laurel, Christ. What is your mother going to think?" His snags his boxers from under the bed.

"That I'm finally happy," I reply with the utmost sincerity.

Roth stops. He stares at me as if I've sprouted a pair of black angel wings.

"What?" I tip my head and wait. *Hiccup*.

Have I never told him that before? That he lights me up from the inside?

"I love you today, Laurel Linnea Collins."

Mush. Out-and-out mush.

"And I'll love you tomorrow, Roth Warren Keswick."

Sliding on his underwear, he leans in for a kiss. "I'm glad I make you happy." His lips brush mine. It tickles.

"I'm sorry I haven't told you before."

"I knew it. I was just waiting for you to figure it out." He slips a brown belt through his short loops and buckles it.

I push myself up on my elbows. "Is that so?"

"It *is* so."

He's so straight-faced I don't even argue.

Roth throws on a fresh blue tee. This one reads, CHICKENS, THE PET THAT POOPS BREAKFAST. My PooPa would have gotten a kick of out of it.

Propping his hands on his hips, he stares at the closed bedroom door like Lizzy Borden might be on the other side waiting with an ax.

"Want to see something?" I ask. The devil twinkles in his eyes. "Not that." Although I would be game. My mother already thinks we did the deed anyway. Snatching the robe, I'd dropped on the chair, I wrap it around me. My hiccups are gone anyway. I don't need the water. But I do need caffeine. Lots and lots of caffeine. "Let me throw something on and I'll meet you downstairs."

"I'm not going out there without you."

"Are you serious?"

One brow meets his hairline.

He's serious.

"Good thing I didn't need water then."

I laugh all the way to my room.

"This is truly stunning," he says softly.

We sit atop a picnic table at the banks of my favorite place on Earth.

I drove Roth by the campground we used to frequent with PooPa but couldn't stop because it was packed with tents and cars and people who wanted to escape the city for a few days. And the shore was already lined with fathers helping their kids bait hooks and cast lines. So, we headed to a less-crowded boat launch that is far more peaceful.

"That it is."

The breeze blows light. The air smells of salt and distant memories. Bass waiting to be fed break the surface every so often. Warm sun rays bounce off pristine waters, blinding us. I cup a hand over my squinty eyes. I forgot my sunglasses back at my mom's.

I spot an older man and two little girls in a fishing boat not too far offshore. The girls drop something over the bow and giggle. It takes me back, and if I listen close enough, I can hear PooPa shushing Esther and me to be quiet, or we'll scare the fish away. I close my eyes and concentrate harder, but their voices fade until I can't hear them anymore. Instead of being melancholy, though, I am...I don't know what exactly. At peace, maybe?

I open my eyes and watch the girls. I hope they're soaking these days in the way I did.

"So, this is it, huh? Anywhere in the world?"

I look over at Roth, remembering my answer to his question on the place I'd pick to go above all others. *Branched Oak Lake.* This inexplicable joy fills me up until I feel I may burst. I smile. "Yes."

"Who knew a place this beautiful would be in Nebraska."

"Hey." I smack him on the arm in jest. "There are lots of beautiful places in Nebraska."

"Hate to break it to you, love, but there's nary a tree in sight except here. It's just...open fields and cornstalks."

"Nary?" I giggle. "Did you seriously use *nary* in a sentence?"

"My vocabulary is quite extensive." He shrugs like he can't help his innate intelligence. It's so endearing.

"We have more than cornstalks and open fields, you know. The Henry Doorly Zoo is regularly named as one of the best zoos in the United States."

"Really? Well, I feel like I might need to be the judge of that. I am an animal connoisseur after all."

"Wow, a mustard whisperer, a walking lexicon, *and* an animal connoisseur? You are a multifaceted, impressive human being, Roth Keswick."

"I am." He blows on his knuckles and pretends to shine them on his chicken shirt.

I love this man. So much.

"How did I luck into you?" I ask him, in a little bit of awe.

"You fell into me, is probably more accurate. Or onto me, I should say."

"Hey. I think it's the other way around." I elbow him, remembering that night at Rudy's vividly.

"I fell into you all right." His voice is deep. His stare is intense. Smoldering. *Whew.*

I need to do something quick, or I'll be dragging him behind a thicket of trees and stripping him naked. I think about that orgasm I missed earlier.

"I caught my first fish right over there." I point to a finger off the main lake right around the bend. "A twenty-four-inch walleye. I was four."

"Did you hog them all on that trip too?"

I double over laughing. Roth tried his hand at fishing for the first time a few weekends ago when we went camping. I caught four bluegill and two catfish. Roth caught a big fat goose egg. He was quite devastated.

"Hey, maybe I'm the *fish* whisperer?"

"I'd believe that," he says sardonically, but I think he's impressed. "Okay, question time."

"Uh-oh." I roll my eyes.

"Hush now. If you could learn one thing you haven't learned yet, what would it be?"

"Well, I would say swing dancing, but...that was never on my list to begin with."

He barks a laugh, which is carried away by the breeze. "Glad I could check an invisible box."

"You check a lot of them," I reply softly.

"Good to know," he says in a tone that reflects mine.

Finishing what we started this morning sounds awfully tempting. And by the expansion of Roth's pupils, I'd say his thoughts went to the same place.

"Okay." I clear my throat before I do something that will get us both arrested. Or a bad case of poison ivy. "Anything?"

"Anything."

I ponder it, while watching how the blue skyline's perfect shades bleed beautifully into the slightly darker ones of the water below it. The hues' differences are subtle and would be hard to capture in a...then suddenly it comes to me. "Photography."

"Photography?"

"Yah. I've always been interested in photography but haven't found the time. And with a real camera, not one of those." I point to the cell phone in his hand. "An expensive one where you have to know what you're doing. That's probably why I haven't done it. It's not a cheap hobby."

"Always keep your dreams in sight, Laurel. Don't let them go, no matter what."

"They are and I won't," I murmur, not referring to photography at all. He knows it.

He's my dream now. I can't mess that up.

We sip coffee from my favorite coffee shop, Scooters, and watch the early morning boaters tootle on the lake. I wish we had time to make a day of it. I'd love to rent a kayak and take a hike on the wildflower trail. Maybe we'd even find a secluded place to skinny dip. Only, my mother has a full day planned of parading her long-lost daughter and her daughter's new boyfriend around town, but when she texts me, asking where we've gone and I tell her we're at the lake, she surprises me by responding, *Take your time and enjoy yourself. I'll save us a spot at the river.*

"Everything okay?" Roth asks. I'm still staring at my phone.

"I suppose."

"Want to talk about it?" His attention flits to my screen, then back to me.

Do I? Will *I* sound like the crazy one? I mean she did tell me to take my time, but today is the Fourth and we traditionally start the day at the parade, followed by a pancake breakfast at the airport hangar, and watch the talent show before heading to the river to get our seats early.

Is she being genuine, or will I hear about this all night tonight? As I got older and learned what gaslighting was, I half wondered if it applied to my mother. Carmen thinks it does, but I believe she's simply clueless about how her words and actions affect me.

"It's my mother."

"She giving you a hard time?"

"I'm not sure." Is she? It's always difficult to tell.

I hand him my phone and let him read the message for himself, sinking my teeth into my lower lip.

He scans it and hands it back. "Do you think she's being disingenuous?"

I blow out the breath I was holding. He gets it. I'm not sure how he gets it, but he does.

"I don't know."

"Does she do that often?"

"She can."

Roth slips off his sunglasses and lets them dangle between two fingers. "I don't want to overstep my bounds here."

"You're not overstepping." I return the phone to my back shorts pocket without replying to her.

"Your mother's problems aren't your problems, Laurel. She can't say what she means—that's on her, not you. Passive-aggressive people tend not to be able to express their feelings in an open and honest way, so they go about it backhanded."

"Backhanded. Good analogy."

"It has put a wedge between you." Not a question.

"Is it that obvious?"

"Unfortunately." He slides his sunglasses up on his head. "Have you talked to her about it?"

"I tried once." It was the night before I left for college. She left me an article on the kitchen table of a girl who had been brutally raped near Belmont University campus, which isn't too far from where I'd be attending Vanderbilt. I didn't bother reading it at the time but later discovered the rape wasn't recent...it was from several years earlier, and when I confronted her on it, she said she didn't know. I never confronted my mother. Ever. But I was so upset and disappointed she couldn't be happy for me that I called her a liar, asking why she couldn't have bought me a rape whistle if she was so worried. She sat there with a straight face and told me that *I* misunderstood. That she was only trying to make sure I was aware of the dangers of a big city like Nashville. I spent my last night at my grandparents' and left the next morning for college without saying goodbye. "It didn't end well."

"I'm sorry."

"Me too. I wish it wasn't this way."

"Of course, you don't. She's your mother. And no matter what she has done or what she says or how she acts, she's still your mother and you love her."

I do, but I hate to admit it's with a dozen asterisks. And I realize love shouldn't be predicated on caveats. You should accept a person as they are, and you should love them equally regardless of flaws. But the reality is...you don't.

I gaze out over the bright blue water, trying to gather my stray thoughts. "Every time I talk to her, I hope the outcome is different, you know? I hope she's supportive or encouraging and every time, she's not—the disappointment is as fresh as it was the first time. I want her to be a better mother, and she's just not."

"Have you ever thought that maybe she's the best mother *she* can be, Laurel?"

Have I? It's a fair question. One I've never thought of. Maybe I'm too busy trying to set her into a mold of my own making. I realize that I don't know my mother. Not really. She's closed off for sure, but maybe I also haven't taken the appropriate interest either.

"I don't suppose I have."

"For what it's worth, it's obvious she loves you."

"I know she does."

"So, what do you say we take her up on her offer, sincere or not, and make a day of it. Let everything go for today, Laurel. Your mother, your guilt, your fears. Obligation. All of it. Let's have a great day, just you and me. I want to hear every story you can remember about this place if you want to share them."

This is a unique gift of Roth's. He makes living in the now seem so easy.

"I would love that."

I text my mother a quick *Be home in time for the ceremony,* then push guilt aside and make a day of it.

We rent a kayak and my arms are wet noodles by the time we paddle back. We take that hike. I pick a huge bunch of wild-flowers to take home to my mother. Roth tucks one behind my ear. We get two fishing poles and buy some live bait, dropping our lines off a secluded bank. I lose every single worm to fish that are far too crafty and the only thing Roth catches is a nice wad of underwater tree branches, which is more than he caught last time. I tell him he's making progress. He isn't amused.

We have a blast.

I let everything go and soak in this day for the blessing that it is. I retell every story I can remember about childhood summers spent camping here, like getting poison ivy in my private parts when I peed in what I thought was a bush and how I thought a fish nibbled on my foot once when we were swimming but it was only Esther playing a joke. I live in the now. If you live in the memories, you might as well already be dead yourself. And I've immersed myself inside memories for far too long. Allowed them to hold me prisoner. Let fear win. It's because of Roth that I don't want to live there anymore, but it hasn't been easy, and I haven't made it easy on *him*. He is patient and persistent and understanding. I am so immensely grateful, though I'll never be able to adequately explain it to him.

"Ready to go?" he calls as he walks down the boat dock toward me after returning our poles. He carries two bottles that I hope contain ice cold water. I am dying of thirst.

"I suppose," I reply reluctantly. "We should probably get back." We both need a quick shower before we head to the park. I take a water he hands me, twist off the top, and drink in very unladylike gulps. It burns my teeth and freezes my esophagus. It's so good.

"I had a great day, Laurel. Thank you for bringing me to anywhere in the world." He wipes off a stray droplet of water dangling from my bottom lip.

I tilt my chin up. The sun would be in my eyes, but Roth blocks it perfectly. A bright yellow aura surrounds him, wholly representing the light he brings to my life. Heaven surely must exist, for how else would I have found this man?

"I wouldn't bring just anyone, you know."

"Yes," he says with a nod. "I do."

He places a soft, chaste kiss on my lips, and we head up to the car, sticky, sunburned, and exhausted yet happier than I can remember.

The rest of the night is as magical as the day was. I cry during the ceremony for my PooPaa. I stand by my mother's side. Roth stands by mine. He holds my hand. We eat blue cotton candy and drink frosty root beer Mother brought in a cooler, while we watch the ski show. We endure her dragging over half the town to introduce them to Roth. Most of the time she remembers I'm there too.

"Thank you for a great day," I tell Roth as we lie side by side on the blanket, watching fireworks burst to life in the night sky.

He pops up to lean on an elbow and bends down until his nose brushes mine. His eyes volley frantically back and forth between mine, like he's searching for an unspoken answer.

"This is by far the best Fourth of July I've ever had, Laurel," he whispers. "I am honored you took me on this walk through your past. I know it wasn't easy."

I'm glad it's dark, because I instantly well up.

I didn't think this day would ever hold the same magic as it once did, and somehow Roth understood that without me saying a word.

He is all I've been waiting for, and I tell him, "I could not have asked for more," right before my mouth reaches up to cover his, not caring that we're amid a crowd of thousands or right next to my mother.

FOURTEEN

AT LAST

Laurel

Ten Years Earlier
November 25, 8:16 p.m.

UGH.

My stomach churns one way first, then the other. It feels like girls gone wild down there. I thought meeting my mother was a true test of our relationship, but I had it wrong.

Today is.

Though Roth and I have been together for eight months, I'm meeting his parents for the first time. Roth is incredibly close to Frank and Elana and their opinions carry a lot of weight.

How do I compare to others before me?

Will they think I'm enough for their son?

I finger the beginnings of a stress zit on my chin.

I often don't feel as though I'm enough for anyone, let alone an amazing guy like Roth, but he goes above and beyond to assuage my neurosis. He accepts every flaw and imperfection, and I have a lot of them. I'm forgetful and socially inept and recently discovered I can't make a maidrite to save my soul. I tried every week for three months in a row and never got it right. How hard is it to throw ground beef, onions, and seasonings into a crock pot that does the work for you? Apparently, very. Mine were either too salty or too oniony or too bland. I gave up. I hope Elana doesn't need help in the kitchen or I'll be disqualified as wife material before the gate even opens.

"Earth to Laurel." Roth kneads the muscles in my neck until they loosen their death grip on my skull. "Damn, you're tense."

"That feels so good." I battle to keep my eyes open.

"Laurel, they love you already. You know that, right?"

"How?" I ask, all thoughts of my kitchen failings now simmering on the back burner. *Ha ha.* "They haven't met me yet."

"Trust me."

"You say that a lot." I moan when he hits a particularly rough spot between my neck and shoulder blade.

"You need reminding a lot."

"I know. I'm just..."

"Nervous?" he fills in, but that's not what I was going to say. I was going for insecure. Petrified. Borderline manic. I'm ten clicks beyond nervous. "You don't need to be anxious. My parents are laid back and easy to get along with."

Let's say, for the sake of argument, that's true. It's not only his parents I'm meeting this weekend, though. I'm meeting his *entire* extended family. Aunts and uncles, cousins and second cousins. His eighty-eight-year-old grandmother, Margaret, will be here. The matriarch of the family. And if that wasn't enough, Roth said close friends and neighbors are also invited. Elana apparently likes to make sure that everyone who has no one has someplace to go during Thanksgiving. She's an amazing woman, but the thought of that many people with eyes on me has wreaked havoc on my digestion. I've taken enough Imodium to plug the Suez Canal for a solid month.

This could be a long and uncomfortable four days.

"Everything will be fine."

"If you say so," I reply, not feeling a shred of his confidence.

Our Lyft driver slows to a stop and every muscle that Roth has worked to unknot balls up again.

"We're here," Roth announces in delight. He gives me one quick squeeze. "We're going to have a great time."

I can only nod.

Roth exits first and gathers our luggage from the trunk, and for a split second I think about telling Kyle, our driver, to step on it, whisking me back to the Sarasota airport. The instinct to flee and hide out in the quiet shadows of my apartment with Meringue as my only comfort is very, very real. But then Roth is back at my door, hand out, lips turned up, reading my mind.

"If you can overcome your fear of swing dancing, Laurel, this is a walk in the park."

I consider that, glancing back at Kyle. His eyes are encouraging. Or maybe they're demanding me to get the heck out of his Chevy Impala, which has so many stickers wallpapered on the back end you can't mistake his political affiliations.

I twist my thumb rings back and forth. "A walk in the park?"

Roth shrugs, wiggling his hand for me to take it. "Central Park, perhaps."

Central Park?

Not helping your case, Roth.

"You got this," Kyle whispers.

Wow. This guy really wants me gone.

Since I guess I can no longer rely on Kyle, I repeat, "I got this," and with a giant gulp of fortitude, I set my hand in Roth's. The moment we are skin to skin, I am centered again. Nervous, but grounded. I step from the air-conditioned vehicle into the pleasantly mild Florida evening.

Roth sets his palm to the small of my back and guides me forward. Snagging the handle of my carry on, I follow him, partially guiding me, partially dragging me toward the front door of an adorable cottage-like beachside home where I will spend the next four days trying to convince myself I am someone remotely worthy of a man who calms my crazy with effortless ease.

Suddenly, I have an epiphany of sorts.

Roth isn't just the mustard whisperer...

He is the Laurel whisperer.

The air is still and crisp. The sun has barely snuck over the horizon, the sky its blank canvas.

It's serene and calm and so, so beautiful.

I love sunrises, much more than sunsets. Especially over the ocean. There's something extraordinary about the freshness of a new day. Its smell is intoxicating and invigorating. It makes you believe anything is possible.

"It's peaceful out here, isn't it?" Elana breaks the morning quiet. I didn't even hear the door open.

"Uh, yah, it is," I reply, surprised she's up so early.

"Do you drink coffee, Laurel?"

"I do."

"Good." She hands me one of the steaming mugs she's holding and takes a seat on the chaise next to mine. "I love this time of the morning." She leans back, crosses one leg over the other, and sighs a long, contented sigh.

Elana Keswick is a firecracker encased in a ring box. She's fiery and electric. She's one of those women who takes no bull and probably got into a load of trouble in her younger days. But she's also real and is clearly okay being exactly who she is. It's obvious where Roth gets his personality from. She is so much fun to talk to, and we connected immediately with our mutual backgrounds in education. I like her immensely. I like Roth's father as well. Frank is cordial and sweet, but he's far more reserved than Elana. She and I clicked, very much like Roth and I did. In retrospect, I feel silly acting like a basket case about meeting them.

I take a sip of what is about the most delicious coffee I've ever tasted and embarrassingly moan. It sure isn't store brand.

"This is wonderful. Thank you and thank you for having me."

When we walked through the door last night, she made me feel wholeheartedly welcome, as did Frank. Theirs is a tight-knit family unit, that much was evident. The way they interacted, their easy laughter. There is a tranquility in this house that is enviable. I'm not sure I've felt at home anywhere else the way I do here...except maybe my at grandparents'. And with Roth, of course. But now that makes sense.

"No need for thanks, Laurel. You're already part of the family."

I am?

I clench my teeth together to shut down a burning flare in my nose.

"How did you sleep?" Elana asks me, turning my way.

I didn't. I finally got up right before dawn, not wanting to disturb Roth. I'm not going to tell her that, though.

"I'm an early riser."

She smiles a smile that tells me she's onto me. Roth is definitely her son.

"I remember when I met Frank's mother, Maggie." She doesn't elaborate, but by the twisting of her mouth she doesn't need to. "We get along well now, but she didn't make it easy at first. Frank is her only son, and she thought no woman would be good enough, you know?" She lowers her voice, apparently mocking Frank's mother who I will meet later today.

"Thankfully, I don't," I answer honestly. Of course, that was my biggest fear in meeting them, but it was unfounded. They have been nothing but kind. And now I'm clogged up for no reason. "You've been wonderful."

"Well, I vowed never to make a single one of Roth's girls feel like an ant under a boot heel."

A *single* girl? Gosh. How many have there been? Roth is not only handsome, he's sexy and magnetic. There must have been dozens of—

"And before you let your mind go a-wanderin', you're only the second he's brought home in twenty-nine years."

Two? And *I* am one of them? Roth and I haven't talked about our exes, not really. Who wants to hear about someone who stole your partner's heart for even the briefest of time? I don't. But this...this is quite new information Roth failed to share with me.

I school my face, but my mouth...she wants to celebrate this small victory.

I'm number two. So...

"Who was the other?"

Good gravy.

Why, Laurel?

Whyyy?

Elana titters. I can hardly stand how cute it is. "Her name was Charlie." Charlie? What a timeless name. I'm already jealous. "She was wild and adorable, and we fell in love with her instantly."

Wild?

Adorable?

They loved her *instantly*?

That delicious coffee starts to retreat back up.

I wait for Elana to continue. She pauses for so long that I start making things up about Charlie. I bet she was exotic. Maybe she was an author who found herself on a trip to Bali. Or a deep-sea diver, who recovered lost treasures from sunken ships. Or an astrophysicist who discovered a star that she named after Roth. *How did it end? Was Roth heartbroken?* I want to ask but I keep my mouth firmly zipped. I swallow hard.

Finally, Elana puts me out of my misery. And not a second too early.

"She tended to pee everywhere, though."

"She..." *Huh?* "What?"

"She was a pee-er," Elana tells me with such a straight face she can't possibly be lying.

"She was a..." *Did I hear that right?* "A pee-er?"

Charlie wasn't a bestseller or a treasure hunter or an astronomy guru? She was...*incontinent?*

What is happening?

The edge of Elana's mouth tips up ever so slightly. Her eyes twinkle. One second connects to the next and yet one more before I realize what *is* happening. I am being played. Elana Keswick has the same sense of humor as Roth does. I could be any number of things...humiliated or mad or even worse, indignant. But I'm not. Not in the least.

I'm elated.

I giggle.

Elana giggles too. I think she's relieved.

And our giggles transform into all-out laughter. We laugh until my sides hurt and water runs down my face. Hers too.

"Charlie was a Maine Coon Roth brought home from the pound when he was fourteen."

"Stop," I chorth. "You're making this up."

"I'm serious," she cackles. "We found out two weeks later she had heart disease and hip dysplasia. She couldn't help her uncontrollable bladder."

Poor baby.

"What happened to her?" I ask, unable to help myself. Roth has not once mentioned he had a cat, and he seems to love Meringue as much as she loves him.

Elana wipes her eyes and sobers up. She takes a drink of her coffee, then stares off into the morning sun. "We eventually had to put her down. Roth was devastated."

"That's awful. I'm sorry."

"So was I. But it was because his heart was broken for the

very first time, and I never wanted it to happen again." *So, his first girl did break his heart after all.* "As a parent, you want to protect your children from harm and heartbreak and all the horrors the world has to callously drop at their doorstep."

My thoughts briefly turn to my mother. Does she feel that way about me? Does she have this rabid protective instinct that Elana clearly does? I can honestly say I don't know the answer to that. I think maybe it's no.

"I won't break his heart," I assure her softly.

"I know you won't." She stretches her hand out to mine. "You're the first woman he's brought home to meet me. He said you were something special, Laurel. He was right."

We have a moment. Except it's more. It's poignant and it's tender. And it will last forever.

"What do you say we go get things ready for the crew?" she asks, patting my arm. "Not much left to do but get out a few refreshments and make a big batch of mimosas. The rest is being catered."

The relief my cooking skills won't be put to the test is very, very real.

"Mimosas and a catered feast? I say I would love to."

"I'm glad you're here, Laurel," Elana tells me. I want to cry.

"So, am I."

"Now let's go get ourselves that mimosa."

It doesn't matter that it's barely even eight o'clock in the morning. I jump to my feet, suddenly energized, and dare say almost excited for the day to come.

"That sounds like a plan."

"Did you have a good time today?" Roth asks me as we step outside and close the door.

"I did. I especially loved the songs you texted me." Every

once in a while, my phone would vibrate, and we'd lock eyes and grin like lovestruck fools.

"Which one was your favorite?"

I think for a minute. "There were so many good ones." *Brave. Right Here Waiting. Count on Me.* "*Under Pressure* was pretty funny."

"Well, you were getting grilled pretty hard by my aunt Erma."

"It wasn't that bad." It was. She was relentless. "But I'd say it has to be a toss-up between *Hungry Eyes* and *Your Body Is A Wonderland.*" That last one made me blush and when Elana saw pink crawl up my face, she simply smiled and asked her mother-in-law if she wanted another mimosa."

"Isn't it magical how much can be conveyed simply by a song title?"

"It is," I agree, warmth finding its way between my legs. What I'd give to be able to push him onto the chaise, pull aside my panties and mount him. Instead, I say, "Your grandmother was a hoot."

"Yah. I should have warned you. G'ma Maggie has a sailor's mouth and a deadpan humor that comedians envy. But that's part of her charm, don't you think?"

It totally was.

"I don't know how many times she dropped the f-bomb." The first time she did it, Roth had to reach over and close my gaping mouth.

He chuckles. "That was my first word, according to my mother."

"It was not." I know he's teasing me. I'm not falling for it this time.

"It was my second then. I said it early and I said it often."

"Bad, bad grandma," I tease, laughing along with him.

"Damn I love that woman. She would always have Frosted

Flakes and chocolate milk waiting for me when I went to stay with her. We'd eat it for dinner while watching *Jeopardy.*"

"You didn't eat them *together*, though, did you?"

He cocks his head as if I've gone mad. "Of course, we did."

I wrinkle my nose. "That's disgusting."

"It's *not* disgusting, Laurel, it's trend setting."

"Trend setting? Really? Was this a craze I missed?"

"You did live in the sticks, so..." His shoulders rise. "Not all crazes made it through the thick of the cornstalks, I guess."

"The thick of the cornstalks? You're ridiculous."

"Trend setting," he corrects, grinning wide. "Come here." He spins and sits on the chaise, waiting for me to join him.

I gaze through the glass, watching Roth's parents chat and laugh with Elana's sister, Elsa and her husband, Hank. Elsa and Hank's daughter, Elisa, and her new husband, John, are at the kitchen table with them. It took me half a day to get all their names straight. So many "E's".

"What about the others? Shouldn't we go join them?" They're playing cards. I suck at cards.

"No. I've shared you all day." When I hesitate, he hooks an arm around my waist and tugs on me. "There. That's better," he moans when he finally has me tucked into his side.

It is. Roth is warm and comfy and it's nice to have a moment alone, but... "Are you sure we shouldn't go in?"

"No need. They'll be out here in a few minutes. Mark my words." He sounds so sure of himself.

"Why do you say that?"

"Because my mother cheats."

I tilt my head up so I can see him. "She cheats?" I repeat in disbelief. Sweet, innocent Elana? "Nooo. No way."

"Yes. Way."

"You're pulling my leg."

"I'm not," he tells me adamantly, throwing up three fingers pressed together. "Scout's honor."

"You were a Boy Scout too?"

"No, but that's the universal sign of truth. Everyone knows you can't lie when you use it."

"I'm not really sure I'd align myself with the Boy Scouts right now if I were you. You know..." I lower my voice and whisper, "Sex scandal and all."

"Ooohhh. Good point. But I'm not lying about my mom. She's a cheater, that one."

Just as Roth is ending his sentence, we hear the glass sliding door run along its rails.

"I heard that, Roth Warren," Elana belts. A ruckus of voices talking over each other follows her onto the patio. "It was *one* time."

"*One* time, Elana? That's what you're going with?" Frank chides. He sits in the love seat across from us.

I try to put a more appropriate distance between Roth and me, but he grips me and keeps me close. "Stay," he whispers.

"I agree with Frank," Elsa seconds. "Remember how no one wanted to play games with you as a child because you cheated at everything?"

"You're all exaggerating." Elana waves them off as if they don't know what they're talking about, but she's laughing. *Sweet, funny, confident Elana is a cheater.* Color me surprised. She takes a seat next to Frank. He puts his arm around her and kisses her lovingly on the forehead. It warms my insides.

"Well, Laurel, we didn't manage to scare you away yet, did we?" Frank asks as Elana snuggles into him. The others have found seats around the patio too, and relaxing, bluesy music is now playing.

I am in heaven.

"It will take more than a foul-mouthed eighty-eight-year-old and a cheater to scare me away."

Hand to God, I don't know where that came from, but it felt like the right thing to say.

Frank tosses that around for a few seconds and then roars. So does Elana. Roth chuckles and squeezes me tighter. "Good one." *Whew, that was close.*

Frank points a finger at Roth. "I like this one."

"So, do I, Dad." Roth's throaty reply heats me from the bottoms of my feet up, and suddenly I wish we were alone. I want to make love to him out here with moonbeams in our hair and ocean waves for ambience. It's late and I'm tired and admittedly a little tipsy from all the mimosas, and I want nothing more than to go into our bedroom to see if I have improved at the quiet game, but I am also thoroughly enjoying our conversation.

Roth's parents tell stories about his childhood, and Roth and Elisa reminisce about summers surfing and swing dance competitions. She was Roth's partner until they were sixteen. She also "accidentally" spills the beans about Roth's short "modeling" career. Elana promises to show me his portfolio in the morning against Roth's rabid protests. I can't wait.

An hour later, we finally decide to go to bed. As we stand to head in, the sweet strings of one of my favorite songs by Etta James cuts through the quiet evening.

"Oh, no," Roth mumbles. He steps behind me and places his hands around my middle.

"What?" I murmur back, leaning against him, exhausted.

"Just wait for it."

As if they've done it a thousand times and this makes a thousand and one, Roth's parents slip into each other's arms and begin to sway.

"They're dancing."

"Every time," Roth says quietly.

We all raptly watch as Frank and Elana seem to step from this world into their own, forgetting everyone around them. They're encased in glass, mesmerized with each other. Their love is blinding, and it's beautiful and romantic and about the sweetest thing I have ever witnessed.

"Shall we?" Roth asks.

"Shall we, what?" I glance from his parents to him. His hand is raised, palm up, waiting for me to take it. "Dance?" No. We can't intrude on this moment.

"Yes, dance."

Only Roth doesn't wait for my reply.

He whisks me onto the makeshift dance floor, and whatever invisible door Frank and Elana have stepped through, we follow. And when we get to the other side, my protests die right on my tongue.

In Roth's arms, this space around us becomes magical. Hypnotic.

It's ours.

A place only we exist.

I melt when he rasps, "I have been patiently waiting for my love to come along...and she's finally here."

Roth never takes his eyes from mine as he sings Etta's lyrics to me. He knows every word. Every note. He's heard this song a thousand and one times too. He's seen it played out.

His body is fluid. We glide on clouds. He leans his forehead against mine. He sweeps his lips along my cheek. He holds me captive.

He sings the lyrics to "At Last" in a whisper, his mouth next to my ear.

I can't breathe.

I can't think.

I am in heaven.

I am spellbound.

I am someone's...

At last.

FIFTEEN

I'M GONNA BE
(500 MILES)

Roth

Present
June 25, 11:39 a.m.

"WHERE HAVE YOU BEEE…?" The last part of Laurel's question tapers off as she stares at the steel-gray monstrosity parked on the street.

She's a beauty. And this is not your average motor home. It's nothing like the one my parents used to own. It's pure opulence. Granite throughout. Heated tile floors. Full-sized refrigerator. Gas fireplace. King bed. Mounted sixty-inch TV. Glassed-in shower with a rainfall waterhead. Every lavish piece of furniture is leather, its shade matching the beautiful exterior. And it's surprisingly homey for such a luxurious beast. I can't imagine she costs less than a million dollars.

So, driving the *Songbird* off the lot made me incredibly jumpy. What if I scratched her? Backed her into something? Ran her off the road? It took me a few miles to get my legs underneath me, remembering turning radius rules, trusting my mirrors, and the tricks of merging into traffic. I was careful with her…maybe overly so. It took me ninety minutes to drive twenty-eight miles. This could be a long trip.

"Roth, what is this?"

"It's a motor home, my love."

"I know that." She walks down the two front steps to come stand beside me, never taking her eyes from the *Songbird*. "What I don't know is why it's here, parked in front of our house."

My father's awed voice belts from behind me, "Holy Lamb of God, would you look at that." He whistles long and low, obviously impressed.

"Roth," Laurel says. I don't like the way she drags out my name, like it's stuck in mud. "What have you done?"

I pivot directly in front of her. She blinks a few times before she focuses on me. "I didn't buy it," I tell her.

She does that cute laugh-snort thing she hates but I think is endearing. "Well, I'd certainly hope not. What is it doing here?"

"It's our home away from home for as long as we're away from home."

"Roth."

"Laurel." I match her censure.

"I didn't agree."

"You didn't disagree." I move behind her and grip her shoulders, whispering in her ear, "Just go inside and look at her before you make up your mind."

"Her?"

"Yes, love. Her. All vehicles are female."

"Is that so?" She rests her head on my shoulder, so I wrap my arms around her and pull her closer. She seems thinner today. More fragile. Her rib bones poke my forearms. And it's in this moment I wonder who I'm truly doing this for...her or me?

I don't want the answer.

"That is so," I say quietly. I press my lips to her neck and breathe in her scent. Today she smells like vanilla, but there is also a distinct, faint chemical tinge that I'm not sure is disease or lingering chemo. Or maybe it's neither. Maybe it's just my overactive imagination. Either way, I feel a renewed sense of urgency to get the hell out of here, as if by leaving Nashville behind we can leave our new stark reality behind too. "Do you want to go inside?"

"I do," my father answers, pushing past us. My mother is on his heels. She looks over her shoulder at us, eyes alight, clearly caught up in the moment. He whistles again when he opens the door, and I can even hear my mother gasp from here. Pretty sure I made the same noise when I walked inside.

"I can take it back if you want," I offer, only half-heartedly meaning it. "I wanted to give you something you've always dreamed of, Laurel, but if you don't think you're up to it, I understand. I don't want to push you. We don't have to go, and it will be okay, I promise."

Laurel is quiet for what feels as long as an eternity. Occasionally, one of my parents' stupefied comments floats out from the motor home. "There are four TVs in here." "Can you believe how soft this leather is?" "This kitchen is to die for." But when my mother shrieks, I can tell they've reached the bathroom. It is *very* impressive.

"Where did you get this?" Laurel asks, nearly resigned.

I knew this question would come up and Laurel would be quite upset if she knew I'd planned to quit, so I decided to keep the story as high level as possible. "Pat Anderson."

"Pat?" She shifts in my arms to face me. "How? Why?"

"He offered." This is true, but I don't serve up the rest of the story.

"It's his personal camper?"

"Motor home," I teasingly correct. "It's a motor home, Laurel. Or a recreational vehicle, or even a motor coach. It is *not* a camper."

"Mo—tor—home," she mocks, swinging her head back and forth with each exaggerated syllable.

"Funny girl." I poke a finger into each side of her waist where she's ticklish. She squees and jumps a foot off the ground.

It's moments like these, little things like a sweet giggle or a quick-witted comeback, that I will miss the most by far. Time stamps, my father calls them. And there are so many of them. So many. How do you begin to pack them all away so you can pick them out when you need them? It's an impossible, daunting task.

"Yes, it's Pat's personal motor home," I tell her, giving a quick kiss to her forehead.

"And the Jeep hitched to the back?"

Yeah. He forgot to tell me the *Songbird* also came complete with our own toad.

"We need a way to get around when we're parked."

"And he doesn't mind?"

A breeze kicks up and catches the edges of Laurel's cotton dress, dragging it upward as if in a vacuum. She secures it in the nick of time, bunching the fabric to tighten it around her knees. Too bad. I was hoping for a Marilyn Monroe moment.

"He insisted, actually."

"That was nice of him."

"It surely was."

"Don't you have to work, Roth?"

"I'm taking a leave absence, Laurel." Not exactly the truth, but not a lie, either.

"For how long?" she asks.

I don't respond. She knows the answer to that.

She gnaws on the inside of her cheek, a habit she has when her wheels are turning. I practically see them whirling, making her beautiful brown eyes murky. "Where would we go?"

I have some very specific goals to accomplish with this trip, so while I'll make subtle suggestions, ultimately, it's up to her and I'll have to work in my surprises along the way.

"Wherever you want, Laurel."

She rises on her tiptoes and mashes her lips to mine, and I hold on to her like she's a life raft in the middle of the Pacific.

She gently cups my cheeks, blinks her eyes open, and I drown in her anyway. She faces the *Songbird* once again, taking two steps toward it.

"It is beautiful."

"She's more beautiful inside."

My mother darts her head out of the *Songbird's* door. "Laurel, dear, you simply must come look at this. It's incredible." That draws Laurel in and the second she steps foot into the "camper" she is done for.

The next day, with our agenda roughly mapped out and emergency plans in place, I throw on our road trip playlist, and we head out, bopping our heads and singing along with The Proclaimers at the top of our lungs.

And with that full-on grin splitting her face in two, I can almost forget it will be our last road trip together.

Almost.

SIXTEEN

Laurel
Six Years Earlier
December 10, 2:49 p.m.

"I CAN'T BELIEVE I'm doing this."

"Stop it," I shush Carmen, wiping a mascara smudge from underneath her left eye. I step back and let my gaze fall down the length of her.

Her hair is coifed perfectly atop her head, each curled strand that shapes her face intentionally placed. Her cheeks sparkle, as do the diamond studs in her earlobes. The gold beaded gown she selected conforms to every curve on her body, hugging her like a gentle lover.

I draw in a sharp breath.

She is stunning.

Manny will bawl his eyes out. I have twenty bucks on the line that says so.

"What's wrong?" she asks in a panic, turning back to the mirror. She skims her hands from her breasts to her torso and sucks in her waist. Her thumbs almost touch when she spans it.

"Nothing." I wipe a drop of moisture away from the corner of my eye.

"I look fat, don't I?"

"What?" I ask incredulously. If she's fat, then I'm the Goodyear blimp's first cousin. "No. You are *not* fat."

"Look at me. I'm bloated. My boobs are giant." Her hands are like suction cups on them, lifting them up and down. They *are* plump, but I think they are rather perfect on her. She obviously disagrees. "Ima...Ima...I'm a horse."

"A horse? Carmen—"

"I can't wear this. What was I thinking?"

Her hands fly to the back of her neck. She starts to unzip the most beautiful wedding dress in the history of wedding dresses.

"Carmen, stop." I grip her fingers with mine. She bats me away.

"Tell everyone the wedding is off."

"What? No."

"Yes. I can't do this."

A few more teeth separate.

"You can. You *are*. You are marrying him."

"No, I can't—"

"Yes. You. Can!"

I go at her again. We fumble and fight and end up on a nearby couch in a thrash of arms and hands and fingers. I grip her shoulders and push them into the cushions. Hard. Her hair is now a mess. She has to walk down the aisle in three minutes.

"Get. Your. *Shit*. Together," I hiss. My chest heaves. My knuckles are white.

Carmen's eyes round. Her nostrils flare. She pulls in a long breath. "You swore," she declares in shock.

"What?" *I don't swear.*

I push myself up. This woman is marrying a man who raises her up on a pedestal and she's about to screw it all to heck because...because...because I don't know why. "What in the *hell* is the matter with you?"

"You swore again. Twice, in like...twenty seconds."

"Well, you...you..." I shake my head clear and pinch my

fingers into her flesh until they scream. "This isn't about *me*. It's about *you*. Why are you acting so...insane? You love Manny. He loves you. You are meant to be. What's the matter? Isn't his credit score high enough yet?"

Her body deflates beneath my verbal punch. She shifts her eyes away. I'm a crappy friend.

"It's seven hundred and fifty-two," she mutters under her breath.

"Good gravy," I say. I heave my leg back to the floor, hearing the distinctive parting of fabric. Lovely. "Then what is it?"

"What if I'm not enough?" Her chest rises and falls in rapid succession. Worry sinks into her forehead. It pulls down the corners of her crimson lips, creating frown lines.

This is not like Carmen.

She's poised and confident and as hard as titanium. Her middle name is "Efyou," for heaven's sakes.

"What did he do?" I ask, suddenly worried Manny may have brought this on by doing something stupid, like men can without thinking.

"Nothing. He did nothing." She sounds very defensive of him. "He has been amazing."

"Then what is it?" I offer her a hand, which she takes. I help her off her back and sit down next to her. With her thumb she begins twirling her two-carat diamond around on her finger.

"Estoy embarazada."

I've been friends with Carmen long enough to know a lot of Spanish by proxy, but I'm out on this one.

"English, please."

Her sigh is weary as she places her hands over a flat belly that I am incredibly envious of. She does work her butt off for it, I'll give her that, and I just don't seem to care quite that much. I poke at mine. It's a little squishy. Maybe a little *too* squishy. Maybe I should care more about the fact that it's squishier than it was when I met Roth. Maybe when we get back from Carmen's destination wedding, I should start—

"I'm pregnant."

Saaay...*what*? All thoughts of firm abs dissipate. Not like I was really considering acting on it anyway.

"You're pregnant?"

She nods.

Holy crap.

Well.

This is unexpected.

"Are you sure?"

Carmen reaches into the cushion of the couch and yanks out a pregnancy test as if she was just waiting for me to ask.

Ewww.

I peek at it, because I am *not* touching it. I know how those work.

There are two pink lines in the little clear window.

"Maybe it's false," I tell her. "That happens all the time, right?"

Carmen reaches into the cushion of the couch and yanks out *another* pregnancy test. How many of those things does she have stuffed down there? She doesn't say anything as she shows me this one too.

Pink lines. Two of them.

"Maybe the whole box was defective—"

"I bought three boxes, Laurel," she says, unsmiling. She goes back into the cushions several more times until six used pregnancy tests rest in peace on her lap.

That's a lot of pink lines.

And a lot of peeing.

Carmen is definitely, 100 percent pregnant.

"Does Manny know?"

She moves her head slowly from side to side.

Oh my.

"Well, how…" *That's obvious, Laurel.* "I mean, when…" Also, fairly obvious. "You know what?"

Now I understand what's driving her angst. It's not marrying Manny. It's the overwhelming thought of raising another human being. I can understand why.

"What?" She scoots down, resting her head against mine. I slot my fingers between hers, her enormous engagement ring cutting into my flesh.

"You're going to be a perfectly imperfect mama."

She splutters. "You got half of that right."

"It's *all* right. Don't strive for perfection, Carmen. Just love that baby unconditionally." I place my palm on her stomach. "Be perfectly imperfect. That will be enough. *You* will be enough."

She doesn't say anything right away. Then, "You think so?"

"No doubt in my mind. This is an amazing wedding gift you will be able to give Manny. My personalized Nashville skyline cutting board will pale in comparison."

"I wanted that, though."

"And when the shock wears off, you'll realize you want this too," I tell her.

"I…I do. I'm scared," she whispers. "Terrified."

And there it is. "We can be terrified together."

"I'm going to get fat."

"I hate to say this but…" She tips her face to mine, waiting for me to finish. "You'll be even more stunning than you already are."

Her lips do a half turn up. "You think so?"

"As if that's even possible."

"Te quiero."

"I love you too."

"I'm going to be a mama," she murmurs in a bit of disbelief.

"You are," I reply excitedly.

We laugh and cry tears of joy. We hug and squeal and

Carmen announces Roth and I will, "of course" be the godparents.

A minute or two later, there's a knock on the door. Carmen's spitfire mother pokes her head in. "Es hora, estas lista? Manny nos espera."

"Si, mama. Ahora vengo."

Mrs. Morales stays frozen, staring at her daughter. Pretty soon her cheeks are wet. Her smile quivers. "You are glowing, mi cielito. Perfecto."

Now *my* face is wet. How perfecto was that? I don't know exactly what they said but it was beautiful and heartfelt.

A glance at Carmen and she's not faring much better.

"Gracias, Mama."

"Now…" Mrs. Morales swipes at her cheeks, the moment gone. "Wipe your tears and vamos. Your new life awaits you."

"Si."

With one last loving smile, Carmen's mother closes the door.

"Does she know?" I ask. She sure acted like she knew. We made sure to toss all the pregnancy tests in the bathroom garbage…except for one, which Carmen tucked into her purse for later.

"I haven't told her yet, but she's like a black witch. Her powers are beyond comprehension. She knows."

"If that's true, she looked happy about it."

"One word. Grandbabies."

I snicker. "Good point." Candice has been after me since we left Leone on the Fourth of July three years ago. As usual, she dances around the bush instead of coming outright and asking. And it's the same conversation Every. Single. Time.

"Is everything all right between you two?"

"Everything is great," I tell her.

"Okay, well…" She always adds a dramatic pause for effect, to which I fill with silence. *"I'm just checking."*

I'm thirty-two years old, yes, but I am in no rush. I don't

need a ring on my finger to know Roth and I will be together forever. I still have plenty of life left for marriage and babies and I'm not going to let her make me doubt Roth the way she does myself.

Carmen steps in front of the mirror and in a flash both her hair and her makeup are once again flawless as if she simply wiggled her nose. Her mother isn't the only one with black magic. We snag our bouquets, and we head out of the bride's room to get Carmen hitched.

It's a warm, cloudless day today in San Juan. We stand at the edge of a white walkway lined with clusters of pink and white flowers. On the other side, on the walkway spanning a small pool, Manny stands at the center with Roth behind him.

He's mesmerized by her.

And he's bawling.

I win.

The song Manny asked Carmen to walk down the aisle to begins to play. It's a romantic Spanish love song, "Llegaste Tú," translated to *you showed up* in English. I kiss Carmen on the cheek and go first before I bawl myself, striding slowly to the twang of dual guitars and a beautifully harmonized duet that, of course, made me sob the first time Carmen played it for me. That's what's amazing to me about music. Sometimes you don't need to understand what's being said...you feel it in your very soul.

Too late, I realize that I didn't bother to check where my dress had ripped in our little scuffle, but as I head down the aisle, all eyes let me know.

I glance down and cringe.

The slit that had originally ended midthigh, is now just shy of midhip.

I think my panties might be showing.

Roth's eyes bug. Then they heat up.

"Wow," he mouths. He shifts back and forth and moves his clasped hands down over his crotch.

Oh my word.

"Stop," I mouth back. My face is red hot, but I square my shoulders. The remaining few steps might as well be over a bed of fiery coals, but I never falter or lose the smile pasted on my face.

The only good news in this scenario is that as high maintenance as Carmen can be, she wanted a small, intimate ceremony.

So, only thirty-one people witness my humiliation.

"How are you feeling?"

Fuck.

I don't say it, but damn, I think it.

Yes, the cuss vault is standing wide open.

Kill me.

Kill me now, please.

I roll over, throwing an arm over my eyes to block out sunbeams that are trying their best to sear them out of their sockets.

"Seen better days," I mutter.

I feel sick.

Fuck.

I feel *veeery* sick.

Bolting from bed faster than an Olympic sprinter, I make it to the bathroom in the nick of time, projectile vomiting the remains of last night's champagne. And vodka. And three shots of Fireball.

"Ugh."

I'm never drinking again.

I flush and lean my forehead against the cold porcelain. I don't even know if it's clean. And I don't care. Right now, it feels like the breath of life. I can't move. I may never move again.

"Overdo it a little?" Roth asks on a chuckle. He takes a seat beside me and rubs my back. That feels good too.

I turn my head so the other cheek can get equal treatment, catching Roth's eye. "What gives you that idea?" I answer. I'm going for sassy, but I sound awfully pathetic.

"How much do you remember?"

I try to think but thinking hurts too.

"Did the officiant go skinny-dipping or did I dream that?"

Roth busts out in laughter. "Oh, that happened."

"Yikes. I was hoping that was a bad dream. Please don't tell me that I—"

"Ah, no. But you had your dress unzipped before I scooped you up and took you to bed. Now, Carmen's mother? That's a different story."

I drag my head off the toilet. "Nooo." *Sweet Mrs. Morales?*

"She didn't get completely naked, buuut…there was plenty o' skin that I cannot unsee."

"Oh my God." I slap a hand over my gaping mouth. "What did Carmen do?"

"She whipped out her phone, of course. I think Isabella will be in about the same shape as you this morning."

The afternoon and evening come rolling back in snippets but not in order.

The tear-jerking toast Roth gave during the reception.

The swing dancing until my feet hurt.

The tears as Carmen and Manny said their I dos.

The coconut-encrusted mahi-mahi…

"Oh God."

I slam up the lid up and vomit again, not even having a chance to tell Roth to leave me in private. He never flinches.

When I'm through this time, I feel better. But I stay close to the bowl anyway. I know exactly how my hangovers work. I will be here for a while. Scooting back, I lean up against the wall and close my eyes.

"Remember anything else?"

I pop one open. Something in his tone niggles at my memory. Something I am supposed to know but don't quite.

I'm beginning to get a bad feeling. And this time it's not fish or leftover alcohol. It's bigger.

"I forgot something, didn't I?"

"Did you?" he lobs back lightly, bumping one of his feet against mine.

"I..." Crap. What happened? "I..." Did I get on a table and pull a Coyote Ugly? Did I...*oh no*. Did I *sing*? I sang, didn't I?

This just gets worse and worse.

I have loosened up considerably in the years Roth and I have been together. I'm not as outgoing as Roth is. I never will be, but I no longer want to be a wallflower, either. He calls it growing. I call it breathing. He allows me the opportunity to inhale and exhale at my own pace. To laugh. To be. And now occasionally it gets me into trouble.

"I'm sorry," I say.

"For what?"

"Singing..." I suggest, but it's a fishing expedition, not a confession. I don't remember crap. Other than the snippets, last night is a big black blur.

"Singing?" He smirks.

What does that mean, exactly?

"I know I need to stay in my lane," I keep going, not sure I'm on the right road. I stay focused on the windshield though, not the rearview. Can't see potholes that way. "I'm an elementary school teacher. I am not Beyoncé."

"Yet...you *diiid* ask me to put a ring on it."

Shut up.

"I did not."

Roth's lips flatten into a thin line.

Oh, snap.

I did?

"What did you..." Gulp. I take a long, stuttered breath in. "What did you say?"

He doesn't react for so long, I start to believe he's trying to pull another fast one. But then he pushes himself from sitting onto all fours and he crawls over to me until we are nose to nose. His arms are wedged on either side of me. His knees hug mine. His breath smells of mint, mostly, with a slight hint of coffee. Mine smells of puke. Great. His eyes volley between mine, making me a bit woozy again.

"I said yes."

He said yes?

Confession time.

I said I was in no hurry to get married, and while that is true, it doesn't mean that I haven't fantasized about how Roth would ask me. He is an incredibly romantic man, and I envisioned that night to be something of a fairy tale.

But instead, I got blackout drunk, channeled my inner Destiny's Child, and demanded he put a ring on it.

Wow.

Way to go, Laurel.

Those negative thoughts run in a ticker tape across my frontal lobe. And then they're gone.

He said yes.

"You said yes?"

"I did, but now I'm not sure you meant it."

Is he teasing? Please tell me he's teasing.

"I *did* mean it."

"But you don't remember it so..."

Maybe not, but "I meant it." I am adamant now. "I want it."

"Want what?" He nuzzles his nose along my jaw. Runs it up right underneath my ear. Nibbles on my lobe.

"You."

"What about me do you want?"

When he nips at my neck, sucking on the spot at base of my throat, I...

I want...

I want him...

..."To put a ring on it?"

He backs up a touch. Stares me straight in the eye. "You don't sound too sure about that."

"I am."

"Hmm, you're not very believable right now," he teases, shaking his head. He moves to sit down and from out of nowhere, this kinetic energy shoots from my heart into my fists. I forget about tequila and mahi-mahi and grab him by the collar, yanking him into me so our breath is one.

"I want you to."

"You want me to what?"

"Put a ring on it!" I demand. "I want you to put a ring on it!"

He blinks once, then twice, then a slow, satisfied smile curves his lips, and he declares, "Yes, Laurel Linnea Collins, I will marry you."

Holy crap on a stick.

I just asked Roth to marry me.

And he said yes.

I am getting married.

Married.

Me.

I throw my hands over my mouth and giggle.

Then I lean over the toilet once more and vomit.

SEVENTEEN

A SAFE PLACE TO LAND

Laurel

Four Years Earlier
August 22, 6:09 p.m.

"Do it." I angle my bare butt higher in the air.

Roth groans, draping the sheet over me until it rests low on my hips. "I can't intentionally hurt you, Laurel. It's not in my DNA."

"You aren't hurting me," I insist, dragging the sheet back down.

His fingertip feathers over my side and I jump.

"Then why are you flinching." He doesn't sound at all amused.

"You startled me, is all."

"Laurel."

I hear the anxiety mixing him up, and I hate that we're having to go through this, but the end result will be worth it. I hope.

"Here." I fling Buzzy back to him. It lands on the mattress.

"What the hell?"

I glance over my shoulder. He's turning it over in his hand. It's almost comical, the muddled look on his face.

"This is a toy," he says blandly.

"It just looks like a toy. It's actually a very useful device. It numbs me."

His eyes lift to mine. Only his eyes. His grin is nothing short of mischievous. "Anyone overhearing this conversation would think we're planning to do something very salacious."

"Salacious?" I draw the question out and his grin widens. "Salacious. You kill me." I love his off-the-wall vocabulary. "Just put the cold part where you're going to stick me."

"Really, Laurel?"

We both lose it.

I can barely get the next part out. "Then turn Buzzy on." My pitch sounds like I swallowed helium.

He flicks the switch and nearly drops Buzzy to the bed when it starts to vibrate. "You've got to be kidding me."

I crisscross my arms and lay my cheek on them. "It's supposed to take the sting out of the injection. The nurse at the clinic recommended it."

He flips it over, studying it. "Could be useful other places too."

"Oh my God." That makes me tingle everywhere. "I don't think Buzzy is supposed to be used a sex toy."

"I don't know. Could be dual purpose."

"Roth," I say, though now he has me thinking...

"Fine. Do you have the instructions?"

I nod. I've memorized them. "Place it directly on the site of the injection for thirty to sixty seconds. Then move it up a bit, making sure the power switch is pointed away from where you'll put the needle. Hold it secure while you give me the shot in the spot you just numbed. It's supposed to work best when the buzzing is between the pain and the brain. Make sense?"

"Easy peasy," he mocks.

"Nothing to it. You got this." I hand him the syringe filled with my ovulation-stimulating concoction.

Roth sets the buzzing bee, ice pack side down, to my left hip.

I watch the clock and tell him when it's time to move it up. He does and with one quick glance to me and a loud swallow, he sticks me and pushes the plunger down slowly.

It hurts, but it doesn't hurt as badly as the first few times. Either he's getting better or the Buzzy really works.

Tugging the needle out, he places pressure with his thumb and gently rubs circles to better distribute the medication, so it doesn't pool underneath the skin. Then he kisses me sweetly on the tender spot, muttering, "How many days left of this?"

He slips the underwear around my thighs back up over my backside and gives me a light tap.

"Six to ten, maybe? Depends on the blood work. I go back in tomorrow."

"I'll be glad when this part is done."

"The needle part?"

"Yah." He disposes of the syringe in a special box they gave us and comes to sit beside me.

"Hate to break it to you, but it will be a while before we're done with needles. After the transfer, I have to take progesterone injections for a few weeks. It increases chances of the embryo staying implanted."

"Well, then…" Roth bunches up my hair into a loose ponytail. "I shall endeavor to be the best shot giver of all shot givers, so you don't even feel them."

For the millionth time, I wonder how I got so lucky.

"I love you, today, Roth."

"And I'll love you tomorrow, Laurel. No matter what happens."

He means if this doesn't work. If I don't get pregnant, yet again, even with intensive medical intervention. After countless blood draws and cavity searches, our infertility issues were "undetermined," whatever that means. We had multiple options the doctors provided us, but since I am thirty-four, considered high risk because of the fertility issues, and the clock is ticking loudly, we decided to go with in vitro fertilization, which they said was the most effective assisted reproductive technology.

The last couple of years have been a whirlwind.

Roth and I married in a private ceremony in the Great Smoky Mountains National Park nine months after I asked him to marry me. Eloped would probably be more accurate, much to the chagrin of our friends and family. But planning a wedding got to be too stressful. My mother was out of control. She had an opinion on everything. Invitations. The gown. The menu. The venue. The wedding list. She'd invited the whole town of Leone already for crying out loud. *"You must get married in the church."* But we wanted a destination wedding. *"Your bouquet must include calla lilies, dear. Everybody loves calla lilies."* Um, I am allergic to calla lilies, Mother. *"Goat cheese? Are you thinking about the lactose intolerant?"* She was taking over, and I spent so many nights crying about it that Roth suggested we elope. So, we found a couple to marry us and they were amazing. Jason was the official pastor and Brianna, his wife, was the photographer. We canceled the wedding and had the ceremony *we* envisioned in a place that was special to *us* and we have the most magical wedding pictures with backdrops of rivers and trees and mountains that look like something a studio would envy.

Our friends...our real friends...totally understood. Even Roth's parents were supportive. My mother, however, hasn't stopped digging me about it to this day.

Since Roth and I have married, we've bought our first home together in a subdivision of Nashville called Bellevue. It was close to where I taught school and twenty minutes from the action of downtown. I've upped my swing dance game considerably and earned my master's degree in education as a literacy specialist. Roth has risen to vice president of marketing at the entertainment company he works for. He puts in a lot of hours, but they love him, and they pay him well. We still find time to see live music (Rudy's is a favorite), dine at new restaurants

(Sambuca is still our go-to), dance at our favorite club (No. 308), and spend nights and afternoons with Carmen and Manny and our sweet goddaughters.

All in all, our life has been one that most would envy, but in the procreation area we've fallen a bit short. Right after we married, we started trying to have a baby. And you know what happens when you *really* want a baby? You don't get one. Month after month after month when I get my period, I have stayed up late at night stressing about it. Month after month after month, Roth never says he blames me.

But does he? How can he not?

"I'm sorry about all of this." I roll onto my back, using one hand as a pillow.

"Sorry? Jesus, Laurel. Don't even say that."

I think back to my conversation with my mother a few years back, the first time she met Roth when she asked me if I thought Roth would stick by me in the lowest of the lows, when the hardest decision is *not* whether to stay, but if he should have stayed to begin with.

Is this what she meant?

"Do you...?" *Don't ask, Laurel. Don't. Ask. Trust him. Trust in* him. He's done nothing, ever, to make you question whether he'd make different choices given the chance. Don't do it now. "Do you want a root beer float?" I ask him instead.

"Only if we have A&W root beer." Roth thinks A&W is the best root beer he's ever tasted, now. That's because it is. Hands down.

"It's not fresh jug A&W, but it'll do."

"In that case, I'd still love one."

"So would I."

I pop up and head into the kitchen in my lacy underwear and a navy blue tank, vowing to never question Roth's loyalty again. I know he'll see us through absolutely anything life throws at us.

EIGHTEEN

ANGEL

Laurel

Two Years Earlier
March 6, 7:13 p.m.

"MAMA, I'M DONE," Sofia whines. She slumps her little body in her chair and flings her head back against the wood so hard it protests.

"Me too," Lucia joins in. She mimics her sister, watching from the corner of her eye to make sure she's doing it right. I stifle a smile with the back of my hand.

"You haven't touched your broccoli." Manny points with his fork to both of their plates. "You're going to insult Auntie Laurel if you don't at least try a bite."

"Si," Carmen agrees, pursing her lips together.

Carmen didn't merely surprise Manny with one baby; she surprised him with two. Twin rambunctious girls who are the spitting image of their mama in both looks and personality. God help Manny.

"Don't pin this on me," I tell the two of them. Personally, I hate broccoli, so I'm in the girls' camp, but it's Roth's favorite vegetable, so it gets table time.

"Broccoli makes you strong," Roth says in a deep voice, posing like Popeye.

"I *am* strong." Lucia shows us her itty-bitty bicep with pride. Roth oohs and aahs and Sofia grins ear to ear. She adores Roth.

"Girls, broccoli," Manny instructs. His tone leaves no room for argument.

But where there are kids and anything green…

"I did, Papa," Sofia insists to her father. "See?" She screws her eyes shut and opens her mouth wide. It's empty.

Lucia does the same thing, but she had just taken a big bite of her macaroni and cheese, so we're treated to a mouthful of yellow mush.

"Una mordida," Carmen demands of the girls. "And no more arguing. One bite right now and only then are you excused."

Sofia and Lucia lock eyes. I watch them communicate in their unique language only twins can hear. It's the same language Esther and I used.

They nod in unison. While their will is no match for their mother's, and they lost this particular battle, they still make a production of it to get their point across. They each find the smallest piece of broccoli available and shove it into their mouths. After holding their noses as they chew, they wash down the remnants with swallows of milk.

It's amazing what three-year-olds already know.

"Muy buena." Carmen dismisses them after she checks they've actually swallowed, and they scramble off of their chairs like their behinds are on fire. "Hey, hey, hey, no running in the house!" To me, she adds, "Sorry. I swear they're the devil's spawn wearing pretty blue dresses."

"They're kids being kids. No need to be sorry."

I place my hands over my belly, excitement running through me at the thought of my own child running around and me yelling at her to stop. At just over three months along, my pants are starting to get snug, and my morning sickness is waning. The minute we passed that twelve-week mark, I relaxed considerably. And at our last visit, while the doctor told me the baby is a tad smaller than she would like, everything seems to be on track.

"You say that now." She reaches for another biscuit. "But once they break that antique crystal vase, you'll be sorry."

"I don't have an antique crystal vase."

"Whatever, Laurel." She waves the biscuit around. Ribbons of crumbs fall to the table. "Let me be dramatic, okay?"

"Drama has always been your forte."

"I know." She takes a bite of bread, followed by a healthy swallow of Chardonnay. "What happened there?" Carmen asks me, pointing to the bruise on my forearm.

"I don't know." I shrug. I've always bruised easily but it seems worse since I've gotten pregnant.

"You done with that, or should I leave it?" Roth stands and gestures to the one remaining biscuit.

Carmen's chewing slows. She stares at that basket longingly. I get it. They *are* delicious. Roth is a fabulous cook and has mastered Southern biscuit making, for sure. He even took a class from a local expert. My biscuits are door stops by comparison. "Yes, I'm done," Carmen finally answers. When Roth reaches for the basket, though, Carmen stops him with a "No!" and snatches it away. Her face becomes almost feral.

"Whoa there, Nelly." Roth chuckles. "Have you been getting enough sleep, Carmen?"

"No judgment, Keswick," she snaps. "Three-year-olds are hard work. You wouldn't, ah…happen to have any of that homemade strawberry jam left, though, would you?"

"Anything for you," he replies on a wink.

"I'll get it," Manny interjects. "Anything else you need while I'm up, carino?"

From the other room we hear one of the girls scream at the other to "give it back" and Carmen replies snidely, "A bourbon, neat?"

Manny cocks his head, as in *"Are you serious?"* Carmen cocks hers right back, as in *"Damn straight."*

"I'm driving home," he announces.

"And I will let you, dulzura."

"You sure you don't need a room instead?" Roth jibes. "We have two extras, all ready to go."

"The girls get up at five thirty," Carmen tells him, straight-faced.

"Manny, you're driving."

We all laugh at Roth's response as he starts to clear the table. I jump up to help.

"Stop. Go sit down." He nods to the couch in the living room.

"No. I can help."

Ever since I found out I'm pregnant, Roth has been overly worried. Almost annoyingly so. He won't let me lift so much as a salad bowl without assistance. I understand this has been hard for him too, though. The last eighteen months have been a roller coaster.

When everything was said and done with our ovulation stimulation and subsequent insemination, we ended up getting four quality embryos, which we froze. We debated for a long time about whether to implant one or two embryos. There was a large part of me that wanted to have twins, so they could experience the same connection that Esther and I did, but twins weren't guaranteed, of course. A pregnancy wasn't guaranteed period, even if we transferred two. In the end, we decided to do what was best for both me and the baby. We opted for a single embryo transfer.

And it didn't take.

We were devastated. I have to be honest; I was terrified to try again. What if the next didn't take either? What if none of the four did? Was there something more wrong with me that they didn't find?

But Roth told me we hadn't come this far to give up, so we tried again.

And the second one...

She is already amazing, though I haven't met her yet.

We are finally, finally going to grow our family. I can't wait.

I grab the salad and the macaroni bowls and carry them to the counter, ignoring Roth's side-eye.

"I said, go sit down."

He snatches the salad bowl and places it in the sink.

"And I said I'm fi—"

The macaroni bowl I still have in my other hand crashes to the floor and shatters into a hundred pieces, as a white-hot pain rips through my abdomen. I double over in agony. It takes my very breath away.

Oh. No.

"What's wrong?" Roth leans over me in a panic. Carmen dashes to my side. Both are holding on to me to keep me from falling to the ground.

But I am holding on to my belly.

To my baby girl.

"Something," I gasp through waves of anguish that are grueling to ride. "Is..." *Oh God. What is happening?* Another swell brings me to my knees. "Wrong."

"Call 9-1-1," Carmen yells. Her fingers dig into my elbow, my shoulder. The bite pales in comparison.

"No, I'll take her," Roth cries.

"Call...Dr....Covington," I pant.

Another surge hits me.

Wetness coats my inner thighs.

I look down.

It's red.

Nooo. Please. Nooo.

"I'll get the car," Manny cries.

"Hurry," Roth replies frantically.

"It will be okay, chica," Carmen tells me. She's trying to reassure me. She is as terrified as I am.

They chatter back and forth but their depth is off. Their tone is muted. They are miles away. They are out of reach.

I am loaded into the car.

Roth holds my hand. He talks to me. The drive is torture. I cry.

It won't be okay.

Blood pools in my seat.

It won't be okay.

We arrive at the ER. They lay me on a stretcher. They roll me into a room. They check my vital signs and scan my belly. Their eyes are grim.

I won't be okay.

They can't help me.

No one can help me.

She's supposed to be okay.

Why isn't she okay?

Then I am leveled by a single soul-sucking, dream-killing spasm that would bring me to my knees if I were standing.

I scream through the pain.

Roth is beside himself.

I beg them to save her.

Please save her.

Take me.

Save *her*.

I fight to stay conscious, but I lose the battle. Darkness envelops me. It's a blessing. It's a curse. I sink into obscurity, and my last conscious thought is I know...I just know...

When I wake, my daughter won't be with me anymore.

I won't be okay...

"Take care of her for me, Esther," I choke out.

Then my world goes black.

NINETEEN

GRAVITY

Laurel
One Year Earlier
August 12, 7:33 p.m.

"WANT SOME POPCORN?" Roth asks, already assuming the answer is a given.

I don't. My stomach is sour, and I feel like an alien invaded my body in the middle of the night. I am off, though I don't know how exactly. But Roth loves popcorn and peanut M&Ms during Tuesday movie nights, so, "Sure. I'd love some."

I listen to the kernels pop in the microwave, one after the other. Pop. Pop. Pop. My mouth waters, only not in an *I can't wait to have some* kinda way. I need to lie down.

Bowls clang in the kitchen as Roth gets our treats and drinks ready. I want to crawl out of my skin and leave it behind. I can't even describe why.

"You okay?" Roth asks, taking a seat next to me on the couch. His brows are sewn together in concern. I can't add one more burden to his broad shoulders. I've given him so many already.

"Yes," I reply, taking the bowl he's prepared specifically for me. Snagging a single seed of popcorn, I pop it in my mouth and chew slowly, trying not to vomit.

I am tired. So very tired since I lost...*don't think about it, Laurel. Don't think, period.*

Halfway through *Lady Bird* I fall asleep, waking when Roth carries me to bed. He crawls in beside me and is softly snoring in record time. But as exhausted as I am, sleep eludes me. I take two of the sleeping pills I was prescribed a few months ago and eventually they do their job.

I wake up the next morning in a fog. It's a school day. I'm dragging. I can barely make it through my morning routine.

"How are you feeling this morning?" Roth pours me a to-go cup of coffee, watching me closely.

"Exhausted. I don't know why. I slept so much last night."

"Your coloring looks off."

"Does it?" I pinch my cheeks. They're warm.

"You should call in sick."

"I can't. The school year just started, Roth. Plus, today is yoga day and the kids are excited to learn down dog."

"Someone else can't teach them down dog?" His tenor is as tight as his clenched jaw.

"Roth."

He sighs, then hands me my insulated mug of life. "I'm worried about you, Laurel. You haven't been yourself since...lately."

Since I lost the baby, is what he means. And I would agree with him. I've been sick. Depressed. I've not been myself; I know. But it will get easier. It will. I simply need to shake this...whatever this is.

"I'm fine."

"You're *not* fine, Laurel. Last month you had bronchitis. The month before that a cold. The month before that another quote unquote respiratory infection. You've lost ten pounds." *Twelve.* "Something is not right."

"It's fine." I sit heavily on the kitchen stool. I could go back to bed and sleep for a month. "Dr. Covington said my body has just been through a lot. It needs time to heal."

"It's been more than nine months, Laurel. And you've been sick practically that entire time. You had to go the ER last month you were so sick."

"My immunity is down. That's all."

I feel as if I'm slogging through soup. Every day it gets thicker and harder to wade through. I'm over it. I want to be me again.

"It's more." Roth grips the counter behind him. His elbows splay to the sides, stretching his fancy olive linen button-down. He is incredibly handsome today. He's always handsome.

"I'll call in if you play hooky with me?" I tease, tucking a finger in between two buttonholes over his six-pack abs. I'm not sure I'm up for it, but I could give it a go.

His lip ticks up. Barely. *Yes, I am changing the subject, Mr. Keswick.* "As much as I would love to, I can't. I have a big meeting with Pat Anderson today to pitch our national marketing campaign."

"Well, that's a darn shame. It could have been fun."

"Laurel." He grips my shoulders with serious intent, but his hold is gentle. "I think you need to go back to the doctor."

"What am I going to say?" *That I am in mourning?* The mind does terrible things to the body when it's under stress. It's a scientific fact. That's all this is. I push myself up from the stool. My bones hurt. "Trust me."

Roth hangs his head. His line turned on him. "I'm worried."

I throw my arms around his neck and squeeze him until I can't breathe. "I'm fine. I'll be fine. I will eat better. I will rest more. I'll take more vitamins and drink protein shakes. I'll do sit-ups and meditate, and I'll get better so..."

So, we can try for a baby again.

I don't say it.

We don't talk about it. Not since my miscarriage. And it's

not because Roth doesn't want to. He begs me to talk about it. It's the elephant in the room. But I can't, because I feel like such a failure. I can't give him what he wants...what I want.

Just as there was no explanation for my infertility, Dr. Covington told me there was no explanation for my miscarriage.

"It happens," she said, clasping my hand in empathy. "There is no reason you can't try again in three months, Laurel."

Isn't there, though?

What if I can't get pregnant again?

What if I can't carry a baby to term?

What if I am defective?

What if I'm forever defective?

What if this tears Roth and me apart?

He says it won't, that it hasn't, but how can I not doubt myself? He wants a child as much as I do. What if I can't give him that?

And honestly, I think that's what's been eating at me for the last several months. Yes, I have felt awful. Yes, I have been sick a lot, but it's these thoughts of inadequacy that are the real culprit. They keep me up at night, the gravity of what-ifs holding me down.

That's why I'm so tired. I'm sure of it.

That's all it is.

"I'm going to be late," I whisper, reluctantly stepping out of his arms. "I was going to try to hit a yoga class on the way home."

He purses his lips but doesn't comment. It's okay, I can read him like the front page of the *Nashville Business Journal*. He thinks I should rest.

"Want to make homemade pizza tonight?" I ask him, slinging my purse over my shoulder. I hold in a wince.

"Sure. We haven't done that in a while."

"Will you pick up cheese and crust mix from the store?"

"Of course. Anything else?"

"Maybe some craft beer?" I wink. We both know what craft beer does to me with its high alcohol content.

He smirks and picks up his keys off the counter. "Sounds like a Tuesday with possibilities."

"It will be." I promise in as sultry a tone as I can muster. I press my mouth firmly to his. "Thank you. It will get better, you'll see."

"I just want you to be healthy, Laurel. That's all."

I miss you too, my love. So much.

"You'll see. I'll kick this bug's ass and then we can go camping like we've talked about. Maybe for Labor Day?"

"Really?" That perks him up. I feel more energized already.

"Yeah. And maybe I'll let you catch more fish than me this time."

Roth closes the front door behind us. Meringue perches herself in the kitchen windowsill. She watches us leave every morning. She's in the same spot waiting for us when we return.

"Oh, this time I will best you on my cunning and my fish prowess."

"Your *fish* prowess?"

"I've been studying up on lures and bait and fishing techniques." Roth grips my elbow to help me down the two front stairs. I fell three months ago. He can't let it go.

"You have not."

"I have," he replies excitedly. "There's this thing called a casting spoon and it wobbles to attract fish. There's a skill to fishing. Did you know that?"

My God…he's telling the truth. I want to laugh but he's so serious right now I can't. I guess he does want to "best me" at fishing. It's the one thing I can still hold over his head.

"Yes," I answer lightly as we get to my car. I gaze up at him, arching my hand over my eyes to block the sun. "It's called patience."

He leans into me and I think he's going to kiss me, but he

doesn't. "Patience pitted against skill. We'll see who comes out on top."

I will. "You're on."

Now he kisses me, and I let my hand wander down south of his belt. The neighbors could be watching for all I care. I haven't been this turned on in weeks. My fingers graze the length of him. He groans. He's thick and pulsing. Maybe it's not too late to call in a sub. We can do down dog tomorrow. I could have him back in the house and naked in under sixty seconds.

Sadly, he halts my advances.

"Tonight," he mumbles against my wet mouth.

"Nooo…" I groan. I try to palm him, but he steps back, leaving me wanting.

"Hold that thought." He opens my car door and ushers me inside. He's flush. I'm panting. Brigette Parker, our seventy-six-year-old next-door neighbor we take to the pharmacy when her daughter doesn't show up, is watching us with a grin. I wave. She wiggles her fingers back. She saw our little show. I think she liked it.

And like that, the gravitational pull that's held me flat to the wall eases, and I can breathe a full breath for the first time in months.

"I love you today, mi amado," I tell him.

His eyes warm. It still amazes me that *I* can do that. "And I will love you tomorrow, my beloved. Have a good day."

"Knock 'em dead at your meeting," I call after him.

He spins and he smiles and everything that was wrong with the world is right again.

As I back out of the driveway, I decide I need to get whatever this is under control. I want to go camping. I want to stay awake past nine. I want to smile and mean it. And I think maybe, just maybe, I want to try for another baby.

So, I dial my primary doctor's number and make an appointment for day after tomorrow.

TWENTY

AUTUMN
LEAVES

Laurel
Present
June 15, 11:15 a.m.

I'VE BEEN in love twice in my life, or so I thought. Well, three times if you count the one-sided love affair I had with Justin Timberlake when I was thirteen.

The first time was when I was eleven and the outgoing and carefree, Benny McCarran caught my eye. We held hands walking home from school. He gave me one of his 4-H recognition pins, which I stuck to my backpack like a trophy. We traded "will you go out with me" and "do you want to kiss me" notes during school. The answer was "yes" to both, of course, and Benny and I had our first kiss behind Mr. Hull's lumber mill.

We didn't know what we were doing. Our tongues dueled awkwardly and there was way too much spit. I didn't know which lip I should kiss, the top or the bottom. Neither did Benny, but we were managing. Until he tried to touch my boob, that is. So I clocked him with a right hook. I left Mr. Hull's with a splinter in my left butt cheek that I got when I fell backward from the blow. It took Esther twenty minutes to extract it while she made me tell her the story over and over because she couldn't stop laughing.

Needless to say, I didn't kiss Benny McCarran again. And I kept his pin.

After Benny McCarran, I dated a couple of boys in high school who were nice, but neither could be taken seriously. And neither lasted long.

Jim Barret was the first. He picked his nose when he thought I wasn't watching. And yes, he ate them. And then he tried to kiss me. Toodle-oo, Jimbo.

Raymond Tucker was the second. He had a vocal tic that sounded like he was constantly trying to hock a spitball. I later found out he had Tourette's. For real. He told me this over a Frappuccino when he asked if that would change my mind about dating him again. Boy, that was rough. I felt bad. Raymond was such a gentleman I nearly agreed. But no.

A few months after I broke Raymond's heart, I went to college and met the second man I thought I fell in love with. But as we've already established, Ace Wallace was a liar and a thief, plus he made this horrible sucking noise as if he was struggling to dislodge a piece of food from his teeth. It was disgusting. In retrospect, I only dated him because I felt pressured by Mother to "find someone" and it was nice for a while to have her off my back. In the post Ace era, I had dates here and there, mostly set up by Carmen, but they always ended before they began.

Reflecting on all of these brief encounters, there is one constant that sticks out. And it's not their uncultured penchants for phlegm.

I didn't cry when they ended.

I didn't lie awake at night, asking myself where I went wrong.

I didn't wonder what I should do to change for the next guy I met.

Mainly because I didn't care.

I didn't care about love or romance or happily ever afters. I didn't need men. I didn't need anyone. I thought I could make it on my own. Be *better* on my own.

They say ignorance is bliss, but sometimes ignorance is just ignorance. The unfamiliar often makes no sense, because how can you understand something that is undefined? On the flip side, how do you define something you don't understand?

It was a circular puzzle that took falling ass first into a heap of splinters and gin and murky hazel eyes to solve.

Roth has not only shown me what love is, he has demarcated it. And he continues to do that day after day, hill after valley. He has given me purpose. Wrinkles from laughing. A reason to dance. He's been a teacher. A lover. A constant. A hand to hold on to.

I squeeze that hand now.

I need that hand now more than ever.

I can't do this on my own. I am *not* better by myself. I am only good because of Roth. I am only me because he loves me.

And I hate this far more for him than I do for myself.

"Are you sure?" I ask Dr. Nuess.

My oncologist's mouth turns south. He's a kind man. Gentle, I can tell. But I wonder how he can do this day in and day out. How do you stare death in the face, unable to defeat it, then have dreamless nights? He probably doesn't. It makes me sad for him.

"I am sorry, Laurel," he tells me. His voice cracks. It's hard for him to maintain eye contact.

I'm sorry too. I let my grief run as wild as my mind.

I had hoped differently, of course, but if you listen to your body, it talks to you. A lesson I learned a bit too late, I'm afraid. I should have listened harder. Taken action quicker. Would that have made a difference? I'm not sure.

I thought those months of illness were the result of losing my baby girl, but now I'm convinced losing my baby girl was the result of my illness. After being sick for months, I did see my primary care doctor as Roth wanted. Dr. Valier is a sweet seventy-nine-year-old man who still runs his own private primary care practice. But after a couple of visits, he wasn't giving me answers so I finally went to see Carmen's doctor, a highly rated internist at Vanderbilt, whom it took me close to two months to get into.

Dr. Thomas did a full workup on me. Blood work followed by a bone scan. An MRI. A PET scan. A CAT scan. And when the results were in, I was immediately referred to an oncologist.

From there, events moved at both warp speed and a snail's pace.

They admitted me, took liters of blood, drilled into my bones, and sucked out the insides. They pumped me full of poison they said would heal me and gave me yet more medication to combat the brutal side effects.

I have spent 89 days in the hospital since diagnosis. That's 89 nights of falling asleep alone, and 89 mornings of waking up lonely. All told, it's been 89 days away from my life, my friends, my lover, my students, my normal.

I have been poked and prodded and had my butt wiped by strangers. I've had tubes shoved in almost every available orifice. Blood clots have clogged my veins. Machines have pumped oxygen into my lungs. I've lost my hair, my eyebrows, my eyelashes. I've thrown up so many times I've popped blood vessels in both eyes, not only once or twice, but dozens of times. My nose and gums bleed without warning and my breath has stunk so bad even I couldn't stand it. I couldn't think. I couldn't sleep. I couldn't be intimate with my husband.

Basically, I have been through the dregs of hell.

Acute myelogenous leukemia is no joke.

The treatment, however, is worse than the disease. I was battle-ready for a bone marrow transplant, knowing the end result may justify the means, but this...

This, I can't do again.

This, I *won't* do again.

I won't live what's left of my life away from Roth. Not one second. I don't want the stench of rot lingering in my nostrils when I close my eyes. I don't want nurses waking me every two hours to take vitals. I don't want bed sores or atrophied muscles or foreign toxins dripping through a central line. I don't want to be some scientist's Frankenstein.

I won't do it again and the mere thought that Roth will beg me to go to extraordinary lengths is enough to send me into a panic. He can't, because we agreed that if we got to this point, we'd be done and we'd both be okay with it. He can't, because I love him so much, I don't know how I would tell him no.

My gaze catches his. The forlorn devastation in them is heartbreaking. He is literally breaking my heart in two.

He palms my cheek. My tears wet his hand. A stilted silence falls over the room, or maybe it's only over us.

I'm sorry, I tell him silently.

Nothing for you to be sorry for, love, he tells me back.

"How long?" Roth demands of Dr. Nuess, dropping his hand back to his lap. But I already know and so does Roth. Remission wasn't expected and obviously it was short-lived. If remission held and the bone marrow transplant was successful...if, if, if... my life expectancy was maybe five years. Without remission, however, I'll be lucky to have six months.

I've been preparing myself for this day since we were given my diagnosis.

And that day is here.

Only much sooner than I expected.

"Roth, it's okay," I whisper.

"No. No. It's not fucking okay. We came in today thinking we'd discuss the next treatment plan and instead we're told all bets are off. That there is nothing more you can do for the person who is my entire..." His voice is shredded. He's spiraling downward fast. "So...How. Long. Do. We. Have?"

As Roth pushes himself up off his chair, Dr. Nuess pushes himself back into his. Roth is rather intimidating when he's not angry. But when he is... I tug on his arm and he sits back down in a huff.

"You'd better start talking," he demands. Dr. Nuess responds, but I fade out of the conversation.

Roth is shattering into pieces. He needs me. We should go.

"What's next, then?" I ask Dr. Nuess calmly.

His gaze bobs between mine and Roth's. It settles on me. Then he speaks to me matter-of-factly and I appreciate that.

"We manage your symptoms the way we've been doing. Pain and nausea. Anything else that comes up. We'll adjust your medication as necessary. Infections are a main cause of hospitalization in cancer patients, Laurel, so you need to exercise caution around others the way you have been." He pauses briefly to wet his lips. "We should also discuss hospice and put an end-of-life plan in place before you need it."

Hospice. End of life. *Shit*. Those words are a cold slap of reality across the face.

"I don't want to die in the hospital," I tell him. I don't know how Roth will feel about me dying in our home, but dying in the hospital is a no-go. I don't get to choose when I die, but I damn well will get to choose where.

"Many people decide to stay in their homes, Laurel. We can arrange for stronger pain control when needed. Hospice will help with that as well."

"Okay."

He hands me a couple of brochures. The one on top is titled *What to Expect at End of Life*. I fill my lungs. This doesn't seem real. "Call my office with whatever you need, whenever you need it. Whatever questions you have, we're here for you and your husband. Again, I'm terribly sorry, Laurel."

And I guess that's that.

"Thank you, Dr. Nuess."

I stand up and shake his hand. His hold lingers. He doesn't want to let go. His sleep won't be dreamless tonight.

It's not your fault, Dr. Nuess. You did all you could.

The drive home is long and quiet. I ask Roth to stop at Wendy's for a Frosty. He does but he doesn't get anything. He says he's not hungry. I don't eat it anyway. It tastes spoiled. Roth calls his parents. I hear Elana keen in denial. I think about Esther. I wonder why my father didn't want me. I contemplate what my last breath will feel like. I imagine holding my baby girl in my arms.

"You should call your mother," Roth tells me. I should. He reaches over and lightly brushes my knuckles. She's going to lose her shit. I know. I swore again. Maybe suddenly I don't care. I decide I do.

"Okay," I agree, thoroughly drained.

I don't call my mother.

I fall asleep instead.

I wake.

We're only halfway there.

I fall asleep again.

I dream of four horses. One of them is white.

I wake.

I'm in Roth's arms. He lays me in our bed.

I fall asleep once more.

I don't dream.

When I wake again, it's still dark outside. This time, I can't force my eyes closed. The ceiling needs painting. A lightbulb is out in the hallway. Meringue needs more cat food. I have a dentist's appointment next Tuesday.

My thoughts are inane. Erratic. My chest feels hollow. I have this urgency inside me with everywhere to be and nowhere to go. What do I do now? Tomorrow? The day after that? What was important yesterday is suddenly meaningless today.

I went to see Dr. Valier hoping to get my health back on track. Hoping to be able to try for a family again. Instead...

Instead.

Rising quietly, I grab a pen and a piece of paper from my nightstand and take a seat on the settee. Moonlight spills over my lap. I trace the yellowish beams as I watch Roth sleep. He's restless. He's so beautiful. I miss him already.

I sob silently. I don't want to leave him. I don't want to die. I wish I could stay.

How do you accept that your road has hit an unexpected dead end with a fatal drop on either side? That your best friend will be left to deal with life without you? That your dreams stop here before all of them were fulfilled?

Did you *do* enough?

Give enough?

Live enough?

Love enough?

Laugh enough?

Dare enough?

Dance enough?

Play enough?

Pray enough?

Sing enough?

Learn enough?

Try enough?

Forgive enough?

Were *you* enough?

Of course, the answer is no, because enough is never enough when death's rancid stench trickles down your neck. There's always more. Only that's not up to you. It never was, honestly.

There's a part of me that wants to scream and wail at the injustice of it or pretend this isn't real. It's tempting...the denial. The anger. I could easily let it consume me, but it's not me. It's not how I choose to live the little time I have left. And it *is* a choice, my reaction. It's the only bit of control I *do* have in this entire situation.

I sit there for what feels like hours, before I finally begin to write.

And I write and I write until my hands ache and I run out of words. The important ones, at least. When I'm done, I fold up the paper I've scribbled on and tuck it into my nightstand, not knowing what to do with it quite yet.

Then I slip back into bed and pull the sheet up over me. Sliding my arms around my husband, I sigh in contentment and finally let the darkness fall back over me, acutely aware of how short and precarious life really is.

TWENTY-ONE

A SKY FULL OF STARS

Roth
Present
June 25, 4:59 p.m.

"Good job," Laurel says, giving me a thumbs-up through the open door. "It only took you three tries."

"Ha ha. Stand-up comedy night?"

I throw the *Songbird* into park and wipe off a profuse layer of sweat from my forehead. *That was close.* I almost hit the electric hookup the first two times I tried backing this monster into our spot for the week.

I step out into heavy mugginess and take a look around our campsite. We are in *The Meadows* area of the campground, which was a whole ten dollars extra per night but offers more spacious sites and fewer campers. I was skeptical. Turns out they didn't oversell it.

"This is surprisingly nice," I say, coming to stand beside Laurel on the cement slab that doubles as a patio. We have a lovely view of Little Pigeon River as long as the spaces behind us don't fill up with RVs.

"Did you see the lazy river when we drove in?" Laurel asks, laying her head against my shoulder. "It looks relaxing."

"It does," I lie.

It won't be relaxing in the least. Lazy rivers are a haven full of screaming, unsupervised kids, but if she wants to go, it will be without complaint from me. This trip is for her, after all.

She unfolds the map we were handed when we checked in and scans it. "They have bocce ball and horseshoes and cornhole and oh!" she pops her head off my shoulder, squealing. She is so melodramatic over the littlest things. I will miss that. "An outdoor cinema. I wonder what that's about?"

Not much, but I'll let her discover that on her own.

"Only one way to find out."

"There's a barbecue on Saturday night. Want to go?"

"Are you asking me on a date, Mrs. Keswick?"

She tilts her face up to me. She's beaming. It reminds me of the first time I went camping with my parents. I wanted to do every single activity they had. And we did. From bicycle races to tie-dyeing T-shirts to pool games. We did it all. And if that's what Laurel wants to do, that's what we'll do.

"Why, yes. Yes, I am."

I love it when she plays along.

"Pick me up at five?"

She giggles. "Five it is."

It makes me happy she's happy. Pat said it best. If this only lasts for a day, it's a day well spent. It already has been.

"Wanna check the place out?" I ask her.

"I thought you'd never ask."

I take her hand in mine. We make our way first to the bank of the river, not a hundred yards from our site. We pick a few flat rocks from beneath our feet and try to skip them across the flowing surface. Laurel is far better at it than I am, though I tell her that I let her win.

We wander and find ourselves in Patriot Park, which isn't much to speak of, and end up winding our way back around the outer edges of the campground, past the cabins, until we're up by the lazy river and the recreational area.

"*That's* the outdoor cinema?"

She sounds starkly disappointed as we stare at what I would describe as a weathered, oversized, mounted set of dry-erase boards cobbled together, along with a couple of scattered picnic tables and a few tree stumps for seats.

"I'm sure it's better in the dark," I assure her, holding back a laugh.

"It doesn't matter." She pulls me back toward the walking path. "We're going to a movie one night anyway," she proclaims with attitude.

"I'm all in."

"Good."

We stroll lazily, planning what we'll do in the Smoky Mountains while we're here. A drive through Great Smoky Mountains National Park to where we were married is definitely on the agenda, as well as the SkyLift to the SkyBridge.

She mentions having dinner tomorrow night at one of our favorite places here, the Old Mill. I hum in agreement, not caring what we do as long as it's not the night before we leave. I have a surprise planned that will knock her socks off. In fact, I have a few of those planned along the way.

"I found this place called the Sinks in Gatlinburg. It's supposed to be a very beautiful waterfall," Laurel says.

"I love beautiful waterfalls."

"Can we go?"

"Of course, love."

I make a note to Google it when we get back, wondering if it includes extensive hiking, as so many hidden wonders in the Smokies do. If it does, it's out. Laurel is no shape for that, despite her assertions otherwise. But no reason to start an argument about something that hasn't happened yet.

"Why don't you lie down while I get things settled," I suggest once we make it back to the *Songbird*. She's getting steamy inside already. I need to get her hooked up so we can get some air.

"No. I'm helping."

"Laurel…" I guide her to one of the leather rocking chairs and gently help her sit. I practically have to smack the backs of her knees to get her to go down. "You need to rest."

I snag a cold bottle of water from the fridge and pop open the cap, handing it to her, but *that woman*…she is so stubborn that she just holds the water in her hand and glowers at me, although I know for a fact she's thirsty. She said so only two minutes ago.

"I don't want to rest. I want to help. I can do *something*."

I bend down, hovering in front of her. I grab one hand of hers in mine. "You *can* do something." That surly look she has going evens a little, but it won't last long. "It would make me happy if you went to lie down."

She snaps her gaze away from mine, staring out the window. "That's not fair, Roth." She sounds defeated. She knows I only go there when I'm adamant about something.

"We need to make a deal, right now," I tell her.

"What?" she replies brusquely.

I tip her face toward me. My legs are tingling from the restricted blood flow. "We need to trust each other."

"I *do* trust you."

"Good. I need to be able to trust you too, Laurel. I need to trust that you'll tell me when you're tired. When you need to sit. Or eat or sleep or if you're in so much pain you need an early dose of pain medication. This doesn't work unless we trust each other to be truthful. I'm already worried out of my fucking mind this is the wrong thing to do."

She averts her eyes again and I feel like a prick. I don't want this trip to be about cancer or last days or making up for lost time we won't have. I want it to be about us. Just us. But it *is* about all of those things, regardless. It would be irresponsible to ignore it.

"I want this time, these memories as much as you do, but I won't sacrifice *you* in the process. Understand?"

She purses her lips and nods reluctantly.

"I guess I could lie down for a few minutes. If it would make you happy," she tacks on. I refrain from sighing. It's a start.

"It would."

I help her up and back to the massive king-sized bed. She moans when she sinks into the soft mattress, her eyelids already droopy. *Not tired, my ass.*

"I could probably use a pain pill too."

I figured as much.

"Of course, my love."

I grab her mix of pain medication, a hydrocodone and a steroid, along with a glass of water. She washes them down, then snuggles into a mountain of pillows and closes her eyes.

"Roth," she calls as I reach the door.

I turn. She's watching me. And when she says, "I love you today," I know she intended to say something else, but I don't press it.

"I'll love you tomorrow," I reply, smiling even though I don't much feel like it.

It doesn't take me long to get electric and water set up, and by the time I make it back inside the RV, Laurel is out cold. I quietly shut the door to the bedroom and get to work.

I text my parents that we made it. I adjust the thermostat to a comfortable sixty-eight degrees. I confirm with my contact that we're a go for the end of the week.

weather looks nearly perfect. be here by 7 sharp.

we'll be there, I reply.

Then I hop into the Jeep I unhitched before I backed in and head into town to pick up groceries and supplies.

"This is so cool," Laurel marvels as we stroll the gravel streets of Elkmont's ghost town, unhurried. Well, Laurel is in no hurry. I keep glancing at my watch on the sly to ensure we won't be late. We need to leave in about thirty minutes to make it to the meeting place on time for my surprise tonight. "I didn't even know this was here." She turns to me. "How did you?"

"I have mad research skills of my own too, you know."

Actually, Travis, our guide for this evening, is the one who told me to arrive early if we wanted to tour the most historic ghost town in all of Tennessee. I didn't know it existed but knew it would be right up Laurel's alley, and I have to admit...it is *very* cool. Brick fireplaces are all that remain of some homes that were built in the 1840s in an old town that is now owned by the national park. Only nineteen of the original seventy-plus buildings stand today.

We've had a fabulous week here, eating at the Old Mill and visiting the Salt and Pepper Museum. We bought donuts at the best place in Gatlinburg, the Donut Friar, and ate them as we drove around Cades Cove. We spent a fabulous afternoon in some of the spots we took wedding photos but found some new ones too. We took our lawn chairs and saw that outdoor movie, the live-action version of *The Jungle Book*. Laurel had so much fun she didn't even mind watching it on that crappy little screen.

And she has been true to her word. She's told me when she needs a break, even if that means cutting our day short. Overall, she appears as if she's doing okay, but I don't exactly know what to expect or when to expect it.

"Look." Laurel points to a crude wood sign hanging between two tall craggy wooden posts tall enough we can walk underneath. "The old Elkmont cemetery. Do you want to go in?"

Do I want to go in?

Fuck no. I don't want to go in. I'll be spending a lifetime at a cemetery near me sooner than I'd like to think about.

"How are you feeling?" I ask, trying to find any excuse possible to turn and hightail it.

"I'm fine, Roth. Please. I want to go."

Cemeteries. Another weird thing Laurel is fascinated with. I've never known someone who loves to walk around the dead the way she does. I don't get it. To me, the air is steeped in torment, the grass muddy with sorrow. There is nothing serene or welcoming about them.

"Please."

She bats her lids coyly and cocks her head just so. She is irresistible, as usual.

I breathe in and blow it out, even and slow. Guess I'm not talking my way out of this one. If she wants to go, we're going. I glance at my watch again. Twenty minutes before go time.

"If you're sure you're fine."

"I am. I promise."

I search her face for pretense, the lilt of her stance for deceit. I see none. She seems to be holding up okay.

"If the walk is too long, we're turning around, okay?"

Please let it be too long. I'll give it three minutes, tops, then I'm calling it.

"Yes, sir."

I roll my eyes and lead us down the dirt path toward the cemetery, twigs and pebbles crunching underfoot. My heart beats faster and aches more with every inch closer. Unfortunately, it isn't far before we come to an opening in a grove of trees where I'd estimate fifty or so battered and crumbling headstones mark those gone.

It's quiet here.

Not peaceful, mind you. Simply silent.

While the ghost town is fairly busy, we are the only ones in this place in this time. It's a bit eerie, if I'm being honest.

"Wow," Laurel breathes.

Her hand slips from mine as she starts to wander and gape. I follow her. Many of the headstones lean to one side and have been wind and rain whipped for so many years they are unreadable.

I stop and take it all in. And what I notice is...nothing.

Absolutely nothing.

There are no flowers. No knickknacks sitting on top of gravestones. No visible knee prints in the dirt. No signs of family coming to grieve their deaths or celebrate their lives or commemorate their accomplishments.

It's as if the villagers of Elkmont have been forgotten along the way. As though their lives were unimportant, fading into nothingness after everyone was long gone. And that hits me like a motherfucking blow straight to the chest, knocking the wind from me.

Who will visit Laurel when I no longer can?

Who will stories be passed down to?

Who will I gush over pictures and replay memories with?

Will Laurel simply be forgotten like these people of Elkmont?

I can hardly bear that thought.

I find myself stooping in front of a marker flush with the ground. I reach out to trace the faint markings.

Margaret Townsend, June 1, 1825 - July 3, 1863.

"Are you okay?"

I hear Laurel's faint voice in the background but don't register it. I'm too busy wondering if the imprints of my knees fit where Margaret Townsend's husband's used to. Did his tears saturate the ground? Did his cries pierce the silence? Was someone here in his stead after he couldn't be?

By the thick dirt coating my finger, it doesn't appear that way.

"Roth, what's wrong?" Laurel shakes me.

What's wrong? Jesus Christ, what isn't?

"She was your age," I mumble, outlining the date of her

death over and over. "So young, so much life ahead of her."

"Who?" she asks, perplexed.

"Margaret."

"Who is...oh, Roth." Then, she's thigh to thigh, shoulder to shoulder with me. "I'm sorry," she whispers, wrapping an arm around me. "I wasn't thinking. This was a bad idea. I am so sorry."

Water races down my cheeks.

This isn't how today was supposed to go.

I am the rock. I *need to be* the rock.

But even rocks have microscopic fissures, don't they?

"I'm sorry," she repeats, her voice cracking.

So am I.

I sit back on my haunches. Laurel mirrors me.

We stay quiet, both of us staring at Margaret Townsend's grave.

"I don't know how to do this, Laurel," I quietly confess. "To be without you. It almost paralyzes me some days, the thought."

As soon as it's out of my mouth, I regret it, wishing the breeze would have carried off my profession before it reached her ears.

She's scared. Though she rarely speaks of it, I know it. And I've put all of my focus into quelling that fear the best I know how, though there isn't a playbook on it, that's for damn sure.

But I am equally as terrified. We're both facing an unknown without the other by our side and though each of them is markedly different, I can't saddle her with my burdens too. She has enough of her own.

"I want you to be comfortable telling me how you feel, Roth," she pleads quietly. She slides her arm from my shoulder and grips my hand in solidarity. We're both going through our own shit but we're doing it together.

"I know." And I am, in everything else but this. This is so raw even I can't touch it.

I hear voices coming down the path toward us. Time's up. We need to go anyway.

I push myself to stand, then help Laurel up. She keeps her hand in mine. We start back the way we came, passing a family of four. And as we pass them, I hear the father tell his teenage children, "This is where your great-great-great-grandmother is buried," and for some reason, that takes away part of the sting of the last few minutes.

I don't know what possesses me to pry, because it's none of my damn business, but I do anyway, lobbing it like a shot in the dark. "Your great-great-great-grandmother wouldn't happen to be Margaret Townsend, would she?"

The family comes to a halt and spins back toward us. The man's eyes are wide and confused.

Well, holy shit. What are the chances?

"Why, yes," the woman replies. It's more of a question. She grips one of the kids by the shirt collar and pulls him into to her. Her eyes narrow. "Do you know her?"

"No," I say with a tad of wistfulness. *Good for you, Margaret.* "But I'm quite sure she would love a visitor."

And without waiting for their response, I turn, with Laurel in tow, and head out of the park to meet Travis before we're too late.

———

I've never heard of a synchronous firefly before my mother mentioned it to me a few weeks ago. Fireflies are fireflies, right?

No.

They're not.

Synchronous fireflies are the only fireflies that synchronize their flashing patterns. No one is sure why they do it, but for about a two-week period every year in early to midsummer, Elkmont houses the largest population of synchronous fireflies in the Western Hemisphere. And we happen to be lucky this year, because the timing of the synchronization is later in June than usual. People flock from all over the country by the thousands to see it. It's so popular, in fact, that getting a seat works on a lottery system.

And I didn't win the lottery, because you have to have the foresight to apply for that in April, but my mother knew someone who knew someone who knew someone and when they heard why we were taking this trip and how much Laurel loves fireflies, we were lucky enough to get hooked up with a personal guide who takes small groups into the viewing. They even provide the chairs and heavy hors d'oeuvres.

Laurel has no clue.

Well... "Oh my God, Roth, I can't believe this!" She does now.

She's bouncing up and down in her chair, she's so excited.

Me? I was worried about how late it would be. I was worried about how worn out she might be. I was worried about the walk. I was worried about the weather. I was worried about her pain threshold. I was worried about her being around so many others. And after we left the cemetery, I was worried she was worried and wouldn't enjoy it.

But she is fine. She is more than fine.

"You excited?" I ask, just because I want to hear her say it.

"Excited?" she quips. "I haven't been this excited since I was eight and I knew I was getting a Barbie Dream House for Christmas after I saw it in my mother's closet. It had an elevator and everything."

"An elevator? Jump back."

"Yes. It was amazing. But this is *so* much better."

I chuckle. Synchronous fireflies for the win.

The moon is bright tonight, which they said could delay the show. But to me, it's a gift. It highlights the wrinkles along the edges of her nose when she smiles. Her skin is radiant. Her eyes glow. And for a few moments you could almost believe this death sentence we're facing is a bunch of made-up bullshit.

"I'm glad I'm sharing this with you," I tell her.

"It's about the best thing we've ever done."

"Even better than Moab?"

She does that snort thing I love. "You're not going to wander off by yourself now, are you?"

That's a story for later.

"I wasn't planning on it, no."

"Then my answer is yes. This is better. Look," she whispers and points with such animation my cheeks hurt. "It's begun."

I stare into the wilderness and the thicket before me twinkles. It's almost psychedelic. As if the stars have descended into the trees themselves and are shining all at once. Then not. Then deciding to give us a show once again. The synchronization comes and goes, mere seconds in between each. The forest breathes and pulses to its own heartbeat.

"Amazing," I hum.

The light show is nothing short of bizarre and spectacular. Unlike anything I've seen before. It's something I will never forget. A memorable stamp in our book.

It's dark now. Almost pitch black, save the moonlight. But when Laurel turns my way and tells me with tears in her voice, "Thank you, Roth. I...thank you," her smile is absolute. Not to be missed.

I did that. I did good.

The show lasts for another hour, maybe a bit more, and then we're trekking toward the parking lot. Laurel falls asleep in seconds when we get into the Jeep, and when we arrive back at the campground, I gingerly carry her inside. I undress her. I slip on her nightgown. I give her her medication.

And then I tuck her into bed next to me, trying hard to only concentrate on the positive instead of the fact yet another day has slipped through our fingers.

TWENTY-TWO

ESCAPE (THE PINA COLADA SONG)

Roth

Present

June 30, 6:13 a.m.

"You're going the wrong way," Laurel tells me as I merge onto I-81 North. The sun has barely peaked over the horizon, casting a rainbow of pastels as far as the eye can see. Looks to be another beautiful day in store for us.

"No, I'm not."

I push the gas pedal down, slowly picking up speed. It's roughly fifteen hours to our next destination, and I haven't had nearly enough coffee yet. But it's my second surprise, so I'm stoked.

"Charlotte is that way." She points out her window to the south.

"Very good." I wink. "You're usually directionally challenged."

"Hey! That's not true." It is. I dodge her tiny fist coming at me. It wouldn't hurt anyway. "Where are we going, then?" She scootches in her seat until she's facing me.

"It's a surprise."

"A surprise?" I love the high rise of her voice. She leans her cheek against the headrest. She seems tired already. Or not fully awake. I told her to stay in bed, but, well, I think we've discussed her less desirable personality trait by now.

"Yes, a surprise."

"We're not going to Charlotte?"

"We're going to Charlotte, love." I reach over to take her hand. "We'll just be a little delayed."

"How delayed?"

"Does it matter?" I counter. We both know we're simultaneously racing time yet have no time line at all.

She contemplates that, and I wonder if she's thinking the same thing.

"No, I suppose it doesn't," she answers.

"Are you tired?" I ask when she holds her hand to her mouth to hide a yawn. She starts to respond, but I can tell by the twist of her upper lip the truth isn't what's coming out. "We'll be driving all day, Laurel. No reason to push yourself."

She glances out the front window, ignoring me. "Look at the sunrise. It's so beautiful today."

She *is* the one who is beautiful today, the one who innately radiates. The rest is…watered-down paint. But I agree, "It is."

We drive a few more miles in quiet before she says, "I think I may lie down for a while."

"Okay."

Unbuckling herself, she shuffles out of her seat, her motions sluggish. I ease my foot off the gas slightly, gripping the wheel tighter.

Setting her hand on my shoulder, she asks, "Are you okay on coffee?"

Always thinking of me. Even when she should be thinking of herself.

"I'm good. Thank you."

"Roth?" She stops halfway to the bedroom. "I'm going to love my surprise, aren't I?"

239

That lifts me higher than she could possibly imagine. "Damn straight you will."

"Thank you in advance."

"You are welcome in advance."

She closes the bedroom door, but not before I see her stuff her earplugs into both ears. Earplugs are a saving grace when camping, let me tell you.

She sleeps for the next four hours, then rejoins me in time to stop for a Wendy's pick-me-up lunch. I order a breaded chicken sandwich; hers is grilled, no bun. We both get Frosties. I eat all of mine and more than half of hers. She lies down again, this time complaining of nausea.

Around dinnertime, I pick up a candy bar and bag of Doritos from the gas station while we fill up. Laurel makes herself a quick piece of dry toast in the RV's kitchen. She seems to do better with that. We play music and road trip games. We pass a skunk at one point. Laurel gets to it before I do.

"You ate a skunk." She giggles, pointing a finger at me.

Little does she know I'd eat a thousand stinky skunks to see that childlike joy on her face.

What was supposed to be a fifteen-hour drive turns into over seventeen because of an accident near Roanoke and construction north of Baltimore. She keeps trying to guess where we're going, but I don't think she's going to remember the conversation we had when we were very first dating, trying to make light of what makes her heart happy and her soul sing.

That's one of the main purposes of this trip. If her soul harmonizes like the Philharmonic Choir, I will have accomplished my goal. I want to give her memories she wants and ones she doesn't even remember she's missing.

Memories matter.

In fact, they are all that matter in the end.

Close to midnight, I pull into Coastal Acres campground in Provincetown, Massachusetts, which sits at the very tip of Cape

Cod. They have only a handful of spots large enough for an RV of this size and the angels were shining down on me when I made reservations, as someone had canceled only minutes before I called. Otherwise, the entirety of the Cape was booked solid for what I guess is a very popular event this weekend.

Provincetown's Portuguese Annual Festival & Blessing of the Fleet.

That's not why I brought her here, but it may be fun to see what's going on. We'll get some fantastically fresh seafood, of that I'm sure.

It's too late for the office to be open, but they told me where to go and to settle up with them in the morning. Laurel has long gone to bed, so I easily find the only open spot and park. I get us hooked up to electric only. I'll do water in the morning. Then I shuck my clothes and crawl into bed, quietly snuggling up next to her, exhausted and sore.

She stirs, muttering sleepily, "Did we make it?"

"We did, love. Go back to sleep." I wrap an arm around her waist and notch her perfectly into me.

"Where are we?"

I fully expect her to shoot out of bed and try to figure it out. But she doesn't move, which is indicative of how wiped out she is. I think we'll take it easy tomorrow. Maybe go into the local park, set our bag chairs next to the water, and watch the fishing boats come up and go.

"Right where we need to be." Kissing her on the neck, I whisper, "I love you today, Laurel."

"I'll love you even more tomorrow, Roth. I'm sure of it."

Then, as quickly as she awoke, she falls back into a deep, deep sleep.

It's nearly morning before I follow suit.

241

I can't see a thing.

I blink.

I blink again.

My lids open and close, yet there is nothing but darkness in front of me.

It's as if I've gone blind.

I reach out, groping, desperate.

My search returns nothing but thick air.

It smells of tar and ash.

Anguish lingers on my taste buds.

I can't spit it out.

A sharp crack startles me.

An immediate earsplitting boom shakes the ground beneath my feet.

I think I may split in two.

Then the sky opens, and torrential shards of rain pelt my flesh.

Each droplet burns like the tip of a pitchfork heated over thousand-degree heat.

My scalp is on fire.

My face is melting.

I welcome the pain.

My sight returns.

I look down.

I am covered in thousands upon thousands of raw blisters.

Blood liberally oozes from each one.

It's up to my ankles.

It's rising.

There is so much I may drown in it.

I wait for my flayed skin to fall off.

It does.

It regrows.

The rain doesn't stop.

The blisters reappear.

The agony doesn't ebb.

The process repeats.

"Roth."

Someone calls to me from the shadows.

It's a blip.

Here, then gone.

"Roth."

Blip.

Come back.

Save me.

"Roth."

Blip.

It's *her*.

Come back.

Save me.

"Roth, wake up. Wake up."

Wake up.

Wake up.

"That's it," I hear.

It's her.

She came.

She'll save me.

I reach for her.

I blink my lids open.

The fog slowly clears, and Laurel comes into view. I immediately drop into familiar puddles of mud. It's comforting there, soothing my ache. The physical torment I felt is gone, as if it never existed. But my heart...fuck. That's a different story. It pounds like an angry fist against the inside of my chest.

Was that a nightmare or some sort of premonition? Is that what life will be like without her? Perpetual, unbearable persecution?

Yes.

Fuck...yes. It will be.

"Roth, what's wrong?" Laurel asks. Her voice sounds muted.

I scrub my palms down my face, unnerved. I study my hands and my arms. There are no blisters. My skin is intact, unmarred.

"Roth, what is wrong? What happened?"

"Nothing," I mumble. I can't possibly talk about a nightmare that feels so real I'm still trembling. I sit up in bed, the sheet dropping to my waist. "What time is it? How long have you been up? How are you feeling? Is there any coffee made?"

"That was a lot of questions at once." Laurel's eyes are large and apprehensive.

"I'm sorry, I..." I clear my throat and rub the sleepy out with balled-up fists, trying to shake off the last of this lingering edginess.

"Let's see." Laurel holds up four fingers. "It's a little after ten. I've been up since eight fifteen. I am feeling much better today, and yes, that's coffee you smell." She straddles my legs, knees sinking into the mattress on either side of me. She rests her palms on my shoulders. "Are you sure you're okay?"

I nod. "I'm sure." *Not even close.*

"Want that coffee now?"

I span the smallness of her waist. "I'm supposed to be waiting on you, not the other way around."

Nibbling the tip of my nose, she utters, "Indulge me." Placing little pecks along my jaw, she kisses her way down my neck and across the top of my shoulder. Her hips roll in a small, but unmistakable invitation.

I guess she *is* feeling better, and I may very well kick my own ass later for not taking advantage of it, but that dream... I'd be making love to her out of my own desperate fear, not the adoration she deserves.

I won't do that.

"In that case, I would love coffee."

"You got it." She doesn't bat a lash, not appearing remotely disappointed as she darts up and pours me a cup.

"Thank you." I blow on the hot liquid and take a small sip. Exactly what I needed. I lean against the headboard and slide the blackout blinds up. The sun is already high in a cloudless, crisp sky. "What a gorgeous day."

Laurel sits at my feet, crisscross applesauce, as she calls it. "Sure is."

"Do you know where we are?" I ask, feeling better with each passing minute.

"No. I didn't want to ruin my surprise."

I'm glad, actually. I wanted to be able to watch her piece it all together. Maybe throw in a clue or two.

"Well, then, what do you say we hop on the bikes hooked to the back and take a look around?"

"I say, I thought you'd never ask."

Laurel is already dressed in tan shorts and a white tank. She slips on her socks and shoes while I finish my coffee, do my morning business, and get dressed. I snag two waters, a couple of protein bars, and a bottle of sunscreen and throw them into a light nylon bag that I strap to my back. We're out the door in under fifteen minutes and pedaling away from the *Songbird* in five more.

The other day when I talked to the manager, she gave me a brief lay of the land and I did quite a bit of research on my own as well. Herring Cove is a couple of short miles from the campground, so that's where I think we'll head first.

Tomorrow I have a private pedicab reserved, which takes us around Provincetown and the point. It's a good way to see a few of the sights in a way that won't wear Laurel out. But it's the night after that I'm most stoked about.

"Follow me," I yell over my shoulder. "And let me know if it's too much, okay?"

"Sir, yes, sir." She salutes me, the bike not even wobbling. She is in a sassy mood today.

We head out on the blacktop, keeping to the side of the road, and it's not long until we're rounding the curve and the first sandy dune comes into focus. The rickety picket fences the Cape is synonymous with should be a dead giveaway.

I look back.

Nothing seems to have registered yet, though she's grinning ear to ear. There is sand everywhere, piled up on the shoulders, so I slow us down to be sure we don't hit a patch and wipe out. A few minutes later, we find a place to park our bikes and head to the water. Laurel stops as we approach a sign that can't be missed.

"Shark warning. Great whites hunt seals here," she reads. "Huh. Guess a swim is out."

"I think I'll keep you company onshore." Grasping her hand, I lead us to the bay. "Do you know where we are yet?"

"Would it be…" She pauses for effect. "Herring Cove?"

"The girl can read," I tease.

"Ha ha ha." She tilts her head back and forth in time. "How about the town of Chatham?"

The sign next to the shark warning did say that, but "Technically, yes."

"Technically?"

"Do you know where Chatham is?" I ask.

She shrugs sheepishly. "Geography was never my strong suit." We mosey down to the water. There are people swimming, despite the warnings. "We're north, right?"

"Very. I'll give you a hint."

"A hint would be helpful." I spot a pod of seals out about three hundred yards taking turns breaking the surface. Laurel spots them too and yelps. After she's done fawning over them, she says, "Okay, okay, a hint."

"It's a great place to be if you like pina coladas and getting caught in the rain."

Her gaze shoots to mine momentarily before she spins in a slow circle, and when she gets back around, the edges of those candied lips are up so high, they'd be lost in the clouds if there were any.

"The dunes of the Cape," she whispers.

"I heard you like making love at midnight in them, so..."

Her eyes glisten. Her bottom lip quivers.

"Roth."

She jumps completely into my arms, legs wrapped around me and everything. It takes me by surprise and I nearly fall on my ass, but I right myself and spin her around as she giggles and cries and tells me over and again how this couldn't be more perfect.

"How long are we here?" she asks, as I set her to her feet once more.

"How many midnights do you want?"

She doesn't answer right away, but when she says, "All of them," it hurts. It hurts so fucking bad. I wish I could give her every midnight from here until eternity.

Maybe Manny isn't wrong. Maybe we should find a hundred experimental treatments and try them all. Maybe I could convince Laurel that we shouldn't throw in the towel based on what the doctors have said. What if they're wrong? They're not infallible. They make mistakes too. What if they've made one here? What if we're losing precious time by glamping around the fucking United States and we should be on a plane to a specialized cancer center in the Netherlands or Australia?

A fist of horror reaches into my chest cavity and wraps its deathly fingers around my heart. It squeezes and squeezes until it cuts off my air.

What the hell are we doing?

"Laurel, maybe we should—"

"Go for a walk? I was thinking the same thing."

"*No!*" I want to scream. "*Fuck Cape Cod. Fuck pina coladas and fireflies and every other surprise I have planned! I'm not going to let you die! We need to do something! Anything but this! Why are we simply giving up!"*

Only, I don't say any of that. I don't suggest we run back to the *Songbird* and pull up Google. I don't drop to my knees and beg her to fight.

I don't, because as I gaze down at Laurel, the stars in her eyes and the resolve in her mind are as plain as her heart is pure.

She has accepted what is to come.

I am the one who hasn't.

"I'd love to," I utter throatily.

Holding hands, we turn our task to finding the perfect dune for midnight.

Several years ago, a coworker of mine told me about this tour he and his wife took while on a trip to Boston. He said it was one of the most awe-inspiring experiences he's ever had, and it's always stuck in my head as something Laurel and I should do.

And finally, after being postponed for the past two nights due to rainy weather, we're here. I was honestly worried the reason I brought Laurel to the Cape was going to go bust before we're scheduled to leave day after next.

All she knows about tonight is that we're going to view the island far differently under the night sky. She has no idea that she will be the star pupil in our own private night photography tour.

We exit the Jeep, the Nikon camera I bought her for our first Christmas together hanging around my neck. I snag the bag I tucked in the back seat that has the other mandatory gear we'll need for tonight, including a tripod.

Our host, Tim, waves to us. I throw a hand up in acknowledgment.

"Do you know him?" Laurel asks, apprehensive. The sun has almost set and while there are other cars parked, we are the only ones in the lot at Harding Beach.

"Sort of." I set a palm to the small of Laurel's back and guide her forward. "It's all good."

"Mr. Keswick?" Tim shakes my hand vigorously when we reach him.

Tim looks as though he was plucked straight from Ireland and dropped in the Cape. His beard is thick and red with a streak of white here and there, matching his eyebrows. A painter's cap covers his hair, but I'd imagine it's much the same. His glasses are a bit big on his face, but they work for him.

He is artsy, for sure.

"Roth, please."

"Roth, great. Nice to meet you. And you must be Laurel."

She gazes up at me. "I am?"

"Are you asking me?" I grin, amused.

"No, silly. I just…" She searches the area for others, then lowers her voice. "Who is this?"

"Sorry, ma'am. I'm Tim Tuttle, organizer of this little nighttime photography rendezvous."

"Nighttime photography rendezvous?" She can't hide her bewilderment…or her excitement.

"Did she not—"

"Surprise," I interrupt.

Tim seems pleased. "Happens more than you think. You're in for a treat," he says to Laurel. "Special occasion you're celebrating or were you simply wanting to learn some nighttime photography skills?" That was addressed to me.

I didn't mention anything to Tim about why we are here. I don't plan to now.

"We're celebrating life, Tim."

I throw a glance to Laurel. Her eyes are still wide.

"And life is worth celebrating, my friend. It's a perfect night for stargazing and picture taking. You have all your gear there?"

"We do," I reply, liking this guy more by the passing minute.

"Great. You two can ride with me. I have water and snacks in the van."

"You wouldn't happen to have a little chocolate as part of that snack pack, would you?"

Tim pats his semiround belly. "Don't go anywhere without it."

"Sold," I tell him. Anything chocolate is Laurel's favorite.

"What are we doing, exactly?" Laurel asks me. Her brows are squished up tight.

I hand my bag to Tim, who loads it into the back of his van, then turn to Laurel. "Exploring the dunes of the Cape, love."

The lines on her forehead deepen. Her gaze darts anxiously between me and Tim, who's paying us no attention. "Roth—"

"Not that," I tell her on a low chuckle. We found a deserted dune on our first night here. I'm still digging sand out of places no one should dig sand from. But it *was* memorable, if I do say so. Laurel's shoulders come down from her ears, visibly relaxing. I step into her. "A long time ago, I asked you what you wanted to learn but hadn't taken the time to yet. Remember what you said?"

She quietly assesses me. I see those cogs a turning, trying to pull that memory up. "Photography," she finally answers. Her eyes glisten under the light of the moon.

"Photography," I repeat. "And Tim Tuttle is supposed to be one of the best there is at night photography."

"I think I'm going to cry."

"Me too," Tim piles on. He pretends to wipe moisture from the corner of one eye. Laurel laughs, and that cloud of our certain uncertainty parts. The reprieve couldn't be more welcome. "Ready?"

"Ready?" I, in turn, ask Laurel.

Her smile is instantaneous and so mind-blowing even Tim sucks in an audible breath. She is something extraordinary. I'm glad others notice it too.

"Ready," she replies, bouncing on her toes.

We pack into Tim's van, and he puts her into gear. "First stop is Nauset Light. It's about a thirty-minute drive. Have you two been there yet?"

Nauset Lighthouse is a must-see on the Cape. Laurel wanted to go yesterday, but it was raining, and she wasn't feeling well anyway. She spent a good part of the day battling nausea and other less desirable digestive issues. I hate this.

"Not yet," I answer. "And Laurel will be your pupil tonight. I'll simply be a spectator."

I hand her the camera. Our fingers brush, and she lets them linger for several poignant moments before she slips the strap over her head.

"Thank you, Roth."

"No thanks necessary, my love."

"Newlyweds?" Tim asks us, taking a left out of the parking lot.

We look at each other, both smiling. She replies, "No," at the same time I say, "Yes."

"What?" I ask when she scrunches up her face. "I am more in love with you every morning than I was the night before, so I'd say that qualifies for newlywed status."

She rolls her eyes, but that happiness she's still wearing is a dead giveaway. "You're so weird."

"Admit it. It wasn't the mustard whisperer T-shirt that sucked you in. It's my weirdness."

"I think they're directly related." She giggles.

"Is someone a big mustard fan?" Tim asks, clueless.

Laurel and I hold our connection for all of two seconds before we lose it. Goddamn, this feels so normal it's hard to wrap my head around what's in store for us.

"Oh, I am a huge mustard fan," I manage to get out. Tears roll down Laurel's face.

That first night I met her when she asked if I was a ketchup fan, I have to admit it threw me for a loop. *What an outright odd thing to ask*, I thought. But as the night progressed, I put two and two together. And, to this day, I still remember that yellow dress she had on, down to the little white flowers that decorated it.

"I think tonight is going to be a memorable night," Tim tells us when our laughter finally dies down.

"I think I agree, Tim," I reply, clearing my throat.

Laurel reaches from behind me to take my hand. "Me too."

"Did you two make it to the festival at all?"

"We did between rain showers," Laurel responds. "The town is decorated so cute. So many flags. We caught the parade and ate some linguica rolls. And the clam chowder was incredible. I've never had seafood that tasted that fantastic in my life. And the rooster paintings on the roads were absolutely adorable."

"Tradition," Tim says. "The Barcelos cock is believed to bring extraordinarily good luck."

"I heard. That's a neat tradition. There's such a sense of community here. You could feel it in the air. Everyone is so friendly and welcoming."

We continue to make idle chitchat on the way to the lighthouse. Tim tells Laurel what she'll be learning. Something about low ISO long exposure versus high ISO short exposure, whatever that means. Light painting. White balance. It all sounds complicated and boring as hell, but Laurel is excited and engaged.

"I've always wanted to learn how to photograph at night," she tells Tim. "I can never get the light balance quite right."

"What have you tried to photograph?"

"The mountains. The moon. The moon over the mountains."

Tim chuckles. "Well, the settings are entirely dependent on

what you're trying to capture, the weather conditions, and the type of lighting you have available."

"What shutter speed should I use?"

"That's a pretty broad question. The aperture and shutter speed depend entirely on the lighting. In full darkness, the aperture opens as much as possible, probably f/2.8 or f/1.4 but that also depends on the capabilities of your lens. And the shutter speed also depends on the ambient light. You should experiment with long shutter speeds of ten to thirty seconds and select an appropriate aperture to match that. In total darkness, the aperture will be the lowest possible, but during the blue hour or with other artificial light, I may stop down to around f/8. We'll take our time practicing and I promise you'll walk away with some great tips to hone your skills on your own."

Greek to me. Thank God, Laurel speaks his same language.

They move on to discussing noise reduction and the finer points of painting with light, which sounds complicated but cool.

It's not long before we make it to the lighthouse. We unload and set up our tripods, getting our cameras secured atop them. Tim points out the constellations with his laser beam. He's incredibly knowledgeable.

It's a clear, bright night with a nearly full moon and we spend the next four hours learning the finer nuances of nighttime photography. I say "we," but I mean Laurel. She sucks up everything Tim says like a sponge, and from what I can tell on her little screen, most of her pictures have turned out fabulous.

There is one set I am particularly excited to see.

We had transitioned from the lighthouse to an amazing stretch of beach running along Vineyard Sound in Falmouth. It was a bit of a drive from where we were, but Tim convinced us it was a spectacular sight not to be missed. As we made our way down this beach to find a spot to shoot, we stumbled upon two overturned fishing boats sitting in the grass of the dunes. They were so picture perfect, it's as if they were staged. After Laurel set up her camera and took a few shots, she wandered down to the boats. She sat on one and looked up at the moon with the lights of the Vineyard in the background, and Tim whispered to me at the same time I thought, "That would be a beautiful shot."

"Would you like me to capture it?" he asks me.

"You have no idea how much that would mean." No idea.

"Let me grab a few of her on her camera. Then why don't you join her, and I'll get some of you two as well."

"Don't let her know you're doing it. I want it to be natural, not forced."

"Of course," Tim replies.

I have a feeling I may need to view them by myself in a dark corner.

"I had so much fun," Laurel mumbles sleepily against my chest. It's after midnight. She's exhausted, no doubt. But we're almost back to our Jeep, so we'll be in bed within the next ten minutes, max.

"You gonna make it?"

She nods, silent. I squeeze her tighter. Tim eyes us in the rearview. I get the feeling he knows something's up.

"Everyone okay back there?" he asks.

"Just tired," I answer for us.

Laurel is quiet, her breaths are even. She's out.

Two minutes later, Tim maneuvers into the lot. It's deserted except for our vehicle and one other. I gently shake Laurel awake and get her into the Jeep before I ensure I have all our camera gear accounted for.

"Thanks, man," I tell Tim, shaking his hand. "We had a fantastic time."

"My pleasure. I enjoyed showing Laurel the ropes. She has a keen eye."

"That she does."

"Hey, if you two are ever back in the Cape around the holidays, I have a holiday night tour that's pretty spectacular. I'd love to have you. Maybe you could even try your hand."

I almost can't speak.

I'm sure Laurel would love that. Next to summer solstice, the holidays are her favorite time of the year. But I have no idea what six months down the road will bring for us, and the year after that...I don't want to think about it.

"We'll keep that in mind. Thanks again."

"Nice to meet you, Roth." He dips his head to tell Laurel, "And you too," but she's already fast asleep again. "You've got a special one there," he adds.

With my throat closing fast, I choke out, "I do," before I can't.

Sliding into the driver's seat, I turn the radio off and listen to Laurel's breathing all the way back to the *Songbird*.

TWENTY-THREE

**GROW OLD
WITH ME**

Roth

Present

July 5, 10:02 a.m.

IT'S TEN O'CLOCK ALREADY. I should get up. We need to head out. I don't, though. I lie with Laurel instead. I soak in her warmth. I watch her eyelids twitch in dream. She mumbles something about cats. She probably misses Meringue, whom we left home with Carmen and Manny to babysit. She doesn't travel well, as most cats don't. We tried that once. Didn't end well.

Yesterday was the Fourth and Laurel was beat from our long and exciting photography adventure the night before, so we had a leisurely day hanging around the campground and then we took in what I would say was the most spectacular fireworks show I've ever seen over the harbor and called it an early night. I tried not to think about the fact it would be my last Fourth of July with her. I try hard not to think about how many days I have left with her period.

My phone vibrates and I pick it up to see it's my mom. I haven't talked to her in a few days, so I answer and quietly tell her to hold on, while I ease my way out from underneath Laurel, careful not to wake her.

I step outside and catch my parents up on the last few days.

We chat for a few more minutes, but I'm not paying attention. My mind is on Laurel.

"How is she doing?" Mom asks.

"I don't know. Depends on the day, I suppose."

My mom is quiet. "This is important to Laurel too."

"I'm worried."

"And you'll be worried sitting in Nashville. Geography won't change that, Roth."

She has a point, though I could come up with a thousand reasons to return.

"I'll let you know when we'll be there. Maybe a week or so?"

"Whenever works for you two, dear. We'll be here. Take your time."

"Thanks, Mom. I love you."

"We love you too, don't we Frank?"

"We do," I hear Dad yell from the background.

"Let us know if you need anything," she adds.

"I will, Mom."

As long as I'm up, I start my packing routine, doing as much as I can on the outside so as not to disturb Laurel. She wakes about an hour later and we eat a lazy breakfast. Well, I eat. She complains of nausea again and doesn't even nibble her toast. She's also coughing and is wearing a Preds hoodie even though it's over eighty out already and a tad humid in the RV.

I've pushed her too far. This is too much. We should go home.

"What's wrong?" Laurel asks me. Tucking her feet on the cushion, she pulls her knees up to her chest and drags her sweatshirt over them. She reminds me of a tiny yellow dandelion who might blow away in a light breeze.

"Nothing," I answer absently.

Has she lost more weight? I think she has. She doesn't eat much. She wasn't a big eater before, but now...

"Roth."

Her clothes are baggier on her. I noticed that a couple of days ago but didn't want to acknowledge it. I think we should head ho—

"Stop."

Definitely. We're going home. We've visited two fantastic places, stacked memories upon memories, and that should be enough. She'll be madder than a murder hornet, for sure, but it doesn't matter. She'll see—

"Roth Warren Keswick." Out of nowhere pink painted toes fly at me and connect with the very tip of my chin. My head snaps back out of shock more than anything else.

"What the hell, Laurel. Did you just *kick* me?"

Her lips part. Her teeth clench together. Her neck disappears into her shoulders. "Whoops. Guess I got a little close."

"Close? You almost took my head off." I rub my chin in exaggeration. She barely touched me.

She watches me, eyes narrowed. "Are you okay?"

Her tenor doesn't exactly exemplify sincerity, so I push the envelope.

"I'm not sure yet." I move my lower jaw back and forth, rubbing the temporomandibular ligaments for effect. "I think my jaw is seizing up."

"We're not going home, Mr. Drama Queen," she announces with a heaping dose of vinegar.

This woman is no one's fool. I love that about her.

"Home? Who said anything about going home?"

"Seriously?" Could her eyebrows get any higher? "You can drop the act."

"Act? Now you're just being insensitive, Laurel."

"Insensitive?" Her voice rises two octaves in defense. Might have gone too far.

Before I take my next breath, she's straddling my lap with my face in her hands. "I know you like you know me."

"Uh-huh," I reply. Her eyes are so dark today. They remind me of raw umber.

"Roth."

"What?"

"Look at me."

"I am." *I am enthralled by you.*

"You're not. You're looking through me."

I'm looking in you, Laurel. There's a difference. I'm sifting through the muck to get to the riches you keep buried and protected. I want them all. I need every last one of them before you leave me. Please, let me have them.

"It's going to be okay."

"It's not," I answer, not mincing words for once. "Not without you."

She sighs slowly. "I'm sorry I kicked you."

"You didn't hurt me."

"I know."

"How are you feeling?" I ask her.

She blinks once. Twice. Three times. She licks her lips and I want to crawl inside of her and rip the truth out myself.

"It's not one of my better days."

"I'm sor—"

"Nope. I will have bad days for no other reason than the obvious. I know what you were doing over here. You were beating yourself up, but I have had a fabulous time here. Do *not* apologize or you will make me mad."

"Do we—"

"No, we don't need to go home. I am going to have bad days and you need to let me have them without freaking out. I promised you I would let you know if I need to go home."

"You won't."

"I will. I keep my promises, Roth. You know I do."

I consider her words, examine her body language. "I'm worried."

She runs her fingers through my hair. It feels so damn good, I moan and shut my eyes.

"How about we take our time getting to Charlotte. Make a few pit stops off the beaten path. Take it slow and easy."

Slow an' easy. Now I can't get that Whitesnake song of the same name out of my head.

My cock stirs. Laurel notices. She giggles and tilts her pelvis forward, rubbing herself along my now-engorged cock. God help me.

"Want to go back to bed?" she asks, voice husky.

Fuck yes, but "No." I want my wife every second of every day, but I'm definitely not a selfish asshole. She's having a bad day.

"No?" Laurel snakes a hand between us and grips me over my shorts with intent. "Doesn't feel like a *no* to me."

"Laurel." I move to stop her, but she bats my hand away.

"Let me do this, Roth." She peppers my jaw with kisses, working the mechanics on my shorts before I have a chance to protest again.

I can't let this happen. It doesn't feel right.

I join my hand with hers, intent on putting a halt to this, but she's now inside my boxers, stroking my taut, greedy flesh. And between the second that I'm lost in sweet sensation and my sense of self kicks back in, she turns the tables on me, switching our hands so mine is doing the stroking and hers is doing the leading. She draws back and watches me as I watch her, scooting down my legs to give us space to work.

This is certainly *not* how I envisioned this conversation would turn out, yet aren't those the best memories? The unexpected ones? This is definitely one for the vault.

"I want you to come," she croaks, pushing our pace faster and faster. She glides her thumb under and over my head with every pass, pausing to press ever so lightly into the very tip. I jerk and shove my cock into my hand, squeezing tighter. She's making my head spin. My balls twitch and tighten. Fuck, I'm bordering on embarrassment.

I try to reciprocate, slipping my fingers under the edges of her loose gym shorts, but she throws up her knee, blocking me. "Ladies first," I insist. I'm close. So fucking close.

"This is about you. For once, let it *be* about you."

I want to tell that that's not how I'm wired, but she snags the edges of her sweatshirt and drags it up over her head. She's bare underneath. Gloriously, beautifully, wondrously bare. She palms her breasts, running her thumbs over her tight, pert nipples the way she did with the tip of my cock. My grip gets fiercer. My speed more urgent. I lunge forward and snag a nipple with my teeth, and the honeyed nectar of her taste is all I need to push me into a pure oblivion only my Laurel could evoke.

I moan around her flesh as my hot seed coats her belly in pearly white ribbons. Laurel leans her forehead against mine and watches. She runs a finger over my sensitive crown, massaging the last few drops in gently.

I let my breath calm as my mind whirls. I am spent and born again. That's the way it feels every time I am with her.

"I love you, today, mi amado," she whispers.

"I want to grow old with you," I whisper back, unable to help myself.

Her voice crackles when she replies, "I was sorta looking forward to that too."

We stay that way. Our heads pressed together. Our chests heaving. My seed cooling on her flesh. Our wishes outstretched in an empty hand. I want to stay here, just the two of us. Make *this* our reality instead of what is.

"I don't want to go home."

Neither do I. Finality lives there now.

"Then we won't," I promise. "Not until you're ready."

We do as Laurel wants. We mosey our way toward Charlotte, taking a more scenic, leisurely route than the interstate. I only agreed to go rogue if she agrees not to be more than two hours away from a major hospital. Having settled on a new plan, we embark on a trip that could be made in one long day but ends up taking us five. And we actually never make it Charlotte at all.

We drive down the Jersey coast to our first stop, Tom's River. They have a Midway on the Seaside Heights boardwalk, which makes Laurel giddy. We ride the Ferris wheel and the carousel. She picks a unicorn and I stand beside her to make sure she doesn't fall. We play PAC-MAN in the arcade—I win—and we eat ice cream cones as we watch the melee below us from the comfort of the Sky Ride.

The next day as we pass through Philadelphia, we grab a Philly cheesesteak at Joe's Steaks + Soda Shop, a restaurant that should be on *Diners, Drive-Ins and Dives*. I can still taste that tender roast beef melting in my mouth.

Our next stop is Monkton, Maryland, where Laurel finds an exquisite topiary garden that's like stepping directly into Asia. From there we spend a couple of days in Baltimore. We wander the stunning and endless George Peabody Library and on the entire end of the spectrum, we stumble across a quaint yet brilliant bookstore near Johns Hopkins, called The Book Thing of Baltimore. Run entirely by volunteers, unbelievably all of their used books are free. We leave with three thrillers Laurel picks out. We eat crab cakes and pit beef and Berger cookies and find a bizarre place, fittingly called Bazaar, an oddity store that features eccentric relics, such as urine bottles, taxidermy, and jewelry crafted out of bones. I have to admit it's a pretty disturbing place.

Virginia, our next location, is simply spectacular. Who knew that a few clicks from concrete highways and our nation's capital there are cinematography-worthy, serene wetlands with connecting boardwalks and abundant wildlife? And we find a place in Chesapeake so eerily beautiful, it could inspire poetry. In fact, it did. Apparently, Thomas Moore wrote about the Lady of the Lake there. The massive cypress trees emerging from the dark waters are stunning beyond words. We sit for an hour and eat a picnic lunch while watching four turtles perched on a log sunning themselves.

In Georgia, we stop at a roadside peach stand, eat world-renowned barbecue, and take our picture in front of Lover's Oak in Brunswick. But out of all the spectacular places we end up, my favorite has to be Blackville, South Carolina. A literal blip on the map you'd miss if you blinked.

"What can I get you two?"

Our waitress at Miller's Bread Basket could have stepped straight from the movie *Grease*. White hair. Button-size earrings. Two dark, prominent moles on the left side of her nose. Makeup cakes the insides of deep wrinkles that have to house countless time stamps. And she sounds as if she's smoked two packs a day for the last seventy years. Her name is even Vi. I gaze around, expecting Frankie Avalon to descend from the ceiling any second singing "Beauty School Dropout."

"I'll have the meatloaf and he'll have the chicken livers," Laurel replies.

I'll have the...*what*? "Uh, no I won't," I pipe in. The liver acts as a filter of toxins in the body. I don't understand how it's fit for consumption under any circumstances. "Disgusting."

Laurel laughs. Vi joins her. "Just seeing if you were paying attention."

I wasn't. I was waiting for a white spotlight and women with mile-high tin rollers in their hair to appear.

"I'll take a hamburger," I say, slapping the menu down on the table without looking at it.

"Pepper steak is the closest we have," Vi replies. Twirling the pen she's holding in her hand, she snaps gum I only now realize she's chewing and all I can think of is that can't be good for her dentures.

"Pepper steak it is."

"And for your side?"

"Mashed potatoes?" Laurel suggests.

"I love mashed potatoes."

"I know." She winks at me and I can't help myself. I snag her hand in mine. Vi falters for a second but recovers quickly. The smile on her face is now wide.

"Gravy? No gravy?"

"Why gravy, of course."

"Best in Barnwell County."

"Then double it."

"You got it." She pulls two place settings from her apron and sets them down. "You two traveling through?" she asks.

"Yes," I answer.

"Have you been to the springs yet?"

"Springs?" I ask, unwrapping my silverware bundle.

"Why yes. People travel from all over the world to drink water from God's Acre Healing Springs."

I roll that through my brain.

"God's healing springs? What's that exactly?"

I glance at Laurel. She's listening to Vi intently.

"It's an old Native American belief that these springs hold healing powers when you drink of its water." Vi looks to Laurel. She places her hand on Laurel's. "You should check them out," she adds, as if she has a sixth sense Laurel needs a miracle.

"Where are these springs?" I ask, sitting up straighter.

"North of town about six miles. Take Solomon Blatt Ave. until you see the signs. Make sure you take plenty of empty bottles to fill."

Empty bottles. Plenty of them. Got it.

"Will do. Thank you."

Vi's smile is soft and warm. "I've heard many a miracle stem-

ming from that spring. I always say, who knows, you know?"
Yes. Who knows? "I'll get your order in. Shouldn't take long."

"Thanks," I mumble as she walks away.

"What do you think that's all about? Magic water?" Laurel
asks skeptically, as soon as Vi is out of earshot.

But miracles happen every day, right? People wake up from
terminal illnesses spontaneously cured. Why not today? Why
not us? Why not from the magical water of God's Acre Healing
Springs? It's worth a try. It surely can't hurt.

"Possibilities," I reply.

Laurel purses her lips but doesn't say anything back.

We're unusually quiet while we wait for our food. Laurel is
on her phone. I map our way to this healing springs place,
which is our very next stop.

Our meals come. We eat, making small talk. My steak is
tender and delicious. The potatoes are to die for. The bread
melts on our tongues. Laurel's meatloaf is hands down the best
meatloaf I've ever had. *Sorry, Mom.*

For dessert we order, what else…peach cobbler, which comes
with a healthy scoop of homemade vanilla ice cream. By the
time we leave, I could use a nap.

I tip Vi well and we load back into the *Songbird.*

"Why are we going to this place?" Laurel asks tersely.

"Why not?" I reply, unable to keep the bite on my tongue
from snapping.

"Roth."

"Laurel." I take in a long breath. "You have been gung ho to
do anything on this trip so far. What's up now?"

She stares out the front windshield. She digs invisible dirt
from underneath her fingernails. She fidgets and avoids eye
contact.

"Tell me," I demand, growing more annoyed by the second.

"You don't want to hear it."

"Well, I can't hear it if you don't say it."

Her head whips my way, and her tongue is as sharp as mine was when she replies, "Okay, then. Here it is. I don't think you've accepted that I'm going to die. I think you think that we'll find some magic fairy dust or happen across some enchanted river." She jabs her index finger angrily at the road in front of us. "I think you think I'll be a one in a million medical miracle that no one will be able to explain and that we'll live together until we're ninety and die holding hands like Noah and Allie did in *The Notebook*. But we won't find a cure, Roth. No matter how hard we look or how much time we spend or how many magic waterholes I drink from. And don't you think that time we have could be better spent watching fireflies or gazing at stars or making new memories? This trip has been fabulous. Why are you ruining it now?"

I can't push the lump in my throat down no matter how many times I swallow. She is correct. On all accounts. I put on a good front but...she's right. I look for a place to pull this behemoth over, but the shoulder is too narrow. I have to keep driving.

"I don't want you to get your hopes up, Roth. I am *going* to die. I need you to tell me that you understand that, because you haven't even said the words yet."

Haven't I?

I have certainly thought them plenty of times. That's all I fucking think about.

"In one mile, turn right on Healing Springs Road," our Google Maps assistant pleasantly advises us.

Laurel shakes her head.

"Aren't you going to say anything?" she asks, calmer now.

What is there to say?

I slow and turn on my blinker. Right.

"Roth."

"It's one stop, Laurel. A half hour. Can't you give me that?"

I am being a grade-A asshole and she has every right to rake me over the coals for it. She doesn't. And for the rest of the five- or six-minute drive we don't speak.

Following the signs, I pull into the small parking lot at the bend in the road. Luckily there is room for us. I shut the engine off. Neither of us moves. Neither of us looks at the other. Long minutes pass.

"You're right. I don't want to accept this," I tell her quietly. "I don't think I'll ever *accept* this, Laurel, so please…please don't ask me to say it." I grip the wheel with both hands and straighten my arms to the point my elbows scream. "I know it's our reality. I know we all die. I know we don't control the circumstances of it. I know all of that. But it's still not fair." She takes in a breath. I know what she's going to say. She's lived through unfair in the worst of ways. "And please don't tell me life isn't fair, because I already fucking know that." I give her my attention now. "I wish I were the one who has cancer, because quite frankly I don't want to be the one here without you. I know it's an incredibly selfish thing to think and more selfish to say, but I don't know how to do that, Laurel. I don't know how to be here without you. Please let me have hope, because everything else will be gone."

After unclicking her seatbelt, she kneels in the space between our seats. She peels my hands from the wheel. I wrap my fingers around the side of her neck and run my thumb along her cheek. It comes away wet.

"I'm sorry I was being a brat," she whispers. "We can go to the springs."

"Logically I know it's only water, but…"

"It's okay. I was wrong to try to take that away from you."

I put my lips to her temple. "Don't apologize. I know where your heart was."

"Let's go get some water."

"All right," I agree, not nearly as enthusiastic as I was a few minutes ago.

We gather as many bottles as we can carry and walk down the beaten rock path to the springs. When we arrive, I stop and take stock. A small stream of water runs in between tall, sparce trees and brush. There are several cluster of pipelike systems with water pouring freely from four spigots each. It's unremarkable, really. Surely miracles don't happen here?

"This is...different than I expected," Laurel says softly.

"Yeah."

Outside of a man and his son catching water from one of the contraptions, we are alone.

"Papi, this water tastes so good," the little boy with two leg braces announces. I would put him around five or six. He has buck teeth and a tuft of blond hair, and his shirt hangs on him. But the grin on his face is the very essence of innocence. He's a cutie.

The boy's father, who is disheveled and could use a hearty, home-cooked meal at Miller's Bread Basket, smiles at the boy, telling him, "Drink more, my son. Drink as much as you want." He trades a full five-gallon water jug for an empty one, while three more are filling. He has close to a dozen full already and at least a dozen more to go. This guy means business.

Laurel heads over to them and starts making conversation. We find out they drove over three hundred miles from Georgia and that Logan has a moderate form of cerebral palsy and they've been coming to these springs for water for three years now.

"Obviously it ain't cured him," Greg, Logan's father tells us, a little tongue-in-cheek. "But whenever we run out of this holy water, Logan cries all night that his knees hurt and his feet hurt and his back hurts. When he drinks it, he doesn't, so...here we are. If it helps him even a little, it's worth the trip. If Logan swears by it, so do I."

"I do!" Logan yells. "I love it! You should try some." He

generously holds out a repurposed Mountain Dew bottle with the label missing to Laurel.

"Why thank you, Logan. That is very kind of you. But you should save that for yourself. I have one of my own that I can fill."

"Hurry," he urges Laurel. "All the water's gettin' away."

"God sees to it that everyone has what they need, remember Logan?"

"I know, Papi. I just want her to see for herself."

"How often do you come here?" I ask him.

Greg stands straight and sets his hands to his hips. "This here will last us about a month. Usually, my wife comes with us and it goes faster, but our daughter came down with a cold."

"You drive ten hours roundtrip to get *water*?" I ask incredulously.

He examines me as if I have bugs crawling from my eyes. "Sometimes twelve. Sometimes sixteen, dependin' on Atlanta traffic. But make no mistake—I'd drive ten days if need be. Would just bring more jugs."

Greg removes another container and motions for Laurel to place hers in the empty space. When it's full a few seconds later, she takes a drink and swishes it around in her mouth before swallowing.

"Well?" I ask, anxious for her report. Is this a hoax? Is there any truth to what this man from Georgia wants to believe? To the stories Vi has heard through the grapevine?

"It's...crisp and refreshing and...I believe the purest water I have ever tasted. In fact, it has no taste at all." She glances at the puddle beneath our feet. "It's quite amazing, actually. Here." She hands me the bottle and I drink.

She's right. It is quite amazing. *From God,* someone whispers in my ear.

That voice gives me pause and I think about all that Laurel has been through over this past year. The doctor appointments, the chemicals, the pain, the sleepless nights. Could the miracle of miracles have been under our nose all along? Could we have saved her from all of that if we'd known this place existed sooner?

Suddenly I wish we had as many five-gallon jugs as Greg does, instead of the handful of empty sixteen-ounce Dasani ones I've stuffed in the crook of my arm. I wonder if I can get empties anywhere in town. I ask him and he tells me no. He made that mistake the first time he came.

We fill all the containers we brought with us. I manage to drum up a few more, but it's not enough and will be gone in few days' time. After we get our precious stash back to the *Songbird*, I help Greg with his load. The walk to the parking lot is short, so it doesn't take us long to get them all into the back of his truck. Laurel chats with Logan while we work, and I decide he has a crush on her. Can't blame the kid. She is rather magnetic.

"Hope you don't mind me askin', and you feel free to tell me it's none of my business, but somethin' wrong with your wife?" Greg asks me on our walk back to retrieve the last two bottles.

My steps falter, then I'm back in step with him. "Can you tell?" I ask. Am I that blind to her state? Once again, I question whether we should be on this damn trip.

"Her colorin's off, but it was more the way she was buried in her thoughts. This place can do that to ya, though. My wife swears she feels spirits here."

Come to think of it, he's right. Laurel didn't say much.

"She has cancer," I admit to a perfect stranger.

"Is it bad?"

We both pick up a jug. Greg holds roughly forty pounds with relative ease, waiting for me to reply.

"She's dying," I admit out loud, finally putting those vile words out into the universe. It is not a weight off my chest, however. It's simply a burden I have placed on someone else now.

"I'm real sorry to hear that, Ross."

I smirk, remembering the night I met Laurel and how she thought that was my name too. I don't correct Greg the way I did her.

"So am I."

"My wife and me will pray for her. And you."

I've had countless people tell me they'd pray for us...it's part of the script after all...but for some reason when this total stranger says it, I feel the power that simple act holds.

"Thank you."

When we get to the parking lot, Greg heads to the door of the *Songbird* instead of his own vehicle.

"What are you doing?" I ask, as he balances his load on one knee and reaches for the handle.

"I figure you need this more than I do." He walks up a step and sets the water right inside the door, gesturing for the one in my hand.

"No, I couldn't—"

"I don't have much to offer folks, Ross," Greg interrupts. "Logan's medical bills have put us in so much debt I ain't seeing a way out in my lifetime, and I'm not complainin' 'cuz I love my boy and would do anythin' for him. But my papi taught me to always give a humble thank-you when someone offers you a kindness. I never understood what that meant 'til I was grown. 'Til *I* was the one needin' a kindness."

He plucks the jug from my hand and places it next to the other one.

I stand stock-still, overcome with emotion and gratitude for something as simple as the reminder of good in people and ten gallons of free water.

"Thank you," I croak.

"Most welcome."

He holds out his hand, which I take. His grip is firm. His

eyes are kind. But it's his heart I can clearly see. This is a good man I am humbled to have met.

"Take care of your boy."

"You take care of your wife."

"I'll do my best."

"Our best is all any of us can do, my friend."

How strange. I don't know this man, yet I feel his friendship. His kinship. Maybe there is something to this place after all.

"Papi, I'm hungry!" Logan yells from the other side of the RV.

Greg shrugs. "Duty calls."

"Thank you, again."

His nod is short and curt. "I believe in paying it forward."

"Papi, can we go to that bread place?" Logan asks as we round the corner. "Pleeaaase?" Logan has his hands pressed into prayer position, his big blue eyes rounded and pleading. "Pretty pleeaaase? We never get to eat there and I wanna so bad."

Greg's shoulders, which were held high with his good deed, slump several inches. "I'm sorry, son, I—"

Shit. No.

"Hey, Greg, you dropped this back there." I hold out a wad of bills I'd slipped surreptitiously from my front pocket. My change from the diner earlier. A fifty is on top.

He stares at it, then at me. His eyes say no, his head is even shaking, but I close the distance between us and stuff it in his limp hand, whispering, "I, too, believe in paying it forward."

His jaw sharpens and he swallows hard.

"Thank you," he chokes out. He gathers his wits before turning to Logan. "The bread place it is."

Logan cheers.

Laurel wraps an arm around me and asks quietly, "What was that all about?" as Greg loads Logan into the passenger side of his old beat-up pickup truck. She knows Greg didn't drop a roll of bills.

"Serendipity, I believe."

We wave to Logan and Greg and I feel inexplicably sad as I watch them drive away.

"I like this place," Laurel sighs, laying her head on my shoulder. "Is it weird that it may be my favorite stop so far?"

"No," I confess, feeling the same way, yet not understanding why, except this ground feels hallowed in some way. "I think it may be mine too."

Maybe miracles *do* happen here.

Maybe one will happen for us.

TWENTY-FOUR

DON'T FORGET ABOUT ME

Roth

Present
July 11, 8:44 p.m.

"HOW ARE YOU FEELING?" I ask Laurel for about the thousandth time.

After a quick stop at Barbie Beach in Georgia and a drive through the gator park in Wildwood, Florida, we arrived earlier today at Turtle Beach, a stone's throw from my parents in Sarasota. We're having dinner with them tomorrow night, but all I can think about is hightailing it back to Blackville. We've gone through nearly half of the water already. How much is enough for cells to change? For divine intervention? One sip? One hundred? How long do we wait? One week? One month? Do we have that much time?

Laurel looks up from the crossword puzzle she's solving in the *USA Today* and blinks. "I still have cancer."

I am so taken aback with her unusually cavalier attitude; I don't know how to respond. Normally, I would be pissed, but I am simply stunned. "Laurel, that's not—" I stutter, not finishing through on my thin lie.

"It is, Roth." She sets her pencil down calmly. "It *is* what you meant. It may be the same question you asked before the spring, but it carries a far different tenor now."

"And what tenor would that be?" I keep my "tenor" even. It's fucking hard.

She bites into her lower lip and shuffles her attention to the paper on the table. She folds one of the edges into a triangle, then runs her fingernail along the crease until it could easily tear off. We both know what she's thinking, only she won't say it.

Guess I have my answer.

Kids shriek right outside our window, and the tension between us fizzles. A group of them are running around with jars, catching fireflies. Laurel's screwed-up face softens into a hint of a smile. Then it's gone.

"I'm sorry." She sinks back into the plush cushions of the *Songbird's* couch. "That was mean."

It wasn't nice, only I keep that comment to myself because the flames are still hot and one slight waft could ignite them again.

One of the things I admire so much about Laurel is how she's managed to stay positive throughout this whole ordeal. It's more than I think I could do. She has a right to be snippy on occasion, and she deserves nothing but grace.

"So, am I. I thought..."

"Maybe it will happen yet," she finishes for me. She doesn't believe it. Neither do I.

"Maybe."

She picks up the pencil and rolls it between her thumb and forefinger. "This trip has been absolutely amazing, Roth. A dream come true. Thank you for talking me into it."

A change of subject. Okay by me.

"I'm sorry we didn't take it sooner."

"We took it at the exact right time," she tells me reassuringly. "When we were meant to." Then she knocks me completely from my chair when she announces flatly, "I think I need to see my mother."

"Your mother?"

"Yes. Do you think we could do that?"

We have had many a conversation about Laurel's relationship with her mother over the years. There is bad blood on Laurel's side, and I can understand why to a degree. I can't quite figure Candice out. She loves Laurel, of that I'm sure, but I think she may be one of those people who truly don't understand how to show it. I've asked Laurel several times how she wants to handle this with her mother, but she's chosen to ignore it. I don't even think Candice knows Laurel is terminal yet.

And the fact she wants to do it now, and in person, is telling. And a heavy fucking blow I admit I wasn't prepared for.

"Of course, yes. Yes, we can do that."

She nods slowly. Her eyes are unfocused as she adds, "The sooner, the better, I think."

The sooner, the better.

The sooner, the better.

The sooner, the fucking better.

Whaaam. Thwack. Blow number three.

"I'm going to take a shower, okay?" Her benign words hold a weightiness that hangs heavy between us. It's hard to focus on which way is up. *Making amends is part of the dying process*, I remind myself. I want to fucking punch something.

"I'll a..." I have to clear the anguish that's settled in the back of my throat before I can continue. "I'll have a cup of tea waiting for you when you get out?"

"That would be amazing. Thank you."

She rises and kisses me softly on the lips. Her movements are stiff. Slow. She holds her lower back as she lumbers to the bathroom and slides the door closed.

She's worsening.

This, right here, is the very definition of torture. Watching your loved one suffer and deteriorate right before your eyes is cruel and unusual punishment. I've read every fucking book and article and tip sheet about helping your loved one die: "Don't ask how to help." "Don't make them talk about it." "Listen."

"Reassure." "Create a peaceful atmosphere." "Give them permission to go."

Fuck me.

I don't know how to do *that*.

I don't know how to do *this*.

Any of it.

The walls I've built around myself for protection and leverage are cracking. In some places, they are crumbling faster than I can reinforce them. And I need reinforcements. Badly. We have far darker places to travel to yet.

So, as soon as the shower turns on, I pick up my phone.

"Roth? Is everything okay?" my mom asks, not bothering to say hello first. She's only miles from me. She may as well be a world away.

I open my mouth to reply, but the only noise that escapes is the sorrowful, pitiful, wounded sound of an animal in the throes of utter anguish. I can't get anything else to come out, no matter how hard I try.

So, I stop trying, and I let self-pity bend and break me.

And my mother, she listens silently while I cry, offering the only two words she can.

"I'm here."

It took me a solid five minutes to pull my shit together earlier. When I hung up with my mother, I felt purged enough to keep going. And when I saw Laurel appear from the steamy lavatory with a fluffy navy towel around her slim frame, my purpose was renewed.

This is about both of us, yes, but she is my focus. My reason. My priority. I'll deal with my grief later. Alone. Without witnesses.

Now we cuddle in stillness as we've done countless times

before, listening to the soft sounds of the night through the open windows. Bullfrogs. Crickets. Water lapping the Gulf shore. A cool breeze blows in, rustling the sheet covering us.

It's peaceful, lying here with her, so for a while I slip back a square to the denial phase and pretend everything is normal. Maybe tomorrow we'll talk about buying our own *Songbird*, or we'll plan dinner with Carmen and Manny when we get home, or maybe we'll start training for our next 5K together.

It's nice, even if it is a fantasy.

"Are you still awake?" I ask her sometime later when I notice her breathing even out.

"I'm scared, Roth."

Her soft admission violently shatters my fantasy, like a bread knife uppercut into the gut. Its blow is vicious. The pain, debilitating. I'm right back where I was before she showered.

I am the male. The protector. I'd kill anything and everything that posed a danger to Laurel. And *this* is anything and everything. This is total and complete warfare. But there is no implement in my arsenal to battle an enemy that is invisible and untouchable, leaving nothing but annihilation in its wake.

I am utterly helpless.

"I am too," I confess, holding her as tightly as I dare. My whole body feels weak, like I haven't eaten in a month, or I just finished back-to-back-to-back iron mans.

"Roth, I want you to promise me something."

Under any other circumstances, my immediate response would be, *"Anything you want, my love,"* but if she asks me to move on with my life or find someone else or, God forbid, try to be happy without her, how can I promise that?

I don't think I can. And what kind of husband would I be to deny my dying wife a single thing? I can't do that either.

"What?" I croak, my heart pounding in my chest.

"When I'm gone—"

"Don't say that."

"Roth." Laurel wriggles until I loosen my grip. With some effort, she fluffs her pillow and positions herself until she seems comfortable. By way of the wince, she's trying to hide, she's far from it. "I realize you don't want to talk about this, but *I* need to. It's important to me."

My emotions get caught in a traffic jam, fighting to get through a one-lane road that has a bridge out. I want to turn around, but I am caged in on all sides with nowhere to go.

"I'm listening." That's all I can promise. And even that is tough.

"I know my death will be hard for you."

"Laurel, please," I choke out. *I can't.* I don't want to have this conversation. Not now. Not ever. It's not denial, I decide. It's called being selective.

"Roth." She twines our hands together and brings them to her mouth. She kisses the tips of each finger, doing it again before saying, "I know you'll grieve. I'd never not ask you to do that. But you have so much to offer—"

"I have no one to offer it to besides you, Laurel."

"I'm not telling you to find someone else, though it would be okay with me if you did."

"I won't," I tell her almost angrily. I think of Pat's story about his dead wife and how seemingly happy he is now with his new one. But I am not Pat. I won't go on to remarry and have four kids. Won't happen.

"If you say so." She runs two fingers over the length of my jaw, trying to calm me.

"I do say so." And I mean it, dammit. I clamp my teeth so tightly together my jaw aches.

No one could ever compare to her. How does she not understand that? And even if I did "find someone else," which won't happen, I would never be able to give that person 100 percent of me, because Laurel will take half of me with her. No woman would settle for that. No woman *should.*

"I'm sorry. I didn't mean to upset you."

"I'm not..." I let go of a breath I've been holding for weeks. I *am* upset. I won't disrespect her by lying. "I have to face a life without you in it, Laurel. Yes, I am upset."

She doesn't say anything for the longest time and, of course, I fill that silence with self-loathing. I am a selfish piece of shit. *She* is the one who is dying.

"Do you remember when we took that road trip to Moab?" she asks.

"Of course, I do."

It was spur of the moment. We talked about it one night and the next day we hopped in the car and drove fifteen hundred miles straight through. It took us almost twenty-four hours. We stayed for forty-eight. It was an insanely, stupidly spontaneous idea that was the best one we ever had.

We camped under the night sky.

We stargazed, in awe of how brilliant the Milky Way is away from city lights.

We got drunk on a case of Corona.

That trip was probably one of my best memories of us, outside of the day we married.

"Do you remember when you got lost hiking?"

"I didn't get lost, Laurel."

She always says that. It's not true. Mostly.

"You did, Roth," she insists.

It was the morning of day two. Laurel was sleeping off the Corona and I woke early, wanting to get in a quick hike. I planned to be back before she even knew I was gone but may have gotten myself turned around a bit. It's not a big deal. She always makes it a big deal.

"A park ranger had to guide you back," she adds, her voice rising with each word spoken.

"And your point is?" I sigh.

She giggles and tucks both hands under the cheek she's lying on, knowing she's got me.

"My point is I was terrified that I'd lost you."

"Laurel—"

"Stop. Hear me out."

I clamp my mouth shut, trapping my feeble protests behind enamel bars. Laurel was actually quite upset when I returned with the diminutive park ranger, Carrie, who scolded me in front of her for relying on GPS versus a park map. Carrie went on to tell me, also in front of Laurel, that they'd just found a hiker who had been lost for twenty days. He was found a mere two hundred yards from a path that would have led him to safety. He didn't make it. I think Carrie was being a tad melodramatic if you ask me, but she got her point across. And served to terrify Laurel more in the process.

"For those four hours that I didn't know where you were or how to get ahold of you or if you were going to make it back to me, do you know what I thought of?"

"How you were going to rip me a new one?" Because that happened. I admit I may have deserved it. Maybe.

The edges of her lips curl up like ribbons. "No. After they found your lifeless body picked apart by vultures and we had to ID you by your dental records and then I had to bury what was left, I envisioned what my new future without the person who made me *me* would look like."

Well, that deflates me flat.

"And do you know what I saw, Roth?"

I do, Laurel. Because that's exactly what I see.

Nothing except utter, total darkness.

But I shake my head, unable to squeak out a simple *no.*

"Cats."

I snort, turning that over once or twice. Is she serious? She saw *cats?* I see nothing and she sees cats?

"Cats?" I draw out my question, letting her hear my disbelief.

"Yes, cats," she replies matter-of-factly. I wait for her to elaborate. She doesn't.

"So..." She didn't see eternal solitude while drowning in a river of tears? She saw... "Cats?"

Her laugh is bright and melodic. She's enjoying my confusion. Then she sobers and drops her chin so I can't see through the windows that lead to her heart. I don't like that. I won't get to look through them much longer.

"Do you know what Esther used to tell me?" She plucks at the sheet, so serious now.

"No."

And what does this have to do with cats?

"She truly believed cats were spirits reincarnated. She was convinced our meema was a scraggly rescue she found wandering down our street a month after Meema passed away. She named her Lena because that was our meema's first name." I listen in fascination. She's never told me this. "So, this cat, Lena, she had a limp. Our meema had a limp. Meema loved to cuddle, and Lena loved to cuddle. Meema always wore her nails long and sharp and Lena hated getting her nails clipped so they always scratched the heck out of us. And that was all it took. Esther was sure Meema had found her way back to us and no one could tell her otherwise."

She lifts her eyes to capture mine, and I am captivated by her. Not unlike the first time she caught me staring in Rudy's.

"So, yeah...cats. I thought maybe if I got enough, one of them would eventually be you, because I was sure you would find your way back to me. And when everyone called me the crazy cat lady, I wouldn't care in the least. I would have you however I could take you."

Oh hell. That is powerful stuff.

I cup her cheek, stroking her soft skin. I would definitely

come back as a cat. I'd never leave her lap. And I could go so many places with this one, but I don't.

"You never told me that."

"You already thought I was being overly dramatic."

"You're kind of known for your theatrics."

Her smile is sweetly sassy. "Whimsically alluring, remember?"

"Oh, yes. I couldn't possibly forget." We stay quiet for a while. I replay her story. "Are you coming back to me as a cat, Laurel? Is that what you're telling me?"

I expect she'll demand I case every animal shelter until I find the sassiest, quirkiest, most whimsical cat and then check for a mole on its belly, where Laurel has one. I love to lick it. Maybe we'd even work out a code in advance to be sure it was her. Instead, she averts her eyes. But just as I'm thinking how odd her reaction is, it's over and her attention is back on me, her face all lit up.

"Maybe I will be with you in the most unexpected of ways."

That catches me off guard.

I don't believe in reincarnation. Or ghosts or spirits. Or even purgatory. But I do believe in something bigger than us. Call it God or Allah or Yahweh. Whatever it is, whatever that place beyond our understanding is…I have to believe in it. If I don't… well, that's not an option. Because that means I won't see Laurel again and that I will not accept.

"Maybe."

"That day in Moab, I felt desperate and isolated and devastated to my very core." Everything about her falls. Her face. Her spirit. Her voice. "So, I *do* know what you're going through to some degree, and I am so very sorry to be the one to put you through it this time."

"Laur—" She sets a finger to my lips to silence me.

"It's my turn. Let me have my turn."

When I nod, she drops her fingers. The tips land lightly on

my chest.

"I'm sorry that when I leave, I won't be coming back with some surly park ranger."

I don't have words. They're all jumbled together in the middle of my gut.

"I'm sorry our time together will be cut short."

"I wouldn't change a thing." Though, I don't know who I am without her. I was pretty solid on who I was before her, but not anymore.

"And I'm really sorry we couldn't have a baby."

"Stop," I snip. "It's not your fault. *None* of this is your fault, Laurel. Not the baby, or the cancer. It's our lot, our hand. You did nothing wrong."

"I'm not saying I did. I'm only saying I wish you had a part of me when I'm gone."

"I will always have a part of you, Laurel. You're here." I flatten her palm over my heart. "You will always be here."

"It's not the same."

"It's enough."

It has to be. Even if it wasn't, not a damn thing we can do about it anyway. Besides, how would I handle a kid by myself?

"And I want you to know that..." She looks as though she's organizing her thoughts. I want to press my mouth to hers, trading my life force with hers. I have tried. Over and over. I have tried and I have failed. "The day I met you I felt like I was dropped inside a kaleidoscope, and no matter what angle I view life through now, all I see is beautiful brilliance. Even through all of this."

"You're the shards of glass," I tell her, my voice hoarse. I trace the outer edges of her lips, lingering in the divot on top. "You are what creates the beauty, Laurel. You *are* the beauty."

"You're the mirrors. And the light. You are what allows me to see it, Roth. Thank you."

Thank *me*? *She* is the blessing. The blue in the sky. The

sparkle in a star. The universe shines for her.

"I wouldn't change a thing, Laurel. Not a day, not a word, not a kiss, not an argument, not a Tuesday." If I had only one day with her, I would take it without complaint.

"Don't forget about me, okay?"

Forget about her? Beyond the bounds of comprehension. I say the only thing she needs to hear.

"You are unforgettable, Laurel."

Her whole body relaxes. "Make love to me."

It's a request and a plea and I want nothing more, but...

"Are you sure? I don't want to hurt you."

"You won't."

"You're weak."

"I want to *feel* normal. I don't want to think about tomorrow." She reaches down, snaking her hand underneath the sheet. She traces the outline of my cock, which saluted her the second she put the words *make* and *love* together. "Please, Roth."

"Laurel," I moan. Grasping her wrist, I stop her. If I'm going to make love to her, it will be on my terms. Not because I'm some controlling, call-me-daddy sex freak. I need to watch her every second for signs she'll try to hide. Like pain. Or exhaustion.

"Here." I gently position her hands above her head. She readily complies, and her wiggle matches her victorious smile. This woman. Incredible.

I move her with care from side to side as I slide her nightgown up and over her, throwing it to the side once off. As I let my gaze caress over flat planes where there were once luscious curves, I have to shove down every feeling that threatens to overwhelm me except for one.

The intense, immense, undying love I have for her.

Nothing else belongs in this space with us.

"You are pure beauty, Laurel."

I run a finger between the valley of her breasts, then move to that mole that's now sunk in the concave of her belly. She moans lightly and both her hands shoot up to grip my hair. The nip of her tugs spurns me downward until my mouth centers over her core.

I lift my gaze to hers. My breaths are hot.

She's watching raptly, expectantly. She shifts her hips upward, her need silent but clear.

I chuckle and snake my tongue out, barely grazing her.

"Roth, yes," she moans.

Her eyes drift shut. Her lips part. Her nails bite me.

Laurel and I have always had this combustive connection when we make love. We are more attuned to each other than I have been with anyone else. It's powerful. Alive. I daresay damn fucking close to nirvana. It's intoxicating and I can't get enough.

So, I don't disappoint.

I make love to my wife. With my mouth. My fingers. My cock.

I take it slow. I drink it in. I tuck away every stuttered catch of her breath. I memorize the brush of her fingers along my shoulder blades. I soak in every liquid writhe of her body against mine.

I feel her on me, surrounding me.

And when she finally falls sound asleep in my arms, sated but clearly drained, I recognize Time for the cruel, heartless bitch that she is.

Time is not a benediction, a miracle, or even a fucking gift as I once thought.

She is the enemy.

A coldhearted adversary that always wins without fail.

And I have learned when *She* says it's up, there is no amount of bartering or negotiating or praying or pleading that will change her mind.

What *She* says goes.

The end.

TWENTY-FIVE

SORRY SEEMS
TO BE THE
HARDEST WORD

Laurel
Present
July 14, 7:23 p.m.

EVERY FAMILY UNIT has their own dysfunction, I know. Except Roth's...his is absolutely perfect, trash-talking grandma, game-cheating mother and all. But for the other 99.999 percent of us, we have to decide how to deal with wounded feelings and ill will from people we may not necessarily choose but who are tied to us through nothing other than DNA. These people, our family, they are supposed to be truthful and have our backs. They are supposed to love us without expecting a thing in return. They should be indignant on our behalf when others hurt us and lay down their lives to protect ours. They should celebrate us in our moments of triumph and carry us when both legs have been snapped off at the knees. They are who we call when we want to unburden our souls without judgment. We should know we can count on them any time of the day or night. They are our family from cradle to grave, like it or not.

My mother is none of those things she is supposed to be. She's engaged in my life; then she's not. She offers words of encouragement, then effortlessly backs over them with a Mack truck without remorse. When I tell people our relationship is complicated, what I mean is that it's tied up in so many knots of bruises and resentments and disappointments and scars that I genuinely do not know how to unwind it. There is no beginning. There is no end. Those two points of origin are buried in the middle of that ball somewhere and yanking on any individual strand will only serve to wind it up tighter. The only way to rid yourself of a knot of this magnitude is to cut it out, piece by piece.

But that also poses its own challenges, because often what's concealed at the center isn't a chewy, chocolaty Tootsie Roll. It's a living, breathing metastases that you've now unearthed, and giving it fresh oxygen gives it new life.

Some people don't even know what lives in their center. They think they do, but they don't.

I do. I can trace that ball back to one singular event.

And it's not what you'd think.

When we were four, Esther accidentally stuck gum in the crown of my hair. *Yeah, I didn't think it was an accident either.* After an hour of trying, the only way my mother could get it out was to snip a half dollar-sized clump of hair at the scalp. And the only way to fix me from there was to cut the rest of my long locks off. I cried for days because I looked like a boy. About two weeks later, we were with Mother in the local Shopko and a woman stopped us and said, "I have twins myself, also a boy and a girl." I made such a scene we had to ditch our cart without checking out, and all the way home Esther dogged Mother to cut her hair too, so people would think we were *both* boys. She even gave us boy names. She was Alvin and I was Simon. Our dog's name was Theodore. Ted, for short. Even at four, Esther had a sense of humor. Anyway, I digress.

Mother refused, of course. "Short hair is great for the summer!" she tried convincing me. Summer was six months away, mind you.

Esther's smart-ass reply was, "If it's so great, why can't I have short hair too?"

Mother huffed and refused to talk about it anymore.

Esther tried Father, only Father always deferred to Mother. But as she usually did, my sister eventually got her way. Somehow, she sweet-talked our father into taking her anyway. She told him Mother had agreed, but had been too busy with school to take her.

That day, apart from any other I can recall, stands out to me as vividly as if it was yesterday. Father told jokes. He never told jokes. He gave us each a dollar to spend at Beck's Five and Dime. He never gave us money. I bought ten banana and ten strawberry pieces of taffy, and Esther bought a box of oatmeal cream pies and a twenty-five-cent Cherry Coke, both of which she shared with me. We stopped at the park. He never took us to the park. We played until the sun went down. We didn't have coats and were freezing, but we didn't care.

We came rolling in past dinner, laughing and as high as two kids could be from eating loads of sugar and spending a great day with their dad.

Candice was not only livid, she was livid with *me*, like it was somehow *my* fault.

Not Esther.

Not Father.

Me.

The day after that was when our father left us.

And I've spent thirty-four years blaming myself for it.

That's what's burning in my very center and you'd think by now, at the mature age of thirty-eight, I would have asked my mother why. Only I was brought up in a home where you didn't challenge authority. Adults were the rule makers. They were smarter. More experienced. What they said went. To ask questions was disrespectful. And this feeling that the parental bond is sacred and shouldn't be poked for fear of unleashing a swarm of bees has carried over into adulthood. That respect remains, even though it's undeserved. Even if it's unearned.

But now the rules have changed.

I am dying.

And I need something from her now that she's been unwilling to give me before.

Honesty.

"Honey?" My mom blinks rapidly as though she's gripped by a hallucination. Sometimes when she looks at me, I think she sees Esther. She leans around me and notices Roth standing at my back. "What are you...?" I know she's spotted the *Songbird* when she sucks in a breath. "Is that yours?"

We drove fifteen hundred miles in two days. This leg of the trip didn't consist of quirky oddity stops and five-star dive restaurants. We made a quick overnight at home since it was about halfway, and we had to pass through Nashville anyway. Meringue wouldn't even look at me. Early this morning, we left for Leone.

And now we're standing on the porch while my mom ogles the camper...RV, I mean.

"It's borrowed," Roth replies tersely. He gets his point across.

"Well, come in, come in." She stands aside and waves us on by. "If I'd have known you were coming, I would have made up the guest room and bought some food."

"It's okay, Mom. We'll sleep in the *Songbird*."

Feeling a bit dizzy, I walk straight to the sofa and sit down. Roth stands in the entryway, his attention dialed in on me. I rub a cramp in my calf. It's ached for the last few days. And I'm tired. I've been more tired lately, even though I sleep a lot. I sigh heavily. I definitely don't have a year. I don't even know that I have a month.

"The Songbird?"

"The borrowed RV."

My mother stares at Roth, confused by his demeanor. Roth is always warm and easygoing. Today he is curt, bordering on caustic. He's acting totally out of character. I raise my hand toward him, palm up. He practically pushes my mother aside to get to me.

"Mother, you didn't tell me you painted the porch." Gone is the mint green. In its place are sheets of stark white that look ill placed. It's the color I always wished it were. Now it makes me sad.

"Well, we haven't spoken in a while, dear. I planned to tell you next time you called."

"Candice," Roth barks, startling us both. "Cut the bullshit."

Woah.

"Cut the...*what?*" My mother's voice fades into nothing as she finally looks at me. *Really* looks at me long and hard. And then it hits her why I'm here. And why Roth is acting like a rabid animal protecting his spoil. "No," she chokes, clutching at her chest. Her cheeks pale and her legs wobble and if Roth wasn't watching for it, she'd be flat out on the floor.

"Here," he says, back to his sweet self. He helps her to a chair across from me and fetches her a cold glass of water. She grips it with both hands, liquid spilling over the sides as she brings it to her mouth. Agony radiates from her, crashing into me in tight waves, one after the other. It makes it harder to breathe.

I hate that I have to be here...for so many different reasons. I'm getting ready to dig into that knot and unearth unbelievable hurts I try not to think much about.

Roth thought I was being obstinate about not calling my mother, but the truth of the matter is this is not news you deliver over a telephone line. No matter what's between my mother and me, she deserves more than that. I am her only living child. What's to be said should only be done in person.

I want answers, yes.

I want honesty, of course.

But the real reason I'm here is that *I need* amends. I do believe the lines of pain someone else has caused you can start to blur just a little. And eventually, if you let them, they could bleed together, creating a fresh canvas to work from.

And I need a fresh canvas, even if I don't have much time to paint on it.

"Is there nothing they can do?" she asks me for the third time. Roth gave us some privacy after we broke the news, going back to the *Songbird*. She cried for the first hour. She drank for the next. And now she's finally ready to talk.

"Nothing, Mother. I'm sorry."

"Not even experimental?" She's gripping my hand so tightly I wince. She loosens her hold.

"I don't want to live that way, Mom. Quality of life matters to me, not simply quantity."

"No extraordinary measures, then, huh?" She says this in jest, but she's still clinging to finding a *yes*.

"That's not what I want. And I need some measure of control over something."

She sits on that for a full minute before replying, "I understand that," as if she's walked a mile in my shoes. It feels like a start.

Mother and I sit on the back side of the porch that overlooks the treehouse. The light is off so as not to attract mosquitoes and beetles. The tire swing creaks back and forth with the breeze. It smells of rain. A storm is expected after midnight.

"You're pretty strong for a sixty-three-year-old woman," I tease.

"Hey, I won't be sixty-three until September."

"I know. Just seeing if you're paying attention."

Silence rests heavy between us. Neither of us knows where to begin.

"I haven't been a good mother." I start to protest, but she stops me. "It's okay, dear. You don't have to lie to make me feel better. A mother knows when she's failed. But even a failure of a mother shouldn't have to bury two children."

"No," I reply softly. "She shouldn't." Rocks churn in my stomach. Everyone I have lost, so has she. She has suffered as greatly as I have. She probably has a knot that mirrors mine. Somehow, now it feels wrong to dig up buried bones. Maybe some skeletons should stay deep beneath our feet.

Ultimately, I decide to respect that hallowed ground, but my mother already has a shovel in her hand.

"I think it's time I tell you a couple of stories. Would that be okay?"

I stare at that shovel, poised, ready to break soil, and my mouth waters wildly.

Do I want the answers I originally sought?

I won't get another chance. This I know. I nod once.

"I imagine you have lots of questions." No. Just one, actually. *Why did my father leave?* "But every story starts at the beginning."

"Okay." My heart leaps into my throat, choking me. *This is it.* The moment I've been waiting my entire life for.

"I don't want this to taint your view or your memories of him, but my father was an alcoholic."

Snap.

What? That is so not what I thought she was going to say.

"Your father was an alcoholic?" I ask incredulously.

"Yes," she answers.

"*My* grandfather was an alcoholic?"

293

"Yes," she answers in the same even tone she used the first time.

"My PooPa was an alcoholic?"

"Laurel, the answer isn't going to change no matter how many times you ask."

I replay every memory I have of my *perfect* grandfather. Family dinners. Holidays. Summer barbecues. Fourth of July. Sleepovers. My graduation. Camping trips. Every possible event alcohol would be available, and I realize...it wasn't.

We didn't have beer in the garage fridge or wine above the stove or cabinets full of liquor I could steal from like my friends did. Neither did my grandparents.

And I never questioned why. Frankly, I thought my family was better than others in that regard. Which is maybe why I've always been so responsible when it comes to alcohol.

"But he never touched alcohol," I reply, having a hard time wrapping my mind around this new reality.

"He used to, I'm afraid. When I told him I was pregnant with you girls and that regardless if he wanted me to or not I was marrying your father, Dan," she adds his name as if I don't know it, "I told him that if he didn't quit drinking, he'd never see you two after you were born."

"What?" I don't believe this. This can't be true. "But I never knew..."

"I never wanted you to know." My mother changes right before my eyes. She regresses to a childlike state. She shrinks in her chair, becoming so small I don't recognize her. "I loved your grandfather, Laurel, so very much, but he was not a nice man when he drank. When I was a child, he was not the PooPa you knew when you were a child. He was the polar opposite, in fact."

I shrink in my own chair. "I don't understand."

"It's hard to believe, I know. He had been an alcoholic since before I was born, but my mother loved him and thought she could change him, so she married him anyway. And that's how *I* remember him, you see. The volatile moods. Sneaking into the garage where he hid his bottle. The yelling late at night. He left me in the car while he drank in the bar countless times. He scared off boyfriends. He broke things. He even crashed the car when I was six." She traces the scar along her hairline, barely visible. She'd told me she fell riding her bike.

"You got that from…"

"Yes. Eight stitches."

"Not a bike accident?"

"I'm afraid not."

This isn't real. It makes no sense. That was *not* the grandfather I knew. I put him on a pedestal. I revered him. He tickled me. He taught me to fish. He took me camping. He scratched my back. He gave me full-sugared Pepsi. We ate watermelon with salt and Wheaties for dinner. I looked up to him. He was perfection.

"Why didn't you tell me? Why didn't *he* tell me?"

"Because he changed after you and Esther were born. He loved you enough…" She doesn't need to say anymore. He loved us enough to quit drinking. From her point of view, he must have loved us more than her. "He wanted to be part of your lives, Laurel. He quit drinking the day you two were born."

"That must have been hard for you," I offer truthfully.

"It was, but it was enough that he did it for you girls."

"Was it?" I ask, because I don't think it was. It wouldn't be for me.

"He never wanted you to know, Laurel," she says, evading my question.

"Then why did you tell me?"

"Understanding starts at the beginning, remember?"

She means her. She wants me to understand *her*. And while she doesn't offer anything else on that subject, she moves on to the reason I'm here, without even prompting.

"I fell in love with your father at the tail end of college. He was..." She pauses, her face suddenly glowing as if she were plugged into a socket. "Gosh, he was magnetic. He courted me in old-school style."

"What does that mean?" I ask. Is she still in love with him?

"He was a gentleman. He opened my door. He refused to let me pay on our dates. He told me I was special. He treated me special. He wanted to...wait. I was the aggressor that night I ended up pregnant."

Oh boy. I do *not* want to hear this.

"He insisted on asking my father for my hand, even though he knew my father didn't like him. It was so archaic and traditional, but he was adamant. I thought it was sweet."

Recalling the story, she told me years ago, how my grandfather said he wasn't the One, I surmise the answer my father received.

"He said no, didn't he?"

Her face screws up. "I'm not sure I've seen him so mad. But we married anyway, as you know. And do you know why I married him, Laurel?"

I wipe sweat from my brow. I'm not feeling at all well.

"Because you were pregnant?" I answer.

"No." Her eyes grab mine in the moonlight, holding on tight. I couldn't look away if I wanted to. "Because that child in me lived to defy my father even as an adult."

I am seeing a whole new side to my mother.

"That doesn't seem like a very good reason."

"It wasn't. It was absolutely the wrong reason." Her attention turns to the treehouse now. Crickets chirp at earsplitting decibels in the background. I want this story. This is why I came, but I long for my bed. I need my husband. I can hardly keep my eyes open. "You're wondering why he left?"

"Yes," I mutter.

This is it. Honesty. Answers.

Mother breathes in. Her inhale is slow.

She breathes back out. Her exhale stretches out.

I wait for. For the wrongs I committed. Every muscle is tensed in anticipation.

You were too loud.

You talked back too much.

You didn't pick up your toys when you were told.

You let him cut Esther's hair.

But what I hear is the exact opposite of what I've believed all these years.

"It wasn't you, Laurel." Her tone is adamant. Pleading, almost. She reaches for my hand and I let her take it. Her eyes are wide and wild. "It wasn't you. It wasn't Esther. And it wasn't me. Your father…"

"My father, what?" I prompt her when she doesn't continue. She's on the verge of tears.

"A few months after you girls were born, your father lost his supervisor's job at the box company. We definitely weren't rich before, but money was more than tight living on a teacher's salary with two new babies. We only managed thanks to your grandparents. They watched you so we didn't have to pay for daycare. They had us over for meals, gave us money for groceries. They bought you clothes and diapers and toys. Your father was very prideful, and it was a severe blow to his ego to take help from someone else, especially my parents, because he knew my father didn't care for him in the first place. He felt emasculated and defeated and he did what I never thought he would do."

"Did he hit you?" I ask. She won't look at me now.

He *hit* her?

"Did he hit *us*?"

"He changed. He was different when he drank."

"He drank?" I spit angrily. I am not a mean person, but I

297

hope that fucker screams for eternity in the fiery bowels of hell. "Don't defend him. He doesn't deserve that."

"I'm not. He wasn't like that when I married him. Your father didn't drink but on occasion before we got married. He knew that was a nonstarter for me. But he spiraled out of control when he lost his job. And a few beers a night turned into a twelve-pack a night, which turned into a whiskey fixation. He spent money we didn't have on alcohol and he didn't care. It took him six months to land a new job and when he did, it was at half the pay he was making. And then he got fired because he either wouldn't show up or he'd show up late. He repeated this cycle for years, his drinking escalating. His anger building. Sometimes he didn't even come home at night. I couldn't trust him at all with you girls. I was never more grateful for your grandparents."

I am stunned.

"Unbelievable."

"When I told him I was kicking him out and that he'd never see you or Esther again, he sobered up. For a while anyway. I thought maybe we'd been through the worst of it and were on the upside. That we'd get our family back, but..."

But...

Then it all clicks.

"The day he took Esther to get her hair cut?" It was such a great day. *Wasn't it?*

"He was drunk off his ass, Laurel. He gave you two money to spend in Beck's but went next door to the bar and took four shots of Jack. He took you to the park but only so he could sit in his car and get smashed."

No, he didn't. He was with us the whole time. Wasn't he?

I strain to remember, but all that comes to mind is Esther and I taking turns pushing each other on the swing and playing on the seesaw and giggling while we helped each other pick out our treats.

"How do you know that?"

"Small towns have their benefits, I suppose. Plus, he smelled like he'd fallen into a distillery vat when he walked through the door."

"But you were mad at *me* when we came home that night?"

"Mad at you?" Her forehead wrinkles in confusion. "Laurel, I was *not* mad at *you*. I was terrified for you and Esther. If anything happened to you..." Her voice cracks and she cups her hand over her mouth.

"He came back, and you sent him away," I mumble more to myself than to her.

She nods. "He called me and told me he'd been six months sober and wanted to see you two. I reluctantly agreed because if he could be a part of your life, I didn't want to stand in the way of that. But when he got there, it was obvious he'd been drinking. I told him to leave and never come back. Ever. Your grandfather threatened to shoot him dead cold if he did. He meant it."

"I'm sorry, Mom."

How could I have been so blind? My mother wasn't keeping me from my father. She was *protecting* me from him.

"You have not a thing to be sorry for. It's all on me. *I* am the one who is sorry, Laurel. I loved him and I tried to make it work, but I should never have let him stay that long. I couldn't imagine your childhood the way mine was. I made many mistakes, I admit, but that was *not* going to be one of them. I heard from his sister that he drank himself into an early grave several years ago. I'm sorry I never told you. I should have. Even though I know I did the right thing by making him leave, I've felt guilty about it ever since. I was the reason you didn't have a father, and I asked myself every night when I went to bed what I did wrong, you know? Why wasn't I enough? For anyone."

In my short life, I have come to learn many things. The most important being that you should not judge others, for you do not understand their trials. Everyone holds their own secrets and buried stories and hidden scars and because of that, everyone deserves grace, even though you may not think they do.

"Thank you for putting Esther and me first." I push my way out of my chair. My body is stiff. My right leg throbs. But I grit through the discomfort and kneel at her feet, gripping her hands. A river that carries freed secrets and deep wounds runs off the tip of her chin. "You're enough, Mom." She tries to stifle her sobs, but her entire body quivers. "You are enough."

"So, are you, my sweet girl," she tells me, her voice tight and strangled. "And I'm sorry that I didn't make you feel that way."

This is the second most important thing I have learned in my short life: When someone who has hurt you tells you they are sorry, they don't need you to belittle their apology with an "It's okay." They need something far more valuable and far more difficult to offer.

"You're forgiven."

My mother loses it then. And so, do I. We hold each other and openly weep.

This brings me to the third most important thing I have learned in my short life: Forgiveness isn't for the other person; it's for you. It's only with this release that you'll be able to see a path forward.

Mine is finally clear.

"Mom, I have a confession to make too."

"Oh?" she asks, wiping her cheeks clean.

"Remember those hot dogs that went missing that summer when Esther and I were eight?"

"Yes?"

I sit back on my heels and shrug sheepishly. "Esther and I took them. We had a hot dog eating contest in the treehouse."

My mother's lips rise like someone held them on both sides and pushed. She starts to slowly rock in her chair and announces casually, "I know, dear."

"You knew?"

"Why, of course."

She knew. Of course, she knew. Mother's always know.

Regardless...now my canvas is finally clean. And so is my mother's.

TWENTY-SIX

NEVER STOP

Laurel
Present
October 29, 8:02 p.m.

"We saw *The Lion King* last night at the Performing Arts Center," I tell my mother excitedly. "Roth surprised me with tickets. Can you believe that?"

It was a good day yesterday. Roth left me a card on the counter with simple instructions to be dressed in cocktail attire by 6:00 p.m. sharp for *the surprise of a lifetime*. Of course, he hovered around all day, making sure I was feeling well enough to go, and told me multiple times that it was okay if I wasn't up to it. But I was able to manage the pain better for some reason. And even if I wasn't, I wouldn't have missed the "surprise of a lifetime" for anything. Yesterday was a blessing.

"He's a great husband, so of course I can. Was it amazing?" my mother asks, though she has to already know the answer to that.

Our trip to Leone a few months ago diametrically changed our relationship for the better. Once the air was cleared and the tears were shed, we spent a surprisingly pleasant two weeks with her. Roth took us roller skating, and we laughed for an hour solid. Balancing on eight wheels was harder than I remembered.

We also took a couple of days out at Branched Oak, where my mother happily joined us. That's the first time she's ever been camping with me. Roth canoed us around the lake. He caught three fish. I caught four. But Mother was the trophy winner, snagging herself a baker's dozen. She even surprised us by fileting a couple of the walleye we caught and making us fabulous fish tacos. I didn't know she could do either, and when she said, "My father taught me. It's one of my best memories of him," I knew we were both on the mend.

That two weeks was a time of healing for us both. We laughed and joked and talked like old sorority sisters. Mother was relaxed and genuine, not a single slight or dig either then or since. It felt like a home, something I missed out on growing up.

I can truthfully say I've never had a better time with my mother. Roth agreed. It's as if a coat of armor has been peeled from my body and I am so much lighter in mind and spirit. Now Mother and I talk every day, sometimes more than once. She's actually a very funny person.

"So amazing!" I gush. I babble about the costumes and the interaction with the audience. "And the singing. The singing was so unbelievably incredible. I want to go back tonight."

But today is not a great day. I'm glad *The Lion King* isn't tonight. Every bone in my body aches in a way I can't describe. Literally down to the marrow. I am cozied up in the corner of the couch, my feet propped up on Roth's legs. I'm dressed in sweats, a hoodie, and have a thick quilt pulled up over me. My blood is still chilled. Roth, on the other hand, is wearing gym shorts and a baggy tee and he appears to be sweating his ass off. He calls me the human radiator.

"How are you feeling today, dear?" Mother asks with concern. I do a great job trying to hide behind my stories and charisma, but the fact of the matter is, I am sliding backward pretty quickly. Everyone knows it.

"It's not my best day," I admit on a half smile. Roth slips his hand under the blanket and strokes my thigh.

"I'm sorry," Mother says, her voice creaking. Her eyes water.

"Tomorrow will be better. Guess what my old students did for me today?"

I don't have an official class anymore. I haven't since I was diagnosed with cancer and had to take a leave of absence to receive treatment. I wasn't allowed back during my short remission because of the infection potential, and then, of course, the worst of the worst happened. I've missed an entire school year, and now I won't return at all.

I miss teaching. I miss the excitement of getting to know my kids and witness the pop in their eyes when they learn something new and the small satisfaction that I had some sort of influence in their lives.

"I'm sure they miss you too, Laurel." Who knew my mother was so intuitive?

"Do you need a pain pill, love?" Roth mouths.

I do, but right now it's my heart that's aching more than anything. No pill can dull that exact pain, I've found. Plus, I hate the way they make me feel. Loopy and groggy. Forgetful. I'm living my last days sleeping and that's not what I wanted either, but I cannot function without them. And I've been taking more and more because they aren't working as effectively as they once did.

So, I nod reluctantly, not wanting a one-way trip back to the emergency room. I've been there six times in the last four months. I've had two infections, a blood clot, two visits for what amounted to pain management issues, and last week we were there again because I couldn't catch my breath. *"Dyspnea,"* the ER doc said dryly. *"A common complaint among cancer patients, especially toward the end of life."* He had a real bedside manner about him, that one (insert eye roll here). They wanted to admit me, but I refused, terrified I would die there, and I don't want to die in the hospital. If they put you in the hospice wing, you're going straight to the funeral home. So, they gave me yet another pill to treat my dyspnea and a printout on *at-home methods to manage shortness of breath*. I threw it in the garbage on the way out.

"What did they do for you, dear? I bet it was wonderful."

It was. "They made the cutest get-well video. Roth was in on it too. He sent them some pictures and the kids each gave their own individual messages. I cried."

"It sounds wonderful."

"I'll send it to you. Get a tissue or two ready. I went through five."

Roth brings my pills and I make small talk with my mother for a few more minutes until they kick in and I can't keep my eyes open any longer.

"I love you, Laureli."

"I love you too, Mom."

"Want to head into bed?" Roth asks when we hang up. He takes the phone I'd propped on my lap and sets it on the end table.

"No. I want to be with you."

"Okay, then. Come here." He pats his lap and I lumber around to lay my head on it. After readjusting the blanket over me, he tucks one of the couch pillows underneath my head. He runs his fingers through my hair that's now about four or five inches long. It's thin and patchy in places, but I feel a bit more like me again, regardless.

"Like this?" he asks when I moan.

"Very much." I'll be asleep in sixty seconds if he keeps this up.

"What do you want to watch?"

"You decide," I tell him, fighting to stay awake.

"Okay." He clicks around until he gets to the National Geographic channel. It's big cat week and there's a show on about the queen of the jungle. "Perfect show for you, my queen."

"Thank you, my king." I giggle, snuggling closer. I'm almost under. "Roth?"

"Yes, my love?"

Ask him, Laurel. Ask him. Every time I go to broach the subject, I chicken out. This time is no different. Maybe it's not a fair last request to lay at his feet, anyway.

"Watch for stray cats, okay?"

Roth stills, then leans over so he can search my eyes. "Do we need to go to the ER?" he asks, concern threading every inflection of his voice.

"I love you today, Roth Warren Keswick." He doesn't answer right away. His lips are pinched as tightly as his brows. I crane my arm so my fingers can brush his jaw. "I'm fine," I tell him. It takes a few seconds, but he finally relaxes, and I know I've made the right decision. Maybe tomorrow, then.

"I'll love you tomorrow, my love."

I drift off...

Sometime later, Roth wakes me. His face is aglow.

"What is it?" I ask groggily.

"Come here." He doesn't wait for me to rise. He scoops me up in his arms, tucking the blanket around my shoulders, and whisks me onto the back porch. "Look," he says in awe, as he sits us down on the cement step.

I lift my head from his shoulder and untuck my arm. I hold out my hand and let wet flakes coat my palm.

"It's snowing."

It's cold. It's magnificent.

I eye the yard. A thick white film already covers it. Esther waves to me in her blue snowsuit to come make snow angels, her chubby cheeks already red. In twin speak, I tell her I'll see her soon.

"It's really coming down," I marvel.

"It is."

"It's beautiful."

"It is."

Roth isn't staring at the snow. He's staring at me. "All these years, Laurel, and I haven't been able to catch my breath yet."

"Roth." My eyes well.

"I will always choose you. I will *always* love you. Always."

"Ditto," I croak, wiping away a flyaway tear.

He smiles that smile of his that goes straight to my belly. And then he yells to the Alexa speaker we have outside. "Alexa, play classic Christmas music."

"It's October," I tell him, my laugh watery.

"I know."

"Have Yourself a Merry Little Christmas" is the first song that plays.

"How did you do that?"

His smile is quick. "Divine intervention, I think."

I ponder that. Sadly, death puts life into perspective.

"Does this complete your list?" I ask him quietly.

It didn't take me long to put the pieces of the last few months together. Once again, Roth demonstrated he could be trusted with my vulnerabilities, and the fact he remembered my laundry list of what makes my heart happy was surprising, though it shouldn't have been.

"It does," he answers. He sounds so far away, though he's right next to me.

We're nearing the finish line. We both know it.

"There is one more thing I don't think I told you."

He perks up. "There is?"

"Yeah. I can't believe I forgot." I drop the blanket to the side and scoop up a handful of snow that's gathered on the concrete. I press it between my palms into a tiny, compact ball, then summon the energy to stand. "It's my favorite winter tradition, actually."

"What's that?" he asks, watching as I bend to grab more snow.

I walk farther out into the yard, frozen water crunching under my slippers, then turn around and toss the clump in my hand at him, hitting him square in the face before he knows what's coming.

"Snowball fight!" I yell before I pivot and take off.

"Hey!"

A tuft of snow catches me in the back. Weak. Roth is out of his league.

I pick up another handful and expertly shape and pack it, heaving it out of my hand before he's taken two steps, then ducking behind a bush for cover.

"You're gonna pay for that," he promises, wiping off the remnants clinging to the "Looking At My Wife I Think Damn She's A Lucky Woman" tee I got for him.

"You can try." I already have four more snowballs made in the time he's still trying to gauge his next move. I can't feel my fingers, but I don't care. This is the happiest I've been in weeks. "Whatcha got, Keswick?" I taunt.

Peeking around the bush, I see him pressing snow between his two big hands. This time it's no little weeny baby ball. It's a good one. He's catching on quicker than fishing.

"You sure you're up for this?" he asks tentatively.

I pop over the hedge and bam! He takes one on the shoulder.

"This is war, love."

"Bring it on."

The last few months have been rough for us both, but they've also been a blessing. We get what so many others don't.

Ironically...time.

Like nearly all of us, I've spent my life wishing Time away. I've wasted it, squandered it, loathed it, and cursed it. I've counted down seconds and wished years would move faster.

But when you know you don't have much of it left, you're

ravenous for lost moments. You savor the next one. They are priceless and coveted and you wonder why you didn't make the most of it when you had more of it.

We make the most of Time tonight. We let loose and we laugh. We spin in circles with our tongues out. We make snow angles. Our socks get wet. Our fingertips stiffen up. Our throats go raw from laughing.

We cling to the present. We don't allow ourselves to see tomorrow.

But the fact is we *are* racing against Time.

It's a race we all run, whether we actively participate or not.

And she is fast and she is cunning and she has an unfair advantage.

And—*spoiler alert*—she always, always...always edges you out at the finish line.

TWENTY-SEVEN

BRIGHTER SIDE · OF GREY

Roth

Present
December 8, 10:13 a.m.

"How is she?"

The whites of Carmen's eyes are bloodshot. I take her hand and usher her inside. Manny follows. Though he can hardly maintain eye contact, empathy hemorrhages from him. I grip his shoulder and close the front door.

"She's sleeping right now." *That's about all she does,* but it doesn't need saying.

"Should we leave?"

"Of course not." *I need you two,* but I don't need to say that either. "Come on in."

Carmen and Manny follow me into the living room. The fireplace is on and it's so hot in here it's downright miserable, but Laurel is always cold, so I'll gladly suffer to make her comfortable.

"Mr. and Mrs. Keswick." Carmen greets my parents who are sitting on the couch. My father has a small fan sitting on the end table that's blowing directly on him. He never complains about the heat in the house, either. God bless him.

"Please, Carmen. It's Frank and Elana."

She offers my father a swift smile as she sits on the edge of the love seat, Manny beside her. Next time, she will call my parents Mr. and Mrs. Keswick.

"Can I get you two something to drink or eat?" my mother asks them.

They both shake their heads no, but my mother doesn't stick around for their reply. She's already halfway to the kitchen. I take her vacated spot, heaviness sucking me into the cushions.

"She doesn't know what else to do," my father says.

"None of us do," Manny replies quietly. "Is she in pain?"

Pursing my lips, I shake my head. Laurel is on so much morphine it concerns me. But the nurse says it's perfectly normal to have to increase painkillers toward the end. *"The goal is to keep Laurel comfortable,"* she told me. *"Do what you have to do,"* I directed her. I can't stand the thought of her suffering at all, let alone a second longer than she needs to. She's already been through so much.

"They're keeping her comfortable."

"What does the doctor say?"

I don't want to say Manny has been in denial, but he's definitely been the most positive among us. He's refused to accept Laurel won't pull through this, that some miracle won't be found at the bitter end. He thinks this will end like it does in a Hallmark movie with some unexpected happily ever after and years from now we'll all look back over a glass of champagne, able to say, "Remember when..."

But it won't. It's been a journey through hell for me to accept that.

And it's time he does. The fact is Laurel has gone downhill severely in the last few days. She has conversations with Esther and her grandfather. *"Hallucinations,"* our hospice nurse, Alice said. And per Alice, who left a while ago, Laurel doesn't have long, which is why I asked Carmen and Manny to come over.

But I can't seem to push the words out of my mouth.

They're stuck in the crook of my throat and no matter how hard I try, they're lodged well and good.

"Would it be okay if I went to sit with her?" Carmen asks me. "I'll be quiet as a church mouse, I promise."

I hesitate, but it's not because I care if Carmen sits with Laurel. I *want* her to. It's because I need to warn her first. I don't want Carmen to be shocked.

Only I don't know how to do that exactly. Laurel is a shell of her former self. Her skin is sallow and paper thin, stretched over nothing but protruding bones. Her breathing is shallow, with a slight wet crackle. The nurse said that's one of the last signs of final organ failure.

Today has been absolutely fucking brutal. And it will only get worse.

"She's..." I glance at my father, my vision unclear. He quietly lends me his strength and I greedily take it, knowing I'll need every damn ounce to get through this. "She's different since you last saw her, Carmen." A mere days ago.

"How so?"

I take her hand, saying nothing.

What is there to say?

Her eyes drop to the floor. Her shoulders begin to shake. Manny comforts her as best as he can, but he is just as rattled.

"I wouldn't leave anything unsaid," I offer on a hush, feeling hypocritical. I've yet to take my own advice.

How do you say goodbye to the person who makes your heart beat and your soul hum?

Unfathomable. It's wholly unfathomable. This entire situation is.

Yet I realize I can't delay much longer.

Carmen mewls as if she's in physical pain. She tucks her head into Manny's shoulder and sobs. Then my mother comes back, carrying a tray filled with meats and cheeses and crackers and sodas, as if this is some sort of unplanned social visit.

I can't take it.

I feel as if I might literally explode into oblivion.

I jump up and pace, fingers pinching the bridge of my nose until it hurts.

I am so angry. So, fucking angry. At God, who has abandoned us. At the doctors, who have failed us. At this godforsaken disease that is taking her from us.

I would trade places with her in a heartbeat so she could live and continue to brighten dark places. Laurel is the most beautiful woman, the most beautiful life force. The most beautiful of everything beautiful. She's had an impact on so many people, so many lives. It's mind-boggling how one person's reach extends so far beyond themselves.

Life is so motherfucking unfair.

"It's okay, son," my father whispers. He grips the back of my neck and squeezes in solidarity.

"You two can go in," I choke to Carmen and Manny, barely able to hold it together.

"We won't stay long," Manny tells me, helping Carmen up. I snatch a few tissues from the box closest to me and hand them to her. She dabs at her eyes, but it's no use. The tears keep coming.

"Take your time. And talk to her, please. It doesn't matter what you say, but if you talk to her, I know she will hear you."

I watch Carmen and Manny head down the hallway and disappear into our bedroom to say their last goodbyes. I overhear Carmen say, "Hey, chica," and I listen to her break down.

My heart cracks into a hundred thousand pieces that scatter inside my chest cavity. The shards pierce vital organs. It's agony. Incapacitating. I feel myself bleeding out from very real, but invisible wounds that I can't die from, no matter how much I pray otherwise.

"Roth." My mother comes to stand in front of me. Her eyes are puffy. Her mouth is pressed flat. "Laurel..." She stops and looks down. It's then that I notice she's clutching a piece of paper to her chest with both hands. She rubs her thumbs along the folded edges, unconsciously, nervously. *This is bad*, a voice whispers. Very bad. "The other day Laurel gave me this to give to you."

She holds out the paper to me. Her hands are shaking.

She what?

"What do you..." I swallow hard, staring at the paper as if it has poison tentacles. My name is scrawled on the outside in her beautifully perfect penmanship. "What do you mean she gave this to you to give to me?"

"Just as I said." She prods me to take it. I don't want to. "Roth." My mother reaches down and brings my hand up to meet hers. She places what I can only assume is a letter to me from Laurel in it. "I didn't question her request. I didn't read the letter. She simply asked that I give this to you when I knew it was time."

"When it was time?" I repeat quietly. My legs feel like they're made of string holding up a lead balloon. They give. Luckily the chair catches me.

My mother crouches at my feet, taking my hands in hers. Compassion pours from her heart. Her eyes are faucets. "It is time, Roth. I'm sorry. It's time."

It's time. It can't be time. I don't *want* it to be time.

"We'll be in the kitchen if you need us."

Then I'm left alone. Just me and what are likely Laurel's last words to me.

Staring at the squiggly lines Laurel always swirls under my name, I trace them with my finger over and over.

Fuck me.

Fuck.

Two fists grip my chest, squeezing it until I can't inhale. Goddamn. It hurts.

With shaky hands, I begin to open the letter and read, and at the very opening line, time stills, stamping my book in big, motherfucking neon letters.

This is a moment you simply don't forget.

Not ever.

And you don't need a book to remember it.

Mi amado ~

I'm writing this while sitting in the corner of our room, watching you restlessly toss and turn. My grief wets the pages, but I don't weep for me. I weep for you. Obviously, this is a letter I never, in my wildest dreams, thought I would have to write, yet here we are.

It's hard to know where to start. Where to grab the right mix of words from, because frankly I don't think they exist. How do you sum up the greatest happiness you've ever known in a few measly paragraphs? I want to be profound, yet I'm not a profound thinker. I want to leave you something that you can come back to when you're missing me so much you physically ache, yet I wonder if they will only make you ache more.

My PooPa used to tell me that a wound never heals if you keep touching it. Boy, do I understand that. And I don't want this to be a wound you constantly reopen. But I've decided that some wounds are worth the beautiful scars that reopening them creates. Our love is one of them.

So here it goes.

It's no secret I haven't always been confident in myself. It's definitely no secret that I've held others at arm's length, because letting them get too close opened up this place of vulnerability that was more terrifying than being alone. But then you came along, and you blew my wall down with a single puff. I fell in love with you the moment you told me mustard was your condiment of choice. Your Mustard Whisperer T-shirt only sealed the deal.

I tried to fight it, though. You fought harder. You never gave up when I threw up crazy after crazy. You made me want things I'd long decided I didn't. You taught me to dance, to believe in myself again, to have faith, to love without reserve. You have given me a home and grace when I didn't deserve it and kicked my ass when I've needed it (I said ass...lol). You are my rock, my sounding board, my strength, my guide, my supporter, my best friend. I love our life and all that we have built with each other. Your love is and always has been unconditional and unwavering. Honestly, it is all that's carried me through the darkest of days and it's all that will get me through what is to come.

I know you're scared. I know you're angry. You're in denial, though you'll deny it. I'm scared too. And I'm incredibly sad, but from the moment I was diagnosed I had a sixth sense this is how the end would be. If there is one hard lesson life has taught me, it's that we have no control over it, not really. We control how we react to events and circumstances, and that's about it. That is how we're remembered.

So, I choose to spend this little time we have left together not in denial, not wishing things were different, not praying for some miracle that will not come. I accept my fate and I am at peace with it.

I choose to die while I am living.

The best part is that I married a man who will push me to do that anyway without asking.

You are the best thing to happen to me, and I am so sorry that our time has been cut shorter than we'd like. Though, if we had a thousand years together, we both know that still wouldn't be enough.

I don't want this to sound trite but thank you. Thank you for loving me. For being my person. For picking up tissues after me. For making me laugh. For broadening my musical tastes. For being the other half of me. Thank you for fighting for me. And thank you in advance for everything I know you will do to make the time we have left something I will take with me after I leave you.

The love we have lights the darkest of spaces. It will do so for eternity, regardless of if I am here or somewhere else. When I take my last breath, know I will never be far away. I will come back to you some way, some-

how, in the most unexpected of ways. We will see each other again; of that I am certain. How can we not? Our love transcends even the cruelty of time.

I love you today, Roth Warren Keswick. I love you today, but I will love you even more tomorrow and the tomorrow after that and the tomorrow after that and…

Your whimsically alluring, fish whispering, mustard hating wife,
Laurel

When I finish with the last word, I hang my head and weep until my tears run dry.

TWENTY-EIGHT

I'LL FOLLOW
YOU

Roth

Present

December 8, 2:23 p.m.

LAUREL'S MOTHER arrives shortly after Carmen and Manny leave. She spends several hours at Laurel's bedside and when she emerges, she is an absolute wreck.

"She didn't open her eyes." Candice clutches me as if she'll fall to her death without me.

"She knew you were there."

"I hope so. I hope so. I made so many mistakes with her."

I am losing my wife, yes, but I have to say that no matter the water under the bridge between those two, Candice is losing a second child and I can't even fathom the pain she is having to endure.

Well, yes, actually, I can.

"She did," I assure her.

"I don't know what I'm going to do." She buries her head in my chest, sobbing uncontrollably.

Neither do I.

Laurel is our anchor and without her, we are untethered and doomed to float aimlessly forever.

I hold Candice through the worst of it, anxious and woozy. I want to be supportive and empathetic, but I have this blistering need to get to Laurel before it's too late.

I catch my mother's eye and hand Candice off so I can be with my wife.

"Go." She clasps my hand. My throat closes. Her eyes brim with tears.

"Thank you, Mom."

I turn and walk toward our bedroom. It could take me an hour to get there or two clicks of a second hand. I don't know. I've lost all sense of reality, except for one. Each step I take is singular. Agonizing. Leading me to an inevitability I'll never be ready for, no matter the time allowed to prepare.

Josh Emory, a high school friend of mine, was killed on his way home from basketball practice when he was seventeen. He was captain of the debate team. Honor student. He volunteered at the animal shelter. He was a great kid with a bright future who happened to cross the center line and get hit head-on by a Dodge minivan. His death was tragic and unexpected and all we could talk about at his funeral was how we didn't get the chance to say goodbye.

But what I've come to discover in this process is that goodbyes don't give us closure. There can never *be* "closure" regardless of the circumstances.

Goodbyes taste bitter.

Death is absolute.

Gone is forever.

The door to our bedroom stands wide open. For several moments, I am frozen in the entry. The stench of lavender oil, sickly flowers, and vast, immeasurable grief threaten to level me flat.

Laurel lies stone-still in her hospital bed. She's the color of paste. Her eyes are closed. Her lids don't jerk with the tell of sweet dreams. They're silent.

It's time.

I want to be anywhere else but here.

I want to be nowhere else but here.

I want to take us away from here.

I enter the room and close the door behind me.

I sit and take Laurel's cool hand between mine and work to clear the dam of grief that is buried miles deep in my chest. I can't find the end of it.

"Hey," I croak. "Busy day, huh?"

She doesn't move. She doesn't giggle. She has no witty comeback. She doesn't even flinch.

I am broken.

Today will be our final entry. Our last stamp.

I know it.

Time has come knocking and *She* won't take no for an answer.

I can barely breathe. My chest hurts. My stomach hurts. My everything hurts.

I don't say anything for a while, not knowing where to start. When I finally do, I don't stop.

"You have made me the man I am today, Laurel. You're my greatest accomplishment, my only love, my favorite swing partner. Thank you for taking a chance on me and for teaching me to fish. Thank you for making me laugh. For being my rock. Thank you for making me better than I could have ever been without you."

I've told her all this before, of course. But it all bears repeating. And repeating.

I recite as much of *The Lion King* as I can remember. I sing her "Some Kind of Love" by the Killers. I read her get-well letters from her former students and colleagues. I play her YouTube videos of cat shenanigans and our favorite scenes from *Dirty Dancing*, because nobody puts Baby in the corner. I turn on *The*

Music Man and fast-forward to her favorite song, "Goodnight My Someone," knowing the words are from me to her this time, not from Marian to Harold.

I promise her I'll watch for stray cats.

I apologize I couldn't save her.

Meringue joins us at some point. So do my parents and so does Candice. I call Carmen and Manny back. We tell stories. We cry. We even manage a laugh or two.

Laurel's fingers twitch occasionally, and I let myself believe it's to encourage me, to give me strength. But she doesn't completely regain consciousness, and I decide that's okay. I don't think I could look into her eyes and tell her goodbye. I'm sure she feels the same.

When her skin becomes increasingly cool and mottled, and her breathing turns more irregular, I know we're close. Alice warned me not to panic. It's harder than I thought.

Dad clasps my shoulder.

The mothers softly cry.

Carmen and Manny start chanting in Spanish. A prayer, I assume.

"I am so proud of you, Laurel," I tell her. "You fought so bravely, so fiercely. You were a gallant warrior, and you gave it your all, as you did everything in life."

In that moment I remember the story Laurel told me the first night I made to love her. About how she held Esther's hand and told her it was okay to let go even though she didn't mean it. If a twelve-year-old can be that selfless, surely I can too.

Uncaring that we're not alone, I crawl into bed with Laurel. Spooning behind her, I hold her chilled body against mine. Her breathing has slowed considerably now, and I swear I feel her relax into me. Instinctually I know we don't have long.

I lower my voice and whisper what she needs from me.

"I love you, mi amada. You are the very light of my life. I

don't know what I'm going to do tomorrow when I wake up and you're not here, but I'm going to figure it out. It's okay. It's okay to go now." That hurt like a motherfucking two-ton boulder pinning me to a bed of box cutters. "Tell our baby girl that daddy loves her. Catch a walleye with your PooPa. Lie under the maples with Esther and watch whirlers fall. I will be fine until we are together again. It's okay," I assure her. I keep repeating this quietly. "It's okay. It's okay. It's okay." If I say it enough maybe I'll believe it too.

Laurel's fingers and legs twitch, which is more movement than she's had in nearly twenty-four hours.

And then a miracle of miracles happens.

She opens her eyes.

They latch onto mine. I swear they do. They focus. I know she knows it's me.

"Hello, my love." I cup her cheek and stroke skin that's so cold it chills me. "I'm here."

She doesn't blink. Her pupils don't swell. Her lips don't turn. The anxiety in the room is tangible. Everyone wants their opportunity to say goodbye, yet they gift it to me, not intruding. And I will look back on our last moment together always believing she heard it.

"It has been an honor to have been loved by you, Laurel." *Is that a tear?* My God, I can barely breathe. She has a tear. "I love you. My heart will be yours for all of my days and nights, every second in between, and every second after." I kiss her chastely on the lips, whispering, "It's okay to rest now if you want. It's okay."

We gaze at each other for a few more slow beats of her heart. She uses the last of her energy to hang on, for me. I can't stop crying.

Then she closes her eyes and gasps.

Everyone quiets.

She gasps again.

You could hear a pin drop.
She gasps a third and final time.
We wait, but she doesn't make another sound.
She is gone.
My Laurel is gone.

EPILOGUE

HEAVEN

Dear Readers ~

I promised you I'd meet you at the end of our story, and so here we are. It was a rough ride, I know. It was rough for me as well. I have no doubt you fell in love with Laurel as much as I did, and that you are mourning her loss almost as deeply as I am. Laurel was one of a kind, don't you agree?

You probably never gave up hope that a miracle would be waiting for us, and in truth, I never gave up hope either. While we accepted Laurel had to leave us, there was no amount of time that could prepare us. Her death was a grievous, painful blow. One I have never quite recovered from.

You may feel robbed, or you may be cursing about how unfair life is, much as I did, but I would tell you that it's okay. Grief is the souvenir of a great love, and I hope you are as fortunate as I have been to have the greatest of the great in your life too. You see, my hope in sharing our set of time stamps with you isn't for you to see how Laurel died, for we all die. It is to witness how Laurel *lived*.

Make everyday a Tuesday. Dance under the moonlight. Stargaze. Watch fireflies. Learn a new hobby. Recite your favorite movie. Mourn your losses. Mend broken fences.

Die while you are living, the way she did.

I had ten wonderful years with Laurel. It was more than some, far less than others. What we shared, for the briefest of time we shared it, was beautiful and extraordinary. She was my perfection. She was mi amada, as I was hers.

I can truthfully say I have been blessed. I have lived a full and happy life. Some days are harder than others, of course. There is not a morning I wake that I don't look at the empty side of my bed without stark longing for those puddles of mud. There is not an evening I turn out the light that I don't yearn for the warmth of her body nestled against mine.

Laurel has been gone from my life for thirty-nine years now. Thirty-nine summer solstices without my love, my partner, my companion, my lover, my best friend. If you're trying to do the math, let me help you: I am now seventy-eight, and my time has finally come to an end. I get to go home to be reunited with my love. My Laurel.

Death comes for us all. That's a given, inevitable, the cycle of life. And my friends, I am ready. But before we bid each other adieu, if you'd indulge a dying old man a final wish, I'd like to share one last chapter with you. A remarkable, unexpected set of stamps I never thought would be part of my collection. These have not only completed it, they have made my life whole. Laurel was true to her word. She found me again in the most unexpected of ways.

Meet Esther.

~ Roth Warren Keswick

"You look like shit."

I don't reply. I give Manny my back and make my way over to the couch. I throw myself on it, staring at the picture of me and Laurel in the moonlight at Cape Cod, which rests on the mantle. I choke up. I register the faint snick of the front door closing, but Manny's whistle is loud and shrilling. And fucking judgmental.

"Wow. When is the last time you took a dust rag to the place?"

He's being overly kind. I'm ashamed to say he picks up a few empty fifths of vodka and takes them into the kitchen. He's trying to shove them in the garbage, but it's full. I know because that's why the empties are lying around the living room in the first place. That, and I don't particularly care. No one to impress.

The fridge door opens and closes.

"No Red Bull?"

Red Bull? That shit keeps you awake. I don't want to be awake. I want to sleep and never gain consciousness.

Manny speaks in a low voice in a short, one-sided conversation, and I half wonder if he's called my mother. My parents left four days ago after I told them I was okay. In retrospect, I'm not sure that was a good decision on my part or theirs.

It has been three weeks since I put my wife in the cold, hard, dank ground. Twenty-one days. Five hundred and four hours. Thirty thousand two hundred and forty minutes. I don't know how many seconds. Each one is more agonizing than the previous one. I need to stop counting. I wish I would stop breathing.

"When is the last time you showered, bro?"

When my mother made me. That would be funny if it weren't true.

"What are you doing about work?"

Work? Breathing is work. Living is work. Making it from the bed to the couch is fucking work.

Manny peppers me with a few more questions, "When was the last time you ate?" "Did your parents make it home okay?" "Did you know you're out of trash bags?" before he gives up and busies himself picking up my mess in quiet. And I let him, unashamed, uncaring. Then he sits in the chair to my right and joins me in stilted silence. We stay that way for a long, long time. Or maybe it's only seconds. Doesn't matter much.

"You know," Manny says carefully, almost as if he's had some sort of epiphany, "Laurel wouldn't want to see you this way."

A thousand and one snide comments snap across my tongue, but the one with the biggest bite is, *Laurel isn't here, is she?*

Only, I don't say it, because while it may be true, it's still far too agonizing to give it sound. And if I say those words out loud, then that gives her death finality. It means I'll never see her sweep through the front door again. I'll never hear her snort when she laughs or go behind her picking up used tissues. Logically, I know I won't anyway, but...

I am lost. Utterly, painfully adrift without her. A limb may as well have been chopped from my body. Hell, all of them may as well be gone. That's how I feel...like an amputee with phantom limb pain that will never subside.

Though Manny is right...Laurel wouldn't want this. She told me to grieve, but she also begged me to live. I don't know how to do that. I don't know how to honor her deathbed wishes by moving on with a life that was supposed to include her but no longer will.

I simply don't.

———

"Uncle Roth!" tiny voices scream in unison moments before I have a monkey hanging from each leg.

"Hey, hey, careful," I chuckle, trying to balance a gift in each hand without toppling over. Who knew two six-year-olds could wield so much momentum?

"You came!" Sofia yells up at me, head flung all the way back. Her round toffee eyes are alight with joy. She's going to be a heartbreaker, that one.

"Of course, I came. I wouldn't miss it for the world."

"Look." Lucia yanks on the bottom of my cargo shorts. "I lost a tooth." She pulls her lower lip down to the bottom of her chin, exposing the empty space where a baby tooth used to be. The permanent one is barely peeking through the gumline.

"Mine is loose," Sofia announces, trying to compete with her twin. She wiggles the same tooth back and forth that Lucia is now missing. It looks as though it's hanging on by a thread.

"It'd be out by now if she'd just let me give it a little twist," Manny says, stepping into the foyer.

"No way, Papa!" Sofia shrieks, running out of the room with both hands slapped across her mouth. Lucia takes off after her, calling her a chicken. I hear Carmen tell the girls to be nice.

"Thanks for coming."

Manny takes the gifts I'm holding. I follow him into the dining room where he sets them on a long table. It's already overflowing with birthday packages for the girls.

"Why is everyone surprised that I'm here?" I grumble, irritated.

"Because you've been pretty antisocial."

He's not wrong. I think I've been out a handful of times since Laurel died. But being around other people, especially those who are happy, only makes that black hole Laurel left feel wider and emptier.

"My wife died."

Manny pins me with stoic regard, ignoring my cutting snarl. "It's been almost a year, Roth."

My hackles rise. If this is the way today is going to go, I'm outta here.

"Don't tell me to move on, man. That will never happen."

"And I would never say it." He looks me up and down, head to toe. "What I am saying, though, is that Laurel would hate this."

This.

He doesn't need to expand.

I know how I look. My hair desperately needs a cut. I'm now sporting a beard, but it is not trimmed and tight. It is shaggy and unruly. My shirt hangs from my thin shoulders and I'm not gonna lie...my shorts are held up by a belt that needs another hole punched in it. Hell, some may even compare me to a homeless man who was lured out from under the Jefferson Street Bridge by the Bridge Ministry for a hot meal. The heavy trials of life are carved into the sharp edges of my face. You can tell I've been through shit and that I've let it best me.

I'm not proud. In fact, I am ashamed of how far I've let myself slide.

Biting the inside of my cheek, I swing my gaze to the kitchen. Carmen is watching, listening. Worry lines frame her compressed lips. The girls have long gone outside where the party is being held. Through the window I watch them laugh and sprint around the yard, playing tag with several other girls. They are so full of life and wonder. So carefree. They remind me of all I will miss.

"Duly noted."

"Beer?"

I don't want one, but I also don't want any more shit. "Sure."

We mosey to the kitchen where Carmen kisses me on the cheek, whispering, "It's nice to see you," before handing me a Corona. I stare at it and am yanked back to the night Laurel and I sat under the stars in Moab, drinking by the light of the campfire. My chest feels heavy.

"How are you?" I ask her, taking a deep swig from my bottle. It's bitter and it hangs out on my tongue too long.

"Oh...you know."

I know.

Do I ever.

An unexpected pang of guilt hits me suddenly and harshly. I

have spent very little time with Manny and Carmen in the last several months. To be honest, it's hard to be around them. I have so many memories intertwined with the four of us, it's impossible to separate the two. But I know they are grieving also.

"Anything I can help with?"

"Absolutely not. You go enjoy yourself." She pats me on the forearm. Dismissed.

All I can give her is a wry smile. We both know I won't be enjoying anything. But hey, I'm here and at least that's one step more than I took yesterday or the day before it.

"Roth," Carmen calls after me when I've started walking away.

"Yeah?"

"Uh, can I talk to you about something first?" She sucks on her top lip and bounces from one foot to another. Carmen is always a force to be reckoned with, and this nervousness is so unlike her that I get an incredibly uneasy feeling.

"Sure."

"I don't really know how to start this."

"Just say it," I nudge, wondering what in the hell has her so outside herself.

She picks up a bag of chips and moves it two inches, setting it down again.

"Carmen, spit it out."

"Laurel wanted me to carry your baby," she blurts.

What. The. Actual. *Fuck?*

"What?"

"Laurel wanted me to carry your baby," she repeats, as if I didn't hear her clearly the first time. I did. I just don't understand it.

I am stunned. Bowled over from left field. Completely blindsided.

"Say something."

Say something? What the fuck do I say to that?

"When she got home after your trip to MD Anderson...after her..." She stops and swallows. "She asked me if I would be willing to be a surrogate."

My body takes over, my head vehemently shaking long before I spit, "No."

I am trembling, almost uncontrollably. Laurel had this conversation with Carmen but not with me? I don't believe it.

"Roth."

"No," I spew venomously.

"It's what she wanted."

"It's what *she* wanted? What about *me*, Carmen? What about what *I* wanted? What I want? I want my wife, dammit! I want *her* to carry our child, to be a mother, to grow old with me, but what I want doesn't matter now, does it?"

I want to destroy things. Anything. Everything.

"Roth," she pleads.

"Not another word, Carmen." I hang my head and breathe long, slow breaths, anger building at an astonishing rate.

"Just think—"

"Not. Another. Word," I grit through clenched teeth.

I should have left then. If my brain wasn't scrambled from this bizarre, wholly unexpected conversation I would have. Instead, I make a beeline for the patio door. There are a few other parents there, mostly paired in the couples I know them to be. I can't even conjure up a pang that should be there because...

I am numb.

What Carmen said has deafened me like a ten-decibel alarm.

"Laurel wanted me to carry your baby."

I can't even wrap my head around that.

Manny is lounging in a lawn chair, beer in hand. He's chatting with a woman whom I've not seen before. She is by herself.

"Hey," he says, nodding at the empty seat beside her.

I take it but not before sliding my chair over a good two feet. If she thinks I'm rude, so be it.

"Roth, this is Sarah."

"Sarah." I give her a stiff nod and sit down, trying to clear these muddled shades of red clouding my vision. How dare Carmen spring this on me now, here.

"Hello." Her eyes dart shyly to the ground, then back to mine, and the warning bell peals.

"Sarah just moved into the neighborhood. Her and her daughter, Meghan," Manny tells me.

That's it.

I'm done.

Maybe this is a setup. Maybe it's entirely innocent. Maybe her husband was accidentally left off the introductory checklist. Regardless, I don't intend to sit here and make idle chitchat with Sarah about how my wife died from cancer at the young of thirty-eight or how Carmen just offered to be a surrogate or how I feel accomplished if I can manage to put on fresh underwear daily.

I am halfway out of my seat when Lucia comes barreling toward me. "Uncle Roth," she squeals. She jumps into my arms and I end up falling back into the chair with her in my lap.

"What, beauty?" I choke out. She throws her arms around me and I bury my head next to hers, hanging on to this little girl with every shred of sanity I have left. It's a thin, thin line, believe me. Almost anything could snap it in two.

"You're not leaving, are you?"

I am. I can't stay. How can I explain this swirling sphere of agony I have become to a six-year-old?

"Of course not," I lie.

"I missed you," she says against the shell of my ear.

"I've missed you too, nugget." I have ignored my sweet, innocent goddaughters in favor of self-pity. I don't deserve their adoration.

She hangs on for a minute, her grip on me tightening. Then she says, "Auntie Laurel came to visit me last night," so quietly it takes a moment to register. My eyes instantly burn, and I struggle to hold my shit together.

"Did she?"

She yanks herself back so she can look into my watery eyes. "Yeah," she tells me excitedly. "She wished me happy birthday. She wanted to be here."

I can't speak. She didn't do anything of the sort. Only, how can I break Lucia's spirit the way mine is broken? If she believes this happened, as painful as it is to hear, I need to listen. I owe her that much.

"And she told me..." Lucia's gaze darts all around us. She leans in closer, dropping her voice to a hush. "She told me to tell you something."

In an instant, it's as if someone has unplugged me from an outlet that's been keeping me alive for the past year. Every ounce of energy is gone. I feel dusty and barren. And even this six-year-old is intuitive enough to know I'm a hairsbreadth away from crumbling into a pile of ash right here.

"Do you want to hear?"

I don't believe Laurel came to visit Lucia any more than I believe the Tooth Fairy put four quarters under my pillow when I lost a tooth. But I find myself waiting with bated breath anyway. Swallowing past a ball of emotion, I try to paste on a smile, but it's weak and shaky at best.

Lucia leans forward to cup her hands around my ear.

When I reflect back on this moment in the years to come, the one that ultimately put my future squarely back into focus, what I will remember is a six-year-old's selflessness, where I had none. She is also grieving Laurel's death, but her faith is what carried me beyond what is to what could be.

It is because of Lucia that I have my Esther.

And I will never forget it.

"Almost there," the doctor in white scrubs coaches. She is so calm. How can she be so damn calm?

"Ahhhhhhhhh," Carmen screams. And I mean screams. It's so much worse than on TV or in the movies. It is a bloodcurdling, horror film, I-am-coming-after-you-with-a-sharp-knife-when-this-is-over howl of pure, unadulterated agony.

Good God Almighty.

I can't believe the human race has survived this.

"You're doing great, babe," Manny encourages, brushing a sweat-stuck strand of hair away from her brow. She releases her death grip on the bedsheet and throws her hand in the air, where she clasps it with Manny's. All twenty-seven bones may be crushed under her vise before this is over. If he's in pain, he's containing it remarkably well. Without a doubt, he knows better than to say anything.

While I'm out of the melee, standing in a corner to give Carmen her privacy, it's strange to be in this room witnessing the buzz of a private, yet remarkably beautiful occasion. I belong, but I don't. I was invited, yet I'm an interloper, a voyeur.

In my dreams, this happens under far different circumstances. Only this is not a dream. This is truly happening. Without my wife.

The longing I still have for Laurel hasn't abated, not an ounce. I physically ache without her some days. Today is one of those days. But what has changed is that it's far easier now to let the good memories in...and to allow them to linger. It's not enough, it could never be enough, but it's what I have. I told my mother the other day that it was like opening a window in a stuffy house, allowing fresh air to push out the mustiness. I realized that I control that window and I'm getting better at using it. I have it open a lot.

"One more big push, Carmen. One more."

Manny's eyes dart up, connecting with mine. *This is it,* they say. My heart races, beating wildly against the walls of my chest. This is it.

I am terrified. I am exhilarated. Mostly I'm terrified.

I've waffled on this life-altering decision so many times. The responsibility of it is enormous. Daunting. But Lucia's words, they haunted me day and night for weeks and months on end. Then one day, nineteen months after Laurel's death, I received another sign...and then the pieces started falling into place from there.

Walking through the door, I throw my car keys on the counter. Meringue swims around my ankles, purring, probably hungry. "Me too," I tell her. I reach down to give her a scratch and she meows at me and takes off. She's not been the same since Laurel's death. I can relate.

Flipping on the kitchen light, I throw the mail on the counter. I pour a scoop of cat food into Meringue's bowl and check the fridge for leftovers.

A dried piece of pepperoni pizza and two slices of American cheese.

A grilled cheese sandwich it is, then.

Minutes later, my buttered bread is sizzling when I notice the return address on one of the envelopes. I push the other mail aside, tear open the end, and stare at it for long minutes. So long I burn my grilled cheese and set off the fire alarm. So long I miss dinner altogether.

Dear Mrs. Keswick,

This is to inform you that your embryos will be sent to us for long-

term storage from The Center for Reproductive Health in Nashville, TN. Before we take your samples, we need to get the storage length and payment information from you. I have enclosed a form you may fill out and return to us at your earliest convenience. If you have questions, please contact us at the below number.

Thank you,

Cryoton Labs

Eventually, I set the letter aside on the kitchen counter, appetite gone, and go to bed. I don't sleep a wink. Next day is a repeat. And the day after that. And the day after that. I do this same thing week after week. The letter never moves. All the while, Carmen's offer and Lucia's "dream" plague me even more relentlessly than they did before.

As if all of these aren't enough signs from Laurel, I stumbled across one more. The final push I guess I needed.

"Where did you find this?" Carmen asks, looking up from the letter to me. Her face is wet. Her bottom lip is quivering.

"In the back of her nightstand drawer. I was searching for the thermometer, actually." I hadn't been in Laurel's drawer since the last days before she died. I haven't been through any of her things, for that matter.

She passes it to Manny for him to read. I watch him, choking back waterworks of my own when I see two droplets fall from his eyes to the paper.

"Did Lucia ever tell you about her dream?" I ask them.

"What dream?" Carmen replies.

"About Laurel."

"What?" Guess that's a no. "Did she tell you?" Manny turns to his wife. She shakes her head. "When was this?"

"The day of their sixth birthday party."

"She dreamt about Laurel?" Carmen asks me. I nod. "What was the dream about?"

I tell the long and short of what I thought was the imagination only a child could conjure. Now, I'm wondering if it didn't actually happen. I think it might have. "And then she cupped her hands over my ear and told me to remember Esther."

"Remember Esther?" they both reply in unison. Again, I nod. Their eyes immediately fall to the letter written in Laurel's beautifully neat script.

"I know. I can't believe it myself. You know her sister, Esther, died when she was twelve years old, right?"

"Yes," Carmen answers solemnly. She's dumbfounded by this unbelievable story, same as I still am.

"Laurel and I had talked about Esther a lot, of course. And I thought maybe the girls had overheard us or you two talking about her. That's how I thought Lucia knew the name. But that dream and now this. I know Laurel wrote this before we lost..." The words stick in my throat. It's still hard to say. "Before we lost the baby. But it all feels too coincidental. Laurel wanted this. She..." I can't believe I'm about to say this. "She still does."

Their attention goes back to the letter. They reread it. Having memorized each and every word, I mentally follow along.

Hey you,

Yes you, in there, my firstborn child. I am feeling many, many things as I write this letter to you. Gratitude. Joy. Anticipation. Impatience. Trepidation. It's surreal and scary and exciting. You have no idea how long I have waited for you or how very much you are wanted. There were so many times along the way that I didn't think you were possible. We went through so much to get to this day, your daddy and me. Every step and every tear have been more than worth it. And here you are, growing inside of me. You're a miracle, mi amada...my beloved.

Though there have been so many ups and downs where you are concerned, I knew from an early age that I wanted to be a mother. When I was seven, I got a Baby Alive for Christmas. She would wet her diaper when you fed her a bottle. I loved that doll. I named her Betty Wetty. I know, it's lacking in imagination, but that was never my strong suit. I carried Betty Wetty everywhere I went. She slept on my pillow with me at night. I pushed her in a plastic stroller around the yard. She sat with me at the dinner table. She played with me in the bathtub. I even put her in my backpack when I went to school. And of course, I would feed and change her. I nurtured and cared for Betty Wetty as if she were real. And it only reaffirmed my calling to be a mother.

But several years later my sister died in a tragic accident. Esther, she was more than just my sister, baby girl. She was my twin. She was my best friend, my coconspirator. She was a part of me as much as I was of her. When we went to bed at night, I'd tell her she was my heart, and she'd tell me I was her soul. This was figurative of course, but when she died, it felt literal. It's as if my heart stopped beating.

Esther was luminous. That is the best way I can describe her. She loved bubble gum and could do a mean Hula-Hoop. She mastered riding a bike months before I could, but she never made fun of me. She brought home stray animals every week, I swear. Animals were her Betty Wetty. She was double-jointed and could turn her elbow almost 360 degrees. I thought it was as cool as it was disgusting. Esther ate it up when everyone cringed. She once snuck one of our mother's cigarettes and we smoked it in our treehouse. We were both sick as dogs and got grounded for a month. I wish you could have met her, my sweet girl. You would have adored her as much I did.

I mourned the loss of my sister deeply, but her death had a far more profound effect on my mother. I watched grief eat her alive. It changed who she was as a person and as a mother. She became cynical and cold and completely withdrew from life. And it was then I swore I wouldn't bear *the same pain she did. I threw Betty Wetty in the trash and didn't give her a second thought.*

But then I met your daddy, and he gave me back the faith that I had lost and helped me dust off the dream of you that I had shelved. Your daddy is extraordinary, mi amada. I love him in ways I didn't think possible. He is the most wonderful human being I know. I could gush on and on, using dozens more adjectives, but you will soon find out for yourself how amazing he is, and I want you to experience that gift of discovering it for yourself.

We love you so much already. It's hard to explain how much, really. My mother used to tell me that it's impossible to fathom how much you can love another person until you have your own child. At the time, I didn't understand what she meant.

Now I do.

And for the first time, I truly comprehend the depth of her loss because if I lost you…well, let's just say for the first time I understand my mother. It's been eye-opening to say the least.

I think the lesson I have learned is that love is the greatest gift we can give and receive in return, no matter the length of time we're allowed to give or receive it. Love transcends loss, not the other way around. And I'd like to honor the person who taught me that.

So, while I still need to talk it over with your daddy, I think he will agree that there is only one suitable name for you…

I think we shall call you Esther.

You will be loved like no one has been loved before, Esther; of that I promise you. I can't wait to meet you. We can't wait.

I love you so so and then more

Your Mommy

———

"So…" I clear the muck from my throat. Manny hands Laurel's letter to our baby back to me. I rub the edges, worn already. "I know I've been a shit friend since Laurel died and I don't deserve the right to even ask but...is the offer still on the table? It's okay if you've changed your—"

"Roth. Stop."

I do. My heart sinks. I'd just gotten my head around this idea and I'm surprised at how disappointed I am that it could be snagged out from underneath me.

Carmen bursts out of her chair and comes to sit at my feet. Her eyes are wet. "I haven't changed my mind, Roth. I want to do this for you and for Laurel. Laurel never asked for a thing. When she did, you knew it was important. And this, she asked of me. It's such a small gesture—"

"It's not," I interrupt. "It's monumental."

"In the scheme of what she did for others, it's not." She clears her throat. "I loved Laurel like a sister. I would be honored to do this one last thing for her."

"It won't be the last thing you do for her. If this works, I'll need help. I can't do this on my own." I'm not even sure I can do it at all.

She snickers. "Like I would let you."

"We," Manny pipes in. "Like *we* would let you."

"We," Carmen corrects. "You don't get to choose your blood, but you do get to choose your family. And you and Laurel will always be mine. And your baby."

"So that's a yes?" I smirk when she calls me an idiot in Spanish, then slugs me in the arm. "Thank you, Carmen."

"Don't thank me again."

I will. Many times over.

"Are you sure you're okay with this, Manny?"

I'm not only asking the world of Carmen, but I am also asking the world of my best friend. Carrying a baby that's not his? That's a tremendous sacrifice.

"My wife is incredibly sexy when she's pregnant." He snags Carmen's hand in his and nibbles on her fingers before she yanks it back, chastising him.

We spend the next few hours talking through specifics and doing some research. Laurel and I only have two viable embryos left and unfortunately, I know how these things go. The chances of an in vitro pregnancy taking are roughly 66 percent. They go up with more embryos implanted, but so does the risk. We debate the merits of both options, much like Laurel and I did, and ultimately, I decide that I only have the stomach to do this one time.

Five months later, after a clean bill of health, the required mental evaluations and the transfer cycle process Carmen had to undergo, both embryos were implanted and one of them took.

Carmen was pregnant.

"Push!" the doctor coaxes, concentrating solely on her task at hand.

Carmen responds with a grunt and more keening. She swears in multiple languages. I hear my name used several times. It's kind of funny, though I don't dare laugh.

Then, the air in the room shifts. The doctor gets serious. The nurses pick up the intensity of their activities. And though I'm sure Carmen's viewpoint will differ substantially from mine, as suddenly as all of this began, it's over.

Carmen's wails morph into choppy, ecstatic, almost manic fits of laughter. She flops against the bed in a drenched twist of exhaustion. Manny sets his forehead to hers and they both close their eyes. The moment is so intimate, so ripe with love and devotion, I have to turn away from it. That agony of wishing this scene were Laurel and me gathers strength, threatening to over-whelm me. I have the urge to run.

What in the hell was I thinking? How can I do this without her?

I can't.

I can't.

I take two steps toward the door, and that's when I hear her for the first time.

My daughter.

Laurel's daughter.

Our daughter.

I want to drop to my knees and weep.

"She's got a good set of lungs on her," the young blond nurse named Kaitlyn tells me.

Does she? I don't see how that can be a good thing.

"Apgar score is nine," another nurse calls out.

Nine? Nine out of what?

"Nine is good," Manny tells me, slapping me on the back. "Stop looking so worried. Congratulations, Papa."

"Yeah," I mutter. "Papa."

Holy shit.

I am a father.

I can't believe it.

I am bombarded by a dozen emotions hitting me from all directions. Shock. Terror. Disbelief. Excitement. Apprehension. Gratitude. Most notably, though, is awe. As I watch them clip the umbilical cord, clean her off, and put an identification band around her ankle, I am hypnotized by her already. She's so small, so fragile.

They put some drops in her eyes, lay her on a small scale, and take a few measurements before wrapping her up like an enchilada. She's still crying when they place her in my arms, and when they do...I finally understand the full spectrum of love, just as Laurel described in her letter.

It's incredible. Life-changing.

"Meet your new daughter, Mr. Keswick," Kaitlyn says with a soft smile.

"Esther," I correct her, so choked up I almost can't speak. "Esther Laurel Lucia Keswick."

"That's a beautiful name."

"After three beautiful souls." My gaze catches Carmen's. Her eyes are red, swollen, and waterlogged. "Thank you," I tell her. How do you adequately thank the woman who gave your child life? Impossible.

"You're welcome," she mouths back.

I stare at my beautiful daughter, stupefied. With tufts of dark hair and the dent in her chin, she looks exactly like her mother. I don't even try to stem the tears from rolling down my cheeks. She is precious. Perfection. I wish Laurel could see her. I think maybe she does.

I walk over to Carmen. "Would you like to hold her?"

She hesitates. "You should let her grandmothers hold her first."

Candice is on her way and my parents are right outside, waiting on news of her birth. When they found out that Carmen was pregnant with their only grandchild, they immediately put their house on the market and bought a condo two miles away from me. Between them, Candice, Carmen, and Manny, this little girl will be loved and spoiled and revered above no other. It won't replace Laurel's absence, because that's a hole that will go forever unfilled, but I hope it will come close for Esther's sake.

"Carmen." I slip Esther into her arms. "You have given my daughter life, and as her godmother, you will be an integral part of hers. Hold her. Love her the way Laurel would want you to."

"I already do, mi amada," she coos to Esther. "I already do."

The End

MUSICAL INSPIRATIONS

In case you didn't figure it out or weren't paying much attention...each chapter heading in *Time Stamps* is a song title that the chapter is inspired by.

- Prologue: "Let Me Hold You" by Josh Krajcik
- Chapter 1: "Haven't Met You Yet" by Michael Bublé
- Chapter 2: "Nice To Meet Ya" by Niall Horan
- Chapter 3: "Today Was A Fairytale" by Taylor Swift
- Chapter 4: "She's Got a Way" by Billy Joel
- Chapter 5: "Just A Kiss" by Lady A
- Chapter 6: "Happy" by C2C, Derek Martin
- Chapter 7: "The One" by Kodaline
- Chapter 8: "Feels Like Letting Go" by Matthew Perryman Jones
- Chapter 9: "Tuesdays" by Jake Scott
- Chapter 10: "Songbird" by Fleetwood Mac
- Chapter 11: "Some King of Love" by The Killers
- Chapter 12: "Tenerife Sea" by Ed Sheeran
- Chapter 13: "I Could Not Ask for More" by Edwin McCain
- Chapter 14: "At Last" by Etta James
- Chapter 15: "I'm Gonna Be (500 Miles)" by The Proclaimers
- Chapter 16: "Single Ladies (Put a Ring on It)" by Beyoncé
- Chapter 17: "A Safe Place to Land" by Sara Bareilles, John Legend
- Chapter 18: "Angel" by Sarah McLachlan
- Chapter 19: "Gravity" by John Mayer
- Chapter 20: "Autumn Leaves" by Ed Sheeran
- Chapter 21: "A Sky Full of Stars" by Coldplay

- Chapter 22: "Escape (The Pina Colada Song)" by Rupert Holmes
- Chapter 23: "Grow Old With Me" by Tom Odell
- Chapter 24: "Don't Forget About Me" by CLOVES
- Chapter 25: "Sorry Seems To Be The Hardest Word" by Elton John
- Chapter 26: "Never Stop" by Safety Suit
- Chapter 27: "Brighter Side of Grey" by Five Finger Death Punch
- Chapter 28: "I'll Follow You" by Shinedown
- Epilogue: "Heaven" by Apollo LTD

Other musical inspirations referenced:

- "Crazy" by Gnarls Barkley
- "Nothing Like You" by Dave Barnes
- "Llegaste Tú" by Luis Fonsi, Juan Luis Guerra
- "24K Magic" by Bruno Mars
- "Slow an' Easy" by Whitesnake
- "Brave" by Sara Bareilles
- "Right Here Waiting" by Richard Marx
- "Count on Me" by Bruno Mars
- "Under Pressure" by Queen, David Bowie
- "Hungry Eyes" by Eric Carmen
- "Your Body Is A Wonderland" by John Mayer

You can also find the *Time Stamps* playlist on Spotify using the below QR Code.

MUSICAL INSPIRATIONS

OTHER WORKS

Interested in a *Time Stamps* swag box, containing a signed paperback, an insulated wine cup (for your tears), a journal and many other fun items? Or perhaps the alternate hardback cover of *Time Stamps*? Or maybe simply a signed paperback of *Time Stamps* or any other works? Order here or check out my store at klkreig.com.

Other works by K. L. Kreig, all of which can be found at Amazon: amazon.com/author/klkreig or through my website at klkreig.com

Finding Me Duet:
  Lost In Between (Book 1)
  Found Underneath (Book 2)

"KL Kreig nailed it! The perfect, heart stopping ending to a fantastic duet, Found Underneath is everything you hope it will be and so much more!" ~ KL Grayson, USA Today Bestselling Author

"Forget Christian Grey, forget Gideon Cross, forget Jesse Ward, ... Shaw Mercer is it for me!" ~ reader Ana Rente

Black Swan Affair (*Standalone*)

"OMG what did I just read? This book... WOW!! It's been years since I read a book straight through. Yes, seven hours I was glued to the pages of this book. A yo-yo of emotions that left me breathless with every scene. *Black Swan Affair* is a must read!!" ~ Nashoda Rose, NYT and USA Today Bestselling Author

"I was rapt from the first page, consumed by its every word, and I still cannot stop thinking about it. This rare gem of a story is a top recommendation from me." ~ Natasha is a Book Junkie

The Colloway Brothers series:

Finding Gray (FREE)
Forsaking Gray
Undeniably Asher
Luke's Absolution
Destination Connelly

"This series is absolutely amazing. Brilliant. Intense. Passionate. Suspenseful. K. L. Kreig really brought her all when she introduced us to the Colloway brothers." ~ **Renee Entress's Blog**

"The Colloway brothers are some of the most swoon-worthy, panty-soaking, endearingly flawed men in contemporary romance today. They are full of grit, intelligence, and sex appeal that will leave you breathless and begging for more." ~ **Rachel Caid, Author of the Finding Home series**

The **Regent Vampire Lords** series:

Surrendering
Belonging
Reawakening
Evading

"If you like J. R. Ward, Sherrilyn Kenyon, or Kresley Cole, you'll love K. L. Kreig. This series just got even better! Books like these are the reason we, the reviewer, should be able to give six stars!" ~ L. A. Wild, Author, Chance The Darkness

"This author has done it again. I was captivated and transported into the story right from the first chapter. A truly fantastic vampire book with romance, suspense, twists and turns, keeping you on the edge of your seat all the way through." ~ Hooked on Books Forever Bookblog

BOOK BABBLES

Babbles...

As always, this is unedited, so overlook the typos and punctuation errors, please.

Gosh, where to start...

Writing is a lonely journey. It's just you, your characters and a blank page, which you hope and pray ends with a story that touches someone somehow. This book, more than any other I've written was an incredibly solitary voyage and very personal to me. It's been FOUR YEARS since I published a full-length novel. FOUR freaking YEARS. A lot in my life has changed in that time. Almost everything, in fact. In those four years, I feel as though I've changed as a person and an author. If you've read my other works maybe you think the same thing, because this was a definite departure from my usual. But that's generally what I do...I try not to follow the troops too closely. I like forging my own path, being my own person. One thing you can usually count on, is that I am not a cookie-cutter author and I'm proud of that fact.

I was actually in the middle of another book (which will be published next!) when this one hit me like a punch to the gut, winding me. I had three chapters written in a record time and knew I needed to shift gears to Roth and Laurel's story. *Time Stamps* is heavy and ends unconventionally, I admit, but if you understood that the idea came from a personal health scare (not mine, but my husband's) would that make it easier? Thankfully, he is okay, yet it got me to thinking...what would *I* want my last few months to look like? How would *I* want to be remembered for navigating a challenge so daunting it would cripple even the best of us?

It came down to one simple thing, and it's not how many assets I've accumulated, or which rung on the corporate ladder I'm currently hanging on or how many likes my Facebook or Instagram posts get. It's the love I leave behind. It's the memories I gift others of me. It's my legacy as a human being, a mother, a wife, a grandmother, a sister, a daughter, a friend. How will *you* be remembered? Because there will be a day (I hope in your very distant future), that you're not here anymore. *That* is the purpose of this book. Do you have changes you need to make in your own life? Fences to mend that are giving you splinters? It's something to think about, isn't it? Reflection can be a powerful tool if you let it .

I'd like to promise you my next novel will not be as angsty, but if you've read my other works, you know that not to be true. #sorrynotsorry. With so many stories blending into the next, I only hope that once the tears dry, you'll be able to say: while I wish it ended differently, *this* is a book I will never forget.

One more final note: you have my sister to thank for the Epilogue. She insisted that I didn't rip her heart out entirely. I think Esther and I accomplished that. Thanks Tara!! I couldn't ask for a better sissy.

Friends, family, bloggers, authors, betas, influencers, and most importantly MY READERS: if you supported me in any way, shape, or form, you know who you are and you know I thank you from the bottom of my heart. I am nothing but sincerely, eternally grateful for your belief in me. Every message and each e-mail I get from someone who wanted to personally reach out and praise me for how my work touched them in some way is *truly* a surreal feeling and *that's* why I do this. Because you all encourage me. For that, I thank you.

For the love of God...help an author out! LEAVE A REVIEW on Goodreads, or wherever you purchased this book. Even one or two sentences or simply rating the book is helpful for other readers. Reviews are critical to getting a book exposure in this vast sea of great reads.

COMING SOON: TINY PAPER AIRPLANES
(Note: Content is unedited and subject to change)

Chapter 1

Fifteen years earlier

I eye the nondescript clock hanging above the door with large numbers and an aggravatingly slow second hand. Seconds tick like hours. Minutes like years. I drum my thumb against the worn wood of my desk in a quick tap, tap, tap, before bringing it to my mouth to bite a nail which is already ground to the nub.

Three more minutes. Three.

I breathe deep, excited. Edgy. Impatient.

Two minutes, forty-nine seconds.

Come on, come on, come on.

Mr. Kinneseck's rich voice drones on in the background, now white noise. I feel the vibrato of each long syllable, but I don't make out the words. I long ago tuned out my English teacher's discussion on *Twelfth Night*, unable to concentrate on this bizarre love triangle that I generally find incredibly disturbing, yet fascinating at the same time.

Two minutes, twenty-two seconds.

I spit out a nail fragment to the floor I managed to chew off.

This is torture. Pure, unfair torture.

"Ms. Bennett."

Two minutes, twelve seconds.

"Ms. Bennett."

The second hand stutters forward one tick and then jolts as if stuck in molasses. My breath whooshes out when it works its way free and continues around.

"Earth to Ms. Bennett."

A jolt against my chair as a shove from behind pushes me

forward on an oomph, involuntarily dragging my eyes from the timepiece. I pivot to give Billy Remmeny a piece of my mind but when my eyes land on him, his oval ones swivel between mine and to somewhere over my shoulder. Bushy brows that nearly touch in the middle arch in an obvious attempt to redirect my ire away from him.

It's only then I notice the boring lull of Mr. Kinneseck has quieted and that I may have heard my name called somewhere in the distance. A sweep over the room validates the gaze of everyone is on me, waiting.

I spin in my chair, forcing my eyes to my teacher versus that spot above the door that continues to mock me.

"Yes, sir?" I reply sweetly. Lacing my fingers together, I set them demurely on my desk and square my shoulders as I straighten my spine.

Mr. Kinneseck is former military. Army, if I remember right. He has a thing for being called sir. And for posture. We all know it. We all exploit it when it serves our purpose. And right now, it does because this is the third time during the hour and a half long class that I've been caught daydreaming about what awaits me afterward.

The smile that upturns Mr. Kinneseck's razor thin lips tells me he's onto my tactics. He is not amused.

"I said—"

The shrill shriek of a bell drowns out his reprimand and probably saves my ass from an extra assignment dissecting Shakespeare using rhetorical strategies. He doesn't have a chance to say anything else because twenty-eight bodies have popped up and started a dozen conversations at once. Even his deep, commanding voice has no chance over the melee of teenagers that have been held down under his tutelage for the last ninety minutes.

I scoop up my textbook, the tablet of extra wide ruled paper and three number two pencils and scurry out the door pretending I don't hear Mr. Kinneseck call my name behind me.

"What has your behind on fire?" Evie asks, catching up to me. She's breathing heavy.

"You can say ass, you know," I shoot over my shoulder, not slowing down my pace to answer my best friend. I power through a group of freshman girls gathered outside Mr. Potter's French class, uncaring that I knocked into two of them. Mr. Potter is the hottest teacher in Arlington High and hanging outside his door to get a glimpse of him between classes is a rite of passage. Somehow, I don't think he minds the attention.

"I know," Evie replies defensively, pumping her short legs to keep up with me.

Huh?

"You know what?" I round the hallway to my right, hugging the corner for maximum efficiency. Almost there.

"That I can say...*that* word."

"What word?" I have no idea what she's going on about. Don't care either. I lengthen my strides; fully aware seconds are ticking off double time now that I want them to slow down.

"You know."

I stop dead in my tracks and turn on Evie, irritated she's keeping me from what's become an anticipated ritual between third and fourth period over the past two months. "What do I know?"

Her face scrunches up. "That I can say it."

It?

"Good God Evie, what the hell are you blathering about?"

She throws her free hand in the air and it slaps against her thigh covered in Miss Me dark wash jeans. "Ass!" she yells in frustration. "I can say ass! Okay?"

A couple students skitter by, giggling at her outburst. We've also managed to garner the attention of Mrs. Granger, a cool, hippie art teacher, standing only ten feet away. I scrunch my face in confusion like I don't know what's happening either and she looks away, shaking her head.

"Okay," I answer evenly. "Good."

"Good? That's it?"

"What do you want? An engraved medal?"

I'm on the move again, Evie on my heels. I zero in on my target. My heartbeat kicks up ten beats per second.

"Some acknowledgement would be nice."

"You're acknowledged," I placate, hoping she'll get the hint and leave. I stop at my locker, 224, and rest my fingers anxiously on the lock. Evie leans her back against the neighboring one and waits. "You can go. I'll catch up."

"I can wait," she replies nonchalantly while examining her fingernails, clueless to my growing annoyance.

"No," I practically bark. Her over-plucked eyebrows crinkle in. "I mean, I need to hit the bathroom yet and I don't want us both to be late." I purposefully relax my stance and try to act cool.

Her gaze flits to my locker then back to me. She pushes herself straight and hugs her books to her chest. "I know you're keeping something from me."

"I'm not," I counter, squeezing the metal between my finger-tips tighter, feeling it heat under my touch. I itch to twist it twice to the right so I can start the process of opening it.

I'm going to be late to fourth period at this rate.

Again.

She smirks. "You're the master of efficiency. In fact, you make me sick with how well organized you are. It takes approximately three and a half minutes to get from English Lit to AP Trig. You always take your Trig textbook to English Lit because stopping at your locker takes an extra minute and a half, which leaves you with less than two minutes to use the bathroom." I start to refute but she mows right over me. "But for the past eight weeks, you've conveniently 'forgotten' your Trig book, so you'll have to stop back at your locker." She eyes it again. "Why?"

Damn her. I should have known I couldn't pull one over on Evie Fredericks. She's observant in an incredibly annoying way sometimes.

"I've just..." I sigh. Gig's up. Evie and I never lie to each other. "I'm not ready to tell you yet."

I want to keep this to myself just a little while longer.

Her chest expands, pushing the books pressed against her ample boobs toward me. "Okay, fine."

I wet my dry lips, then chew on the bottom one. "You're not mad?"

She shrugs, only one shoulder lifting. "No. Everyone's entitled to a secret now and again. I know you'll tell me when you're ready."

That's it? All this worry and angst over how she'll react and she's okay with me keeping this private? "Thanks?" It's a question because I still don't believe her.

"See you in class," she quips, spinning on her heels.

Uh...I offer a small, grateful smile. "Love you, Eve."

"Love you, too, toots."

I watch her walk away, the halls already starting to quiet and thin. I have less than a minute before I will officially be tardy. It will be my third late slip in the past three weeks and will earn me a detention, but I couldn't make myself care enough to divert my mission.

Belying the nerves vibrating inside me, a few nimble, practiced moves later, my locker opens and a tiny paper airplane floats to the ground at my feet. My thirty-seventh one from a secret admirer whom I'm already three-quarters in love with.

I bend to pick it up and gently unfold the intricate pattern I've learned to refold perfectly. I hold the creased paper between trembling fingers, scanning the now familiar, flawless penmanship.

..d sad when you walked down the hallway this morning.
What are we going to do about that?

..ng like a fool, I press the paper flat to my chest and lean forehead against my locker, working to hold back the tears.

How did he know that?

How does a boy who doesn't know anything about me know me so well?

Today is—*was*—my mother's birthday. Six years without her and it feels as if it's a day and six years all at the same time. I swore when I woke up I smelled Channel No. 5 lingering in the air around my bed. I got mad at my sister because sometimes she'll do things like that. She thinks it helps when all it does is hurt more. Or maybe she does it for herself, too. I don't know. I forget sometimes that she lost her parents also, and that days like these are as hard for her, if not harder, because she had to step into their role and raise me.

But the fact a virtual stranger took notice of pain I thought I'd done a good job at hiding, when Evie hasn't even mentioned it, does something weird to my insides.

I pull the paper away from my chest and read the neatly written words again.

I like these notes, the game.

I like the whole secret admirer thing he's got going on.

But I figured out who he was weeks ago. At least I think I did. Only I've been too scared to do anything about it. I've never had a boyfriend. I've never been in love. I've never let myself venture too far outside my comfort zone because the truth is I'm a little socially awkward. Too quiet. A mouse in the corner, content to watch everyone else live happy lives, wishing I could participate too.

The other truth is, I haven't loved many people in my life.

I loved my parents and they died. I love my sister, but she's distant and though I know she loves me, I also know she wants her own life, free from the responsibility *of* me. Who can blame her? I don't. And the only other person I've loved is Evie.

But I could love *him*. I already know it. I'm already falling. Maybe he is, too.

I shift my attention to the locker down the hallway from mine. He's there. He's pretending to dig into his book bag for a pen or a stick of gum, but he's not doing either. He won't leave until I do. He'll follow me to AP Trig. He'll sit to my right and mimic Mr. Brunner's lisp until I laugh. He'll watch me covertly out of the corner of his eye, thinking I don't feel the heavy weight of gaze on me.

I do. I have. I feel it until I fall asleep. It's there when I wake. It sits on me like a weighted blanket in my dreams, a comfort I like too much already.

What do I do? What if I'm wrong? What if he doesn't feel *that* way about me? What if I ruin our tentative friendship?

What if you pass up the greatest love of your life because you're a chicken?

I glance over at him again. He quickly looks away. He's nervous, too.

I could fold up the note and tuck it inside the pocket of my book bag. I could. I want to, the same way I have all the others before it. It's the safest choice. But today I don't. Today I turn that tiny paper airplane over, I scribble a reply, and I do the scariest thing I've ever done in my life, praying this doesn't backfire in a rush of embarrassing flames.

Lungs full of trembling fear, I walk up to him and silently throw my arm out. He looks to my steady hand, then back to me. The corners of his lips round. Stark gray eyes dance with mine in a tango. He runs his tongue over the backs of his teeth, as if he's trying to get something out that's stuck between his molars. He palms the back of his neck, rubbing while he's thinking.

He makes me wait a full thirty agonizing seconds before he

. and slips the refolded airplane from my fingers. I
.ips until they're moist. His stormy gaze drops to them.
co groan. I want to kiss him. My chest flutters under his

With me still standing there he starts to unfold my note and,
nable to stand it any longer, I rush to tell him, "Guess I'll see
you in class," with the last breath I'm holding onto.

He nods once and smiles a smile that I haven't seen on him
before, but it's a smile to end all smiles. It totally upends my
world and I'm suddenly buried under the landslide that is him.
It's a descent he left up to me to trigger and I guess I just did.
But instinct tells me it's a place I'm safe. Where I can breathe
steady and be me even as I get sucked into the darkness below
the light.

I'm halfway down the hall before I hear him call behind me
with sexy confidence, "Yes, you will," and my mouth breaks out
into a grin so big my face cramps. I can't help it. I throw a flirty
look over my shoulder and catch a matching goofy grin lighting
up his face.

Oh, yes. I could love this boy.

And it could be a love to end all loves before it.

Want more? Sign up for my newsletter here to be in the know
on new releases and receive exclusive info!

ABOUT THE AUTHOR

This is the hardest part...talking about myself.

I'm just a regular ol' Midwest girl who moved to the South (Tennessee) and now understands the slight that "Bless Your Heart" really means. I've fallen in love with yoga and Jess Sims from Peleton. I don't do as much running as I used to, but I still eat, and I still love carbs and there is still a love-hate relationship with my ass and thighs. Mostly hate. I like a good cocktail (oh hell...who am I kidding? I love *any* cocktail). I'm a huge creature of habit, but I'll tell you I'm flexible. I swear too much. I love alternative music and in my next life, I want to be a badass female rocker. I still hate, hate, hate spiders, telemarketers, liver, acne, winter, and loose hairs that fall down my shirt (don't ask, it's a thing).

And at fifty-two years of age, I also have a new love. Her name is Vienna Faye. As parents, we love our children deeply, but the love you have for your grandchildren is more, somehow. It's indescribable. And she is spectacular, just like her mother. If you follow me on Instagram, you'll see her once in a while, and I'll bet you agree!

God has blessed me in so many ways ...and I know it.

If you're a stalker, the first step is to admit it. After that, you can find me in the usual social media sites: Facebook and Instagram. Also give me a follow on BookBub, TikTok, Goodreads or Amazon, all of which I use with irregular frequency. Truthfully, if you want to reach out, email (klkreig@gmail.com) is the best way as I check that every day and I respond to every single one.

day and age, with so many great authors and so many uses, it's challenging to keep up with it all, so if you want to miss when my next book is releasing, sign up for ewsletter found on my website at klkreig.com. Promise, no mming and you'll only get it when I have something impor- ant to say, which isn't often.

Happy reading.

~ Kelly

81044050R00213